AN UNLIKELY ASSET

Thomas Hutton

AN UNLIKELY ASSET

Copyright © 2025 Thomas Hutton.

Paperback ISBN: 979-8-9922207-9-7
eBook ISBN: 979-8-9928630-0-0

Book Design by Transcendent Publishing

This book is a work of fiction. Names, characters, countries, and incidents are a product of the author's imagination or used fictitiously. Any resemblance to persons, living or dead, is entirely coincidental.

Printed in the United States of America.

To my mother and father, whose love and devotion to their children has been an ever-present source of strength and inspiration.

And to Chris and Polly - "And with the morn those angel faces smile which I have loved long since still and lost awhile."

TABLE OF CONTENTS

PROLOGUE

December 24, 1974

The Capital Beltway is a sixty-four-mile ribbon of asphalt that encircles the nation's capital. To modern America, it has become a symbol — the demarcation line between politicians and the people they have sworn to serve — fantasyland and the real world. It is also a treacherous superhighway that carries thousands of travelers every day, the rush hour equivalent of Russian roulette.

The irony of this was not lost on Matt, even in his state of near panic. For so long he had been straddling two worlds, knowing all the while that someday they would collide. But not until tonight did he think it might cost the life of someone he loved.

Traffic was mercifully light, giving him a shred of hope that he could get to her in time. That thought had no sooner crossed his mind when up ahead he saw a slowdown.

"No, no, no…" he said, his throat tightening with panic, "This cannot happen."

Gripping the wheel tighter, he rode up on the bumper of one car, then another, weaving in and out and eliciting several angry honks. The Omega shook and pulled to the side in protest, reminding him that he was pushing it past its limits, not to mention his own as a driver.

He looked in the rear-view mirror to see a black sedan mirroring his movements as he threaded the pack. Was this just another impatient driver, or was it something else? It suddenly occurred to him that he was operating from faulty information, that it had all been a ruse to make him frantic, impulsive, get him alone. He let up on the gas a bit and stole more glances in the rearview, hoping to get a glimpse of the driver of the sedan. It was hard to be sure, but he thought he caught sight of a strong, familiar profile.

With his attention divided between the road ahead and the sedan, he didn't notice the old school bus, converted into a hippie van, sloppily rounding a cloverleaf from the road above. It entered the Beltway far too quickly and was veering right into Matt's path.

The bus flipped on its side, shooting like an errant missile across four lanes of traffic. Matt slammed the brakes while ferociously swerving as far to the left as he could. But he was trapped by the Jersey barrier separating his side of the road from oncoming traffic. There was simply no way to avoid the careening bus.

Everything happened so fast — a split moment that seemed to last an eternity. The screech of brakes rent the air, followed by an abrupt, dead silence. Beams of light cast an eerie glow across the road, moistened by light rain. Cars were spread across the road like a child's toys carelessly tossed on a playroom floor. Strange voices reached his ears, but they were fading in and out like a radio station with a weak signal. Matt heard someone say, "I really hate to see head injuries," and wondered vaguely who they were talking about. Suddenly he felt himself being pulled sideways from the Omega. He hung weightless for a moment, then was placed down again on a firm, flat surface.

He heard the voice shout, "This one's bad, get him in the ambulance — now!"

It was only as the "surface" began to move that Matt realized they were talking about him. He tried to open his eyes, but an overpowering wave of nausea stopped him.

He opened his mouth to tell them he was fine, that there was somewhere he needed to be, that a woman was in danger. But his tongue felt swollen, the words blended into one indistinguishable slur.

"Buddy, don't try to talk," the man said, "We're gonna get you to the hospital." He then barked, "Hurry up, guys, we're gonna lose this one!"

"Lose… lose?" Matt began, but a plastic mask was placed over his nose and mouth, ending all attempts to communicate. Then he felt another wave of nausea as he was lifted again.

As the ambulance pulled away a dull tapping from its windshield wipers echoed between the wails of its siren. The plastic mask hurt his cheeks, but the cool oxygen it brought felt good. He felt something warm and sticky creeping across his forehead, and for the first time wondered if he was indeed on his way out. A bitter, feeble attempt at a laugh burst from his lips. Of all the ways this might have ended, a car accident on the Beltway seemed like a cruel cosmic joke. The humor evaporated when images of his devastated parents and shocked friends as they heard of his demise flashed through his mind. But his last thought, before everything went black, was of her.

CHAPTER ONE

Sixteen months earlier…

"Matt, honey, wake up…"

"Huh?" Matt Thomas opened one eye to see his mother turned to the back seat, her brow furrowed slightly.

"Up and at 'em, kiddo," his father added, "We're here."

"Here?" he said vaguely, then sprung into an upright position as he saw the entrance to American University. "Oh, we're *here*. Wow."

It was as if he had closed his eyes in one world and awakened in another. At some point the rural backroads leading from their home in Michigan had given way to the congested lifelines feeding Washington, D.C. American University was a city within a city, with a mix of buildings dating back to the 1800s and more modern office-style structures, all surrounded by lush greenery. He rolled down the window and was immediately blasted by a wave of uncomfortably warm, sticky air, but Matt didn't care. The whole place was abuzz with a kind of electric energy he had never felt before.

Everywhere he looked, students and their parents were scurrying back and forth between their cars and the dorms carrying suitcases, televisions, small refrigerators, and other belongings. Others, their work done, stood together, hugging, or wiping away tears as they said their goodbyes. The incoming freshmen were fresh-faced and wide-eyed; their parents looked, for the most part, like his – the fathers with neatly shorn hair and the mothers in smart summer dresses with box-shaped purses hanging from their wrists.

Matt Sr. slowly navigated the chaos, carefully passing throngs of families and small groups of upperclassmen loitering about, apparently to observe the new batch of students. Several of them, Matt noticed, looked markedly different than their younger counterparts, with longer hair and clothes that looked slightly unkempt; they also carried themselves with a confidence that seemed to border on arrogance, though that could have been his imagination.

The thought occurred to Matt that he didn't know what the hell he had gotten himself into. At military school he and his fellow students had been in lockstep about the hippie counterculture – they most definitely opposed it; now, he wondered whether he would be surrounded by the sort he had seen on TV, burning buildings and fighting the police. If so, he'd be branded a pariah before the first week was out. Somehow, he doubted the man-to-man talk that consisted of his father's warning not to get into "any trouble" (a reference to girls or something else, Matt wasn't exactly sure) was going to help him navigate this new landscape.

Matt recalled the dreaded conversation when he broke the news that he was going to American, rather than the University of Michigan as his parents and sisters had. There had been no argument, but from the way his mother delicately dabbed her eyes and the slight tightening of his stoic father's jaw, he knew the decision had hit them hard. It wasn't one he had made lightly. He would no longer be a short hour from home, but nearly six hundred miles. There wouldn't be "surprise" weekend visits by Mom and Dad, with his favorite burgers from Klimpy Jim's in nearby Ann Arbor. Now the most he could hope for were care packages with – he suspected, knowing his mother – vitamins, pairs of new underwear, and a note telling him to wear a sweater. There would be phone calls and holiday visits, but nothing would ever be the same again. Matt had tried unsuccessfully to articulate the pull of Washington, D.C., but how could he expect them to understand when he didn't? It wasn't about his choice of school (for Matt, college was just something one did, the next logical step toward adulthood), but about a need to be in the locus of a country he'd been taught to love and was now being ripped apart by an unpopular war, the Watergate scandal, and social unrest. Now, as the Thomases eyed some likely supporters, if not perpetrators, of that unrest, Matt could almost feel the unspoken *I-told-you-sos* emanating from the front seat. He had placed himself squarely in the belly of the beast.

Within a few minutes the station wagon pulled up to Matt's new residence, Anderson Hall. A sharp contrast to the stately, Georgian-like homages to academia nearby, Anderson was a simple, unimpressive brick building that looked more like a warehouse with windows than a dorm at a prestigious private university. The car was still rolling when a young man walked over and stuck his head in the driver's window, nearly positioning it on the steering wheel.

"Hi. I'm Tex. I'm from Texas," he announced, moving apace with the vehicle until Matt's father brought it gently to a stop. "Are you moving into Anderson?"

"Yep," Matt replied, avoiding his parents' eyes as he leaned forward between them.

"Great, I'll help you with your stuff." With that, Tex moved to the rear of the station wagon, popped the tailgate, and began unloading suitcases which he set, with surprising gentleness, on the ground.

Matt shared bewildered glances with his mother and father, then slid out of the car to help. He could only imagine what they thought as they took in the scene: their son, clad in khaki pants that went perfectly with his buzzed light brown hair and penny loafers beside this strange, rather sloppy young man with a bushy black mustache that probably had remnants of a previous meal sealed within. A slight paunch, more pronounced due to his small stature, was visible between faded cutoffs and a rumpled T-shirt with Greek letters.

Tex ran a hand across his sweating forehead and turned to Matt's parents. "Why don't you two relax and get a soda while we get Matt moved in?"

Matt's father opened his mouth as if to say something but his mom beat him to it.

"That's a good idea. You go ahead and we'll meet you back here in a few minutes." She then took her husband's arm and led him away, giving their son the opportunity to make acquaintances on his own.

Matt picked up a few small boxes and followed Tex to the building, watching as he juggled three suitcases. Once inside the lobby, Tex located Matt's name and room assignment on a list posted on a wall, then directed him to the elevator.

"Man! That was some party you missed last night!" Tex said as he set a suitcase down and pressed the button for the fourth floor. He flashed Matt a mischievous grin. "Good thing there's another one tonight."

"Really?" Matt had expected to have dinner with his parents, followed by a quiet night getting his room situated.

"Yes, sir. At my fraternity, the PIs." He gestured with his free hand to his t-shirt. "Why don't you come and I'll introduce you to the guys?"

"Sounds great. I have dinner with my folks, though."

"Afterward then. I'll swing by at eight."

Once off the elevator, Tex led the way to Room 432, where he hoisted Matt's suitcases up on the top bunk as if to claim a stake before his roommate arrived.

He took a deep breath and pronounced, "I think you lucked out. Not every freshman gets to live on a floor that's a room-by-room."

"What do you mean?"

"Women!" Tex blurted. "This floor is coed. It's an experiment to see if guys and chicks can live together without turning the place into a Screw-U!"

"Really?" Matt looked at him in wide-eyed amazement, his mind already weighing the potential pros and cons of such a situation.

At that moment his parents appeared in the doorway, his father holding two sodas. Blushing, Matt scanned their faces and was relieved that they didn't appear to have overheard the conversation.

Tex accepted one of the sodas from Mr. Thomas' outstretched hand. "Thank you, sir," he said, bowing slightly. "Well, I'll get out of your hair now – it was great meeting y'all!" He was almost at the door when he turned and said, "Don't forget, Matt, I'll be by at eight sharp!" Then he was gone.

"Seems like you've made a 'friend,'" Mrs. Thomas observed. It was the tone she used when she wasn't quite sure she approved of someone.

"Seems like he's being rushed," Mr. Thomas said.

Matt raised an eyebrow at him. "Really?"

His father had referenced his fraternity days only occasionally and in vague terms, but with an expression that implied the experience was a positive one. "How do you know?"

"Because that's how it happened with me. Right now there are guys just like Tex all over campus looking for freshmen like you. It's tradition, Matty."

"Right." Matt looked down at the floor, embarrassed that he hadn't picked up the ruse and disappointed that Tex's friendly overtures had an ulterior motive.

After unpacking some of his things, Matt and his parents headed to a restaurant in downtown Washington they'd picked out of a guidebook the week before. Over rare steaks and iceberg wedges, they tried to make normal conversation, with Matt's mother updating him on some local gossip and Matt telling his father – a fellow spy novel buff and the one who had gotten him hooked on the genre – that he was rereading *The Spy Who Came in From the Cold.*

His father stopped chewing long enough to raise an eyebrow. "What is this, the third time now?"

"Fourth," Matt said, "It's *that* good."

Matt knew what his father was going to say before the words came out. "I know, I know, everyone loves John le Carré and his George Smiley fellow, but you know…" – and here Matt and his mother chimed in – "…I'm a Graham Greene man."

His father looked at them in surprise, then the three of them burst out laughing. Yet for most of the meal the mood was somber, almost awkward, as if they had in some strange, sad way already started moving away from each other.

Passing the White House on the way back to campus, his father searched Matt out in the rear-view mirror.

"You know, I think you made a good decision coming here. It's a wonderful opportunity." He paused, then added, "Make it a point to meet people."

"I don't think that will be a problem," the younger Matt noted. "If there's only one more person like Tex at this school, I think I'll get along."

His parents smiled, then their faces fell when they realized they had already reached the campus. They would be spending the night in a nearby hotel, then get an early start on the nearly twelve-hour drive home. Matt's father pulled up to Anderson and they all got out to say a proper goodbye. As each one pulled him into a tight embrace, Matt wanted to thank them for the love and devotion they had given him for the last eighteen years, and for the confidence they showed by allowing him to go to school so far away from home. But the words seemed so inadequate he felt they would somehow dimmish the moment. And of course he couldn't tell them that all he wanted at that moment was to be a little boy again, to be back home with them, his dog – heck, even his sisters.

There were more tearful hugs and promises to call soon, then he watched forlornly as the station wagon disappeared into a sea of tail-lights. Matt walked about campus, hoping his sadness was not apparent to strangers he passed. Most were laughing and joking, clearly thrilled to be there.

This is pathetic, he thought, *It's my first night in Washington, D.C. and I'm acting like I'm at a funeral.*

By the time he made it back to Anderson, his mood had begun to lift.

Before returning to his room, he stopped in the men's room to make sure his eyes weren't red. He knew he already looked like a square to these guys; he didn't need to be thought of as a sissy as well. After a quick look in the mirror he splashed water on his face, more to summon confidence than to refresh himself, then drew a deep breath and passed his fingers through his hair. Not too bad, he thought, except for a slightly disheveled shirt.

He unfastened his belt, dropping his pants to his knees to properly arrange the shirt tale. At that vulnerable moment, the door to the bathroom opened and in stepped a pretty young woman. She barely gave him a glance as she moved toward a toilet stall.

"Oh!" Matt exclaimed, scrambling to grab his pants. "Am I in the women's room?"

"No," she shot back. "I think I'm in the men's room!"

Amazed at the casual invasion of the male domain, he zipped up and rushed from the bathroom, where he promptly burst out laughing. It was exactly the type of humiliating scenario he had placed on his "coed cons" list earlier… and yet… He laughed again as he started toward his room, thinking college was going to be pretty cool after all.

CHAPTER TWO

Matt liked to think of himself as having a broad and eclectic taste in music. Some of his favorite childhood memories were of his dad firing up the hi-fi and, with rare abandon, swing dancing with his mother to Glenn Miller and Duke Ellington. Later, his sisters got him hooked on The Beatles, and – much to his parents' dismay – the Rolling Stones played continuously whenever he was home from military school. But he could never get into the folksy ditties that had become so popular over the past few years – not just because of the social message in the lyrics, but the cadence. More than anything, The Grateful Dead "grated" on his nerves like no other, and they made him realize what it was that bothered him so. To Matt, that type of music had a vibe of laziness and lack of direction.

When he got off the elevator a few minutes earlier he'd heard "Mountains of the Moon," faint enough to warrant nothing but an eyeroll. Now, as he moved down the hall, he realized with a groan that the music was actually quite loud – and it was coming from Room 432. Unsure of the proper etiquette – and hoping to establish a mutual respect for privacy – Matt knocked while placing the key in the lock. Before he could grasp the knob, the door swung open, pulling him partially through the entryway.

"Trick or treat," he said, his usual filter on the fritz. Considering the odd cast of characters he had met so far – Tex, the girl in the bathroom, and now this zit-faced stranger (likely, his roommate) with a head of unkempt fuzzy hair – the greeting seemed appropriate. A sweating beer bottle dangled loosely from meaty fingers. The stranger took a slug of it and belched, producing an invisible but odorous reminder that Matt's personal space was no longer his own.

"If you're selling Fuller brushes, you're outta luck. I don't do cleaning and I don't use 'em on my hair!"

"That's evident," Matt replied with a trace of annoyance. "Actually, this is my room."

At that moment, the door to the adjacent room opened and out stepped an attractive girl in cut-off jeans and a tie-dyed shirt.

"You got a phone?" she asked, whisking past them. They watched, surprised by her boldness, as she picked up their phone and began to dial.

"Who is that?" Matt asked without taking his eyes off the girl.

"Beats me," he replied with another slug of beer. "Who the hell are you?"

"I'm Matt, I got here a few hours ago. Who are you?"

"Grossman."

Neither Matt nor Grossman looked at the other during the introduction. Their eyes remained on the coed, who was now engaged in conversation on their phone.

Matt stepped past Grossman into his new home. "I hope she's not talking to Africa!"

"I hope *you* don't mind the top bunk," Grossman said, flopping on the bottom.

Before Matt could respond, Tex appeared. "You guys ready?"

Grossman leaped off his bed. Obviously, he had also been the beneficiary of the Tex treatment and was unabashedly excited about the prospect of a party.

With one last glance at the girl, Matt followed them out of the room and back toward the elevator.

"Who's the babe?" Tex asked.

"No clue, man," Grossman quipped, and Tex glanced back over his shoulder at Matt.

Matt shrugged in support of Grossman's testimony. "She just walked in and made a call."

It was then Matt realized their lack of wisdom in leaving their few possessions in the company of the unknown girl. Yet somehow, in the spirit of the moment, everything seemed not just acceptable but part of a larger, significant narrative he would look back on fondly one day, even if it did include theft and a phone bill that rivaled his tuition.

When the three arrived at the campus watering hole, aptly called The Tavern, they found partying so fierce it seemed to have a determination about it. It was as if the students were putting the summer to rest, but there was no mourning, just excitement. Matt and Grossman quickly got caught up in meeting Tex's fraternity brothers, all of whom were just as outgoing. Beers were immediately shoved into their hands, with Grossman draining his while Matt took small sips to be sociable. At military school, drinking was a high crime that came with the threat of immediate expulsion and usually committed only by guys who didn't want to be there in the first place. But this was a whole new world, and before he knew it a second beer was placed in his other hand and he was being celebrated for "double fisting" it.

Thanks to his father's insight, Matt could easily spot the signs of the campus fraternity system at play. Tex had marked them as new recruits; now, his fraternity brothers were doing their part to lure them in with the promise of beer, women, and song. *Fine by me,* Matt thought. He could think of no better way to make new friends, and besides, guys who were so busy partying and drinking beer were unlikely to be staging the next campus protest. One sip turned to another, each working to erase his inhibitions and perhaps call into question why he had them in the first place.

Three beers later, Matt happily discovered he possessed a skill that would make him a sought-after guest at any college party. At the urging of Tex and Grossman, he joined a race to "chug" beer, and he won... by a substantial margin. Several other chugging matches followed, none of which put Matt's superiority in dispute. By the time The Tavern lights flickered, giving notice of closing time, he had made a name for himself as the champion.

As Matt joined the slow, reluctant exodus to the door, he noticed a strange, rubbery feeling in his limbs. It was unfamiliar – he'd never consumed anywhere near this much alcohol – but not unpleasant; nor was the sensation that everything that had plagued his mind over the past several weeks was simply melting away. The past and the future ceased to matter – there was only this delicious present moment. As he stepped outside into the steamy air, he saw Grossman, who was equally schnockered, and the two embraced like long-lost brothers.

When they arrived at Anderson Hall – a small miracle considering their state – they found their floor engulfed in a massive party that seemed to have spilled out from the room next to theirs. It also looked to be better than the one they'd left at The Tavern, and for one reason: this one was coed. Normally, such circumstances would have triggered Matt's self-consciousness bordering on low-level anxiety – an unfortunate byproduct of going to an all-boys military school. Not tonight, though; thanks to that magical elixir, what the girls thought of him simply didn't matter. He was hot shit, and "love it or leave it" was his new mantra.

No sooner had the two opened the door to their room when the girl from next door, the one they'd left on their phone, appeared.

"Did you behave yourself in our room?" Matt inquired.

"Certainly not! I gave your phone number to my boyfriend. He lives in California. We don't have a phone in our room – rather spend the money on parties."

Matt and Grossman looked at each other and nodded, unable to argue with her logic.

"I'm Kate," she said, a slow smile spreading across her face. "And you two are *really wasted*." Just then, another coed entered their room. "And speaking of wasted, this is my roommate, Sarah."

"Have'n we met sommere?" Sarah slurred as she held out her hand for Matt to shake, trying to place him.

"Have we?" Matt replied, pretending not to remember.

"Yessiree…" With that, she slumped on the bed as if that would help with her recall. "The bath-roooom! You," she giggled, pointing to his crotch, "Pantsss down."

Turned out being drunk didn't cure everything. *Think quickly,* he thought, annoyed at being mocked. *Think of something smart to say.* When a clever comeback eluded him, he settled for glaring at her as she lay across the lower bunk, her head resting on her arm.

"Don' worree," she slurred. "No one cares whiss is whiss. Just use the one you're closess to."

"Really?" Matt was genuinely astonished by her explanation of rest-room protocol.

She lifted her head and nodded in an exaggerated fashion. "Really."

Just as an admiral's entourage follows when the commander changes ships, it wasn't long before the partiers – many of them women – from Kate's room began gravitating to theirs. Matt and Grossman looked around the packed space, unable to believe their luck in scoring such a popular neighbor. Buoyed in his drunk state, Matt engaged in one of his favorite military school pastimes: movie impersonations. He would say a line and the others would have to guess who said it and in what film. Matt's impersonations were legendary at military school, though he had never, nor would he ever, do such a thing in front of girls when sober.

The crowd became silent as he assumed a karate stance and shouted in a surprisingly accurate Mandarin accent, "Destroy the image and break the enemy."

"Bruce Lee!" shouted several men in the crowd, "Enter the Dragon!"

He then turned his back to the audience, took a deep breath, and spun around again, this time adopting the crisp tone of an upper-class Brit. "There's a saying in England: Where there's smoke, there's fire."

"Sean Connery!" they cried out, with several girls now eyeing Matt appreciatively, "From Russia with Love!"

Matt, who by this time badly needed to drain his bladder, went to step away, but the crowd wasn't having it.

Amid shouts of "Another one! Do another one!" he laughed and turned his back to them again, this time for a longer moment. The crowd peered at him curiously, as he appeared to be stuffing something in his mouth. When he spun around, his cheeks were puffed out, thanks to wads of napkins placed by the beer cups.

"A man who doesn't spend time with his family," he rasped as he brushed his fingers against one cheek, "can never be a real man."

With that, the room exploded into an uproar, with everyone screaming, "The Godfather!" and several guys slapping him on the back.

Matt spent a moment enjoying his ovation, then took several small bows as he backed out the door and headed to the bathroom.

On his way back, there were two students bouncing a basketball in the hall. He signaled for a pass, which he received and immediately returned. *Even drunk,* he thought, *I'm outta sight.* Backing away, he was nearly to his room when he received a second pass. This time, before he could return it, a voice rang out from behind him.

"Hey, you little shits, cut out the noise and let the rest of us sleep!"

With the basketball firmly in his hands, Matt turned around to find a weary upperclassman.

"It's three-fucking-o'clock in the fucking morning and nobody can sleep because of you freshman assholes partying. Now you're right outside my fucking door!"

Matt was quick to apologize; then, hoping a little humor might calm the moment, he added, "You want a beer or anything?"

To say the peace offering was not well received would be an understatement.

"What I want is to wring your neck, you little asshole. I was sleeping."

Matt contemplated his next move, aware that his outward calm could be easily mistaken for indifference and add fuel to the fire. Sure enough, the guy stepped forward with his hand outstretched, and he was clearly not intending to shake.

Shit, Matt thought, *and the night was going so well.*

Before he could react, the hand was forcefully seized by someone coming out of Matt's room. The unknown rescuer brushed past Matt, placing himself between the two would-be combatants. He had a heavy, dark mustache that made him look older, very serious, and somewhat threatening. It was the kind of mustache that belonged on a villain. His vice-like grip had the upperclassman recoiling in pain. A cloud of smoke surrounded his head, and the cigar, resting lightly in his mouth, moved with his lips as he spoke.

"You – I don't like your face!"

Matt watched in amazement as the upperclassman looked toward the ground, clearly intimidated.

"Maybe you didn't hear me. I don't like your face!" the rescuer said again, holding up his free fist. "Either you get lost or I'll put this down your throat and pull your lungs out!"

The upperclassman didn't say a word, he just retreated ingloriously down the hallway.

Turning to Matt, the hero exclaimed, "That guy has no sense of humor!"

Matt sauntered away in the opposite direction, then returned to his own room to find Grossman passed out on the floor.

No doubt about it. It was only Day One, and college was already the weirdest experience of his life.

*   *   *

The next morning, the first thing Matt was aware of was the feeling of nails – one for every beer – being driven into his temple. The second was Grossman's deep snoring; his roommate hadn't stirred, not even when Matt, aided by two other guys, lifted him onto his bed the night before.

"Coffee," Matt mumbled. Though he had never been hungover before he instinctively knew a hot, strong cup would be essential to the cure. Getting some was priority one; the thought of anything else, like showering or changing out of yesterday's clothes, was simply too much to bear.

Ten minutes later, he and Grossman made their way to the school cafeteria. On the way Matt was shocked to find his roommate rather chipper as he went on about how great the party was. When Matt finally asked how he was even functioning, Grossman revealed it wasn't fortitude, but experience.

"Dude, I feel like total shit, but that's the way it goes. It passes in a few hours."

Despite Grossman's convincing tone, Matt couldn't imagine a moment when he would not feel this wretched. And, on the off chance his roommate was right and he would, in fact, recover, he made that vow every college student makes and never keeps: "I am never drinking again."

Grossman emitted a dubious snort. "Uh-huh."

As they walked in Matt scanned the room for a free table, his gaze landing instead on the mustached hero from the night before. He was sitting alone.

"Would you like some company?" Matt asked, then plunked his tray down without waiting for an answer.

"Sure." He gestured to the chair.

"I'm Matt, and that's my roommate, Grossman." Matt turned and waved Grossman over. "Thanks for saving me last night."

The mustache twitched almost imperceptibly. He would have fit perfectly in a picture of Fidel Castro with his strongman bodyguards. Another thing: his manner was more mature and self-confident, revealing perhaps, that he had experienced more of life than either of his new acquaintances.

"I didn't save you; I merely corrected that guy's attitude." He paused. "Besides, I saw the way you were looking at him. You would've held your own if it came to that."

Matt was unconvinced but didn't argue. "Well, thanks anyway."

"No sweat. You two are freshmen, I take it?"

"Yeah," the newly arrived Grossman responded with pride. "You?"

"Same. Did your roommate tell you how he almost wiped the floor with an upperclassman last night?" Grossman stared from the stranger to Matt in shock. "Yeah, you're living with a real killer!" His voice was bold and resonant, his intonation lent the words unusual clarity and definition.

"God," remarked Grossman. "You sound like a TV announcer or something. I'm going to call you Walter, like Walter Cronkite!"

The newly anointed Walter accepted the honor, never revealing his real name. He quickly changed the subject back to the previous evening, telling Grossman what had happened in the hallway but, Matt noted, downplaying his own role.

"Yeah, well," Grossman replied, "he went to military school. When they're not marching or jerking off, they actually learn how to do some serious shit."

Matt heard an almost grudging respect in his roommate's voice and wondered if "serious shit" was a compliment or a commentary about the nefariousness of the U.S. armed forces. Maybe a little of both, he decided.

"Here," he said, "I'll show you some 'serious shit.'"

Walter and Grossman watched with quiet intensity while Matt took a pat of butter from his plate and transferred it to the bottom of an empty glass. He then nonchalantly stepped over to the empty table next to theirs, bent over, and placed the glass against the underside of the table a few inches from the edge. The butter bonded the glass to the underside of the table. Matt then situated a chair directly in front of the glass so an unsuspecting victim would sit right there.

Returning to Grossman and Walter, Matt couldn't suppress his pleasure. "It's like denture adhesive. It'll hold 'til someone hits it with their knee."

Much like jungle predators, the three waited for the trap to spring. Sure enough, a few minutes later a delegation of Neanderthals – or jocks, judging from their oversized biceps – claimed the table. Matt couldn't have planned the drama better had he tried. One by one, they sat down, leaving the fateful seat empty. That one would go for the last member of their party, who was currently crossing the room with his tray. He was the perfect target – tall and muscular with an angular jaw and a confident strut that indicated he was not to be messed with. For Matt, who had known plenty of guys like this in military school, it only heightened the anticipation of what was to happen.

When he reached the table, the jock put his tray down, then slowly removed the chair as he joked with his friends. As he sat, he moved his chair closer to the table, propelling his legs beneath it. It went down just like Matt predicted. The second his knee touched the glass it broke free and crashed loudly to the tile floor. The guy screamed and leaped to his feet, sending the chair shooting out behind him.

"Did you see the motherfucker that threw that shit?" he snarled, an angry flush spreading across his face.

Fortunately, his attention was drawn to the opposite side of the room, away from Matt, Walter, and Grossman, who couldn't have contained their laughter if they wanted to. Walter practically inhaled his unlit cigar, wheezing as he slapped his knee. Matt laughed so hard he had to rub his eyes to clear the tears.

When he dared to look again toward the spectacle he had created, Matt caught a stare from a coed at the table beyond the victim. Their eyes locked for only a millisecond, but it was enough. Not only was the childish prank witnessed by a member of the opposite sex, but an exceptionally fine one. The girl's light brown hair was pulled delicately over her ear. Her skin was soft, creamy, and slightly brown, a remnant of a summer spent in the sun. The sloped angle of her slender nose and her recessed cheekbone held a certain sophistication. Her gaze, though sterile, held just a hint of curiosity. Then, as if forgetting Matt just as quickly, she turned to the guy sitting next to her.

Terribly embarrassed, Matt looked back at Grossman and Walter, who were still in the throes of laughter.

Walter took note of Matt's expression. "What's eating you all of a sudden?"

He was saved from answering by the arrival of Tex, who also looked no worse for the wear despite the heavy imbibing the night before.

"Guys!" he boomed as he spun a chair around and slid into it, hanging his arms over its back. "The fraternity is having a party tonight. It's a mixer. Last one before classes."

Matt turned to him, the girl and his shame forgotten at the word "mixer." It would be an opportunity to meet women, and possibly suffer more humiliation in their presence.

As if reading his mind, Tex added, "We have taken the liberty of arranging dates for you guys." He then motioned to a fellow fraternity brother who stood by like a dutiful lieutenant, clipboard in hand. Tex grabbed the board and ran his finger down a list of names, some of which had been scratched off. His finger settled on a name and he announced, "Matt, your date is Janet. She lives in five sixty-two, Letts Hall. She expects you around eight o'clock."

Matt glanced at Grossman and Walter, wondering if they were as unsettled by these rapidly evolving developments as he was. The answer appeared to be no, as they accepted the names from Tex as casually as if he was making a fast-food delivery. Two co-eds, preferably the sort that puts out, coming right up!

"Wait a minute," Matt protested as Tex stood to leave. "We just have to show up? Don't we have to meet them before or something?"

"Nope," Tex grinned. "We've taken care of everything. Just pick 'em up a little before eight. We've taken over The Tavern for the night."

"Really?" Matt asked.

Tex's lieutenant quickly explained that PIs did not have their own house like many fraternities did. Land in that part of D.C. was so valuable that after the first few fraternities were started the University stopped allowing new buildings on campus for private use. The brothers were therefore scattered throughout the dorms and off-campus apartments. For parties, they always rented out The Tavern – a most beloved tradition.

"That means free food and free beer," Tex said, clicking his tongue twice for effect, "along with the free women."

"Life is good!" Grossman exclaimed, while Matt already rethinking his vow to swear off the drink. If ever he needed liquid courage, it would be tonight.

"Okay…" he said slowly, eliciting a raised eyebrow from Tex, "But shouldn't we take them flowers or something?"

"I'd bring a raincoat," Tex replied, not missing a beat, "just in case you get lucky."

The others took in Matt's cocked head and furrowed eyebrows and burst out laughing, the sound accompanied by several pounds of Walter's fist on the table.

"A rubber, you doofus," the lieutenant blurted out, also apparently delighting in Matt's bewilderment.

"Oh, and you're welcome," Tex said, flashing the grin again, then he and his lieutenant left, no doubt to discharge similar assignments to other freshmen.

Suddenly, Matt's headache returned, and it had nothing to do with the hangover. As he and his friends left the cafeteria, he stole a final glance at the beautiful coed. She was still engrossed in conversation with her male companion, who had the pretentious preppy look of a guy who didn't resort to sophomoric antics like gluing a bomb made of glass and butter to a table. Matt shook his head, dismissing them both. Who cared what some random girl thought? He had another party to look forward to… and maybe even a need for a raincoat.

CHAPTER THREE

"You must be a Republican," the bartender said, shaking the martini shaker with the percussive rhythm of a maraca player. He poured it into the chilled glass and, with a subtle flourish, placed it before her.

"Excuse me?"

Anna Ivanovich Aslanov sat at the bar, legs crossed demurely at the ankles, manicured fingers wrapped around the stem of the glass. From her dress and demeanor, anyone would think she belonged in this room, waiting for a date or perhaps a girlfriend for an after-work gossip session.

"Republicans always order martinis…" The bartender grinned in a manner that suggested he appreciated her beauty but knew she was out of his reach. The flirtation would go no further unless she encouraged it.

She did not.

"I did not know this," she replied seriously, with just the hint of an accent. Was there an end to the strange cultural nuances in this country? If so, Anna had seen no evidence of it. It kept her slightly off-balance and on edge, no matter what Vadim had told her. He had his own agenda and her comfort was not a factor in it.

"Do not try too hard to blend in, Annushka," he said when she arrived in D.C. three months earlier. "America prides itself on accepting everyone with open arms. This is hypocrisy, of course, but we can use it."

Slowly, and with pinky extended, she brought the martini glass to her lips and took a sip. The vodka was subpar as it was not Russian, but it was icy cold and would have to do. She took another sip, allowing it to flow through her body, relaxing her ever so slightly.

She nodded her thanks to the bartender, who, thankfully, was flagged down by another customer, then returned her gaze to the mirror behind him. She saw reflected back at her, through a haze of cigarette and cigar smoke, a snapshot encapsulating everything she had heard about America.

The Town & Country Lounge at the Mayflower Hotel was a who's who of D.C. politicos and journalists and had been since the days of Hoover. It was filled primarily with men, dressed in suits and ties, most with cigarettes clenched between their lips or yellow-stained fingers of one hand, with two fingers of single-malt scotch in the other. In a throwback to the old days, they stopped in for a drink before heading home after a day of legislating, lobbying, or reporting on those who did. Some gesticulated as they debated the issues of the day, while others leaned in close and spoke *sotto voce* as they hammered out some behind-the-scenes deal that would affect countless members of the populace. A few Anna had even seen on the news or in the papers. It was the perfect marriage of power and materialism, and perhaps for the first time, Anna truly realized how challenging her job in America would be.

She also knew that every man there had, at one point or another, taken note of her presence at the bar, either with the long, lingering stare of an invitation or a fleeting glance before shyly turning away. Some idly wondered whether her affections came at a price tag.

Anna Ivanovich Aslanov read each stare, quietly assessing, and arrived at one conclusion: men were pigs. It was the same everywhere she went and had been that way since she turned thirteen, from the young comrade standing beside her at the factory to the elderly gent at the K Street newsstand where she bought her paper each morning on the way to work.

Even Vadim had stolen the occasion lustful glance when he thought she wasn't paying attention. He thought he was teaching her to always be aware of her surroundings in this strange place. And, like all men, he didn't understand that this awareness was as natural to her as breathing, and as necessary to her survival.

Anna scanned the reflection again and sighed. None of those vapid male faces matched the photos Vadim had shown her at their last meeting.

"You will befriend him, Anna Ivanovich," he had said, tapping a thick finger on the picture. As always, he spoke in English and insisted she did too, a practice designed to keep her from slipping up in inopportune times. "He can be very helpful to us."

Anna had frowned, for the man was singularly unattractive – with pasty skin and a frame so slim it almost suggested poor health. Vadim's slight emphasis on the word "befriend" was not lost on her.

"Who is he?"

"His name is George Trent and he works for a large American defense company. We also hear he likes to gamble, maybe likes it a little too much." Vadim's lip twitched with humor as he raised a glass of the cheap port he had come to love while in the States. "We will help him pay his debts."

Anna had studied the picture, committing the features to memory. At least Trent looked to be only a few years older than her. The last man she'd been tasked with "befriending" was a government bureaucrat roughly her father's age – or what he would have been had he survived Stalingrad. Unfortunately, the quality of the bureaucrat's information had been grossly overestimated by Vadim; far more unfortunate for Anna was that his sexual appetites had not waned with the passing years.

Suppressing a shiver of revulsion at the memory, she drained the martini glass and signaled for another. A glance at her watch told her it was nearing six p.m. Where was George Trent? Supposedly he stopped in at Town and Country every Friday after work and downed two Old Fashions before heading to his home somewhere in Arlington.

Twenty minutes and a half a martini later, she was about to pay her tab and leave when she saw in the mirror a familiar figure making his way across the room. At first, Anna wasn't even sure it was him. George Trent was much more attractive in person, though she suspected that might be because of the cut of the expensive suit he wore. More than that, she realized, it was the energy with which he weaved through the crowd, responding to several men who greeted him with a curt nod that let them know he was off the clock. In short, he carried himself like a man with a position of authority and the salary to match. A picture might be worth a thousand words, but sometimes the story they told was far from complete.

Trent strode purposefully to the other end of the bar and slid onto a stool as if it had been reserved for him. It would have been easier if he sat next to her, but perhaps this was a blessing in disguise; it gave her a chance to rethink her approach.

"The usual, Mr. Trent?" the bartender asked, already grabbing a rocks glass.

Trent nodded again, but this time it was a more relaxed gesture. The bartender was there to give, not take.

She watched, vaguely fascinated, as he placed a sugar cube in the glass, then added bitters, a dash of water, ice, Maker's Mark, and finally, an orange slice. It looked delicious.

"There you go, Mr. Trent. Old Fashioned, no cherry."

"Cheers," Trent said, raising his glass. As he did, his eyes flicked impassively about the room, much as hers had a few minutes earlier. Anna swiftly focused on her own drink, yet she could still feel that moment, quick as a heartbeat, when his gaze landed on her.

She politely raised a hand to catch the attention of the bartender.

"Excuse me," she said, "Can you tell me where the powder room is?"

He smiled in a way that made Anna wonder whether she had used the right term, then pointed past the crowd to a far corner. He assured her the drink would be waiting, and she slowly slid off her stool.

The ladies' room was spacious and, to Anna's relief, empty. It was *always* a relief to shed the mask, even if only for a few moments. Exhaling, she quickly crossed to the vanity and shrewdly assessed her appearance. She looked good – her makeup, impeccable and understated; her dark hair, parted in the middle with curls resting on her shoulders, had been copied from a photograph of Jacqueline Kennedy Onassis.

She leaned in then for a closer inspection, frowning at the slight shadows under her dark, almond-shaped eyes, her slightly paler than usual skin. Fumbling around in her clutch bag, she retrieved black eyeliner and expertly ran it around her eyes, then pinched her cheeks to a rosy glow. Her full lips, she left nude.

She then looked down at her outfit, satisfied she'd made the right choice: a simple linen dress the color of lilacs that zipped up the back and cinched her waist to a handspan. Slingbacks of the same shade minimized her size-eight foot and emphasized her dainty ankles. It was among the first purchases she made after arriving in D.C. – and one of her favorites, as much for its symbolism as its aesthetics. Oh, what an overwhelming and eye-opening experience that trip to the boutique had been. It was the moment she understood the seductiveness of America: the hope that something even more pure, even more magical, was not only possible but within one's control if they proved themselves worthy. That hope, Anna knew, was poison, and very valuable to those who knew how to use it.

She took one last look in the mirror and exited the bathroom, already rehearsing what she would say to George Trent.

CHAPTER FOUR

At exactly quarter to eight, Matt and Grossman arrived at room five sixty-two, mercifully putting an end to the hours-long speculation on how the night would go. All the banter had only increased Matt's nervousness, which he attempted to assuage through action – a technique that always worked before a test in military school. Not so tonight – he had methodically gone down a predate checklist to find that while he looked and smelled presentable, his anxiety continued unabated. Grossman's disheveled appearance, on the other hand, indicated a much more laissez-faire approach to romance.

Matt resisted the urge to wipe a clammy palm on his sports coat, a parting gift from his mother the week before, and instead knocked twice on the door. He hadn't given much thought to what his date would look like, but simply assumed she was one of the many attractive co-eds he'd seen since arriving at school. As the door opened, however, he realized his folly. Before him stood a short, fat girl with hair trimmed nearly as close as his own. Unrefined features rendered her face nearly nondescript, the exception being the faint shadow of a mustache.

Surely, this can't be my date, he thought.

"Hiya," the girl said. Then, shifting a wad of bubble gum roughly the size of a golf ball from one side of her mouth to the other, she dashed Matt's hopes for the evening. "I'm Janet."

Matt opened his mouth to respond, then closed it again. It was as if once he introduced himself, this would become his reality.

Clearly enjoying the moment, Grossman pointed to him and announced, "This is Matt." He then leaned in closer to Matt and said, "She's beautiful."

If Janet noticed his sarcasm she gave no indication. "Oy vey," she exclaimed as she sized Matt up, "I didn't expect a *goy*!"

Goy? he thought; then, figuring it was some frat lingo he was not familiar with, replied. "Oh, no, I'm not in the fraternity."

A long, uncomfortable pause ensued, punctuated by a puzzled look from Janet and a snicker from Grossman.

"Well, better get going," he offered, then turned and headed for the elevator.

Janet closed her door and with another snap of her gum took Matt by the hand. Deflated and uncomfortable with the physical contact, he nevertheless allowed himself to be led to the elevator, where Grossman was holding the door for them.

Grossman's date, Sue, lived just one floor down, but the ride seemed much longer, thanks to the awkward silence and the feel of Janet's thick fingers entwined with his. Even Grossman was quiet, perhaps for the first time since they had met the day before. Odder still was that when they got off the elevator he moved down the hall tentatively, rather than with his usual sauntering gait. That's when Matt realized gleefully that he was nervous about meeting his own date.

"What's the room number?" he asked innocently.

"Four sixty-two," Grossman mumbled.

"Oh. Right under my room," Janet noted, as if anyone cared. She then produced a huge bubble and popped it, leaving a pink string along her bottom lip.

Grossman continued to drag his feet until Janet impatiently stepped ahead of him, dragging Matt along with her toward the door. As her loud knocks echoed through the hall, Matt looked back at his friend in amusement. The night would be a disaster for sure, but at least he wouldn't experience it alone. To his dismay, the door was answered by a lovely, petite young woman with blond shoulder-length hair. Janet immediately took control of the introductions, but even over her grating voice Matt could hear Grossman's sigh of relief.

Grossman would also be spared the pressure of having to break the ice with his date. As they set off across campus, Janet rambled on, a one-sided conversation that drowned out the possibility for anyone else to participate. Matt listened as she detailed her entire schedule, making note of what places to avoid and when. Then, after a few moments dreading the rest of the evening, he seized the opportunity to take in the quad of American University at dusk. The lights along the walk started to come on, presenting a contrast against the darkening sky. It was a beautiful, serene scene, though it would have been even more so without the snapping of Janet's gum, which she had so skillfully integrated with her inane chattering that it seemed an entirely new form of communication.

*   *   *

They finally arrived at The Tavern to find Walter and his date, Meryl, waiting at the door. Matt immediately noticed that Meryl was also pretty and wondered if he had somehow drawn the short straw. The small band was met by the omnipresent Tex, who was handing out beers that had been thoughtfully arranged on a table by the entrance. Holding two beers above his head, he shouted to be heard over Electric Light Orchestra, booming from the jukebox.

"I'm glad you guys made it. And these…" He paused to scan the three girls, freezing for a beat when his gaze landed on Janet, "…must be your lovely dates."

Walter leaned over to Matt. "Some are lovelier than others! You should have gotten the *shiksa*."

Matt didn't know the meaning of the word but assumed Walter thought Grossman might be better coupled with Janet.

"She's a trophy, alright," he replied, but his eyes were fixed on Tex. He wanted an answer.

As he stepped up to accept his beer, Tex met his gaze and grinned sheepishly. "We all take one for the team sometimes, right Matt?"

Matt grunted in response, then followed the others to a table on the other side of The Tavern. Though it was early the place was already filled with people and the promise of an epic night. Officially billed as a rush party, it was an opportunity for the frat brothers to impress freshmen and get them to join up. For Matt and his friends, it represented something much more significant: classes started in the morning, and this was one last glorious chance to party without guilt.

They had no sooner settled around the table when Janet launched into another monologue that shifted from one uninteresting topic to another, including her father's business and a painfully detailed description of her mother's recent surgery. Matt hid behind a blank stare while listening wistfully to the witty banter going on around him. But when Janet started talking about her nightly beauty regimen, Matt decided he'd definitely earned a break. Realizing she was not going to come up for air, he abruptly stood and announced that he was getting another beer.

As he turned away Janet suddenly complained of being cold. Could she borrow his jacket? Matt groaned inwardly. If he liked her, or at least didn't find her repulsive, he wouldn't have hesitated. But since he couldn't refuse without looking like a total heel, he shrugged out of the jacket and handed it to her. The gesture resulted in no gratitude. Janet simply draped it over her shoulder, then redirected her soliloquy to the others at the table, oblivious to the fact that no one was listening.

Tex met Matt at the bar. Within seconds, Grossman and Walter sidled up. The topic of conversation focused on women. Sue and Meryl certainly had potential. Janet, it was agreed, was another story. Tex again acknowledged the terrible mismatch and offered an apology, but his smirk told Matt he was enjoying it far too much.

"You ought to get Janet as drunk as you can," Walter advised. "She can't get any more obnoxious and it just might make her sleepy and shut her up."

Thinking this was as good an idea as any, Matt drained his beer, then ordered two more and brought them to the table. Fortunately, Janet sipped as much as she spoke and was soon done with both of them. It didn't stop her from talking, but she also didn't argue the next time he slipped from the table to get more. From then on, he stopped by the table only to drop off the drink then headed off to mingle with others. Janet didn't care. She simply kept up her oration with anyone who happened to be nearby.

Walter, he realized, was a bona fide genius.

Later, Matt wouldn't remember who had called the first chugging match, nor would he recall how many he entered. All he knew was that there was no shortage of challengers seeking to take down the recently crowned champion. Tex played the role of the referee, not that one was needed. Matt's supremacy was never in doubt. Between bouts he returned to Janet's table with a beer for her. Each encounter, no matter how brief, was painful, even as he also grew increasingly intoxicated.

It was Sue who approached Matt at the bar with the news that Janet was sick.

"She's in the bathroom, and I think she needs help."

"That makes two of us!" Matt said under his breath. Then, embarrassed by his comment, he asked, "What should I do?"

"Well, try to help her, of course," she replied, but it was clear that her sympathy lay with him.

Matt headed for the restrooms in the hall outside The Tavern. There was a small group of girls gathered there, debating what to do about the person in the ladies' room who was clearly in a bad way. Between sounds of vomiting, he heard a shrill, familiar voice shrieking, "I'm spinning, oh, I'm spinning. It's going so fast!"

"She's really sick," one of the girls said to another.

"She's my date," Matt confessed with embarrassment, then added, "*Blind* date," to place the situation in proper perspective. "Is there anyone else in there?"

The girls shook their heads, and one replied, "Nope! She's alone. Nobody wanted to deal with that."

Matt couldn't argue with her. Unfortunately, he didn't really have a choice.

"Cover me?" he asked them. "I don't want to get in any trouble for being in the ladies'."

They nodded, then he took a deep breath and entered no man's land.

Janet was in a stall. With one eye closed and his face pulled into a grimace, Matt gently opened the door. The scene was horrifying. Janet was on the floor. Her arms and legs were wrapped around the toilet bowl, hands firmly clutching the sides as if she were holding onto a carnival ride. She had apparently missed the mark at some point, for there was a puddle of vomit on the floor as well as in the bowl. Worst of all, she was still wearing Matt's new sport coat. He moaned, not with any regard for her, but disgust that his coat was in contact with the porcelain and God knew what else.

He thought for a moment, contemplating the proper course, then softly placed his hand on her shoulder and helped her to her feet. Thus began a comedy of errors worthy of Laugh-In. Getting her out of the stall proved a challenge, as did propping her up by the sink while he grabbed paper towels and wiped down her face, especially since every time he loosened his grip on her she started sliding toward the floor. Finally, he decided her appearance was as good as it was going to get. Fortunately for her, she was far too drunk to care about what anyone thought. He, however, had plenty of concern. Beyond being embarrassed, he felt guilty knowing that he was at least in part responsible for her condition.

With a sigh of resignation, he wrapped an arm around her shoulders.

"Okay, Janet, here we go."

She searched his face for a moment, almost as if she was trying to place him, then she nodded and they made their way toward the exit. Matt was just about to reach for the knob when the door swung open and standing there was the lovely co-ed who had witnessed his childish prank in the cafeteria that morning.

They both drew back with a start.

"Oh, am I in the wrong place?" she asked, though clearly this was not the case.

"N-no," Matt stammered as the heat rushed to his face. Behind her, he could see the gaggle of females giggling at his discomfort. "I'm just helping her."

"Yer pretty," Janet slurred, for once talking about something other than herself. Then, to Matt's absolute horror, she grabbed his free hand as if staking her claim.

"Um, thanks," the girl replied then, stepped inside the bathroom, her delicate nose wrinkling at the smell of vomit.

Given her unstable condition, Matt slipped Janet out of the side door without telling anyone he was leaving. The walk back to her dorm was long and painful. The fresh air helped her a little, but she was still too drunk to walk unaided. Even worse than the physical contact was the fear that passersby might conclude they were a couple.

"I feel so sick!" she complained several times throughout the journey, "Everything is spinning."

"You're not sick," Matt replied each time. "You're just drunk. It'll be over soon." But he was thinking more about his escape than about her condition, which would no doubt be even worse the next day.

Matt groaned when they arrived at Janet's dorm to find Grossman and Walter in the lobby, having just dropped off their dates. They watched as he awkwardly assisted Janet, making no attempt at hiding their delight. Finally, Matt stopped and looked at her, deciding that she could make it the rest of the way on her own. He was done.

"Goodnight," he said, all business, "Hope you feel better."

"Oh, please!" she said, not about to be cast off so easily. "Come up to my room."

Grossman and Walter burst out laughing as Matt searched for an excuse.

"I can't. The guys are waiting," he said, pointing to his friends. "We've got to help the fraternity clean up The Tavern."

"Matt, we can clean up for you!" Grossman called out good-naturedly, earning a sneer from Matt and a snort of glee from Walter.

Janet smiled and pulled Matt toward her. His mind raced for a solution, but his thoughts were yo-yoing between his repulsion for Janet and his newfound hatred for Grossman.

As the elevator door opened, he made his move. "Really, Janet, if I don't help the guys I'll never get into the fraternity! Hope you feel better; I'll just get my coat some other time."

With that, he abruptly shoved her onto the elevator, leaned in and pushed the button for her floor, then quickly removed his arm just in time to save it from the closing doors. The elevator whooshed away, and he breathed a deep sigh of relief. He thought with annoyance of the sport coat, an unfortunate casualty of the evening, as was his sense of humor.

"Assholes!" he muttered as he walked past Walter and Grossman, which only made them laugh even harder.

"Hey, where're you going?" Walter called as they followed him outside.

"He's going to help clean The Tavern," Grossman snickered.

"I'm going to *bed*," Matt said, picking up the pace, "Maybe when I wake up tomorrow this will have all been a bad dream!"

"But the night is still young…" Walter said with amusement.

"And it's over for me," Matt shot back.

"The whole fraternity is going to the PIO," Grossman added in a sing-song voice.

"I'm not *in* the fraternity, and I've had enough 'fun' for tonight, thank you."

Out of persuasive arguments, Grossman fell back on an old standby: "Oh, don't be a putz!"

The use of yet another word he didn't understand pissed Matt off even more. "I don't know or care what a *putz* is, but I do know, compliments of the fraternity, what hell is, and I'm not going to spend any more time there tonight."

Walter and Grossman looked at each other; then, as if in a perfectly choreographed move, they lunged toward their wayward friend, each grabbing an arm.

"Tomorrow's the first day of school!" Matt protested, trying to shake them off.

"Exactly!" Walter said, deftly managing his cigar as he spoke. "We are packing the rest of the summer into tonight. Besides, we didn't come to college to let school get in the way of our education!"

*   *   *

The PIO, or Pioneer Restaurant, was the only place near American University that was open all night. Its clientele were also people of the night – women whose tight-fitting clothes and cheap makeup and jewelry were an advertisement for their profession, and a myriad of dropouts from society who probably had no place else to go.

Not all the fraternity brothers made the trip; however, there was a hardcore element, led by Tex and large enough to fill two large adjoining booths, who embraced Walter's attitude toward studying. The group settled in and ordered a feast of various breakfast foods, then began a review of the evening which, by all accounts, had been a success. It didn't take very long for the conversation to come around to Matt's date. To his surprise, the discussion turned out to be kind of a catharsis for him. He told them how he'd found Janet in the ladies' room and, now seeing it in his past, was able to laugh along with everyone else. Thus, the awful night ended on a high note. Matt was hailed as a hero for surviving Janet, while she, moving forward, would serve as a sort of litmus test for questionable pledges. If there had ever been any doubts about Matt's suitability as a PI, they were put to rest that night.

CHAPTER FIVE

Matt awoke five minutes after his first class began. Letting fly a series of expletives, he jumped out of bed, threw on his clothes, and dashed down the hall toward the bathroom. Grossman was leaving the bathroom when Matt entered. His roommate was a horrid sight – his face was covered with patches of toilet paper intended to staunch the flow of blood resulting from self-inflicted shaving wounds; his black hair, normally unruly, was matted like spaghetti left on a plate overnight.

"Better hurry! Don't want to be late for class," Grossman said mockingly, then brought up his wrist to look at an imaginary watch. "Oops, looks like that train already left the station."

Matt was in no mood. His head was pounding – he had already renewed his "no drinking" vow – and he was kicking himself for kowtowing to the pressure to stay out late the night before.

Grossman watched Matt as he doused his face with water then chugged a large amount of mouthwash and swished it around.

"Can't be too cautious," he drawled, "Never know when you will meet the girl of your dreams… or in your case, wet dreams."

Matt spat out the mouthwash. "You know, sometimes I think I hate you, Grossman."

"I hate waking up before the end of a wet dream…"

Matt paid no attention. He ran out of the bathroom in a mad rush.

A few minutes later he was sprinting across a barren campus. Obviously, every other student had made it to class on time. His head pounded ferociously with every step, and when he slowed to enter the building, he realized he was queasy as well. He didn't give it much thought, though, as he took a staircase two steps at a time. On the second floor he searched for his classroom. It was an uncomfortable feeling. The halls were also empty, as if the place had been evacuated; however, when he peered through the classroom windows, he saw they were packed with fellow students training their eyes on whatever professor was holding court.

Matt found his classroom and slowly opened the door, hoping not to attract too much attention. Scanning the room for an available desk, he noticed a sweater being removed from an empty seat in the middle – an obvious gesture of charity for the latecomer. He made his way to the desk, staring at the professor who, fortunately, was writing on the blackboard with his back to the class. Proud of himself for having executed a stealthy late arrival, Matt turned to thank the Samaritan and found himself nose-to-nose with the girl who had witnessed his pranks in the cafeteria and his debacle with Janet. His smile instantly turned to a blush. She smiled politely, then quickly returned her attention to the front of the room.

Mortified, Matt also tried to focus on what the professor was saying but realized he was completely lost. He turned to ask the girl, and that's when he saw, seated to her right, the guy who'd been with her in the cafeteria. He was examining Matt as one would a bug they were about to crush.

If looks could kill, Matt thought, *I'd be dead and buried.*

Once again Matt focused on the professor, who was now orating on his philosophy of teaching and learning. Matt was immediately suspicious. For one thing, the middle-aged man was speaking like he was a student, making heavy use of slang terms like "cool" and "man." For another, he wasn't dressed like a teacher. He wore a baggy flannel shirt, jeans, and boat shoes with no socks. When he sat, he leaned back in his chair and perched his feet on his desk.

He's probably having a midlife crisis, Matt decided. He could only hope the guy would be so easygoing when it came to grading exams.

While the professor continued to dispense his philosophies, Matt really started to feel sick. The adrenalin of rushing to class receded, making the aftereffects of his partying more intense. Perspiration trickled down his forehead. He wiped his brow and rested his head on his arms folded across the small desk. That only made things worse. He began to feel dizzy too. Then something happened: someone nudged his arm. He looked up to see her hand retreating from his desk.

"Don't fall asleep," she whispered out of the side of her mouth. "Hey, you look sick. Are you okay?"

"I'm fine," he managed. "Rough night last night."

"Yes, I noticed," she said, reminding him that she had witnessed the bathroom fiasco with Janet.

He wanted to ask what she'd been doing at The Tavern, but then another wave of nausea overtook him. "Actually, I do feel a little sick."

"You should go to the student health center," she suggested.

"I don't want to miss class," he replied, pointing his finger toward the professor, who was now writing on the board.

"Don't be silly. This isn't high school. You can leave if you need to!"

Now she had presented him with a challenge. It no longer mattered how he felt, he had to prove he wasn't a wimp.

"Yeah, I think I'll blow off this class and get some zzz's," he said as coolly as possible, already gathering his books.

I can do whatever I want, he told himself, *This isn't high school.*

He stood and made for the door, only to freeze when he heard the professor say in a decidedly *un*-laidback voice, "Where are you going, young man?"

Matt felt the burn of a dozen laser beams, realizing every eye in the classroom was focused on him.

"I'm sick," he muttered pathetically, then continued out the door without waiting for permission. As he turned back to quietly close the door, the girl mouthed, "I'm sorry," while her companion gave him a loathsome smirk.

He moved slowly across the quad, not quite sure what to think. Had he been set up? Did she intend to embarrass him? She didn't seem the sort. In fact, she seemed to like him, or maybe she was just feigning interest to make that guy jealous. And what was the deal with those two, anyway?

Matt's internal debate was interrupted by the sound of his name being called. When he turned he saw Walter rushing to catch up.

"Wassamatta, you?" Walter said in a surprisingly good imitation of a mobster.

"I feel like shit."

"And ya look like shit," he said, still in character, "What else is new?"

Matt rolled his eyes. "Where are you going?"

"The registrar's office. I gotta get out of U.S. History. You should see the syllabus. We're supposed to read a book a week. A BOOK A WEEK! I didn't come to college to work that hard!"

Matt managed a laugh, then rubbed his roiling stomach.

"You know what you need, man?" Walter paused as if about to impart some life-changing knowledge. "Food."

Matt nodded. He hadn't had anything to eat since the midnight meal at PIO.

"Hey, you wanna come?"

Walter thought a moment. "Sure, the registrar will still be there after a burger, right?"

The two walked into the cafeteria, where Walter ordered a burger with all the fixings and Matt played it safe with eggs, dry toast, and coffee. As they ate, Matt related what happened in class. Walter agreed that he'd had no alternative but to leave once the girl issued the challenge; and, like Matt, he wasn't sure what to read into the situation. One never knew with women, especially the pretty ones.

The conversation then turned to the fraternity. Matt was a bit surprised that Walter was going to join – he seemed more comfortable as an observer and commentator of group activities than a participant – but awfully glad he was. Walter, with his cryptic comments that somehow cut to the heart of the matter, was quickly becoming something of a trusted counselor. Neither knew what to expect from the swearing-in ceremony, other than it would take place within the next few days and was top secret.

By the time they finished eating Matt found he was feeling better – at least good enough to go back to the dorm and take a nice long nap before

Grossman returned. After saying they would meet up later, Walter went to change classes. As Matt walked outside, he nearly collided with the girl from his class.

"It's you!" she exclaimed. "I'm so, so –"

Matt waved away her apology. "Happy to be a source of amusement to the class." He paused. "Your boyfriend certainly seemed to think it was funny."

"Boyfriend?" She looked at him quizzically. "Oh, you mean Michael. He's just a friend from home."

"Oh," Matt said, thinking, *Does Michael know that?*

"Anyway, I'm Catherine Martin."

"Matt Thomas."

Catherine looked at him with a small smile. "Matt Thomas, would you like to take me out Saturday night?"

*   *   *

A few days later, at precisely 9:50 p.m., Matt and Grossman left their dorm and headed to the campus chapel for their initiation into the fraternity. As they crossed the quad, Matt gave his roommate a sideways glance and smiled. In honor of the occasion, Grossman had taken uncharacteristic care with his appearance; unfortunately, his slightly crumpled khakis looked like he had found them at the bottom of a hamper and his valiant attempt to tame his hair with some sort of pomade had resulted in an oily sheen.

Holding an initiation ceremony in the chapel was not the norm; then again, the PIs was not like others. In his initial pitch to the pledges, Tex had focused on the fraternity's reputation for civility. Sure, other fraternities talked trash about them not having their own house, as if this meant they were not a "real" fraternity. To Tex and his brothers, however, not living together was a selling point. Other fraternities, he contended, were more like mobs. They engendered a group mentality that everyone adopted at the sacrifice of his own identity – and with the lousy actions of some bad apples often incriminating the rest. Not so with PIs. Each brother remained his own man, and they came together because they wanted to be together, not because it was geographically desirable. This was the truest form of fraternalism.

Matt and Grossman arrived at the chapel and located the door to the basement, where they had been instructed to go for the top-secret ceremony.

"This is kinda creepy," Matt whispered, as he pulled open the door to reveal a dark, musty-smelling staircase.

"Uh-huh," Grossman replied.

"But cool…"

"Yeah, man. Like, who knows how many people have been down here since the 1800s? It's like something out of a ghost story."

"Actually, the chapel was only added in 1965."

"You *would* know that."

"What? It was in the catalog," Matt muttered, slightly embarrassed.

They reached the end of the stairs to find a rather surreal scene. The basement was dark, save for the light of a single candle on a table in the center. On one side of the table stood Walter and the five other freshmen joining the fraternity; on the other side were several brothers. As president of the fraternity, Tex was officiating the ceremony. Matt stifled a laugh when he saw him. Just two nights earlier, the same guy had been screaming, "Chug, chug, chug," as Matt and some unfortunate opponent gripped sweaty glasses of beer. Now, dressed in a long blue choir robe emblazoned with Greek letters, he was doing his best to project a solemn presence.

"Now that we're *all* here…" Tex began with a pointed glance at Matt and Grossman as if scolding them for being the last to arrive. He then directed the inductees to stand before the brothers, who had formed a small semicircle, before launching into a homily on the bonds of fraternalism.

"Fraternity! Brotherhood!" he declared with staccato intensity. It reminded Matt of watching General Douglas MacArthur's famous speech on TV, when he proclaimed "Duty, Honor, Country" to future soldiers at the United States Military Academy, West Point.

"This fraternal institution," Tex continued, "depends on each of us in this room, and each of us in turn depends upon the other. For the next four years, and throughout our lives, we will be inextricably linked. Like the Musketeers, we must stand for each other. To maintain this bond, we must have faith in ourselves, in each other, and the institution of fraternalism – a faith as everlasting as the candles of the menorah."

Matt leaned toward Walter and without taking his eyes off Tex whispered through closed lips, "What's a menorah?"

"What a putz," Grossman muttered, earning an elbow in the ribs from Matt.

Walter also kept his eyes trained on Tex as he replied, "It's a symbol in the Hebrew faith."

Matt pondered this for a moment. "What's that got to do with anything?"

"This is a Jewish fraternity…"

"Walter, I'm not Jewish!"

Walter's mustache twitched with amusement. "You're circumcised, aren't you?"

Matt whipped his head toward him, thoroughly confused.

"What?"

"Relax! You'll fit right in."

If Matt could have slunk back up the stairs without becoming a spectacle he would have gladly done so. He'd been so caught up in Tex's overtures and beer chugging it never occurred to him that he lacked a basic qualification for joining. On the other hand, no one had asked him if he was Jewish – or even if he was circumcised – so maybe it wasn't a big deal. He liked Tex and the other fraternity guys, and he definitely wanted to be a part of whatever Walter and Grossman were going to be doing.

He leaned toward Walter again. "Does this mean I need to get a menorah?"

It was too much for Grossman, who emitted a loud snort, while Walter's mustache now danced uncontrollably as if it was fighting to be free of his face.

After issuing a warning glare at the wayward inductees, Tex finally concluded his presentation. The fraternity brothers fell in line behind him to congratulate the new members – a ritual that clearly held great meaning for them. Matt, however, was preoccupied with other things, mainly what his mother would say if he was asked to convert. As he observed Tex and the fraternity guys exchanging handshakes and back-slaps, he got the distinct feeling that this was adding up to another night of drinking, which after his recent debacle he was definitely not in the mood for. As soon as he received his congratulations, he said he was going to the men's room, then slipped out of the chapel and into the balmy D.C. night.

Any guilt he felt for ditching the guys was short-lived. The meaning of true brotherhood could wait; right now he had larger concerns, namely his upcoming date with Catherine. He'd spent the better part of a day reeling from her invitation. With no dating experience of his own, his notions of romance had come largely from the stories of his military schoolmates, all of which involved the male leading the courting. Then there was Michael, whose relationship with Catherine seemed like more than a friendship, no matter what she said. Nevertheless, he'd accepted, and though she was the aggressor he had no doubt that the planning of this event fell on his shoulders. What would they do? What would they talk about?

The idea of taking her to The Tavern popped into his mind and was immediately dismissed as completely uncool. They were in D.C., for God's sake, with its endless potential – and therein lay the problem: too many choices and no car to get to most of them. Despite the speech Tex had just delivered, it never occurred to him to go to his new brothers, or even Walter and Grossman, who upon hearing of her invitation expressed suspicion that she was using Matt to step out on Michael.

"Don't fall for it," Grossman had cautioned him, "Girls that fine get away with murder."

"…and even some ugly ones…" added Walter sagely.

As he entered the dorm, Matt was so lost in thought he almost didn't notice Janet, who was on a similar course toward the elevator. Her ever-present gum proved to be his saving grace; the loud pop and snap jerked his awareness back to his surroundings just in time. Pretending not to see her, he picked up his pace and got to the elevator first. Inside, he furiously punched the "close" button, never mind that he knew it wouldn't actually make the doors close faster. It was a near-miss, with the doors closing just as she was about to enter. He saw a flash of surprise in her eyes when she realized he was inside, then heard the loud pop of her bubble gum, which, he imagined gleefully, was now flattened across her face. He was still smiling when he got off on his floor, but it quickly faded when he noticed the door to his room was ajar.

He found Kate lying on the lower bunk, the phone pressed to her ear. With a sigh of annoyance he sat down in his desk chair, propped his feet up on the radiator, and stared out the window with what he imagined was dignity. Rolling her eyes at his unspoken drama, Kate nevertheless ended her call. Then she casually threw his feet off the radiator, nearly knocking him backward off the chair, and plopped herself down in their place.

"You look bothered," she said, watching him struggle to regain his balance.

"Yeah, but it's a good thing… I think."

He told Kate about Catherine, briefly chronicling the series of embarrassing events that had, somehow, led to her asking him out. Though he didn't elaborate on his own lack of experience in this area, Kate's small smile gave him the distinct impression that she was all too aware.

"Two suggestions: Take her to dinner at the top of the Key Bridge Marriott, it's romantic. And get a car. I think Milt Green has one. Maybe you can borrow it."

Matt was relieved by the first suggestion— if Kate thought dinner at the Key Bridge Marriott made for a cool first date, good chance Catherine would also. The latter, however, gave him pause. Milt Green was the

Resident Assistant and Matt had not said more than two words to him. How would he even broach the subject?

"Just ask him," she said, noting his raised eyebrow. "The worst he can say is no, right? Besides, he's lent it out before."

Her logic appealed to him.

"You're great!" Matt exclaimed, then stood up from the chairs and rushed past a startled Kate toward the door. As he approached Milt's room, however, his pace slowed. Though he had not yet conversed with the RA, he had, when passing Milt's room, heard several of his "exchanges" with various co-eds; he'd also seen said co-eds entering and exiting at all hours of the day and night. They always seemed to be having a good time, though Matt doubted they would feel that way if they knew how many other girls Milt had in his rotation.

He paused at the door, listening for a moment lest he interrupt one of Milt's liaisons and embarrass some poor girl – not to mention himself. When he heard a single male voice, Matt decided Milt was either on the phone or talking to himself and debated whether he should just return later. No, he told himself, the stress of planning this date was taking up far too much energy. He needed an answer about the car… now. He raised his hand and gave the door three short raps.

Sure enough, when Milt opened the door he had a phone receiver cradled between his shoulder and right ear. A long cord stretched behind him all the way to his desk, where the base teetered precariously on a stack of books.

"It's going to fall," Matt pointed out, but Milt held up a finger, then opened the door wider and waved him in. Matt stepped into the room just as the phone base crashed to the floor, waking up a half-naked girl in Milt's bed. She looked around the room sleepily, then, deciding the situation warranted no concern, put her head back on the pillow and closed her eyes.

Matt groaned inwardly, then reminded himself his timing could have been far worse. For several minutes he stood there, alternatively looking at the ceiling and out the window – anywhere but the bed.

Milt's part of the conversation was primarily comprised of a series of "uh-huhs" followed by an occasional, "I know." Yet all the while Matt could feel the RA's eyes on him, as if sizing him up.

Probably thinks I look like a square, Matt thought. With Kate in his room, he'd not had a chance to change out of the dress clothes he wore to the ceremony.

Abruptly, Milt exclaimed, "I got an idea! I'll get right back to you." He hung up. "My sister," he said to Matt, "She needs a favor."

"Well, actually," Matt admitted, "I came to ask for one too."

"Who do I look like, the Godfather?" Milt said. "Actually, I heard someone did an imitation of Vito the other night that was *spot-on*. I mean, this guy stuffed his cheeks and –"

"Don Milt…" Matt interrupted before the conversation got too far off track – or he got roped into doing the Corleones' greatest hits.

Milt smiled. "Go ahead. Hit me."

"Well, I met this cute girl and she asked me out and –"

"*She* asked *you* out?" Milt asked with exaggerated incredulity. "You must be something special…"

Matt shrugged. "I don't know, but I want to plan something cool and I heard you have a car and –"

"Say no more," Milt said magnanimously. "You can borrow it."

"Really?"

"Life is complicated enough, right?" Milt gestured to the sleeping girl. "We guys have to stick together. Like how you're going to help me out with my sister…"

Matt raised his eyebrow, unsure of what to say next.

"Look, she works downtown, they need a part-time gopher, and they're driving her crazy to find one. She asked for my help." Milt gave Matt another once-over, nodding appreciatively at his attire and conservative appearance. "If you are willing to go talk to them, I'll let you have the car keys on Saturday."

Matt thought for a minute. He hadn't been planning to work his freshman year, at least not until he got the lay of the land and had a handle on his schoolwork. On the other hand, it would be cool to earn some extra money, and he wanted that car.

Finally, he said, "Maybe I should know a little bit about this…"

"Don't worry, it's a respectable place, sort of. Anyway, there are probably a thousand guys who would give their right ball to work there. It's not just a job," he added with a wide grin, "it's an adventure."

Matt didn't know whether to trust Milt, but he had to admit his interest was piqued.

"Okay, deal," he said, holding out a hand to seal the arrangement.

"Not so fast, Romeo. I have a few questions." Milt's tone suddenly became serious. "Have you ever been in trouble?"

Puzzled, Matt began sifting through events in his life that could possibly fall under the heading of "trouble." Other than a few military school pranks gone awry, there weren't any to speak of.

"You mean like –"

"I mean with the police," Milt interrupted.

"Nope," he replied firmly.

"Do you do drugs?"

"No!" Matt exclaimed, but with a touch of embarrassment at sounding like such a goody-goody.

"Not even a little weed?" Milt asked, eyes wide.

"Really!" Matt shrugged sheepishly. "I went to military school and you'd get in really deep shit for that. Besides, I don't like the smell of it."

"Good," Milt said, thrusting out his hand to shake. "That's what I wanted to hear!"

"What's the deal?" Matt inquired, tentatively extending his own hand. Milt pumped it with the vigor of a used car salesman making a sale.

"The deal is you interview for this job, which gets my sister off my back, and I let you borrow the car. Let's see when they will get you in for an interview." Milt picked up the phone. "Now, I'm gonna call her back…"

By now Matt was more than a little curious and maybe a little suspicious as well. Milt's side of the conversation with his sister didn't answer any questions or allay any concerns, nor could Matt discern why Milt was being so secretive. What had he gotten himself into? He didn't know, but he was getting increasingly annoyed that he had gotten himself into it over a girl, and likely one with a boyfriend at that.

When he hung up Milt said only that his sister would call Matt in the morning to set up the interview, which would be downtown and probably in the afternoon. Beyond that, Milt remained tight-lipped and possibly amused by Matt's discomfort. With growing dismay, Matt thought back to the initiation ceremony, when he found out that he was a *putz* (whatever that was) joining a Jewish fraternity and possibly in need of a *menorah* (another mystery). And who could forget the nightmare fix-up with Janet, or his humiliation when he fled class (on Catherine's suggestion) in his hungover state? This was just the latest in a growing number of situations where he, A) was completely in the dark about something that B) everyone else seemed to know about, and C) was the butt of some joke told by every *goy* or *shiksa* (whatever they were). It was not a trend he wished to continue.

Annoyed, he said goodnight to Milt and headed for the door.

"Hey," Milt called, "Where you going on the big date?"

"Dinner at the Key Bridge Marriott."

"Good choice! You should do a monument run after dinner."

Matt turned back around. "Monument run?"

"Yeah, you take a drive around the monuments at night. You know, the Lincoln, the Jefferson, the Washington. They were all presidents."

Matt raised an eyebrow at him. He might not know much, but he knew his American presidents. He was sure Milt was just playing with him.

"Anyway," Milt continued, "girls love it. It's romantic. Shows 'em you have a sensitive side, and if anything will win their heart, it's knowing you are sensitive!"

"You would know!" Matt muttered with a pointed nod toward the girl in his bed, eliciting a self-assured guffaw from the RA.

Car or no car, he thought as he headed back to his room, if Milt's sister didn't provide immediate clarification he was calling the whole thing off.

The phone rang at eight a.m. sharp the next morning, startling Matt from sleep. He jumped down from his top bunk to answer before Grossman could reach it, only to realize his concern was unfounded. Grossman, nestled fast asleep on the bottom bunk, didn't stir in the slightest. Matt grabbed it on the third ring. The caller introduced herself as Ann Green, Milt's sister, then, without further preamble asked if he could be "down here at four," apologizing that it was so late in the afternoon.

"Down where?" Matt asked, fearing the sister shared Milt's penchant for secrecy.

"Why, the White House," she answered.

That's it, he thought, resisting the urge to slam down the phone. *This is a put-on.*

"Didn't Milt explain?" Ann asked, sensing disbelief at the other end of the line.

"Explain? No, he didn't."

"I'm sorry if there's been any confusion. Let me fill you in."

Matt noted her sincerity and professional manner. Either she was damn good or this might actually be the real thing.

"I'm a secretary in the White House. Our office is in need of a messenger, someone to help out on a part-time basis. Milt thought you would be interested."

Matt felt his skepticism dissipating.

"It's probably only going to be two or three mornings a week, but I'm afraid we have to get the process going because it will take a while to get the proper clearances."

"Excuse me," Matt interrupted. "Are we talking about T H E White House?"

She laughed. "I see. You think I'm putting you on and, considering my brother's reputation I can't say I blame you. Why don't you hang up and call directory information? Ask for the number for The White House. It's four-five-six, one-four-one- four, but you confirm that for yourself. Then call that number and ask the operator for me. That should clear things up for you."

Matt hung up. As he dialed directory assistance he thought of a similar and highly enjoyable school prank, when he would torture some unsuspecting operator with a fake name. Now he wondered if someone, somewhere, was getting back at him. When he reached directory assistance, the number for the White House was confirmed. He nervously dialed. It rang once.

"White House," a voice on the other end announced.

Matt hesitated in disbelief. It occurred to him that he was standing in his insignificant dorm room in his underwear, talking to THE White House.

"Ann Green's extension, please," he asked shyly.

"One moment. I'll connect you," the operator replied briskly. Then he heard the friendly voice of Milt's sister.

"Feel better now?" she teased.

"I'm sorry, it's just sort of hard to believe."

"You'll get used to it," she replied, as if he had already been hired. "Just be here a little before four. It takes a few minutes to be cleared in. See you then."

CHAPTER SIX

That afternoon, as Matt walked briskly across campus, he made a mental note to thank his mother. Just two weeks earlier, he'd fought with her about buying the suit. After years of uniforms at military school, he hadn't thought past the freedom of throwing on a pair of khakis when he went to class. She'd insisted, though, spouting some one-never-knows-what-the-day-will-bring speech that at the time he'd found annoying. In his defense, he couldn't have foreseen an interview at the White House, but regardless, Mom's words had been proven eerily prescient.

Along with his gratitude was a healthy dose of self-consciousness. The crowded quadrangle was alive with guys and girls socializing and enjoying the sun. More than a few were also shooting some judgmental stares his way. Like most universities in the early 1970s, a strong sense of counterculture, largely the result of the antiwar movement, pervaded life at AU. For many students – and from what Matt had seen, a few teachers as well – that attitude was expressed through ripped dungarees and tie-dyed t-shirts. To them, Matt's suit might as well have been a neon sign broadcasting his support for the "establishment." Who he really was as a person was not even a consideration. The thought both angered and made him uncomfortable, but it also made him realize how lucky he was to have met guys like Grossman and Walter, along with Tex and the rest of the brothers. For all their ribbing, they truly accepted him as one of their own. By the time he reached the campus gate on Massachusetts Avenue, just above Ward Circle, his tie-dyed detractors were forgotten and he turned his attention to getting to his interview.

Twenty minutes later, Matt was still standing by the gate, his eyes flicking nervously between his watch and the street. He had seen only a few cabs – all of them occupied – and damp patches that had nothing to do with the heat that had formed under his arms.

Punctual to a fault, he never felt comfortable unless he was early for something. When planning out his day he gave himself an hour to get to the White House – this, allowing for the twenty-minute distance from campus and a fair amount of traffic. But that meant nothing if he couldn't get a cab! It suddenly dawned on him that the area was largely residential and sparsely populated compared with downtown D.C., which likely explained his current predicament. He looked at his watch again – even if he knew the bus schedule he would never make it in time.

Just as he was on the brink of desperation, a yellow cab appeared. Matt waved him down frantically.

The driver waited for Matt to slide in and, without taking his eyes off the road, craned his head back for instructions.

"The White House," Matt said, allowing himself for the first time to feel the excitement of what was to come. Just saying the words made him feel important. *I have business at the White House!* he thought, smiling. If he was expecting the driver to be similarly impressed, he was disappointed. The man emitted a grunt then eased the cab into traffic and continued down Massachusetts Avenue.

With a sigh of relief that he was finally on his way, Matt leaned back and stared out the window. Known as Embassy Row, Mass Ave was where many foreign governments had their official missions to the United States. Most were stately old buildings with colorful flags from their native lands and black limousines in the driveways with diplomatic license plates signifying that the occupants were immune to the laws of the country.

As they drew closer to their destination, Matt was struck by a blinding flash of reality: he was on his way to an interview at the White House with no plan and no clue what to say. And what kind of questions were they going to ask? Grades? Republican or Democrat?

Previous work experience? Then there was information he needed, like how much time he'd be expected to spend there each week and how much he would be paid.

Matt's thoughts were interrupted as the cab turned onto Pennsylvania Avenue. He had seen The White House on TV his whole life, but the sight of it in person literally sent a shiver racing up his spine. The driver pulled to the curb and waited patiently while Matt, all thumbs, nervously counted out dollar bills, then grunted his thanks when he saw the generous tip. Matt hopped out and glanced at his watch, seeing he had ten minutes to spare. He spent two of those minutes just staring awestruck at the executive mansion, a lump forming in his throat.

Quit your worrying, he berated himself, *You're not gonna get a job in there!*

Anne had arranged for Matt to meet her in the lobby of the Old Executive Office Building next to the White House. He knew from high school civics class that The OEOB housed many White House offices; now, as he stared up at the imposing building with its ornately detailed granite façade, he thought it looked somewhat out of place next to the simple architecture of the White House and the modern buildings that lined Pennsylvania Avenue.

Inhaling, he climbed the front steps and entered the lobby, wondering again if he was the victim of an elaborate joke.

"May I help you?" asked a uniformed guard from behind a desk.

"I'm supposed to meet Ann Green here."

The guard looked down to read a paper on the desk.

"Are you Mr. Thomas?"

Matt smiled broadly; his suspicions finally put to rest. This was no joke.

His smile was accepted by the guard as affirmation. "Please be seated, sir. I'll let Miss Green know you have arrived."

He called me sir, Matt thought, stifling a goofy laugh as he stepped over to a seating area. He'd been so nervous entering the building that he didn't even notice the lobby. It was adorned with oversized colorful photographs that left no doubt as to who occupied the Oval Office.

There were pictures of Richard Nixon on the podium of the Republican National Convention, his hands waving victoriously above his head after receiving the nomination for President. Another photograph offered a different view of the same victorious moment; shot from across the convention floor, it spanned the room festooned with balloons, streamers, and hundreds of the Republican faithful wearing silly convention hats with elephant trunks dangling in front of their faces. Yet another photo featured Nixon, hand upon a bible held by Mrs. Nixon, taking the Oath of Office. Still others showed the new President and First Lady walking down a chilly Pennsylvania Avenue in the inaugural parade.

Ann was quick to arrive. Petite, pretty, and blond, she bore absolutely no resemblance to the imposing, dark-haired Milt. She did have his charm, though, greeting Matt with a warm smile and the familiarity one might afford an old acquaintance. Clearly, she considered her brother Milt to be a good filter, giving Matt instant credibility.

Ann guided Matt through the gate past the guard, out of the lobby, and down a long marble corridor. The whole time, Matt's head was on a swivel, his eyes were drinking in every detail, from the ceiling, which seemed to be twenty feet high, to the simple black and white marble floor. Huge mahogany doors surrounded by intricately detailed cast iron frames led to offices on both sides of the hall. Each door had brass doorknobs and engraved hinges, owing to its architectural design dating back to the last century.

"This building is really amazing," Matt said in awe.

"Yes, it is," Ann replied. "It was built just after the Civil War. In some rooms you can actually see pipes on the walls where the original gas lights were mounted."

She led the way up an impressive granite staircase to the second floor. Huge stone stairs protruded from walls with no visible support. No doubt it had been an engineering marvel at the time of its construction, and it was no less of one this day. Matt smiled at the giant shiny mahogany banister atop hundreds of carved bronze posts. He pictured himself sliding down the handrail, the way he had done many times on the much smaller one in his grandmother's house.

On the second floor they passed two men standing in front of an office, the huge wooden door open to reveal an inner lobby to a suite of offices.

"The Vice President's office," Ann said casually. "You can tell he's in because those are his Secret Service agents."

"Really!" Matt said with the wonder of a country boy seeing a Ferris wheel at the county fair for the first time. The agents paid no attention to Matt and Ann.

Further down the hall, they reached a door with a sign reading "Executive Secretariat" beside it. Matt followed her into a small reception area that had two private offices on either side. In the reception area was a tall, slender man with sandy hair that was giving way to gray.

"Mr. Sanford," Ann announced. "This is Matt."

"Hello, son," the man intoned with a deep southern drawl as he clasped Matt's outstretched hand.

"Pleasure to meet you, sir," Matt replied.

Ann politely excused herself and headed for one of the inner offices while Mr. Sanford led Matt into the other. He walked around a large wooden desk and pointed to a chair for Matt, then placed himself in a tall executive leather chair. It produced an inappropriate squeak that forced Matt to wonder if it was the chair or the results of its occupant's greasy lunch.

The hello in the reception area was the totality of the older man's greeting. He immediately launched into a description of the job.

"I have another young fellow working two afternoons a week. I'd like to augment him by having some coverage in the mornings – two, maybe three a week – to help with the 'chores' – opening safes, delivering papers and mail, running errands, keeping the supply room stocked, burning copies." Mr. Sanford noted Matt's raised eyebrow at the words "burning copies" with a hint of humor. "That means making photocopies, son."

Matt nodded, slightly embarrassed for taking the words literally.

"It's not a sexy job," Sanford continued, "but this is the White House and these are interesting times. I get in at seven, and that's when I'd expect you. It's possible we will need some work on the weekends too – probably just a few hours on Saturday morning. You'd probably just be sleeping in anyway, right?" He continued without providing an opportunity for Matt to respond. "You'll start as a GS-3. It's not a lot of money, but you'll earn leave."

Matt opened his mouth to ask a question, but Sanford didn't seem to notice.

"Tell me a little about you, son," he drawled as he leaned back in his chair and crossed his arms.

"Well, I'm from Michigan and I went to a military academy. In the summers, I work in my dad's lumber yard. I –"

Sanford looked at his watch. "Say, we better get you downstairs before it gets too late!"

Matt hadn't realized how much he wanted the job until it appeared he was being dismissed. What more could he have said, in the few seconds he was allotted, to impress Sanford? He was debating whether to ask when Sanford shouted at the top of his voice, startling him.

"Keith!"

It took a split second for a short, stocky man to enter the room. "Matt, this is Keith. Keith, Matt. Would you get Matt downstairs to the Secret Service before they close?"

Matt looked from Sanford to Keith and back again. Why would he be going to the Secret Service? Was there some sort of exit procedure before they officially rejected him?

"Okay, boss," Keith replied, then turned his gaze to Matt. "Come on, Bud," he said, turning around and leaving the office. Matt rose and was about to offer his hand again when Sanford said, "I'll see you later, son."

See you later…?

"Yes, sir," Matt said, still confused. As he followed Keith out, Mr. Sanford shouted, "Say, son, you don't fuck chickens or anything, do you?"

His face turning red like a tomato, Matt reached for a response and said the first thing that came to mind. "I'm allergic to feathers, sir."

Sanford looked at him for a beat then roared with laughter. "That's good! 'Cause if you did, they'd find out!"

Keith, also chuckling, placed a hand on Matt's arm. "Very funny. Now come on, it's almost five."

Matt smiled to himself. Evidently the two men thought he was exchanging witty banter, when all he had done was tell the truth.

As he followed Keith down the hall, Matt had the opportunity to take in his appearance, which was a sharp contrast from Ann and Mr. Sanford. While they looked like typical executives, Keith looked anything but, with light brown hair that flopped across his forehead and a ruffled shirttail that hung out the back like that of a schoolboy. He was, Matt thought with a start, the White House version of Grossman!

Midway down the long corridor, Keith stopped at an elevator bank and pushed the down button. A second later the door slid open.

"I'll sure be glad when you get on board, Bud!" he said as he gestured for Matt to step in ahead of him. "They're running my sorry ass six ways from Sunday."

As he spoke, Matt caught a whiff of stale coffee and cigarettes and got the impression they served as Keith's main source of fuel during his busy days.

"Oh, I don't think I got the job," Matt corrected him, "I mean, that really wasn't much of an interview, and Mr. Sanford didn't offer it to me."

Keith raised his face toward the ceiling and let out a boisterous hoot. "Don't call him mister. It will go to his head. He's Glen, just plain Glen! And it was enough of an interview for him to make up his mind, or we wouldn't be going down to see the Secret Service. Long as you've never been in trouble, Bud, you're good as hired!"

Matt was shocked. "Really?"

"Yup."

As they got off the elevator on the ground floor, Matt saw several doors, the last of which had a seal with a five-pointed blue and gold star and the words United States Secret Service in the center.

Was this really happening?

They slipped inside the door to find a man standing behind a small counter.

"This is young Matt," Keith announced. "We'll be bringing his paperwork down first thing in the morning. Wanted to get his picture and fingerprints done tonight."

Without offering the slightest acknowledgment, the expression-less and tired-looking man pointed to a chair situated in front of a blue screen. Matt took the appointed seat and waited for the man to stroll across the room.

"Look straight at the camera," the man said blandly, as though he had done this a thousand times before and couldn't stand doing it just one more time. A flash of light momentarily lit the room. The man repeated the process, making sure he had a good result. "Over there," he pointed, directing Matt back to the small counter in the center of the room.

Matt watched as he took a small, toothpaste-like tube and squeezed a dab of black ink on a blackened pad. He then took a small roller and with great precision evenly dispersed ink across the board in a smooth, thin layer, taking care to iron out any air bubbles. Having accomplished this to his satisfaction, he reached for Matt's left hand, delicately rolled the pinky finger in the ink, then skillfully rolled it on a white card, leaving the artful impression of a maze of lines and swirls. After repeating the process with the remaining three fingers and left thumb, he took Matt's entire hand, holding all four fingers firmly in his own. He then pressed them on the inkpad and again against the white card, carefully recording their unique patterns together. After re-inking his pad, he did the whole thing again with Matt's right hand.

This must be what it's like when you're arrested, Matt thought, and though he had never done anything even remotely illegal, his palms felt slightly clammy with perspiration.

The man's brusque manner did nothing to put him at ease, though Matt wasn't sure whether he disapproved of him personally or was simply a bureaucrat trying to get out of the office by five o'clock. When he was finished, Keith took Matt back to the Secretariat, where he got a first-hand lesson in what made the government run: paperwork.

"You'll have to fill out this 171 and SF 86," Keith said, as he handed Matt two thick stacks. "You can use that desk."

Matt looked over the two forms, wide-eyed in amazement. Some of the information required, like his work experience, was simple, especially since he had little to report. But other questions covered every detail of the lives of his family members, including places of residence, social security numbers, and even traffic violations. He set about the task, studiously filling in the information he could, saving the hardest stuff for last.

"Keith," he said, "I'm going to need to use the phone."

Keith didn't hesitate. "Knock yourself out."

"It's long distance, though, I have to call Michigan…"

"No sweat, Bud. Everyone has to call somewhere to get information."

Matt sighed as he picked up the receiver. It wasn't that he didn't want to speak to his parents – he had been meaning to call them anyway – but he wanted to be able to give them this news on his own time. Sure enough, the moment he said where he was and why, his mother shrieked with delight and, over Matt's protestations that he would get into it later, called his dad to the phone. For the next several minutes they plied him with questions – most of which he couldn't yet answer – and congratulations, until Matt was finally able to steer them to the business at hand.

Thus began an arduous process of asking each question, waiting for his parents to debate back and forth about the correct date and circumstance. After crossing out several answers, Matt learned to wait until they had reached a consensus before committing it to paper. By the time he hung up the phone it was seven-thirty and he was utterly exhausted.

Keith had left the room but returned shortly, whereupon Matt turned the papers over to him. Keith took one look at Matt and laughed at his now tussled hair, the result of running his hands through it as he slaved to complete the forms. His tie, once expertly knotted, was now loosened and askew.

"You look beat, Bud, you better make tracks." He picked up the phone and called Glen, who was also apparently working late. "Hey, I'm sending young Matt home. Do you need anything else from him?" He paused a moment, then said, "You got it."

A few minutes later Matt and Keith were once again standing in front of Mr. Sanford's desk.

"Keith, did you get everything done?"

"Yes, sir. Everything. Got the picture for his pass. Got his fingerprints. Got both the 171 and SF 86."

"Good! Welcome aboard, son," Glen said with genuine warmth as he stood to shake hands. "When can you start to work?"

"Uh…" Matt said, mentally running through his schedule of classes and fraternity obligations.

"How 'bout Monday?" Keith suggested with a smile. "We can get him a temporary pass 'til his investigation is complete."

Matt nodded with some trepidation, which was either missed or simply not of concern to the two men. It was agreed: the following Monday he would start work in the White House.

Sanford glanced out the window, noting the raindrops illuminated by the security lights on the exterior of the building.

"Say, son, how did you get here today?"

"Cab," Matt responded.

"Keith, see if you can get a car."

Keith picked up Glen's phone and made a quick call. "Car will be at the ramp in five," he said, putting the receiver back on the phone. With that, Glen thanked Matt again, then Keith led him downstairs.

"The ramp," Matt soon learned, was a driveway that ran through the OEOB from West Executive Avenue on the White House side to 17th Street. Within a moment of their arrival, an elegant black limousine drove up. The driver jumped out of the car and rounded the back to open the rear door. Matt noticed he was wearing a suit with the Seal of the President on the jacket.

"Sir?" the driver said as he opened the door.

Matt nodded tentatively and got in. His reluctance was noted by the two men, each of whom realized the young man was embarrassed by the fanfare.

"See you Monday, Bud!" Keith called out as the driver shut the door. A moment later the car headed out of the compound into darkened Washington streets.

"American University, sir?"

"Yes. Hope you know how to get there. I'm a little new around here."

"No problem."

Matt leaned against the back seat, unsure how to react to this royal treatment. He felt like he was somehow cheating by being treated like he was important. At that moment, he caught the driver's glance in the rear-view mirror.

"This is a little embarrassing!" he admitted.

"What's that, sir?"

"I suppose you're used to driving around the President and here you are taking me back to school."

"Actually, the Secret Service drives the President. I drive staff members, so I think you're right where you belong."

The ice was broken. Matt told the driver about his whirlwind interview. He admitted how he wasn't really sure what he had gotten himself into and that he was more than a little nervous. A new job was tough enough, but working in The White House – now, that was intimidating!

"Tell me about it," the driver said. "One day I was in the army motor pool at Fort Hood, Texas, and the next they tell me I'm going to the White House. It makes ya feel pretty special, for sure, but once you're here a while and see people coming and going, you realize that someday it will end for you too. You go back to your life and everything is just a memory. So ya gotta enjoy the place, but don't let it go to your head. Don't let it change ya!"

The two fell into a comfortable silence then as each slipped into his own thoughts. The driver's words struck a chord with Matt. As he stared out the window at the light-filled streets he decided he shouldn't make such a big deal about the job. It would be surely interesting while it lasted, but ultimately it wouldn't change a thing.

CHAPTER SEVEN

The rain was coming down harder as Matt walked back to his dorm, but he barely noticed for the flurry of mental gymnastics going on inside his head. Before stepping into Milt's room he had never even dreamed of working at the White House; now, barely twenty-four hours later, he was riding around in a limousine and waiting for his security clearance to go through. Reality had definitely begun to sink in, and with it the realization that juggling the job with college life could be quite challenging, whether he let it go to his head or not.

He wasn't that concerned about keeping up with his regular classwork, but what about during exams and when term papers were due? Then he recalled the rigorous schedule at military school and how he always rose to meet it. Every hour of every day was accounted for; every night was spent shut in his room studying, He knew he could do that again if need be, but it was not what he wanted, especially if it meant sacrificing fraternity activities, or even horsing around with Grossman and Walter. If worse came to worst, he decided, he would have to let the job go.

For a minute he wondered if it had been a mistake to accept the position at all, but that thought was quickly dismissed. Like most once-in-a-lifetime opportunities, it was too cool to pass up; plus, the ego boost that came from Mr. Sandford hiring him on the spot was not easily dismissed.

Matt walked into this room to find Grossman, wearing only white briefs and a t-shirt, in front of the window with a pair of binoculars pressed to his face.

"Matt, do you know how lucky we are?" Grossman mused without turning around. "Three thousand years of recorded history and we hit college right smack in the middle of the sexual revolution."

Matt didn't know what surprised him more, the realization that his roommate had a somewhat creepy penchant for voyeurism, or that he could focus on any one thing for more than five seconds.

"How did you know it was me?" he asked.

"That would be the aroma of innocence and nervousness," Grossman replied good-naturedly.

"Screw you." Matt crossed the room to the window. "What the hell are you looking at?"

"People having sex."

"You lie like a rug!" Matt exclaimed, then realized he didn't doubt it for a minute.

"Yup. Not more than two minutes ago, this guy and babe – a very hot babe, I might add – were doing it with the lights on. Very considerate of them, I'd say!"

"Where?" Matt stretched his head out the window.

"Third floor, second room from the right." Grossman put the binoculars aside and looked at him. "Has anyone told you that you look like a Ken doll in that suit?" Before Matt had time to summon a response worthy of the insult, Grossman redeemed himself by asking, "How'd the interview go? Did you get the job?"

"I start on Monday."

"No shit! Any hot secretaries? Did you meet The Dick?" he deadpanned.

This time Matt didn't hesitate. "Yes, and he asked me to say hi to you."

Ignoring the retort, Grossman glanced at the clock on the desk.

"Shit! We're late for the fraternity meeting!" He jumped up, grabbed a pair of jeans from the floor and began pulling them up over his briefs.

"What meeting?" Matt groaned. All he wanted right now was food and sleep.

"The special one Tex called to plan the party on Saturday."

"What party on Saturday?"

"The one that's on the night after Friday!"

Matt yanked off his tie. "I don't know about any party, but I'm going out with Catherine on Saturday. And I'm not going to any meeting tonight. I haven't even eaten yet."

"You better go," Grossman warned. "It's the first meeting since we joined."

"I guess it's also the first meeting I'm going to miss. Why don't you take notes for me?"

Just then there was a firm knock on the door. Grossman opened it to find Walter.

"Hellllloooo," Walter intoned. "You ready?"

"I am. Matt's not going to the meeting. He had a stressful day at the office," Grossman quipped.

Walter stepped sideways to allow Grossman to pass him in the doorway, but Grossman paused just short of it. "Oh yeah," he said, looking upward as if trying to remember something. "That chick – Catherine – she called about an hour ago."

"Really?" Matt said, annoyed. "Why didn't you say something earlier?"

"It takes concentration," Grossman replied with a downward sweeping motion, "to look like this."

"Cut the shit," Walter drawled. "Matt, do you want us to wait 'til you change, or should we drag you out of here in that silly suit?"

"Well, did she leave a message?"

"Just for you to call her."

Matt looked at his watch. "Okay, you guys go ahead. I'll change clothes, call her, and catch up with you in ten minutes."

Walter and Grossman exchanged looks as if debating whether to believe him, then Walter nodded.

"Okay, but you better be on the level."

"Yeah," Grossman said, "Don't get so caught up with your *shaina maidel* that you forget what's really important."

Matt raised an eyebrow. "Let me guess – that means hot babe, right?"

Grossman laughed and turned to give Walter a high-five. "Look how far our little goy has come!"

Walter nodded in agreement. "Very good. Just hurry up and get to that meeting."

"I will," Matt promised, already sliding out of his jacket as they stepped into the hallway and shut the door behind them.

A few minutes later, dressed in a fresh shirt and khakis, he fished the piece of paper with Catherine's number from his wallet and reached for the phone. She answered on the third ring.

"Hi Catherine," he said, "It's Matt…" Then, suddenly nervous, he added, "You know, from class…"

Catherine answered with a smile in her voice. "Yes, Matt, I know who you are."

"Right," he said, glad she wasn't there to see his face burning. "My roommate said you called…"

"Yes, I did." She paused, and when she spoke again she sounded serious. "Listen, I'm really sorry to do this but I need a raincheck for Saturday."

"Oh." He hadn't realized until that moment how much he had been looking forward to it. "What's up?" he asked, then attempted a joke. "You have a hot date?"

"Ha, ha. Actually, I have to go to New York. My dad's company is holding its annual dinner and he's insisting we be there. I totally for –"

"Wait, did you say 'we'?" Matt interrupted, his disappointment giving way to suspicion.

"Yes, um, Michael is also invited," she said, then quickly added, "Oh, but it's not a date or anything. Michael –"

Matt cut her off again. "You don't have to explain. Listen, I have to run, though, I'm late for a meeting. I'll see you in class, okay?"

She paused for a moment as if about to say something, then changed her mind. "Okay," she said, sounding almost sad. "See you in class. Take care, Matt."

Matt hung up the phone, livid at himself for ignoring the warning signs. Whether she called Michael her "boyfriend" or not, she clearly had some sort of entanglement with him, as did, apparently, her father! In the meantime, he had been running around like a fool, arranging a car and asking for date advice. Then again, it had also led him to the job at the White House. With that comforting thought, he headed out the door.

CHAPTER EIGHT

At six a.m. the following Monday, Matt arrived at the guard's station of the OEOB.

"Aren't we the eager beaver?" Keith joked as he met Matt and handed him a can of cola. "Drink up, you're gonna need it."

It was the last time Matt would require an escort to enter the building.

Though he was only to work at the White House part-time, Mr. Sanford had suggested he spend that whole first day there so he could start to get the lay of the land and take care of any administrative tasks related to his hire. The first order of business was a meeting with Sanford himself, and he began it without preamble.

"Son, there are two types of people in the White House: the big swinging dicks, and the rest of us. We're all on the same team and we have to work together. Don't ever forget that! Remember, you work for me! Always do your best and I'll look out for you!"

"Yes, sir," Matt replied crisply, already warming to the man. Sanford wasn't polished, but he was a man who got things done. That was evident by his rough exterior and the way he barked orders to Keith. But there was another side to him too, one with which Matt identified. The straightforward way he looked Matt in the eye spoke of a fair man.

"I'd appreciate it if you would call me Glen," Sanford continued, eliciting a grin from Keith, who had already advised in favor of this informality.

"Yes, sir," Matt repeated, drawing a smile from his new boss.

"I know, you went to military school and old habits die hard. You'll get used to it. One more thing, and it's paramount above all else. No matter what's happening, this must be your highest priority."

Matt leaned forward in anticipation of a great mission.

"Every two hours, beginning at ten hundred hours, you must get me a cold Diet Pepsi."

Matt fell back in the chair, while Keith made no attempt to conceal a laugh.

"I see you've already found the machine…" Glen gestured to Matt's soda can, then reached into his pocket and pulled out a five-dollar bill.

At Matt's questioning glance, Keith nodded to indicate that he would show him the way.

"At fifteen cents a pop, this will last you a while. I don't want to have to remind you." He handed the five to Matt. "Just let me know when this runs out and I'll give you more. Understand?"

"Yes, sir," Matt replied, slightly deflated by the mundane task.

"Good! Now Keith, shouldn't you get Matt down to Security?"

"Okay, Bud," Keith said as they headed down the hallway, "This is going to be the most uncomfortable part of your day, but you gotta do it. Before you're official here, Security's gotta blow red, white, and blue smoke up your ass. They do it to everybody."

A few minutes later they were in the Security office suite.

"This is our new guy, Matt," Keith announced to a pretty young secretary upon entering the outer office. She smiled, stood up, and walked around her desk to poke her head into an interior office.

"He's free. Go on in," she told Matt with another smile.

Matt glanced back at Keith, who said, "Go 'head. When you're done meet me back at the Secretariat and I'll show you that soda machine."

Matt walked in and saw a man around thirty seated at the desk.

"Have a seat," he said, all business. "I'm Jerry Jensen."

Matt sized Jensen up as he slid into the chair. He was unusually stern-looking for one so young. He was also neat as a pin, with slick, perfectly manicured hair and a crisp white shirt that contrasted sharply with a blood-red tie. Matt knew he was in for a lecture.

"Let me begin by welcoming you," Jensen said, reaching to shake hands. He then held up a piece of letterhead with an official-looking blue seal centered at the top. "The FBI has notified us that the results of your preliminary background investigation are favorable, meaning you can start work." He paused, his steely eyes meeting Matt's. "Of course, your suitability for appointment to the White House staff is pending the full investigation." He put the paper in a file folder on the corner of his desk.

Though he hadn't really expected a problem, Matt felt an immediate surge of excitement that he had been deemed fit to work there, even if it was only on a temporary basis.

"Later this morning," Jensen continued, "you will be given White House credentials. They carry with them a very serious responsibility."

Here, Matt thought, *comes the red, white, and blue part Keith warned about.*

"Accepting them carries an inherent statement that you not only are an employee of the United States Government, but that you are now working for the President of the United States of America. From now on, everything you do reflects on the President. Now, I know you are young." He shook his head, "I'm not really sure why we hire people so young. But the fact is, you are here, and this is the deal: You can't afford to act like a typical college student. This means no drugs! No drinking!"

No beer? Matt thought. *I'm the chugging champ!*

"You must live clean. You must be loyal and honest. Is this clear?" Jensen looked directly into Matt's eyes as if searching for weakness.

Matt cleared his throat. "Yes, sir," he replied seriously.

"This job is going to provide you with access to very important people and you are going to hear and read things that are very sensitive. Nothing you hear or read here is to be discussed beyond the eighteen acres. Is that clear?"

"Yes, sir," Matt said, suddenly feeling the weight of a great burden. "But what is the eighteen acres?"

Jensen cast his eyes heavenward as if asking for strength. "Oh, you are just too new. The eighteen acres includes the White House proper, the Old Executive Office Building, the New Executive Office Building, and Blair House. It is the White House compound. Now, one more thing. Be careful entering and leaving the White House. There are all kinds of demonstrations going on every day. Steer clear of them. You have a good, clean record. We don't need your picture showing up in intelligence reports, or worse, on the front page of The Washington Post. Is that clear?"

"Yes, sir!"

"Good! Now, enjoy your time here and remember, if you ever need anything, or if someone, anywhere or anytime, shows unusual interest in your activities here, you let me know *immediately*."

"Yes, sir!" Matt repeated, wondering whether Grossman's inquiries about hot secretaries qualified as "unusual interest." He stood up to leave and again accepted Jensen's outstretched hand. "Sir, uh, the part about drinking… I am in a fraternity…"

Jensen rolled his eyes. "Good God!"

"Never mind," Matt shot back, fearing the man might take him by the collar, walk him to the entrance, and throw him out the door.

It was almost imperceptible, but Jensen's expression softened. "I understand you are a college student, and it's unrealistic to think you won't do some partying. But hear me! Don't talk about this place to anyone. Anyone! And if you do drink, make *damn* sure you don't talk about this place!" His tone grew increasingly adamant with each word, as did the intensity of his stare.

After several more "yessirs," Matt backed out of the office, resisting the urge to bow. Young as he might be, Jensen had put the fear of God, not to mention the U.S. government, into him. At that moment, Matt didn't know which was more intimidating.

Keith met him midway down the hall. "I was just coming to get you." He saw the look on Matt's face and grinned. "Bud, don't let Jensen get to you. He's all bark and no bite."

"That remains to be seen," Matt muttered. "At least my preliminary clearance went through – not that I was worried."

The next stop was the personnel office, located on the ground floor. Matt breathed a sigh of relief when he was introduced to a mild-mannered, matronly woman who handed him papers to sign. Still recovering from the Jensen lecture, Matt plopped the papers on a desk and signed them without so much as a casual review. He walked across the room and returned them to the woman, who was seated behind her desk. Taking the papers, she shuffled their order and placed them in a file folder.

"Okay," she said, standing up, "Raise your right hand and repeat after me."

Matt was puzzled but did as he was told.

"I do solemnly swear," the woman continued, indifferently administering the oath of office. Though he realized it was probably a requirement of everyone who worked there, he found it hard to describe what he was feeling – a mix of pride and humility, responsibility, and privilege. He repeated each word with such reverence, he might have been ascending to the highest office in the land. When it was finished, he stuck out his hand and vigorously pumped that of the woman, who looked surprised and possibly a little amused. Matt heard Keith's chuckle from across the room, but he didn't care. He was incredibly moved.

A moment later they were on the move again. There was one more chore, Keith explained, to accomplish before Matt was official. They returned to the Secret Service office, where Matt had previously been photographed and fingerprinted. That time, he had felt like a criminal; now, the very man who had done the mock "booking" managed a polite smile as he handed Matt an identification card. Though small in size, it carried weight. Directly below Matt's color photograph, highlighted against a blue background, were three large white letters "WHS," identifying Matt as a member of the White House Staff.

When they returned to the Secretariat, Keith looked at his watch.

"Where now?" Matt asked.

"Well, *you're* going to the basement." Seeing Matt's questioning stare, he added. "It's nearly ten hundred hours, time to get that Pepsi. You'll find the machine in the northwest corner. I have something else to take care of but I'll see you soon."

The basement of the OEOB was a sharp contrast to the upper floors. It was dark, with a ceiling low and packed with wires and conduits; the walls were bare and crude, exposing stone foundation. The halls were filled with excess furniture, boxes, carts, dollies, and just about everything that needed a place but didn't have one. Matt took a few steps from the elevator and paused, attempting to figure out where northwest was.

"Excuse me," a voice said from behind. "Do you know where the Control Center is?" Matt looked over his shoulder to find an athletic-looking man in a neatly tailored suit.

"Sorry, I'm new here," he replied, "I'm trying to find the soda machine."

The man smiled. "I'm Kent Brown. I'm new too."

As Kent reached to shake hands, Matt noted the blue pass hanging around his neck. It was similar to his own, except for one detail: its white letters were "USSS," indicating that Kent worked for the United States Secret Service.

They continued down the corridor, past two large carts filled with what could best be described as "mush." It was the color of wet cement and emanated a pungent smell that made Matt's stomach turn.

"Gross," he said, recoiling from the stench. "Wonder what this is…"

"Probably the trash," Kent observed. "All trash from the White House is shredded and destroyed with chemicals so it doesn't show up in the newspaper, or in Moscow."

Continuing on, they found an open door. Kent ducked his head inside and motioned for Matt to join him. Inside, two men dressed in green work suits were fitting a large piece of thick iron to the front of what looked like a podium.

"Excuse me," Kent said. "Do you know where the Control Center and soda machine are?"

One of the men looked up from his work. "Yeah, right around the corner." Then, feeling Matt's curious stare, he said, "It's a new podium for the Prez. This is an iron shield to protect him if anyone starts shooting."

"Good to know." Kent pointed to his Secret Service badge and gave Matt a conspiratorial wink.

The soda machines were outside the Control Center Kent had been searching for. As they reached the machines, Kent held out his hand.

"Nice to meet you. I didn't get your name."

"Matt."

"Good to meet you, Matt," Kent said before disappearing into the Control Center. It took a few seconds for its door to swing shut – enough time for Matt to see rows of television and computer screens with images from around the White House. Several men were keeping watch over the comings and goings.

Matt got back on the elevator, Diet Pepsi in hand.

Mission accomplished, he thought wryly, hoping this wasn't indicative of his tasks at The White House.

The elevator stopped on the first floor, and when the door opened, in stepped a scholarly-looking man wearing a tweed jacket and Hush Puppies.

"Hello," he said amiably as he pushed the button for the third floor.

"You're Dr. Stein!" Matt exclaimed before he could stop himself.

"I sure am," the man replied amiably.

Though he was slightly embarrassed by his outburst, Matt decided to cut himself a break. After all, he was within inches from the Chairman of the President's Council of Economic Advisors. More commonly known as the "Nation's Chief Economist," Stein was a regular on the evening news. Matt would have recognized him anywhere.

"How are you doing today, Dr. Stein?" Matt asked in what he hoped was a casual voice.

"I'm fine…" Stein eyed the can of Pepsi. "But I'm a little disconcerted to see that Pepsi in the basement has gone from fifteen to twenty cents a can. That's an increase of more than thirty percent!"

Immediately feeling at ease, Matt chuckled, "That just seems to be the way things are going lately."

"I think I'll stick to buying mine by the case at the grocery store," Dr. Stein said with a grin.

When the elevator came to a stop, Matt wished Dr. Stein a good day and hurried down the hall toward Glen's office. He had no sooner delivered the precious cola when Ann Green walked in.

"Long time, no see," Matt joked, but this time, Ann was all business.

"I need a favor," she said, "Need to get this 'Red Tag' to the Roosevelt Room, asap."

She handed Matt a manila envelope. On the upper right corner, where a postage stamp would normally go, was a red tag about an inch square. In between sips of soda, Glen explained that the red tag meant the item needed immediate attention. The Roosevelt Room, he added, was in the West Wing of the White House, just across the hall from the Oval Office.

Matt accepted the mission with excitement. It was the first time he left the OEOB to cross West Executive Avenue, the private street running between the White House and the OEOB. As he crossed the threshold into the West Wing, he found himself standing in a small vestibule decorated with large colorful photographs of President Nixon. A familiar scent flooded his nostrils, immediately transporting him back to military school. Eyeing the brass door furnishings, he realized the smell was Brasso, the same polishing fluid he'd used to buff the ornaments on his uniform. It gave him a strange sense of continuity, and the feeling that he was exactly where he was meant to be.

Beyond the vestibule's inner doors, down a short narrow corridor, was a desk occupied by a uniformed Secret Service agent. The urgency of his mission momentarily forgotten, Matt slowly proceeded down the corridor, taking in the photographs as he went. Then, fighting the urge to pinch himself, he flashed his new White House Badge at the agent, an older man with a jovial smile and a twinkle in his eye. A small name tag above his heart read "Van."

"You're new, aren't you?" Van asked, eyeing the badge. "What do you do?"

The question momentarily threw Matt, who replied, "I'm a messenger. I guess I messenge."

To his surprise, Van rolled his head back and let loose a laugh that shattered the quiet of the hall. "Where are you headed?"

"The Roosevelt Room, sir."

"Up the stairs on the left. Go through the first-floor lobby."

"Thanks, Sergeant," Matt responded reverently, noting the rank on the man's sleeve.

As he followed Van's directions, he mentally ran through what he knew of the West Wing. Along with the Oval Office and offices of the President's Chief of Staff and National Security Advisor, it housed the Situation Room, Cabinet Room, Press Office, and several other offices, along with the White House Mess, the President's private barber shop, and, of course, The Roosevelt Room.

When he reached the top of the small staircase, to his immediate left was an office with two Secret Service agents posted outside. Matt stifled a gasp when he saw Henry Kissinger, the President's National Security Advisor, walk past the entryway. Directly across from the stairs was another door leading into the main lobby.

As he entered the lobby, he was surprised to find it rather unassuming, given the fact that it served as the waiting room for the President and his highest aides.

"May I help you?"

Matt looked over to see a receptionist studying him. He pointed to the red tag on the envelope and said he was there to deliver it.

"I'll see that the boss gets it," she said, reaching out to take it from him.

That's it? he thought, disappointed. He'd hoped he could see his new boss, maybe even the President, but apparently it was not to be. His all-important mission complete, he turned to leave the lobby and noticed a Marine Guard, in full dress uniform, ceremoniously standing at the door leading to the front lawn. Matt felt the sudden urge to leave through that door, past the guard and out toward Pennsylvania Avenue. Instead, he retraced his steps back down the stairs and through the ground-floor lobby. When he got back downstairs, Sergeant Van was standing in front of his desk with a few people.

"Matt, can you hold up a minute?" he said, "The man is on his way."

Momentarily puzzled as to who "the man" was, Matt stood to the side. Within a minute the doors from the vestibule opened and in walked Richard Nixon, returning to the West Wing from his hideaway office in the OEOB. Just a few steps behind the President, five Secret Service agents followed. Matt stared, transfixed. Nixon was wearing his trademark blue suit. His face was tanned and a little more wrinkled than it appeared on TV. He was also, to Matt's surprise, not as tall.

Again, he was seized by a sense of the surreal. He was a freshman with barely a week of college under his belt, standing inches from the leader of the free world. No ceremony. No big deal. Just a man on his way to his office. Mr. Nixon smiled and nodded politely as he briskly passed. He didn't say a word.

"Hey, Matt," said one of the agents, pointing at him. It was Kent.

Matt smiled, his mind reeling. The simple act of getting Glen's Pepsi had resulted in his meeting one of Nixon's most trusted people. With a start, he realized that in the White House, no task was truly mundane but in some small way contributed to the running of the country. The thought was both sobering and a reminder to be grateful for every mission, red tag or not.

He headed back to the OEOB. Midway across the small West Executive Avenue, he paused and looked back at a news crew gathered on the front lawn. A reporter stood before a camera with a microphone, no doubt filing a report for that night's news. Beyond the reporter and his crew, a few protestors with placards marched back and forth in front of the main gate on Pennsylvania Avenue. He recalled years before when his family visited Washington, how they stood in line for hours to take the White House tour. Now he was on the inside. He thought again of what the limo driver said on the night of the interview and for the first time realized just how easy it was to let this all go to his head.

When he returned to the Secretariat, Keith was waiting with a new assignment.

"Bud, you need to be checked out on the copy machine."

Matt followed him into a room not much larger than a closet, where he learned that "checked out" meant learning how to use the monstrous copier and how to maintain it. Beside the machine were several shelves. They were filled with staplers, pens, pencils, tape, and notepads of several sizes with "*The White House, Washington*" in bold blue lettering across the top. One stack of paper caught Matt's attention. It wasn't white like the others.

"This is cool!" he said, running his finger over the embossed Seal of the President of the United States. "What's this one?"

"It's the President's stationery. He's the only one who can use it. You can tell because it's not white, it's a little green."

Keith rolled his sleeves above his elbows, opened the giant copy machine, and began showing Matt how to clean its filament wires. Just as he was explaining the importance of cleaning the roller drum, Ann ran into the room.

"There you are," she said, spotting Matt with relief. "I need to get this red tag over to the CIA, ASAP. I ordered a car, and it will be at the ramp in five minutes."

Matt took the manilla envelope from her outstretched hand. He was quickly learning that when Ann said she needed to do something, it really meant that *he* had to do something, NOW.

"You better beat feet," Keith confirmed. "Oh, and you might as well have the car drop you off at school. No sense coming back this time of day."

Matt glanced at the clock and was shocked to see it was nearly four o'clock. The day had flown by and he hadn't stopped for a minute. His only nourishment had been the cola Keith gifted him that morning.

When he arrived at the ramp, there was a group of three men waiting for a limousine. He immediately recognized Governor John Love, the "Energy Czar" President Nixon had brought in from Arizona to address America's dependence on foreign oil. Within a minute a limousine arrived and one of the men opened the back door. Governor Love climbed in, only to get back out without his rear end even touching the seat. He looked over at Matt.

"Are you Matt?"

Matt nodded.

"This is your car."

Smiling sheepishly, Matt passed the three gentlemen and slid into the car while they continued their conversation.

"You should have taken the governor," Matt said to the driver.

"His car is on the way," the driver said, completely unconcerned. "It'll be here in a minute."

As the driver was nosing the shiny black limousine into traffic, Matt sat back and stared at the sealed envelope in his hands. What information was so critical it necessitated his immediate departure? Who at the CIA would see it and what action, if any, would result? Suddenly, the enormity of what he didn't know hit Matt like a tidal wave. Part of him wanted desperately to tear open the envelope, while another wanted to set it down on the seat, jump out of the limo, and forget this whole business. Since neither was a viable option, he focused on finishing this task so he could go back to campus and get something to eat.

Suddenly, he was jerked violently forward as the driver slammed on the brakes.

"What the –?"

He looked out the window to see that the driver had stopped just short of colliding with a female pedestrian. She looked truly startled, as though she had been lost in her own thoughts as she stepped off the curb. She froze in place for a moment, then quickly backed up to the safety of the sidewalk.

"Sorry, sir," the driver said, though a glance at the traffic light told Matt she was indeed the one at fault.

As Matt looked back at her, he was struck by how absolutely stunning she was, with shoulder-length hair the color of coal, large eyes, and porcelain skin. She was tall for a woman, possibly five-eight or so, with long, toned limbs that bespoke a life of physical activity. Her dress, which was sleeveless and ended just above the knee, fit her like a glove and accentuated a waist Scarlet O'Hara would have envied. Without a doubt he had never seen anything like her, at least not in real life. His gaze found hers, and though their eyes locked for only a split second, it was enough to make him uncomfortably warm.

"Whew," Matt laughed nervously as the limo slid past her. "You almost had yourself a pretty new hood ornament."

The driver, who failed to see the humor, uttered a curt, "Yes, sir," then announced that, traffic permitting, they would arrive at their destination in approximately fifteen minutes.

"What road are you taking?" Matt asked, resisting the urge to turn around to see if he could still spot the woman.

The driver's eyes met his in the rearview mirror. "The George Washington Parkway, sir."

Matt nodded his thanks, then turned to stare out the window, excited to experience yet another new route. The road was nestled among trees above the Potomac River, west of the city. Through the thick foliage, he caught glimpses of exclusive estates. A break in the trees offered a breathtaking view across the river of the National Cathedral perched high above Northwest Washington. Below, closer to the river, he could see the gothic architecture of Georgetown University.

A few minutes later, Matt saw a sign for the Federal Highway Administration. Thinking the driver had made some mistake, he was about to say something when he noted the fortified entrance, armed guards, and formidable fences. Clearly, they were there to protect something more than the maintenance of highways.

When the limousine approached a gate, an armed guard stepped out of a small security booth and walked over. The driver rolled down his window and nodded, then, without so much as a word, the guard waved to let the car pass.

"Man," Matt said with surprise, "don't they check I.D.?"

"They know the White House cars," said the driver. He pulled the car up to the CIA's front entrance. "Shall I wait?"

"I'd appreciate it. This should only take a minute or so and I was told you would drop me off at school."

Once inside, Matt was in for another surprise. In sharp contrast to the secrecy outside, the lobby boasted a giant insignia of the CIA on the polished stone floor. There was a white marble wall on the left side of the lobby bearing the inscription "In Honor Of Those Members Of The Central Intelligence Agency Who Gave Their Lives In The Service Of Their Country." Below the inscription were neat rows of bronze stars, representing individuals who had perished. There were no names, for even in death their identities were top secret. Inexplicably, this made it even more moving to Matt, who reverently stared at it for a moment before approaching the guard desk. Next to it stood a young man.

"Is this the envelope from the White House?" he asked, sizing Matt up.

Matt nodded.

"Excellent, I've been waiting for you. Thanks very much." He took the package and retreated past the guard into the interior of the secretive building. It was an abrupt end to Matt's trip to the spy agency. Thoughts of what was in the envelope resurfaced as he returned to the waiting limousine.

Twenty minutes later, Matt walked into the dorm, feeling like he had re-entered Earth's orbit after a voyage to a faraway solar system. This feeling was exacerbated by the sight of Grossman stretched across his bed, leafing through a dirty magazine.

"How's the youngest member of the Nixon Administration? Bug anyone today?"

"You know what bugs me, Grossman?" Matt shot back.

"When your dick comes out the little slot in your underwear and rubs against your pants?"

"No! It's that you can't ever be serious."

"Here's something serious, pal," Grossman countered, reaching for a small paper lying next to him on the bed. It was neatly folded in half. "It looks like your little friend left you a note under the door."

"Little friend…?" Matt crossed the room and snatched it from Grossman's hand.

"I could have read it, ya know, but I didn't. I'm sure it would only make me puke."

Matt opened the note to see, in delicate handwriting, *Just wanted to say hi. Give me a call when you get back…Catherine.*

"If you didn't read it," he asked, "then how do you know who it's from?"

"Okay, so I glanced at it to make sure it wasn't for me. From there, it was a simple process of elimination." Grossman pulled his eyes from the centerfold to glance at Matt. "Let's face it – there aren't many girls knocking on your door – or sliding notes under it."

Matt resisted the temptation to point out that it was Grossman's door as well. He was simply too tired and overwhelmed from the day.

"…and that's another thing that bugs me," Grossman stated matter-of-factly. "The way that girl is always hanging with Doofus. I'm telling you; she's playing with one of you, or both!"

"No argument there," Matt replied, crumpling up the note and dunk-shotting it into the trash.

CHAPTER NINE

Anna sat in the tearoom of Garfinckel's department store, an untouched plate of finger sandwiches before her. She was exhausted, and not just in body. It was a weariness of the soul.

George Trent turned out to be another dead-end, her carefully orchestrated meeting beginning and ending with some lustful stares over martinis, followed by his abrupt departure. Desperate and loathing herself for it, she recalled a conversation weeks earlier with Vadim. Clearly disillusioned with her usefulness in America, his encouragement had become thinly veiled threats.

"I am doing everything you asked, Vadim. I have met whomever you told me to meet. But I cannot force them to do or say what we want them to." She put her head in her hands. "This place!" she exclaimed, "I don't understand it!"

"Oh, I think you understand it quite well, Annushka," he replied, his cold blue eyes staring pointedly at her fine dress, the silk scarf tied around her purse. "It is a place that values beautiful things above all else. Success lies in how you use that beauty. If you cannot, well…" He held out his hands as if in supplication to some greater power, "…there is only so much I can do."

Though she'd kept her face carefully neutral, she felt an icy fear running through her body. Failure in America not only meant she would be sent home, doomed to a life of monotony in whatever factory they placed her in. It also meant her mother and brothers would lose the spacious apartment they had been given as a condition of her service. Yes, she had volunteered to come here, but what was her choice?

Vadim made that clucking noise with his tongue that she had come to detest. Then, as if reading her thoughts, he'd said quietly in Russian, "If you're scared of wolves, Annushka, don't go into the woods."

Anna snapped back to the present, shook her head as if to rid herself of the memory, then looked around the tearoom. It was filled with what looked to be the neglected wives of titans in business and politics who substituted any emotional needs for handbags and furs.

They're no better than me, Anna thought. *We all behave as prostitutes. At least I have a higher purpose.*

Anna had first come upon Garfinckel's quite by accident the day after arriving in America. It had been a grueling journey, starting with a train ride from Moscow to East Berlin and a nerve-wracking cross of the border into West Berlin, followed by a flight to New York and, finally, another train to D.C. Vadim, after seeing she was fed and settled in the apartment he had arranged for her, wasted no time in issuing orders.

"You can learn only so much from magazines, Annushka. I want you to explore; observe these people, acquaint yourself with the way they live. This will be very important when we begin our work together."

So, she explored, walking the city streets until she had blisters on her feet. It was summer then, and Washington was a sauna, hot and muggy, at least twenty degrees hotter than back home. It was also noisy, dirty, crowded, and, as far as Anna could see, lacking in any discernible culture. Finally, after meandering aimlessly for what seemed like hours, she was headed back to her apartment when a window display on F Street caught her eye. Female mannequins were posed in confident stances with cigarettes dangling from their lips. Drop cloths were strewn about and ladders leaned against the walls. Blobs of paint decorated the display, but they were seemingly random and certainly incongruous with the tailored, double-knit suits the mannequins wore. Whatever message it was attempting to convey, it was lost on Anna. And yet, she was intrigued.

She backed away from the window, out past the awning and almost onto the street. Garfinckel's was emblazoned against the limestone of the eight-story building. Anna had read of this store in one of the American fashion magazines she had leafed through as part of her training back in Moscow. It was where rich ladies went to shop, have tea or lunch, and gossip.

Entering Garfinckel's that day had been like stepping into another universe for the first time. The store still had the art deco touches of the past. Glass counters offering all kinds of luxuries formed squares along the carpeted floor. Anna took in all the aromas: musty carpet, leather, and cigarette smoke, combined with an unfamiliar scent that she somehow recognized as expensive. The sheer abundance and variety were beyond all imagining – ridiculous and glorious in its excess.

She walked through the store, unsure how to behave. Women behind the counters smiled at her, even as their eyes swept her from head to toe, making Anna suddenly aware of her scuffed heals and hair frizzing in the humidity.

A woman of an age when one is referred to as "handsome" came up beside Anna, who started.

"I'm sorry. I noticed you looked a little lost. Is there something I can help you with?"

Anna smiled stiffly. "It is beautiful in here. I am overwhelmed. What is it you do here?"

"I help you find what you want and I help you find what you didn't know you wanted." She took Anna's hand and lifted it as if about to lead her in a dance. "Let me show you around."

Anna smiled, amused by the woman, and allowed herself to be led to a nearby counter.

The woman sat her in a chair in front of a mirror that magnified her face. Anna took in all the lipsticks, eye shadows, and nail polishes. It seemed every color and shade were available, all in neat rows with wonderful names like "Cornflower" or "Tahitian sky" underneath. She felt something cool and slippery gently stroking her cheek.

"You are a beautiful young woman under all of this," the woman said gently. She then wiped the heavy blue from Anna's eyelids and the war-paint red on her cheekbones, dropping each tissue of cold cream into a little basket by the chair.

Then she quickly began working on this fresh canvas. Anna felt a soft brush against her eyelids and for the first time since her arrival in Washington she allowed herself to relax.

"Tell me. Do any famous people come here?"

"Well, it depends on what you mean by famous. There is Washington-famous and there is Hollywood-famous. I think you know who we prefer." She leveled her face with Anna's and gave a quick wink and a smile. She held a piece of tissue to Anna's lips. "Blot." Anna pulled the tissue in between her lips and let go. "What do you do, honey?"

"I am a graduate student," Anna replied, more aware than ever how much she must have stood out from the usual customer.

"Well, that's exciting, what are you studying?"

"I am studying your government."

The woman pulled back, studying her more closely. "I thought I heard an accent, where are you from?"

"Europe."

"Huh. Well, I'm from a faraway place too – the Bronx – and my accent was even harder to get rid of." She gave a low, throaty laugh. "There, all done."

She flipped the mirror around so it showed a normal reflection. Anna was astonished. Her face was more delicate now, less severely colored. The woman had done some sort of trick that made her jaw and cheekbones more prominent.

"Do you see? I've used the same colors, but I have used them to hide or accentuate your features. You are not painted; you look natural, as you should."

Anna could do nothing but nod. She had always known she was beautiful, but this was different. It was as if she had been handed a passport to a country within a country, one even most Americans never saw, let alone girls from Minsk.

Since then, Garfinckel's had become something of a refuge for her. Sometimes she purchased a new dress or pair of shoes, justifying them as necessary for her role; other times, like today, she just came to escape the confines of her life and surround herself with beautiful things.

Anna glanced at her wrist and realized she'd left her watch at the apartment. How long had she been sitting there? She had no desire to leave this place and return to the packed, sweaty street, but she had no choice. Vadim would want a thorough accounting of her day when they met that evening, and he would not look kindly upon her spending it in a tearoom. For all she knew, he had someone watching her right now. With a sigh, she stood and headed toward the escalator, a feeling of dread settling over her as she recalled their last conversation a few days earlier.

"It is time, Annushka," he'd said, as if she were a child who neglected her chores, "to demonstrate your commitment to our work. Since you have had 'no luck,' as the Americans say, with the men we recommended, you will find someone appropriate to befriend."

There was that word again – "befriend." How enraged her father would have been if he knew his boyhood chum and comrade in the War was treating her so. Beneath the anger, though, was an icy fear of the consequences should she fail to produce results, and fast.

All these thoughts were swirling in her mind as she exited the store and began walking, purposefully but with no destination in mind. The streets were packed with a mix of men in business suits, women carrying shopping bags, and tourists with cameras around their necks and ice cream cones in hand.

How odd these Americans were, with their air of self-importance and their preoccupation with whatever pleased them in the moment.

That is what will defeat them, she thought. *They are aware only of themselves.*

Indeed, everything she observed since coming here only confirmed what she had always been told about the United States. Yet, even with this knowledge and the "special training" she received, she was not living up to the expectations of Vadim and those he reported to. Shame and self-pity, feelings she never entertained back home, were now her constant companions, as if the weakness of this place had infected her. She picked up her pace a bit, an unconscious attempt to leave them behind.

Forty minutes later, she found herself, quite unexpectedly, passing by the White House. As she started to cross Pennsylvania Avenue and 17th Street, Anna sighed, reminded once again of her mission and how short of it she was falling.

The blaring sound of the car horn jolted her back to the present. She jerked her head up to see the limo screeching to a halt to avoid hitting her, the driver's face as it shifted from panic to annoyance. She nodded an apology and scurried back to the curb, scuffing the heel of a new pump in the process. As the limo slid by her, she saw through the cracked side window the face of a man – a boy, really. They locked eyes for a moment, his filled with a familiar shock that had nothing to do with the near accident, but her beauty. Amused, despite her mood, Anna barely noticed the limo's White House plates as it continued on its way.

CHAPTER TEN

Matt very quickly learned his way around the eighteen acres. The duties of a messenger took him throughout the complex, to both the East and West Wings of the White House, the Old Executive Office Building, and the New Executive Office Building (NEOB) across Pennsylvania Avenue. He also became a frequent visitor at many of the offices of the President's cabinet secretaries, who ran federal departments and agencies, and in the Capitol Hill offices of prominent members of Congress. There were several return trips to the CIA as well. Limousine rides were no longer exotic or embarrassing, but just another means of getting his job done quickly and efficiently.

For Matt, each day brought with it a tremendous learning experience, both in and outside the White House. Whenever he returned from a mission, his limo would pass through crowds of angry protestors, demonstrating against the war in Vietnam or the President due to the unfolding Watergate scandal. He began reading newspapers and magazines and watching the evening news so he could keep up with current events, or at least the version of them presented to the public. Matt felt more and more a part of a new and exciting world, one that his friends on campus couldn't share, or even fathom.

It was the visits to the West Wing that Matt enjoyed most, largely because he never knew who he would see there – from cabinet members and Supreme Court justices to senators and even movie stars. It became commonplace for President Nixon and his security detail to rush by him on their way to or from a meeting, yet each time Matt would pause and stare with the same sense of awe-filled disbelief.

During these trips he also became better acquainted with Sergeant Van and with Kent, who could be found standing duty outside the Oval Office whenever Nixon was inside. Matt always made it a point to stop by and say hello and the two would exchange jokes and stories. Oftentimes, a rowdy laugh would be followed with a finger to the lips by one of the other agents, reminding them that on the other side of the door the most powerful man in the world was at work.

On one such visit Kent admitted that protecting the President was boring.

"It's like babysitting!" he exclaimed, "Of course, the motorcades and crowds make it a little terrifying. You never know where a shot could come from."

"Then why do you do it?" Matt asked. He couldn't understand living with that kind of pressure every day, where any misstep could mean injury – or worse.

"Because I love the fieldwork – you know, the other side of the job, tracking down counterfeiters."

"How is that different from this?"

"You get to kick in doors."

Matt was fascinated. "How do you do that, anyway?"

"It's like this," Kent said, turning toward the door of the Oval and raising his foot.

"Hey, man," his partner protested, "Let's not get carried away!"

Flashing a grin, Kent abruptly ended the demonstration. "You get the picture."

Matt glanced at the other agent, a nice enough guy who clearly did not see the humor in their antics. Not wanting to overstay his welcome, he waved goodbye to Kent and headed back toward the OEOB. No matter how many times he visited the West Wing or what happened when he was there, he always had the same thought as he crossed the lobby: America is such an awesome place! It wasn't lost on him that while most people outside the White House took that awesomeness for granted, he and the others on the inside lived it every day.

He returned to the Secretariat to be handed an assignment by Keith to copy a batch of papers. Just as he started to get a rhythm of lifting the cover, placing a document on the glass, pushing the copy button, then removing the document and replacing it with another, an absolutely stunning secretary walked in. She was older than Matt, probably in her late twenties, and about five-foot-four with slim hips, shapely legs, and breasts that were outsized for her frame. Her blonde hair looked streaked by the sun; her smooth, fair complexion was punctuated by deep blue eyes.

Matt felt his jaw go slack and clamped it shut; then, noting the documents in her hand, he quickly stepped back from the machine so she could use it.

"Copy-us interruptus," she laughed, oblivious to Matt's beet-red face, and positioned herself in front of the machine.

As she leaned forward to press the copy button on the far side, her skirt rose up, exposing a stretch of toned upper thigh. Matt stared in disbelief at his good fortune; then, just when he thought this couldn't get any better, it did. Coming upon a document held together with a staple, she glanced at the staple remover on the side of the machine where Matt was standing. She could have simply asked him to hand it to her, but chose instead to reach for it herself, pressing her breast against his hand in the process.

Awkwardly positioned in front of him, she turned her head, her soft breast burning an imaginary hole in his hand, and said, "Excuse me."

She was so close her warm breath produced a tingling sensation as it flowed across his face. Matt managed a slight smile, hoping she couldn't hear the loud, staccato beat of his heart over the noise of the machine. Then, as quickly as she had appeared she was gone, leaving behind the hint of perfume and a curt, "Thanks."

"Bye," Matt managed to croak out, stretching his neck to watch her leave. The second the door closed behind her, he ran into the main room to relay the story to Keith, who listened with the vicarious interest of a juvenile.

Glen heard the story from his office. "Son," he shouted laughingly, "you're oversexed and underfed."

Matt turned red again, this time because he couldn't argue the point.

*   *   *

One month to the day he had started, Matt arrived at work to find Keith waiting with him with two Cokes and a smile.

"Well, Bud, it's official," he said, handing a can to Matt. "The FBI completed your background check. You're officially one of us!"

Feeling a rush of excitement, Matt's first thought was of his parents' reaction when he called them to share the news.

He and Keith popped open their cans and clinked them together.

"That's a relief," Matt said, chuckling. "Not that I was worried about them finding a sordid past. I mean, I've led a pretty boring life so far."

"Well," Keith said, his tone uncharacteristically serious. "If you had done something bad, they would have found it. You know those papers you filled out the day of the interview?"

Matt nodded. He would never forget that torture.

"Well, first thing the next morning I turned them over to the White House Security Officer, who forwarded them to the Director of the FBI. The FBI analyzed them, then instructed special agents across the country to check local police departments, credit bureaus, sheriffs' offices, and schools. Agents also visited every school you attended and interviewed your teachers. They also talked to your friends and neighbors."

"What did they ask?"

"You know, have you ever been in trouble? Were you known to use alcohol or drugs? Did you belong to subversive organizations? Was there any reason to doubt your loyalty to the United States? That kind of thing."

"Holy crap!" Matt exclaimed. It wasn't that he felt violated or that security measures weren't necessary – he just didn't think his lowly position warranted such a thorough search.

"It's all smooth sailing from here," Keith grinned and took another swig of his Coke. "Just don't join any of those 'subversive groups' on your campus."

Matt laughed. Grossman's comments about the President were derogatory and often lewd, but he highly doubted they could be classified as subversive.

"Smooth sailing," he replied, raising the soda can, "I'll drink to that."

He would later look back on that conversation and think he and Keith had been tempting fate.

One morning, Matt arrived for work earlier than usual and before anyone else – his first order of business to open the bank of safes that contained the Secretariat's classified papers. Though the OEOB was protected by the Secret Service, safes were still required for such documents. There were seven of them, each with its own combination lock like those found on bank vaults. Since writing down the combinations was forbidden, the security people had devised a way to help those with access remember: Each safe was given a name. A picture of a telephone, placed on the first safe, could be used to correspond the letters in the name to numbers on the telephone dial pad. For Matt, who'd learned in military school that the simplest solution was usually the most efficient, it was perfect.

He had just begun opening the first safe when the phone rang. The caller got straight to the point, identifying himself as the guard at the front of the building then announcing the arrival of a Mr. Wallace for his meeting with Mr. Sanford. The guard then asked Matt to send down an escort.

Leaving the safe securely locked, Matt trotted down to the Pennsylvania Avenue entrance to collect the visitor. He saw standing next to the guard station a sixtyish man with a kind face, a thin frame, and ramrod-straight posture that hinted of military training.

"This is Mr. Wallace," the guard said. "May I see your pass?"

Matt handed his White House badge to the guard without question – an error he would soon regret. For in handing the guard that little blue credential, he was validating Mr. Wallace's presence there – and accepting responsibility for him. While the guard copied Matt's name onto an official visitor log, Matt turned to Mr. Wallace.

"I understand you have a meeting with Mr. Sanford, sir."

"Yes, at seven o'clock," he replied, in a way that was both mild-mannered and carried a level of authority.

"I'm afraid he hasn't arrived yet…"

"That's fine. I don't mind waiting," Wallace said amiably.

The guard gave Matt back his badge and pressed a button to open the entrance gate, producing an obnoxious buzz designed to make sure the guard knew when the gate was open.

Matt and Mr. Wallace left the lobby and proceeded down the long hallway. As they ascended the staircase to the second floor, Matt took greater notice of the visitor. At first glance he'd seemed dignified enough; now, however, something about his manner struck Matt as strange. Upon closer inspection, Matt noted with surprise that the man's light blue suit was soiled. It was also tattered at the cuffs, which rode a couple of inches above scuffed shoes.

Trained or not, Matt thought, *this is no military man. What business could he possibly have with Glen?*

"Have you known Mr. Sanford long?"

"No, no, we've never met," Wallace replied. "We have some mutual acquaintances."

There was a slight but definite lilt to his accent that reminded Matt of Sanford.

"Well, it seems you're both from the South," he conjectured aloud.

The visitor didn't respond; he just held his head high and straight ahead as they neared the Secretariat.

Once inside, Matt showed Mr. Wallace to a chair near Glen's office, then continued with the task of opening the safes. Occasionally he would peer over at the man, who just sat there waiting patiently. It wasn't like Glen to be late for a meeting, yet this man didn't seem to mind.

At roughly seven-fifteen Glen blew in like a gale-force wind.

"'Morning," he said, walking briskly into his office, not stopping to glance at Matt or Mr. Wallace. Matt was fast on his heels.

"Mr. Wallace is here to see you."

"Who is Mr. Wallace?" Glen asked as he removed his topcoat.

"The gentleman waiting to see you," Matt said, pointing to the man, who continued to stare straight ahead.

Glen leaned over his desk, peeking out the office door.

"Never seen him before. Don't have any appointment."

"Must be some sort of mistake," Matt said, suddenly and inexplicably uncomfortable. "I'll talk to him."

"Sir," he said as he approached Mr. Wallace, "Mr. Sanford doesn't recall having an appointment this morning."

"Mr. Sanford?" the man repeated. "No, no, I have a meeting with Mr. Statum!"

Matt paused, mentally reviewing the exchanges with the guard and Mr. Wallace. He was certain that both men said the appointment was with Mr. Sanford.

"I am sorry for the mistake. Can you tell me what office he is in? I'll be happy to let him know you're here."

Before Mr. Wallace could venture a response, the phone rang. Matt rounded a desk and answered, "Secretariat."

"Mr. Thomas," a voice demanded.

"Yes…"

"Mr. Thomas, this is Agent Dunning, Secret Service Intelligence. Is Mr. Wallace with you?"

Matt felt a lurch in his gut. "Yes."

"He doesn't have an appointment up there, does he?"

"That's right…"

"Mr. Thomas, Mr. Wallace came up on our computer. He is a caller."

"A what?" Matt didn't know what a caller was, but he was sure it wasn't good.

"A caller is someone who tries to visit The White House. He's crazy. We have to get him out without creating any trouble."

Matt felt himself sinking. His hands were clammy, and he could feel cold sweat run down his forehead. He stared at Mr. Wallace, then back at Glen, who was working at his desk, oblivious.

Is this really happening?

"This is what you have to do," the Secret Service agent was saying.

"What *I* have to do?" Matt asked, his voice shaky. "Isn't this more along the lines of your work?"

"Look, we have to get him out without creating a scene. The simplest thing is for you to tell him he'll have to wait in the lobby. Be relaxed, but firm. Now listen, because this is important. The Vice President is in his office, so I want you to walk Wallace down the opposite corridor. You follow? That's the 17th Street corridor. We will have people in the hall in case anything happens."

"In case anything happens…" Matt repeated, more to himself than the agent. He was now sweating from every pore and his stomach was in full revolt. The only thing he could compare it to was when he had first learned to fly, that feeling that one error could result in his ending up in a fiery blaze.

"Lift the nose, Matt," he'd commanded his sixteen-year-old self as the plane, still on the ground, careened toward a fence, "Lift it, now!"

He pulled on the controls, instantly transforming fear into exhilaration as the plane took to the air. It was an experience he'd drawn on ever since when faced with a crisis of confidence.

This was entirely different. In letting Wallace in, he'd already made that error; worse still was that if things went sideways it wouldn't just affect him.

"Are you still on the line?"

"Yes, yes," Matt said, trying to sound in control and failing miserably.

"Okay, then. You get him to the lobby and we'll take it from there. Remember, relaxed but firm!"

Matt hung up the phone and glanced again at Mr. Wallace, who was still patiently waiting, unaware of the forces aligning to remove him.

Be firm! he repeated to himself over and over as he slowly rounded the desk. He longed to take a deep breath, but his lungs were so constricted with fear he felt like gasping for air.

"Excuse me, Mr. Wallace," he said, trying to keep his face neutral as the man looked up at him. "I'm not sure where Mr. Statum is located. It would be best if you waited in the lobby, sir. I'll be happy to take you back there." He motioned toward the door and to his great relief, Mr. Wallace stood and, without a word, began moving in that direction.

The two headed down the 17th Street corridor, which was getting busy with staffers arriving to start their day. To the casual observer Matt had the typical purposeful gait of any young staffer, but every placement of his feet was measured. His sweat-dampened clothes clung to him uncomfortably, and every breath was an effort. Though it appeared he was staring straight ahead, his eyes flicked about the corridor, then to Wallace. He recalled thinking earlier that the man had military training. If he figured out the ruse and bolted, things could get ugly.

After what seemed like an hour, the lobby came into sight. The guard, who had obviously been alerted, was standing by his desk. He said nothing as Matt and Wallace reached the gate but Matt caught his icy glare as "the caller" passed through; across the way, two men in the lobby watched, their jaws tense.

"Mr. Wallace," Matt said in a tone one might use for a visiting dignitary, "if you'll be kind enough to wait here, sir, we'll track down Mr. Statum for you."

Wallace smiled at him with an almost innocent look that, for a split second, invited sympathy. Perhaps, Matt thought, he truly meant no harm, but it didn't matter. His presence posed a threat and had to be removed with as little drama as possible. Matt returned the smile and gestured to a chair, then turned and quickly headed back to the Secretariat, fearing that at any minute he would hear screams or gunfire, or some other awful thing. But that didn't happen, and as his heartrate slowed and his mind began to clear, he thought about how easy it was to deceive

Mr. Wallace. He also recalled the details he'd observed earlier about the man, and his subtle feeling that the situation was not as it seemed. If he was going to survive here, he would have to recognize that feeling and never ignore it again. He would have to recognize when it was time to "lift the nose."

When he returned he found Glen and Keith standing in the outer office.

"What was that all about?" Glen asked, having been alerted to the security breach.

Matt realized his hands were trembling and shoved them into his pockets. "All I know is that this Mr. Wallace said he had an appointment with you at seven. The guard called so I went down and got him."

"You mean to say the guard called my office and said this man had an appointment with me, by name?"

Matt glanced at Keith, whose eyes, other than widening slightly, revealed nothing.

"Yes, sir, that's why I went down and got him."

Glen shook his head, walked back into his office, and sat down, clearly in deep thought.

Suddenly, the door of the Secretariat opened and two uniformed agents walked in carrying handheld radios. Matt and Keith stood motionless, watching as they made a beeline for Glen's office and closed the door behind them. It took only a second for the discussion to turn into an argument.

Matt's gut lurched again, and for a moment he thought he might vomit. Though he couldn't make out the words, it was clear the men were clearly arguing over his actions. Should he go in, or wait to be called? Keith was no help, for when Matt glanced over his eyes were cast toward the floor.

As the argument grew louder, Matt's thoughts went back to his home in Michigan. He wished this was all an ugly dream and he would wake up in the security of his bed. Heck, he would have happily settled for listening to Grossman's snores in the other bunk – as long as he was anywhere but here.

He was jolted back to the present by a burst of Glen's voice. It was loud and filled with venom.

"Cut the shit!" he screamed at the men. "*Your* guard called *my* extension and told *my* young man that this flake had an appointment with me! My man did only what he was told to do."

By this time Glen was screaming so loud it startled people passing by the open door of the Secretariat. Matt saw several freeze for a beat and hurry down the corridor as if they were afraid he was coming for them next.

"And furthermore, this young man has been here less than a month. What training have you given him? I'll tell you what, not a fucking thing! There was a breach of security this morning, it was your own people who screwed the pooch, and I'm not letting you make a scapegoat out of anybody. The responsibility for this goat fuck is going to stay right where it belongs, with you."

"Holy shit," Matt whispered, and this time when he looked over at Keith he saw his arms were crossed and his face was flushed from trying to conceal his laughter.

"Now you sorry sons-a-bitches get your asses out of my office before I get mad!"

The two agents fell silent, no doubt correctly assessing that Glen would not be steamrolled. They left the Secretariat without even a glance at Matt. As they headed down the hall, an eerie silence in the wake of Glen's tongue-lashing was broken only by the fading static on their radios.

Matt was still trembling as he walked into Glen's office. His legs felt rubbery, as if drained of nearly all their strength.

"I – I – I don't know what to say."

Glen looked up over his reading glasses, perched precariously on his nose, and smiled. The explosion, like some kind of cathartic tonic, had completely calmed him down.

"Relax, son," he said, "you didn't screw up! But take it as a lesson. You always gotta cover your six o'clock position. Never be afraid to ask questions! And remember, in this place, when things go to shit someone is always looking for someone else to blame."

Glen then returned to the papers on his desk, the matter closed in his mind, and Matt left the office to find Keith still chuckling.

"Bud," Keith said, "you made some friends today!"

As if on cue, Jensen blew the door open and raced into Glen's office.

"Out! Out!" Glen shouted. "I've wasted enough time on this today."

Jensen wisely retreated, but on his way out he grabbed Matt's shirtsleeve and dragged him down the hall to his office. After depositing Matt into a seat, he calmly shut the door, walked back to his desk, and let loose.

"What the hell just happened?" he shouted. "I… want…every… detail – now!"

Matt quickly recounted the events exactly as they happened, his words pouring out of him in what seemed like one very long exhale.

Surprisingly, Jensen waited for him to finish. "Okay. It sounds like the problem lies with the Secret Service. But I don't know why we hire people so young they don't possess the judgment to see a situation."

Matt bit back an angry retort and settled for an easy escape route instead. "Hey, I'm late for a mission and Glen will lose it again."

"Go ahead. But this better not happen again." He waited until Matt was nearly out the door before firing the parting shot. "I have my eye on you, young man!"

"Don't doubt it for a minute," Matt muttered under his breath. As he headed back to Glen's office he thought of the comment Keith had made a few minutes earlier. There were some people at the White House he indeed considered friends, but Jensen clearly was not one of them.

CHAPTER ELEVEN

"He wants to see you, Bud."

Matt ran a finger under his nose to wipe away the beads of sweat. Of all the days to take a long lunch, he thought, this was the absolute worst.

After what he was already referring in his mind to as the "Wallace Debacle," Matt had gone to fetch Glen's first Pepsi of the day. He grabbed one for himself as well, sipping it as he returned to his task of opening the safes, but instead of the desired fortification the cola just made him more jittery. He was hurting.

Glen agreed.

"Son, you look like shit," he stated matter-of-factly. "Have you eaten today?"

Matt shook his head. It was a good thing, too, because if he'd consumed anything it would have come right back up, if not while dealing with Wallace then surely during the argument between Glen and the agents.

"Okay, here's what's gonna happen. You're going to go out and get yourself some food."

Matt opened his mouth to protest. He didn't want to be seen as not being able to handle the stresses of the job.

"No arguments, just go. That's an order." He looked up from a stack of paperwork. "And I don't want to see you back here for an hour – with my Pepsi, of course."

The minute Matt exited the OEOB and set off on 17th Street, he mentally thanked Glen for insisting he go out. The day was warm. A light breeze brought some relief and the sun felt good on his face. It was the first time he'd taken a full breath in hours. After walking aimlessly for several minutes, he came upon a diner, went in, and ordered a burger deluxe. It wasn't until the waitress placed it before him that he realized how hungry he was.

He didn't know how time got away from him. One minute he was inhaling the burger, which was heavenly, the next he caught sight of a wall clock and saw he only had five minutes left of his break. He paid his bill and hightailed it back to the OEOB, then remembered Glen's Pepsi. Shit! Torn for a moment, he figured he was better off returning late with soda than on time without it. All told, by the time he returned to the Secretariat he had been gone nearly an hour and twenty minutes, and Glen was looking for him.

Fearing Glen would think he had taken advantage of his kindness, he rushed into the office with his tail between his legs and an apology pouring from his lips.

"I'm sorry, Glen. I'm really sorry. I know it was incredibly irresponsible to be gone so long. I'm sorry! Really!"

Glen peered over his glasses with a look of disgust. Matt tried to steel himself, but burger or no burger, he didn't have the strength for another riot act.

"It won't happen again," he said, trying to pre-empt him. "I promise!"

"Son, do you think I'm some kind of ogre?"

"Uh, sir?"

"First, I told you to take a break and I meant it. Second, I told you to dispense with the sir. And third…" He eyed the soda can in Matt's hand, "…you remembered my soda."

"Yes, sir – I mean Glen." Matt handed him the can.

"Now, let's get back to business. The front office called for the boss. He's in a meeting in the Roosevelt Room with Ambassador Dobrynin, whose eyeglasses just broke. They want you to pick up his glasses and get them fixed. You better move out, *toute suite*."

Stifling the urge to salute, Matt turned sharply to leave the office, then called out, "Thanks, Glen!"

As soon as she saw him, the West Wing receptionist smiled and picked up a broken pair of half-rim black reading glasses from her desk.

"It looks like the screw fell out," she said, pointing to the small hinge.

Matt eagerly accepted the glasses as if they symbolized his chance at redemption. The fact that the glasses belonged to Anatoly Dobrynin, well, that made an otherwise small task a matter of vital international implications. Dobrynin, who had served as the Soviet ambassador for the last decade, was a legendary fixture in Washington. Matt had first learned about him in social studies class, when they discussed his role in the Cuban Missile Crisis. For the last few years he had worked closely with National Security Advisor Henry Kissinger to keep the lines of communication, limited though they were, open between the two superpowers. The importance of that communication was not lost on Matt. He clearly remembered how as a child he and his schoolmates had been trained to climb under their desks in case the Soviets decided to bomb America.

Matt held up the glasses. "Any idea where I should take these?"

The receptionist didn't miss a beat. "Atlantic Optical, on the north side of Pennsylvania Avenue, just past 17th Street."

"Wow, thanks," he said, grateful that she had shaved time off his task.

The walk from the West Wing entrance to Pennsylvania Avenue took only a minute. As he neared the front gate, he once again became aware of the world outside the White House. Unlike earlier, when he had simply sought to put distance between himself and the stress of the morning, he now walked with the brisk pace of a man conducting the business of the American people. Just passing through the gate from the protected enclave elicited stares from passersby, tourists, businesspeople, students, and a homeless man who made the north fence his permanent residence. Matt could imagine what they were thinking as he left the prestigious residence. His feeling of self-importance was palpable.

As he headed down Pennsylvania Avenue toward 17th Street, Matt slowly fingered the glasses as if they would magically impart the wealth of the Soviet statesman's experience to him. Had Dobrynin worn them when staring down Kissinger, perhaps even the Presidents Kennedy,

Johnson, and Nixon? In closed-door meetings with Nikita Khrushchev at the Kremlin? What history must have unfolded through those simple half-rim spectacles!

Matt walked into Atlantic Optical, with its wide array of eyewear, confident his little mission would be an easy one. All he had to do was get a new screw from an optician. Instead, after several minutes of searching, the store manager informed him he couldn't find a screw to fit the glasses. Frustrated but undeterred, Matt left, turned onto 18th Street and walked up to K Street, the heart of Washington's commercial section. There he came upon an optical store tended by a middle-aged man whose freshly starched lab coat added an air of authority to his presence.

"Where did you get these glasses?" he asked, studying them through an optician's loop.

"They belong to the Soviet Ambassador," Matt said in a hushed tone so as not to be overheard. "I'm from the White House and I have to get them fixed."

The optician held the glasses at arm's distance and carefully rolled the earpiece around in his fingers.

"I'm afraid we are not going to find a screw to fix these glasses."

"What is so difficult about fixing a pair of ordinary glasses?"

"They may be ordinary in the Soviet Union," the man said, "but they're on the metric system, and their screws are different sizes."

"Geez," Matt said, and leaned over the counter to look at the glasses while the man continued to roll them in his fingertips. They were like two little boys who had come upon a wonderment.

Finally, Matt muttered in resignation, "I guess we'll just have to tape them."

"I can do better than that!" the man said as he set the glasses down, "Won't be perfect, though."

Matt watched as he began rummaging around in a drawer, fishing out a screw a little smaller in diameter and longer than the hinge itself. Turning to the drawer again, he found a tiny nut and secured it to the part of the screw that protruded beyond the hinge. The fit, as the man predicted, was imperfect and caused a slight wobble, but at least the

Soviet Ambassador wouldn't look like some nerd with a piece of tape holding his eyeglasses together. Matt profusely thanked the man, who refused to accept any payment for his good deed. It seemed the excitement of playing a role in the caper was compensation enough.

From K Street, Matt made the short trek back to the White House. When he entered Lafayette Park, he came across a full-throttled, sixties-style protest, with a group of police officers wearing riot helmets positioned between the demonstrators and the White House. Remembering Jensen's warning to steer clear of such activities, he made a U-turn and backtracked through the park, down 17th Street to enter the grounds through the OEOB. It added time to his trip but the last thing he needed, especially today, was to end up in the morning papers.

"Oh," said the receptionist when Matt appeared. "I'm afraid the meeting ended. Can you take those back to the Soviet Embassy? You know where it is, don't you?"

"No," Matt replied as he turned to head out to the ramp, "but I'm sure the limo driver will."

A few minutes later, Matt was relaxing against the plush leather seat, Dobrynin's glasses still clutched in his hand. As the limo eased through the gate his attention was once again drawn toward the demonstration. He noticed that the protesters were about his age, most with very long hair, faded torn blue jeans, and ragged shirts. Their hands clutched homemade signs with the peace symbol or the words "Stop the Killing." Matt stared out the window at the spectacle. And while he recognized the vast differences between the protestors and himself, he knew their cause was good. The war was a horrible thing.

It was no small comfort that the draft, which President Nixon had been winding down for the past few years, was, on January 27, 1973, officially brought to an end. Matt, by virtue of his age, narrowly escaped being called up, but he knew plenty of boys from military school who were either conscripted or joined up.

He realized that the protestors would view him, riding around in a White House limo, as part of a warmongering political machine, part of the problem. He thought of the countless variables, from family background to finances and seemingly random events and split decisions, that resulted in every person's circumstances and even their appearance. How odd, he thought, that the length of people's hair or the clothes they wore could obfuscate their similarities and even position them as enemies – and how often this led to crises and maybe even war. It wasn't often that Matt waxed philosophical – his upbringing and military school background favored decisive action based on the facts before him. When he did, however, the epiphanies struck hard and stuck with him.

His musings were interrupted by the driver, who announced the imminent arrival at their destination. A second later he turned onto 16th Street and pulled up to the gate midway between L and M Streets. Matt asked him to wait, then slid out and pressed the button on the call box. As he waited for someone to respond, he studied the building, not quite able to reconcile its appearance with the formidable reputation of its inhabitants.

Indeed, the Soviet Embassy was an old Victorian, so small and plain it was hard to believe that it represented the world's only other superpower. Its simplicity made it appear almost innocent, but one look at the roof, with its vast array of communications antenna used for eavesdropping, immediately dispelled any doubts as to the true nature of the place.

Eventually, a short man wearing an ill-fitting suit and harsh cologne arrived on the other side of the gate. He spoke no English. Ignoring the assault on his nostrils, Matt tried his best to communicate, slowly annunciating why he was there and holding out the Ambassador's glasses as evidence. But the man in the bad suit was uninterested. He waved Matt away with a careless motion of his hand and was about to retreat into the building when Matt uttered the magic word: Dobrynin. The man's cold eyes flickered with recognition and the grudging acknowledgment that the young man before him may actually be there for something important. He then opened the gate and motioned for Matt to follow him up a small walkway and into the embassy.

Once inside, the man held his hand out in front of Matt like a traffic cop, making it clear the American was to go no further. Then he disappeared through a door off the lobby. Matt perused tapestries that hung on the walls of the dark, foreboding place. Momentarily, a new host appeared.

"May I help you?" the new person said in heavily-accented English that for Matt called to mind the Count on Sesame Street. Biting back a smile, he quickly explained that he was from the White House and had Ambassador Dobrynin's glasses. Then, holding them out, he demonstrated the wobble due to the ill-fitting screw and apologized for not having a better fix, while his new host expressed appreciation with a series of "Tank you, tank yous," accompanied by tiny bows.

Matt suppressed a shiver as he left the embassy. He had only spent about three minutes inside, but it was three minutes too long. As he slipped into the plush seat of the waiting limousine, he suddenly had the strange sensation of being watched. He glanced back at the building just in time to see what appeared to be a slender female form standing in a second-story window. Matt squinted, trying to get a better look, but then a heavy curtain dropped in front of the glass, obscuring her from view.

CHAPTER TWELVE

For most of his life Matt had counted down the days to the end of the school year. Elementary school seemed to drag on forever, and the rigor and regimentation he so loathed in military school began to wear on him as each spring approached. Now, whole weeks were passing in the blink of an eye. It was as if he was on a merry-go-round ride of work, classes, and fraternity events. He woke each morning with an endless to-do list running through his mind and fell into bed each night too exhausted to put together a cohesive thought, let alone pick up the dog-eared, dusty copy of The Spy Who Came in From the Cold on his nightstand. In the space between he was like an endurant swimmer, wringing from each deep breath every ounce of energy until he could steal another. He could feel himself changing. He was less easy-going and more focused; he replaced sleep with splashes of cold water on his face and ignored the faint dark rings he saw around his eyes when he looked in the mirror.

Those closest to him noticed it too; Walter's invitations to get a drink or take in a movie were almost pointless, and even Grossman's daily mantra, "Man, you look like shit," was tinged with concern. Matt barely registered this, even as he flipped off Grossman or declined the drink with a regretful, "Sorry, man, I have to…" followed by a rattling off of items from said to-do list. Before long he dropped the apology and the list, offering just a curt shake of his head and a "too much on my plate." Bottom line: even if he had a choice, he wouldn't have changed a thing. His work at the White House stood out in sharp relief, for though he followed others' directives all day long he had never felt so self-directed; each time he walked through those doors he was reminded that though his tasks were regimented and often boring, he was playing a small but important part in history. Autumn flew by, registering only as more comfortable weather, and even the end of his first semester might have gone unnoticed if not for the sudden flurry of exams and term paper deadlines that felt like an unwelcome distraction from his real life.

Matt's visit home over winter break brought both a welcome relief and a sharp realization.

"Matt!" his mother exclaimed, clearly concerned, when they met him at the airport. "You're skin and bones!"

"Now, now," Matt, Sr. said, placing a gentle hand on his wife's shoulder. But Matt saw his father's eyes shrewdly sweep over him. "You do look a little lean, son. They working you too hard at the White House?"

"No sir," he said, adding with a smile, "Maybe a little."

His mother pulled him into a hug. "Well, you'll get plenty of rest now that you're home. And I made all your favorite foods, so maybe you'll gain a few pounds too."

And he did rest…for about two days. He slept in, ate three squares a day, caught up with some military school buddies. But by the time the family gathered around the dining room table for Christmas dinner, he felt antsy, like a revving motor in a car stuck in park. Though he loved and missed his parents, he couldn't wait to get back to D.C., The White House, and his fraternity brothers' drunken hijinks at The Tavern.

When the spring semester began, Matt made another valiant attempt at balancing school, work, and fraternity life; however, before long he was spending even more time at the White House, more out of personal necessity than any demands placed on him by others. He told himself it was pure pragmatism. Glen's office, with its correctable electric typewriter, made the drudgery of schoolwork, if not more palatable, a bit easier. More importantly, it was private after working hours – Matt could get more done in two hours there than he could in an entire day in the dorm, with Grossman's crass philosophical diatribes and Kate's constant drop-ins. And who could deny the advantages of having the Presidential Library at his fingertips? The ability to get any book or article ever written from Presidential Records in a matter of hours? It was a no-brainer.

Indeed, though Matt enjoyed interacting with the White House staff, he preferred being at the OEOB at night. The normal hubbub of the day – the unique chiming sound of the White House phones, voices in the corridors, and opening and closing of doors gave way to silence broken only by the peaceful hum of vacuums. For study breaks, he chatted with Secret Service agents making their rounds or took walks from the West Wing through the Executive Mansion, out the East Wing entrance and around the South Grounds. The unpleasant tradeoff was missed time with his friends, but for now it was a price Matt was willing to pay. Anything else would have meant dropping the several plates he had spinning. *All I have to do,* he kept telling himself, *is hold on until the end of the semester. Then I can breathe.*

He clung to this thought so tightly that when summer break arrived the wave of melancholy took him completely by surprise. The dorms were filled with the same frenzied activity as when he got there the August before, only now it was in reverse, with students carrying boxes out to their cars or clinging to friends in the packed lobby with promises to call and write. The energy had shifted; the excitement of embarking on a new adventure now felt like an unraveling of close entanglements that may not survive the separation of the summer yet would impact lifetimes.

Watching other students leave to be with their parents, siblings, and childhood friends triggered an emptiness and a deeper realization about his own family. Staying at work this first summer break, before the true responsibilities of adulthood took hold, made it all the less likely that he would ever go home again, save for short visits during holidays. The love and security he had depended on his entire life, though still unshakable at the core, was entering a new phase.

With a start, Matt realized he was mourning the old; yet at the same time he had this odd sense of knowing that something important, something obscured from view, was around the corner. This knowing was the real reason he had accepted Glenn's offer to work full-time this summer, even more so than the daily excitement of the White House or the fact that Grossman and Walter, his adopted family, were also staying in town – though those inducements would have been tempting enough.

He packed sporadically over the last few days, seizing any spare half-hour, sometimes even five minutes, to pull items out of a drawer. With each carefully folded shirt or book he placed in a box, he felt as if he was pushing his feelings further down. Unpacking them – the feelings and the boxes – was simply added to the list. In the meantime, drinking the emotions away would have to suffice.

"Oy, you're like a woman," Grossman said as he shuffled into the room and saw Matt holding a shirt against his chest to fold it. "You're just gonna iron it again when you take it out."

Matt eyed Grossman's crumpled t-shirt, the wild hair. "Or I could just sport the unmade bed look you've made so fashionable…"

"Joke all you want, boychik. Just remember I'm the reason you have a bed to lay your head on after a long day of saving the world."

Matt laughed with the first genuine amusement he'd felt in days. "Touché."

In an uncharacteristic burst of initiative, Grossman had secured the three of them an apartment for the summer, though Matt and Walter speculated that his real motivation had been wooing the outgoing occupant, a busty blonde co-ed. Alas, the co-ed had spurned his clumsy advances, but the apartment, a spacious and surprisingly affordable three-bedroom three blocks from campus, was well worth the hit to his ego.

*   *   *

That Saturday afternoon, Matt dragged himself to the dorm to box up the last of his things. It had been a particularly grueling week at work, topped off by copious drinking on Friday.

Matt could hear the music blasting even before the elevator doors opened, which normally would have been fine but today just grated on his already frayed nerves. Shouldn't everyone be gone already? Indeed, as he walked down the hall he found it was eerily empty, with just a few fellow stragglers who, like him, had waited for the last minute to move out. He nodded to them, moving in the direction of the music: it was coming from his soon-to-be-vacated room.

Grossman, he thought, his annoyance dissipating somewhat when he realized he didn't want to be alone in the empty dorm. It was depressing enough.

Any thought that Grossman was working was dispelled as soon as Matt walked through the open door and saw him sitting on the floor, throwing a ball back and forth against the wall. Walter, a cigar clamped between his teeth, stood looking out the open window. As Matt entered, he turned, nodded, then made a *p'tooey* sound and spat a clump of cigar out the window.

A second later, they heard a startled grunt from the ground below, then the shout of "You son of a bitch!"

Satisfied, Walter turned away from the window, then did a double-take and peered out at something.

"What?" Matt asked and crossed the room; usually if something caught Walter's interest it was worth checking out.

"Nothing... just that girl," Walter drawled.

"Girl?" Matt looked out the window just in time to see Catherine getting into the passenger side of a yellow Alfa Romeo convertible. The trunk was open, and a male figure was lifting a small suitcase to place it inside. Though he already knew who it was, Matt's brow furrowed slightly as the trunk closed to reveal Michael's face. No doubt about it – the guy just bugged him.

Matt turned to Walter and shrugged. "So? We knew she was with him, right?"

As if on cue, Kate appeared in the doorway and called out, "Hey, Matt, your girlfriend left this for you." At his puzzled glance, she walked and handed him a record.

Matt looked at the cover and rolled his eyes.

"Girlfriend?" Grossman raised an eyebrow at him. "And we thought you were spending all your time kissing Tricky Dick's ass!"

"I hate you, Grossman," Matt said indifferently.

"I hate it when that last drop of pee makes a big wet spot on my pants!"

"Whatever. I think the fact that she just drove off with another guy is evidence to the contrary."

Matt didn't give Catherine much thought these days. It was largely a case of out of sight, out of mind – he was at the White House much of the time and they didn't have any classes together during the spring semester. On the few occasions he did see her on campus he'd been taken with her beautiful eyes and easy, kind smile; then he would see the ever-present Michael hanging about like a dark cloud and tell himself their cancelled date was a blessing in disguise.

Just the previous day, he'd run into Catherine as he was crossing the quad. It was a rare moment when he was not rushing to get anywhere; otherwise, he might not even have noticed the box clutched tightly in her arms.

"Whacha got there?" he asked, smiling.

"Records…" she sighed, raising up one knee to balance the box on it. "I could have left them with a friend here but there's no way I'm going the whole summer without them…"

"Well, let me help you." As he took the box from her, he glanced at the one on the top and saw it was Roy Orbison's Greatest Hits. "Oh, this is one of my favorites. Unfortunately, it's my sister's too because I lent it to her and never got it back."

"You look sad about it," Catherine observed.

"About the record? Nah, I'm just missing my family." He shrugged. "I'm staying in D.C. to work over the summer."

Catherine's eyes softened. "Oh, that's too bad…"

"No – it's great! I love the White House!" Matt exclaimed, and immediately felt the heat rushing to his face.

I love the White House? I sound like such a dork!

Catherine didn't seem to notice his nerdiness, or his embarrassment. "I'll be working too, for my dad." She paused. "I'm not leaving until tomorrow. Meet for a drink later…?"

Matt was about to say that yes, a drink would be great – no elaborate date plans this time! – when he saw Michael approaching from behind her.

"You know, Catherine, I'm just really busy…" He saw the disappointment flash across her face, then added pointedly, "Hello, Michael."

Catherine turned to look at him. "Oh, hey."

Michael threw a curt nod at Matt, then gestured to the box in his arms.

"That yours?" At Catherine's answer in the affirmative, he walked over and took it from Matt. "C'mon, we still have a bunch of stuff to pack." The proprietary tone in his voice was unmistakable.

"Right, well…" Catherine looked at Matt as if she wanted to say something more, then thought better of it. "Don't work too hard, Matt."

"I'll try. Have a great summer." With that, he had turned and walked away without a backward glance.

Now, he stood staring at Roy Orbison's face as he recounted the encounter to his friends.

"Boy, she's *good*," Grossman said.

"She certainly gets an A for effort," Walter added between chews of his cigar.

"I know," Matt said, unable to suppress a satisfied grin.

Twenty minutes later, he taped up the last box and stood surveying the room for any last-minute things lying around.

"Fellows," he announced, "I think we're done here."

Walter agreed. "What do you want to do now?"

"I don't know, what do you want to do?" Grossman answered, tossing the ball, and the question, to Matt. "What do you want to do?"

"We could go to the apartment," Walter suggested, "Finish unpacking."

Matt and Grossman looked at him with disdain.

"If I go to the apartment now," Matt said, "It will be to crash."

His friends looked at each other then at him, shaking their heads in unison.

"C'mon, lover boy," Walter said, "Let's go get a drink."

CHAPTER THIRTEEN

The constant yo-yoing between the humdrum and the frantic was like a drug that wreaked havoc with Matt's nervous system but left him wanting more. One day, as he was halfway through some mind-numbing and time-sensitive task, Ann Green entered carrying a manila envelope. He held up a finger for her to wait a moment.

"No, no," she said, waving it impatiently, "This must be hand-delivered to Secretary Kissinger at the State Department – now."

Matt suppressed a rare look of annoyance as he stopped what he was doing and took the envelope, which had the familiar red tag. *Did anyone in the White House ever do anything that didn't require special attention?* he wondered, even as he felt that familiar rush of adrenalin kick in.

He left the OEOB, surprised to see that the White House tour line had wound its way from the East Wing all the way around the South Grounds and up 17th Street. As he headed down 17th toward E Street, his eyes flicked across the sea of faces from all over the country, even the world. He drew closer then so he could hear bits of conversation. It was a little game he often played, listening to what people said and trying to guess where they were from. He considered it a win when he picked up that Midwestern twang that might give away a fellow Michigander. Did they notice his credentials, the manila envelope with its red tag? How impressed they would be to know it was addressed to The Honorable Henry A. Kissinger!

Chiding himself for such thoughts, he tightened his grip on the envelope and pressed it tightly against his side. The only thing he should be thinking about was ensuring the special cargo stayed in his possession.

The walk from the White House to the Department of State was a pleasant one. He passed the park running through the center of E Street, with its rectangular pools filled with large goldfish and lily pads; a lovely, if out-of-place, site saddled between two streets, among the limestone, granite, and marble office buildings. People were always in the park, including, to Matt's delight, young secretaries who spent their lunch hours perched daintily on benches, their heads tilted toward the sky to bask in the summer sun. Today did not disappoint in that regard, and Matt thought briefly how nice it would be to join them, though his imaginings stopped short of initiating conversation. Small talk, especially with attractive women, was not his strong suit.

He passed the Federal Reserve, which looked like a giant marble mausoleum, and proceeded down 21st Street. At the Department of State, the guard took one look at Matt's White House badge and allowed him to enter unchallenged. Matt gave the man an officious nod, then allowed himself a small smile as he headed for the elevators and recalled the first time he'd had business at the State Department.

As he stepped onto the elevator that day he had been shocked to find an elderly woman, barely five feet tall, operating it. The small space was permeated with the scent of the flowers, coming from the corsage on her tiny wrist. As she and Matt exchanged smiles, he had the sense that he had stepped into another age. Later, he mentioned the odd experience to Keith, who explained that she was one of several elderly, corsage-wearing women who'd been fixtures there since the elevators were manually operated; these days, thanks to upgrades in technology, they just pushed the buttons.

Now, as he stepped inside, he gave the woman an almost reverent smile and said, "Seventh floor, please."

Visiting the seventh floor of the Department of State was no small thing. A place of rarified air, it was where the Secretary and his most senior advisors were located; it was also not uncommon to see leaders from all over the world striding purposely among the elegant antiques.

By now Matt had seen Henry Kissinger many times at the White House, and though he was no longer quite as "starstruck" as he'd been the first day, he remained amazed by the man's humble demeanor. No matter what was going on in the world, no matter the incredible weight of responsibility he undoubtedly felt, Kissinger was always quick to greet people with a smile and a congenial, *"Gut morning."* This alone would have been impressive enough, but when Matt took into account that he had arrived in this country a refugee from Nazi Germany in the 1930s, Kissinger became a true giant among men, and the very symbol of America's promise to the world.

When he arrived at the Secretary's private suite, he was again met by a guard who, after glimpsing his blue White House credentials, allowed him to enter. The receptionist and secretary to the Secretary were away from their desks, so, with no one to give the envelope to, Matt simply placed it in the center of the desk right outside Kissinger's office then walked out, content that his mission was complete.

It was nearly noon and he was feeling the ravenous hunger that always struck him this time of day. Just two blocks from the OEOB, the diner where he had eaten the day of the "Wallace Debacle" caught his attention. Matt considered going straight back to work, but the memory of the burger deluxe, and the advertisement in the window with the familiar Coke bottle resting in an Arctic snow scene, drew him in like a mirage calling to a desert wanderer.

He walked inside and scanned the packed place, enjoying the delicious chill of air-conditioned air hitting his hot skin. Finding every table taken, he was about to walk out when he noticed one available stool, sandwiched between two older men, at the lunch counter. Swiftly walking toward it, he begged the frazzled but friendly waitress for a Coke then downed it in front of her before placing his food order. A few minutes later, as he sipped a second Coke, she set a plate with a hamburger and a pile of steaming fries in front of him. He attacked it ravenously, finding it even more delicious than he remembered, and seemed to magically regain his strength within a few bites.

Halfway through his meal, he heard a female voice to his left say in slightly accented English, "Excuse me, is dis stool taken?"

"Um, yeah…" he said distractedly, for between his enjoyment of the food and errant thoughts of work he hadn't even noticed the man next to him leave. He then turned and froze when he found standing beside him a stunningly beautiful young woman.

Matt was aware of his mouth closing and opening in a series of false starts, then words coming in out in a rush. "Oh, sorry, you want the stool, sure, no, not taken."

Her full lips pulled up slightly in a silent, amused acknowledgment that she had taken him aback – likely a regular occurrence when she spoke with men.

Matt searched her face, wrestling with the sense that he had seen her before and coming up empty as to where. Certainly, he would have remembered her face, the voice that sounded like velvet mixed with gravel, and the immediate rush of heat to his face – and every other part of him, for that matter.

Sitting gracefully on these stools was no easy feat, but she managed it effortlessly.

Matt took a few more bites of his burger, suddenly finding it had lost its appeal. He continued eating for something to do, all the while stealing sideways glances at her profile, trying, unsuccessfully, to place her. He saw that slight smile playing on her lips again and had the feeling that she knew she was being observed. Feeling foolish, he cast his eyes downward, only to catch sight of toned calves and delicate, demurely crossed ankles.

"Do you work nearby?" she asked suddenly and while still looking forward, making Matt wonder for a second if she was speaking to him.

"Me? Um, yes, a few blocks away. What about you?"

"I am a student."

Matt again detected the hint of an accent, the way she said "*a student*" as if she had to think about including the article, and knew for sure that he'd never heard her speak before. Yet, he couldn't shake the feeling that he knew her.

"Me too." He paused. "You don't by any chance go to American University, do you?"

"No," she said curtly, then took a sip of her coffee.

"Oh, I thought maybe I had seen you around campus…maybe one of the pubs nearby?"

"Pubs?" she asked quizzically, as if unfamiliar with the word. "Oh, no. No pubs. I am new to Washington and I do not know many people."

Suddenly, she glanced at her watch and started fishing around in her purse. "I must be going now."

"Let me get that," he said, gesturing to her empty coffee cup.

"That is very kind of you." She stood, and for the first time looked directly at Matt, melting him from the inside out. "My name is Anna."

"Matt."

He dared to imagine that he had a window of opportunity, one that was rapidly closing. Thus began an internal tug-of-war about how to prolong the moment that ended with her curt, "Nice speaking with you," followed by the sound of her heels clicking away.

"Damn," he muttered, then glanced at the clock on the wall and saw how late he was. "Oh, damn!"

With that, he fished some bills out of his wallet, placed them on the counter, and rushed out.

*   *   *

Anna Ivanovich Aslanov had always believed in fate; she also believed that sometimes people had to create their own. Seeing Matt, first riding by her in the White House limo and then at the Soviet embassy, was fate handing her a gift. Now she would have to take matters into her own hands.

When she first approached Vadim with the idea of pursuing Matt he had scoffed at the idea.

"He is just a college student, Annushka, a boy! How could we possibly benefit from such a relationship?" His eyes scanned her body as if searching for some lascivious agenda. "Perhaps you are thinking only of how such a 'relationship' could benefit you…"

Anna had kept her face carefully neutral, for it would certainly *not* benefit her for Vadim to know that he made her skin crawl.

"I'm telling you, Vadim, he is not just a college student. He was riding around in a White House limousine – and he came to our embassy!"

Vadim snorted. "Yes, I heard about that. He had the important mission of bringing the ambassador his glasses."

"Yes, he is as you say, low on the ladder," Anna said, "and this is why I can get close to him." She paused, then said pointedly, "Not like the others."

Vadim narrowed his eyes at her. "Are you saying it is my fault that you have failed to get the information we need?"

It wasn't his words, but the slight menace in his tone, that scared her. One call from him and she would be called back home, and suffer the consequences, as would her family.

"No…" she said slowly and logically, "I am acknowledging my failure and saying that we may have another opportunity. I am asking you for the chance to take it."

For a long moment, Vadim swirled his glass of port and stared into it as if he would see the answer there.

"Okay," he said finally, "You will wait while I check into the boy."

For the next two weeks, Anna went about her business, going to school and her job, pretending to be any other immigrant enjoying the freedoms America had to offer. And she *was* enjoying it, going to Garfinckel's for tea and a new black dress that she could ill afford but perfectly fit her curves. And yet, never for one moment did Vadim's looming decision leave her mind.

One afternoon she returned hot and sweaty to her apartment from a walk – how she hated the weather in this city! – and wanting nothing more than to take a cool bath and relax. Instead, she found Vadim sitting on the sofa and staring off at an invisible spot on the wall. He almost appeared to be meditating, but she knew that beneath the serene expression his mind was endlessly calculating, working out some scenario, possibly several at once, to every possible result. This visit to her apartment, his first, indicated that he had come to deliver his decision – and that it did not bode well for her. Anna felt icy beads of sweat gathering under her arms that had nothing to do with the weather.

"Galina could be home any minute," she pointed out coldly as she set her purse on the coffee table. "What then?"

"Why, I would tell her that I am your uncle," he said matter-of-factly, "waiting to take you to dinner. Certainly, the cow would believe that."

Anna couldn't suppress a smile, for her roommate, a rather homely student at a nearby secretarial school, was indeed a cow. Of Belorussian birth, Galina had been in the U.S. for several years, though how her family had obtained permission to immigrate remained a mystery. Her idea of scintillating conversation was limited to reminiscing about the soul-crushingly boring Northwestern town her parents settled in – and making comments to Anna that masqueraded as compliments but only revealed her jealousy.

"Annushka, I have decided to let you pursue the boy."

Anna sat heavily on the couch, unable to hide the relief that flooded her body. Whoever he had follow Matt apparently saw something that validated her idea.

"What did you learn about him?" she asked.

"He is indeed a lowly messenger, but not just for glasses. He delivers documents to the CIA, State Department, and other government buildings. He has access to important information and, providing you do your job, we too can have that access." He paused. "You have your chance, Annushka. Do not waste it."

Before he left, Vadim provided her with Matt's address, the times he typically arrived at work and left, and some M Steet bar he and his friends had gone to two Fridays in a row. He then reiterated what she already knew: that Matt often left the confines of the White House, either on foot or by limo, carrying sensitive documents. Her work would be to find a time and a place to make the initial contact.

"Accidentally" bumping into Matt proved more challenging than she thought. As there were no set times when he made deliveries, Anna had no choice but to go to Pennsylvania Avenue and try to blend in with the tourists while keeping an eye out for him. Once, after seeing his limo ease into midday traffic, she hopped in a cab and followed him, groaning in frustration when he was dropped off right in front of a government building that would certainly require security clearance.

By midweek, Anna's nerves were frayed. Vadim expected daily, detailed reports about her efforts, and each conversation ended with a subtle threat as to what would happen to her if she did not deliver. Then, late Wednesday morning, she saw Matt exit the building and head down 17th Street, a large envelope tucked under his arm. She followed at a safe distance, noting with annoyance his slow pace as he meandered, first by the long line of people waiting to tour the White House, then past a park and, finally, to the State Department. She looked at her watch and hoped he moved faster inside than he had on the street.

Five minutes later, she breathed a sigh of relief when she saw him emerge. Each of those moments had seemed endless as she stood there, feeling uncomfortably exposed, as busy pedestrians, including several leering men, passed her by.

As Matt headed back toward the White House, Anna realized that she did not have a way to actually meet him. With each step he took, her anxiety increased, as did her determination not to let him slip away. When he went into the diner, she almost wept with relief.

*   *   *

Matt was still thinking of Anna, and how he had bungled the opportunity to get her number, when he walked into the Secretariat. One look at Glen's frowning face, however, told him he had much larger problems waiting for him.

"Son," he asked tightly, "did you take a package to Kissinger's office at State?"

"Yeah…" Matt replied slowly, "Is something wrong?"

"Who did you give it to?" Glen asked impatiently.

"No one. No one was there. I left it on his secretary's desk."

"Well, it's not there now. But that's not the worst of it. The document was Top Secret. I've got no choice but to notify security that it's missing."

Glen picked up the phone and began to dial.

"I don't understand," Matt said as Glen waited for someone to pick up. "I left it right out on the desk. Maybe I should go back over there and –"

Glen held up his hand, an obvious gesture for silence, then said, "Yeah, Jensen…"

Jensen? Matt thought, his gut clenching. His mind ran to the incident with Mr. Wallace, and he wondered if this time the results would be more disastrous.

What's next? Being mugged on my way to the CIA?

The call seemed to go on forever, with Jensen doing most of the talking. Finally, Glen uttered a farewell grunt and hung up the phone.

"I'm gonna puke," Matt said, his eyes shifting from the floor to the window – anywhere but Glen.

"You're not going to puke, son," he said reassuringly as he gestured toward the chair in front of his desk, "I'm sure there is a reasonable explanation for all this."

Hearing this, Matt relaxed just a little as he slid into the seat, but any relief quickly dissolved with the arrival of Jensen. Matt hadn't thought the man could be any more disapproving of him than he had at their first meeting. Now, as he looked at Jensen's face, contorted with anger, he realized how wrong he had been.

"Another violation, eh?"

"If it *was* a violation, it *wasn't* Matt's," Glen shot back. "He didn't even know the document was classified." Jensen started to say something but Glen silenced him with a look. "Now, I've already been through this with the front office. They put the thing in an envelope without the proper packaging or a receipt. Matt did exactly what he was asked to do!"

Jensen shot Matt a deadly look. "Well, someone's ass is going to be in a sling over this. Every classified document must be controlled. That means double-wrapped, marked appropriately on the inside, and, for God's sake, we should always have someone sign for it! This is the grossest vio– "

Glen cut him off. "You're preaching to the wrong choir."

"Seems to me that this choir needs a little preaching. This is the second time that *he*," he said, pointing to Matt, "was around during a potential risk to national security. Or do you not remember when our friend from la-la-land got into your office? Two close calls are two too many."

"That's enough," Glen thundered. He then glanced at his watch and back to Matt, his expression softening. "Son, it's nearly one o'clock. I need a Pepsi."

With a nod, Matt stood and retreated silently from the office, feeling much like the recalcitrant child being sent to see the principal, only with exponentially higher stakes. He paused just outside the door, torn between getting the soda or staying and listening to the ensuing conversation that would undoubtedly be about him. The fear of what he might hear proved to be too much and he continued down the hall. As he approached the elevator, he was so engrossed in his own thoughts that he barely registered the party of Secret Service agents exiting it.

"Hello there, young man," a voice said cheerfully, snapping Matt back to the moment. Looking him directly in the face was Vice President Gerald Ford.

"Hello, sir!" Matt replied, standing aside for the Vice President and his party.

Returning with the Pepsi, he braced himself for the renewed encounter with Jensen; however, when he entered the Secretariat, he heard only laughter. He peeked timidly into Glen's office to see his boss' broad grin, while Jensen's thin tight lips broadcasted to Matt a simple, unmistakable message.

He cannot stand me.

"C'mon in, son," Glen boomed. "We found your document, or should I say, Henry Kissinger found it!"

Matt shivered involuntarily, as if his body was releasing the fear. "Oh, thank God."

"Yeah, his secretary just called," Glen continued. "The document was right where you said it was. Ole Henry himself walked by the desk and snatched it up. Put it in his briefcase. He has it."

"Of course, this doesn't negate the fact that proper procedure wasn't followed," Jensen interjected.

"That's right!" Glen retorted. "And it's your job to make sure everyone knows the proper procedure, so I suggest you start right now making sure everyone in the front office gets trained."

As Jensen stiffly stood, buttoned his suit jacket, and stormed out. Matt couldn't suppress a smile.

CHAPTER FOURTEEN

Matt had once read that Washington, D.C. was built on a swamp, and he didn't doubt it for a minute. It was not unusual for the humidity level to equal the temperature, producing a stifling feeling whenever he stepped outside. He'd also learned that in the old days legislators and bureaucrats didn't stay around for the summer, and particularly enjoyed that old tale blaming the rise of the federal bureaucracy on the advent of air conditioning, which made the place tolerable for them to work year-round.

Instead of the reprieve he'd been hoping for, Matt found his summer schedule was as grueling as the heat. Monday through Saturday he was up by five a.m., in the office by seven, and didn't leave until six or seven at night. On Sundays, he took it easy, usually at the pool with Grossman and Walter on the roof of their apartment building.

Their temporary home was populated by a more upscale, mature professional set, but what it lacked in young females to ogle it made up for in opportunities for male bonding. The pool's sauna – or *schvitz*, as Walter called it – was a favorite source of entertainment. The three would ease themselves into the schvitz, force themselves to stay there until they were boiling from the inside out, then burst out the door like banshees and dive into the pool. The water, cool in comparison to the heat of their skin, immediately sent a consciousness-expanding signal to their brains, similar, they imagined, to a drug.

Most of the time, they just sat around the pool talking, and on a deeper level than the dorm environment, and the frenetic pace of parties and classes, permitted. They shared what they wanted for their lives, in college and beyond, some of which they hadn't been aware of until they said it out loud. Matt learned that Walter's economy with words stemmed from a painful childhood stutter and marveled how hard he had worked to overcome it, to the point of transforming himself into a person others considered a source of wisdom. More surprising was that Grossman's indifferent attitude and crass humor were largely a façade developed in response to his parents' divorce and hid a much more serious, sensitive character. These exchanges, often mere snippets of conversation in between dips in the pool, reminded Matt of his military school days, when he and his roommates bonded over the common adversities of marching and hazing. They were the moments that cemented a brotherhood far deeper than dorm room assignments and fraternity ceremonies.

Inevitably, these poolside chats turned to the opposite sex. Grossman was perpetually on the make, with results that rarely mirrored the effort, while Walter was dating Meryl, the girl he had been paired with at the rush party. She was pretty and nice enough, though Matt wasn't sure if they fit together or just preferred it to the messiness of the college dating scene. Both, to Matt's relief, danced around the elephant by the pool: the inexperience he never admitted to but seemed to emanate from every pore. Instead, they contented themselves with alternately teasing him about giving the gum-snapping Janet another chance – "Maybe it's *bashert*, boychik!" – and trashing Catherine as duplicitous and "not that great-looking" – the latter a falsehood and obvious attempt to make Matt feel better.

*   *   *

It began as just another Friday boys' night out, an escape from the shackles of, well, whatever. They really didn't need a reason. Matt started it off on the wrong foot by announcing he wanted to be home by nine p.m. because he had an early morning at the White House. His companions, though disgusted by what they saw as misplaced loyalty, merely nodded, believing that after one or two drinks in a bar filled with hot Washington women Matt's priorities would right themselves.

They got to the Sign of the Whale at 8:30, just as dusk was settling over the city. Originally suggested by Walter, the trendy M Street bar had quickly become their regular Friday watering hole for its neighborhood feel and clientele of working professionals in their mid- to late-twenties. The three friends were so anxious to let loose and let go of the week that they started to cross the street without looking for oncoming traffic.

The sudden screech of car brakes announced a disaster narrowly avoided. Walter and Matt dashed the remaining distance to the safety of the sidewalk, then turned to see Grossman standing defiantly at the bumper of the small black Porsche that nearly ended them. He was waving his hand back and forth in front of his zipper, an economic gesture that combined contempt and obscenity. Mortified, Matt glanced at Walter and saw the mustache flicking in humor. Grossman, quite proud at having made his point, calmly followed them into the bar.

"We don't know you," Matt stated.

"Did you see how I showed that rich shit?" Grossman replied, undaunted.

Walter rolled his eyes in a silent *oy vey*.

"What'll it –?" the bartender began as he stepped forward to take their drink order. Before he could finish, Grossman interrupted.

"Beer! In a bottle. Cold."

Matt shook his head in his embarrassment. "I'll have whatever you've got on draft."

Walter held up two fingers to signify he would have the same.

"Oh, and three shooters of peppermint schnapps too," Grossman demanded, then he glanced around the bar and loudly proclaimed, "Yeah, that was one difficult brain surgery I did today!"

"I wish we had a silence button," Matt said to Walter.

"Or a sledgehammer," Walter added, then picked up one of the beers placed before them. "L'chaim."

The bartender returned with three shot glasses of schnapps.

"This is going to be an ugly night!" Grossman declared, raising the small glass to his lips to down the schnapps with the swagger of a hero in a Western.

On that, Walter and Matt could agree, and they reared their heads back in unison. Grossman turned again to survey the crowd.

"Tally ho!" he shouted above the hum of conversation around them, "I see a fox!"

Matt turned in the direction of his friend's stare and froze; for there, standing at the other end of the bar, was Anna, the woman he had met at the diner. He didn't know what shocked him more: that she was there, or that she looked even more stunning now, in a sleek black dress that left little to the imagination.

"She's beautiful," Grossman said, sounding slightly awestruck. "Look at that body. Look at those –"

Only Walter seemed unaffected. "She's probably the driver of that Porsche," he said with a snort.

"You know," Grossman continued, "a woman like that could make an honest man out of ya…"

"You wouldn't know where to begin with a woman like that."

"Oh, I could make her happy…"

"Only if you left her alone," Walter snapped back.

"Yeah," Grossman shouted as a small group of men and women settled next to them. "I'm pretty happy with my performance before the Supreme Court today." He paused a moment to gauge the reaction but the conversation continued uninterrupted.

Smirking at the failed attempt to draw attention, Walter intoned in his best announcer voice, "Will you look at the time! Gotta run. I've got to do the news at eleven!"

For a long moment the people near them went silent, all eyes turning to the purported media personality among them.

Delighted that he had pulled off the farce – and one-upped Grossman – Walter ordered them three more shots. It was only then that he noticed that Matt wasn't joining in on their hijinks.

"What gives?" he asked quietly.

"That girl," Matt said, speaking from the side of his mouth as if it would make it less likely to be overheard by Grossman, "I met her the other day!"

Walter raised an eyebrow. "*You* met *her* and didn't mention it? Damn…the White House really has gone to your head."

Matt shot him an annoyed look then relaxed when he saw Walter was smiling.

"Nothing like that…I sat next to her at a diner and when I got back to work this crazy situation was going on and –"

He cut himself off when he glanced over and saw Anna looking their way. She was definitely dressed for evening, from the dress to the painted red lips pulled up in that knowing smile, to the eyes, heavily lined with black kohl, that were boring holes into his.

Precisely at that moment, the bartender arrived with three more shot glasses.

"The lady," he said, "sends her compliments."

Matt and Walter looked at each other, then at the bartender, whose expression mirrored their incredulity that a woman like her would make overtures toward schlubs like them.

"See, she's got the hots for me!" an oblivious Grossman said. "Oh, m'God. Here she comes!"

Matt turned to see that Anna was indeed headed toward them.

"What'll I say? Shit! Shit! What am I going to say?" Grossman babbled in a panic.

"I wouldn't worry about it," Walter said, thoroughly enjoying the moment.

With barely a nod in his direction, Anna passed Grossman and walked up to Matt.

"Well, isn't this a strange twist of fate…" she said coolly, that small smile in place.

"Sure is!" Matt blurted out, then immediately commenced to chastising himself for sounding like an exuberant kindergartner. "Um, thank you for the shots."

"I wanted to *tank* you for the coffee. Sometimes a kindness from a stranger can make all the difference."

Matt noted the sudden shadow that crossed her face. "Well, you're welcome. How are you?"

"I am very well. I thought tonight I would be among more strangers and instead I see a friend. Like I said, it is fate."

Matt, who was brought up to believe that what you get in life is directly correlated to what you put in, had never given much thought to the existence of fate.

Grossman stepped forward. "Hello there…"

Behind him, an amused Walter had settled on a stool with his beer to await the show.

"Um, my friend is really quite taken with you," Matt explained unnecessarily.

"Well," she said, leaning in so close that her warm breath caressed his ear, "I'm quite taken with you."

To Matt's complete mortification, he shivered, even as his face flushed hot and red.

Is this really happening?

Anna backed up just a bit and called out to the bartender, "Two more schnapps, please."

Two?

Matt looked at Walter and Grossman, who were already turning toward the door.

"Wait, guys," he called out, "you don't have to go…"

Walter laughed at his half-hearted tone and said, "See you, boychik," while Grossman made an obscene gesture behind Anna's back.

Matt stared after them with a mixture of excitement and anxiety. It was not just that Anna was unusually beautiful, though that would have been enough to terrify him. Unlike the college girls, who were just starting to dabble with their feminine power, she possessed a certain worldliness; she had fully stepped into that power long ago. Every insecurity he'd felt around girls came to the fore, and for the first time he grasped the truth of the saying, "Be careful what you wish for."

Fortunately, he didn't have long to dwell on his fears. As soon as the bartender placed the shots on the bar, Anna put one in Matt's hand, then took the other and downed it with a quick, backward toss of her head.

"Your turn," she said, licking her lips as she placed the glass upside down on the bar as if issuing a challenge.

He looked at her, noting how different she was from the reserved young woman from the diner. Who was she, really? More importantly, why, when she could have any man in the bar, had she chosen him?

As he lifted his glass with a nod to her, then to his lips, Matt decided that he didn't care. That for just once, he would stop thinking about everything he should and could be, and enjoy what was.

CHAPTER FIFTEEN

"Better get out here, Walter!" Grossman boomed gleefully when Matt straggled in the next morning, "The eagle has landed… though I don't think he'll be flying again any time soon."

The usually meticulous Matt was indeed a sight, with his shirt half tucked and his hair so disheveled he could almost give Grossman a run for his money. One might have thought he had been in a fight, except for remnants of red lipstick on his neck and the side of his face. Even his expression seemed indicative of someone returning from battle: a combination of exaltation, shell shock, and perhaps a bit of uncertainty as to whether they had won or lost.

Walter came out of the back bedroom in his undershorts, cigar stub clamped between his lips, just as Matt fell into a chair and groaned. His head felt swollen to twice its size and throbbed viciously.

"What do you have to say for yourself, young man?" Grossman said.

Despite his pain, Matt couldn't hold back a small, self-satisfied smirk. Walter's cigar slipped from his mouth and he broke out into laughter.

"Vell, vell, vell," he said, adopting the high-pitched voice of an aged babushka, "It looks like our little boychik has become a man."

Matt chuckled, the effort sending daggers to his temples and his gut into high revolt.

"Ugggh…uh oh…" he said, then dashed toward the bathroom with the laughter of his friends trailing behind him.

"It's not supposed to make you puke," Grossman called out.

"Screw you!" Matt roared as he bent over the bowl, which only ignited another round of guffawing from his friends.

Once his stomach had emptied its contents of schnapps and the handful of cashews from a bowl on the bar, he curled in a ball on the floor and thanked God for the gift of cool porcelain. *How much did I have to drink?* he thought, trying to recall the number of shots and quickly losing count. All he knew was that Anna had literally and figuratively been calling the shots; he was just along for the ride.

Other flashes from the bar started coming back to him. Swaying sloppily with her to "Joy to the World"; her musical laughter at something he said and his vague sensation that it wasn't all that funny; and the bartender offering them shots of tequila mixed with the schnapps. "Wow, that's smooth," Anna had exclaimed. He also recalled at some point telling her that he should go because he had to get up early for work, which she promptly ignored. Had she asked about his work? She might have, but his memory was tainted by her intoxicating scent and the way she looked at him.

Walter appeared at the bathroom door. "You okay, man?"

"I have to get ready for work," he groaned as he positioned himself again over the bowl, only to be racked by painful dry heaves that brought no relief.

"What you need is to eat something," Walter said over the gagging sounds, "and some coffee."

"Yeah," Grossman added as he slid in the doorway next to Walter, "or you're never going to make it through the day." He paused for a beat. "Sooo, what did happen last night?"

The question brought forth a whole new, much more vivid series of images. Shortly before closing time, they had stumbled out, arms thrown around each other, into the street. Anna elegantly raised an index finger in the air, immediately attracting the attention of a nearby cab driver trolling for fares. They had no sooner hopped into the back seat when he felt her sliding that same hand down the front of his pants, then inside them. His head spinning with booze and lust, he just barely registered that she had only given one unfamiliar address to the driver, and, before he knew it, they were pulling up to her building.

"I really need to go home," he slurred, but Anna ignored him as she passed cash to the driver.

In the two times he met her, Anna had presented as two very different women; now, once in her apartment, he was about to experience a third. She backed him up to the couch, then pushed him down on it and straddled him with her long legs. With Anna's breasts pressed against his face and her warm body on top of him, all insecurities – in fact, all thoughts – were suppressed. What followed was a marathon that far surpassed his virginal imaginings of sex, in every possible way and in every room in the apartment. As they moved from the living room to the bedroom, to the kitchen, and finally to the shower, Matt had no doubt that he was in over his head.

* * *

"Look what the cat drug in," Keith said with a knowing look when Matt got to work an hour late. "Did you forget your way to the White House this morning?"

"Something like that," Matt replied, averting his gaze as if Keith would be able to see in his eyes what had happened the night before.

First I was the eagle who landed, he thought, recalling Grossman's earlier comment when he came home, *Now I'm something the cat dragged in.* He didn't know which animal analogy was more accurate, but he was certainly feeling less than human. At least his stomach had settled down, thanks to the eggs and toast Walter made him.

"So?" Walter had asked as they sat down to eat, "What *did* happen last night?"

"Most of it is a blur." Matt glanced around to make sure Grossman was out of earshot. He wasn't in the mood for lewd comments, belches, or any other disgusting thing he might bring into the conversation. "But once we got to her apartment she turned into an animal. There's no other way to describe it."

"Good for you, man," Walter chuckled. "Are you gonna see her again?"

"I –" Matt cut himself off as another memory flashed through his mind. Anna, looking impossibly gorgeous in nothing but a bedsheet, asking the same question – *Will we see each other again?* – and him, answering in that eager puppy way he loathed.

"Shit…"

He reached into his pants pocket and pulled out the piece of paper with the phone number written in Anna's elegant hand.

"Er…I think I'm supposed to see her tonight."

"So what's the problem?" Walter asked. His eggs finished, he went to relight his cigar, but Matt's desperate look deterred him. He placed the stub back in the ashtray.

"I think I suggested a tour of the monuments."

"You recycled the date idea you had for Catherine…smooth move."

"Yeah, real smooth. How am I supposed to get a car by tonight?"

"Could be a problem…" Walter agreed, picking up the cigar again and placing it unlit in his mouth as if it would help him think. "You know…I think Milt stayed in town for the summer – weren't you going to borrow his car…?"

"Seriously, Bud," Keith said, bringing him back to the present, "You okay? You look a bit rough."

"Sure," Matt said with a nod. Though over the past few months he had come to see Keith as a close friend, it wasn't the same as with Walter and Grossman. More importantly, he wasn't comfortable airing such intimate personal business at work.

Ignoring Keith's curious look, he walked over to the desk, picked up the phone and dialed Milt's sister's extension.

Please pick up, he prayed silently, his heart quickening when Ann Green answered on the second ring.

"Hey, Ann, it's Matt Thomas. Do you think I can get your brother's number?"

An hour later, Matt had everything arranged. Milt, tickled to hear his date idea resurrected with another girl, agreed without hesitation to lend him the car. Matt was so relieved he chose to ignore Milt's reminder that he "owed him one," and the subpar mobster imitation with which it was delivered. After extricating himself from that conversation, he called the Key Bridge Marriott and reserved a table for two at seven p.m. As he went to call Anna and confirm their plans, he realized how nervous he was – and how odd this was given their night together. Maybe it was the alcohol, maybe it was the surrealistic quality of their encounter, but he felt almost as if he had witnessed it from outside himself. Bottom line: he couldn't for the life of him figure out why a woman like her would be interested in him, and his confusion only increased when he finally summoned the courage to call and heard the relief in her voice.

CHAPTER SIXTEEN

Relax, Matt told himself for the hundredth time as he slid into Milt's car, which, to his delight was a cool-looking 1969 BMW. Checking his reflection in the rearview mirror, he decided he looked reasonably presentable, maybe even handsome.

"The name's Bond," he said, then rolled his eyes at himself and headed toward Anna's apartment.

The rest of the workday had dragged, giving him a chance to recover fully from his hangover but also time to obsess over the date. Since he was driving, Matt wouldn't have the luxury of over-imbibing like he did the night before. Would the conversation flow without the benefit of copious amounts of alcohol? Lurking behind that concern, however, was a much larger one: how the evening would end.

After leaving the White House the day shifted into overdrive – cabbing it over to Milt's to pick up the car, then racing back to his own place to pick out and iron the perfect outfit. The fact that he had to do so under the playfully mocking eye of Grossman was an annoying but welcome distraction. Unfortunately, the anxiety returned once he was alone, and with a vengeance.

All thoughts drained from his mind when he saw Anna waiting outside her apartment building. Her dark hair hung just past her shoulders in gentle waves, and the dress of deep purple, though less revealing than the black frock she'd worn the night before, was somehow even sexier. Then again, Matt realized, that might be because he knew what she looked like wearing nothing at all – another vision that, to his mortification, sent the heat rushing to his face as she approached the car.

"Funny meeting you here!" he blurted as he got out to open the passenger door for her.

Great opening, Matt, he thought, but Anna giggled then sweetly leaned in to plant a kiss on his cheek.

"How was your day?" she asked as he slid back behind the wheel.

"It was good. Had a bit of the headache, though."

She laughed again to acknowledge his understatement. "Schnapps can have that effect, but the fun is worth it, no?"

"Yeah! I mean, um, yes, it was fun." He paused to take in the full import of what she had said. "So, what did you do today?"

As she chatted on about meeting a friend for lunch and a shopping trip to someplace called Garfinckel's, Matt nodded in all the right places while mentally reciting Milt's directions to the Marriott. Over the last ten months he had gotten to know parts of the city inside and out; however, he often traveled on foot or while lost in thought in the back of a limo. Now, he realized how different it was to navigate the city while driving.

Once he made the turn onto Foxhall Road he was able to relax. It was a beautiful drive, and a surprisingly comfortable silence fell over them as they took it in. Huge old trees lined the road, which wound through one of the most exclusive sections of Northwest Washington. Manicured lawns and stately mansions were concealed behind security fences, though occasionally, an open gate permitted a glimpse of an inner enclave – and elicited a low gasp from Anna. When Foxhall intersected with Canal Road, the calm Potomac River weaved between the District and Rosslyn, Virginia, where the skyline rose above the banks of the Potomac. At night, streetlights illuminated Key Bridge, which connected Washington to Rosslyn.

The Key Bridge Marriott Hotel occupied a prime sightseeing location at the base of the bridge, where it overlooked the Potomac and Georgetown and provided a breathtaking view of the nation's capital.

As he turned into the parking lot, Anna turned to him, eyebrow raised. "Is a hotel customary for a first date in your country? Perhaps I should have packed a suitcase."

"It's supposed to have the best view of the city," he exclaimed, blushing furiously. "Really!"

Anna looked at him and burst out laughing. "Matt, you are so cute, it is so much fun to tease you!"

Matt had requested a table next to the windows overlooking Washington — another suggestion from Milt; and, just as he promised, the view was magnificent. Streetlamps throughout the city cast a pink hue that hovered like a halo in the night. Red and white lights from distant cars moved back and forth like little toys. Downriver, the white marble of the Kennedy Center stood out against the evening in contrast to the dark sky and the river upon which it sat.

"Wow, this is amazing," Anna said as she looked out the window.

"Sure is," Matt agreed, though the only view he was studying was her reflection in the glass. There, he saw innocence mixed with something else that he couldn't quite put his finger on. Sadness, perhaps? It wasn't an emotion he entertained often, and certainly not a quality he looked for in a girl, but for some reason it only made her more mysterious — and more alluring.

The waiter arrived to take their drink orders — a martini for Anna and a gin and tonic for Matt — and rattle off a seemingly endless list of specials before leaving them to peruse the menu. Matt tried to decide what he wanted but found it hard to focus on anything but her. Everything she did, from the way she sipped her drink to the way she ordered — "Petite filet, rare" — was like a seduction. From the way the waiter was staring at her he clearly thought so too, though Anna didn't seem to notice. Then, feeling the young man's eyes turn to him, Matt also ordered a steak well done, which elicited a disapproving, "Very well, sir."

"It ruins the meat," Anna said, answering Matt's unspoken question of, *What is his problem?*

"I always eat it that way…" He shrugged casually to cover the fact that he felt like a yokel. Matt found he had nothing to worry about, at least not when it came to conversation, which flowed easily as they waited for their meal. It was so easy, in fact, that he was halfway through his steak before he realized he was doing all the talking. He told her about his family and what it was like to grow up in the Midwest, how stressed he had been over the last year – something he had not admitted to anyone else – and that the stress had not abated with the end of the semester as he'd hoped.

The whole time, Anna sat there, silent except for the occasional prompt.

"You must have a very important job…"

He shook his head. "No… I mean, yeah, every job at the White House is important." He paused as the waiter came to clear their plates. "But, hey, what about you? What was it like for you growing up…?"

"Different," she said, bringing her napkin to her lips. "Europe is very different from D.C."

Matt nodded in what he hoped was a manner that conveyed both curiosity and respect for her privacy – something he had learned to do during his time at the White House. He had met people from all over the world, not all of whom wanted to go into details about their homelands, not to mention their personal stories.

"Oh, yeah…?" he asked, hearing the sudden note of formality in his voice, as if he was tiptoeing around something. "How so?"

The small, knowing smile tugged at Anna's lips. "Well, Matt…" she began slowly, seriously, "It is…very… cold."

As she broke out into peals of laughter, Matt realized he'd actually been leaning forward, expecting some details about her country of origin, and maybe some insight into her. But it was not to be, thanks to the return of the haughty waiter with a chocolate souffle and after-dinner drinks that ushered in a more relaxed, decadent mood. He watched, mesmerized, as she enjoyed every bite, without any of the "a moment on the lips, forever on the hips" concern most American women expressed about indulging in such things. When the check came, he was almost annoyed, then reminded himself that the night was just beginning.

*   *   *

"What now?" Anna asked as they walked to the car, her directness making Matt smile. The night air was balmy and electric, though he didn't know whether that was because a thunderstorm was coming or simply her presence beside him.

"Would you like to see the monuments?" he said as he held open the passenger door, "They say they are really something to see at night."

"Sure," Anna replied in a way that left him wondering if she preferred to go to a bar or dancing. Maybe Milt's idea was great for an American girl, but to someone as worldly as Anna, a dud.

"On to the monuments," he muttered, undeterred.

As he put his latest insecurity behind him, he shifted his focus to the beauty of the city before them. Its imposing federal buildings were simple in their massive presence, and the same could be said of its many monuments. They were particularly remarkable at night, when the throngs of tourists had gone and one could almost imagine being transported back to the days when they were first unveiled.

He first drove to the Lincoln Memorial, the giant marble mausoleum presided over by an enormous seated statue of the sixteenth president, that served as a tribute to him and a well-known symbol of freedom. Matt recalled watching on the black and white as Dr. Martin Luther King stood on those massive marble steps and proclaimed, "I have a dream." Though he was just a kid, he recognized it as a pivotal moment in King's journey to move a divided nation toward racial equality.

He parked the car and stared for a beat at the building's white marble highlighted against the dark sky by giant lights, then got out and went around to open the door for Anna. As they climbed its massive marble stairs, turning at the top toward the city, he realized he had made the right choice in taking her there. She was staring with quiet awe at the moon's light reflected in the water of the Reflecting Pool that stretched out like a giant carpet along the National Mall. Mesmerized, he followed her gaze to the Washington Monument at the far end, finally settling to the glittering U.S. Capitol beyond. Inside his marble temple, the statue of Lincoln sat in cool, contemplative silence. She placed her hand gently on his arm, then they slowly walked around the statue, reading the great man's words memorialized on the colossal marble walls.

"This is beautiful," Anna whispered, sounding as surprised as she was moved.

"Lincoln was so amazing! He saved our country!"

Anna looked at him blankly for a moment as if sifting through a collection of facts. "Oh, your civil war," she said finally, "I have read about this."

"Yes! The country was split in two and he got people from all over to come and fight. I mean, this was before television. How did he motivate farmers from all over to do that?"

"Leaders find a way," she said somberly, and from her tone he knew she was speaking not about his country, but her own. This both fascinated and unnerved him. For him, the Memorial fostered a deep sense of what it was to be an American. It connected him with the greatness of America and what men like Lincoln and King wanted America to be. Noting Anna's unreadable expression, he wondered what emotions it was invoking in her. Was she embracing her new country, or was she viewing it through the lens of some other history he did not understand?

She looked at him and smiled. "Thank you, Matt, for bringing me here."

In an instant, his questions were replaced by a deep gratitude for Milt. Whatever favor he requested in the future, Matt knew he would gladly oblige.

"C'mon," he said, taking her hand, "We're not done yet."

They got back in the car and headed down Independence Avenue to the Jefferson Memorial, situated on the bank of a body of water known as the Tidal Basin.

Once inside, Anna remarked, "Wow, this is definitely different from the last one."

The Jefferson was also empty and serene, except for a few birds nesting high above in its dome. Its huge marble columns appeared to cradle a bronze statue of Jefferson, and its curved marble walls were inscribed with his words.

They quietly followed the curve of the building and, as they began to read, were approached by the Memorial's lone attendant, a park ranger wearing a wide-brimmed hat Smokey the Bear would have been proud of.

"Hello," he said, happy to have someone to talk to at the lonely hour. "Is this your first time here?"

"Yes," Anna replied, almost reverently.

"How come you allow birds to fly in and hang out in the ceiling?" Matt wondered aloud, sounding like a little boy.

"The Memorial belongs to them as much as it does to us."

Matt smiled. "Yeah, but we don't poop on Thomas Jefferson!"

"Can I give you a little history?" the man asked, clearly happy to have an audience. He didn't wait for a response. "The memorial is a testament to the profound influence Jefferson had on America. The inscriptions on the walls around you are evidence of his brilliance, as well as his belief in the freedom and democracy that serve as the very foundation of the life of every American. Each spring the cherry trees that surround it on the Tidal Basin are Washington's biggest attraction. Those cherry trees were a gift to the United States from Japan. People come from all over the world to see their delicate blossoms, because they are such an unforgettable sight."

The ranger was on a roll and continued his history lesson, indifferent to his guests' desire, or lack thereof, to be tutored at that late hour. "There is a legend about the Jefferson Memorial: One night, President Kennedy left the White House for a quiet walk. He came all the way across the Ellipse behind you, and around the Tidal Basin. It was a night like tonight, dark and quiet. The President appeared to be in search of inspiration. He carefully read Jefferson's words, just as you were doing. He told the park ranger on duty it would be even more beautiful if it was lighted at night. Not long afterward, the Memorial received nighttime lights, making it possible to be enjoyed all the time."

"That is so cool," Matt said honestly but hurriedly, for what usually would have fascinated him was now preventing him from being alone with Anna. "Thanks so much." Then he and Anna politely bid the ranger goodbye and turned to leave.

"Boy, I thought he would go on forever…" he said almost apologetically once they were out of earshot.

"It was interesting," Anna replied, "though working at the White House you must know all of that already."

"Sure, some of it…"

She glanced at him. "You must know so much about the way your government works."

Matt laughed. "Usually, I'm too busy making copies to see much."

"Making copies?"

"Yeah, you know…" Matt said, torn between being completely honest and fluffing his job a bit. "…with the copy machine. I copy stuff for meetings. Sometimes," he added, "I deliver the papers."

"Not everyone has access to information," she said, matter-of-factly.

She was right, of course. He had gotten so used to the grind, and his lowly status, at the White House that he had forgotten just how privileged he was to be there at all.

He headed down Independence Avenue and parked at the U.S. Capitol, silently thanking Milt again for suggesting the tour. Always impressive, the building was even more so at night, with floodlights bathing the white dome, making it luminescent against the dark sky. It reminded him of a huge wedding cake, with the stars and stripes of the flag in its dome blowing in a mild breeze.

"I think this is my favorite of all," Matt said.

"Really?" Anna asked, genuinely curious. "How come?"

"Because it's not dedicated to one person like the memorials are. It's just a big, beautiful building. But look at the flag flying high and proud, even at night. It's like a beacon of openness and freedom for anybody to come here and see. I mean, all you gotta do is watch the news to see how screwed up the whole world is. Maybe this country has problems too, but even with them, we're so lucky to live here." He stopped himself there. "I mean, uh, not that other places aren't nice…" He trailed off feebly, hoping like hell he hadn't offended her.

"Lucky," she repeated, her tone undiscernible. Then she turned and smiled at him, "Thank you, Matt. This has been a lovely evening."

Thank you, Milt.

They stood there in comfortable silence for a few more minutes, watching the large, billowy white clouds highlighted by the building's lights as they moved across the sky. Out of nowhere, a cool breeze had sprung up, bringing sweet relief from the heat of the day. Then he saw Anna shivering and reluctantly turned to go. As they walked back to the car, he fought the urge to put his arm around her. The "lovely evening" comment, while appreciated, seemed to indicate a conclusion. It filled Matt with both disappointment and a humiliating sense of relief.

They made small talk on the way back to her apartment, mostly about movies they had seen. Matt was delighted that she seemed to love films as much as he did, and Anna joked that she was learning about American culture from John Wayne.

"You can't serve papers on a rat, baby sister," she deadpanned slowly, "You gotta kill him or let him be."

Her voice, brought low but still clearly feminine and tinged with a European accent, made Matt laugh so hard he had to control himself in order to drive. It wasn't easy, especially when she delivered several more lines from *True Grit,* and by the time he pulled up to her apartment he was begging for mercy.

"Can you get me off the hook, Tom?" he rasped.

"What?" Anna looked at him blankly. "Who is this Tom?"

"Tom Hagen! You know, when Tessio is about to be killed? It's one of the best scenes in *The Godfather*."

Anna shrugged. "Oh, I have not seen that one."

Matt drew back and clutched his chest. *"What?* That's an *infamnia*!"

"I do not know this word – infamnia…" Anna gave him a pointed look, then glanced at her building. "Why don't you come in and teach me?"

CHAPTER SEVENTEEN

The next few weeks unfolded at breakneck speed, with each hour taking America closer to the boiling point and threatening to blow the lid right off the White House. The government nearly ground to a halt as two years of ugly revelations, a congressional investigation and a special prosecutor's criminal investigation were about to culminate in the first resignation of a president. The entire world watched as the Judiciary Committee of the House of Representatives voted three articles of impeachment against President Nixon for his part in covering up the Watergate affair.

Each day, Matt could feel the heaviness hanging over the White House like a cloud; each evening he found himself fending off the verbal assaults of Walter and Grossman as they expressed their disgust that he continued to work for the discredited president. Matt saw things in a different way. He read the paper and watched the news, and, like most Americans, he felt let down by revelations of wrongdoing. But he also felt a part of the operations of the White House, and the nearly five thousand other loyal Americans who served there every day, working to end a horrifying war in Southeast Asia, build detente with America's Cold War enemy, the Soviet Union, and build a relationship with China to avoid a new cold war with the world's most populous nation. He also didn't believe that President Richard Nixon was really the sinister and dark character vilified in the media, burned in effigy on the street and on the precipice of impeachment on Capitol Hill.

For Matt personally, the summer was also proving to be one of epic proportions. It was as if the night he and Anna met in the bar represented a line of demarcation. Before crossing that line, he'd always assumed a relationship would be slow burn following a trajectory similar to that of his parents: date through college and, eventually, wind up at the altar. Instead, he felt consumed by a force and speed beyond his ability to control – or articulate, as he found when he returned home a full thirty-six hours after he left for the tour of the monuments to face the judgment of his roommates. In his absence they had morphed from hippies to mother hens, scolding him for not calling then wanting him to account for every minute of his stay, which he staunchly refused to do. In truth, he barely recalled what happened after Anna pulled out that bottle of Smirnoff, and could only offer a constipated smile that Grossman and Walter mistook for a smug smirk.

All he knew was that whatever this thing with Anna was, it was exhilarating and draining him in ways nothing else had. Since then, they'd gone out several times, some nights going to bars or a movie, always ending up in her bed, drunkenly pawing at each other. Yet, instead of getting to know her better, he felt like she had only become more of a mystery – always full of questions about him but rarely sharing about herself.

One morning, he was dialing Anna's number when Glen burst into the office, snapping his fingers. "What's Jensen's number?"

"Two-seven-two-three," Matt answered without thinking, then watched absent-mindedly as Glen returned to his desk, and punched in the numbers.

Almost immediately, the Secretariat's phone chime sounded. Sighing, Matt disconnected from Anna's phone to answer the incoming call.

"Secretariat," he said, then drew back in surprise when he heard his own voice coming from Glen's office.

"Hello?" Glen said.

"Hello?" Matt replied, smiling as the realization dawned that he had given Glen the number to his own office.

"You stupid shit," Glen said, looking out his door at Matt.

"*I'm* the stupid shit?" he said, leaning over the desk so he could peer into Glen's office, "I believe you called me!"

Glen slammed the phone down in frustration, while Matt leaned back in the chair and struggled to stifle a laugh. A second later the phone rang out again.

"I'll get it," Glen snapped. "It's probably just me again."

There was another beat, then he heard Glen say, "I was just about to call you. Okay, he'll be there in a minute." He ended the call, then shouted with real urgency in his voice, "Son, c'mon in here. ASAP!"

Matt slid out of his chair and raced into Glen's office.

"Son, that was Jensen. He needs to see you in his office. And another thing: I just passed the front office. The President's lawyers asked for some extra hands for a special project. One of them is going to come up in an hour or so, so standby."

Matt groaned inwardly at the thought of dealing with Jensen for any reason.

"Okay," he said, picking up the can of Coke he had been sipping, "I'll run over to Jensen's office, then come straight back for the lawyers."

When he opened the tall mahogany door to the security office a secretary looked up from her desk.

"They're waiting for you," she said, shifting her eyes toward an open conference room.

They? he thought. *Who could "they" be?*

Matt entered the conference room to find Jensen and two other men seated silently at the table. Without a word, they rose to their feet in unison, the way people would greet a guest of honor, but their steely expressions told a different story. Matt froze for a beat, then followed Jensen's pointed finger to the seat at the head of the table. Jensen walked behind him and closed the door, then rounded the table and came to stand behind the others.

"Mr. Thomas, these are Special Agents Nelson and Jackson from FBI Counterintelligence."

As Jensen spoke, each man laid his FBI credentials on the table – not that they needed them. With their identical black tailored suits, crisp white shirts, and highly shined shoes reminiscent of Matt's days at military school, they looked like they had just stepped off a Bureau recruitment poster.

"Thank you for joining us," Agent Nelson said, establishing himself as the lead man. He was maybe thirty years old, and trim, with closely shorn hair that also spoke of a military background.

This is not good, Matt thought as he set the soda down on the table and took a seat. There was a storm brewing, and Matt knew it had nothing to do with the political climate. In fact, he got the distinct feeling that some major trespass had been committed and he was named as the perpetrator. And, though he had no idea what this was about, it worked on him, manifesting as a vague sense of guilt and clammy palms.

The three men took their seats, then Jensen mercifully broke the silence.

"Agent Nelson, why don't you begin?"

Nelson nodded. "Without going into a lot of details," he said crisply, as if Matt wasn't deserving of further information, "a few days ago our people picked your name up in a transmission from a source known to be hostile."

"My name?" he repeated dumbly, "A source known to be hostile…?"

Matt had no idea what he was talking about, yet his stomach, which was rolling and pitching like a tiny boat on rough seas, seemed to know something his brain couldn't fathom. Again, he felt this might not be merely something that had happened, that the agent was about to accuse him of something.

"Yes, Mr. Thomas, and it is our belief that this hostile intelligence organization has targeted you. We don't know how you came to their attention. It could be as simple as they saw you coming and going from this building. You wouldn't even know you were being observed."

Nelson paused; his face expressionless but his sharp eyes scanning Matt as if to detect deceit. Fighting to steady his hand, Matt raised the soda can to his lips as, in a move that reminded him of the *Huntley-Brinkley Report* routine, the other FBI man – was it Jackson? Matt couldn't remember – took over the meeting.

"We believe you will be approached by one of their agents."

Matt reached for the soda again, more for something to do with his hands than out of thirst. At that precise moment, Jackson reached toward a projector at the center of the conference table, which Matt had noticed but vaguely assumed it was left there from a previous meeting. As soon as he flicked it on, the breath was literally snatched from Matt's body, igniting a coughing fit that sent droplets of cola all over the table. There, on the screen, was an image of Anna. She was standing on a corner, with one hand brushing a stray lock from her face, a shapely leg pointed out as if she was about to step onto the street. Her gaze was fixed, almost hard, but that may have been because she was eyeing the traffic for an opportunity to safely cross.

In one awful moment, everything clicked into place. The accent she clearly tried to control, her reluctance to discuss herself, and, most importantly, the fact that she had never revealed her country of origin. And then there was him, the dumb shit who never even asked.

Still gasping for breath, his stomach clenching and releasing as if to expel some demon, Matt jumped up and ran out of the room, heading for the nearest restroom. He barely made it into the stall before throwing up the egg sandwich he'd had for breakfast. A second later he heard the door opening, followed by the sound of Jensen's voice.

"Matt, you alright?"

"No!" Matt snapped. "If I don't die right now, I'm going to drown myself in this toilet."

"What is wrong with you?" Jensen pushed, sounding uncharacteristically baffled, and maybe even sympathetic.

"Your friends are a little late…"

"Matt, are you saying she already contacted you?"

Matt groaned. "Oh, she made contact alright!"

"Where?" Jensen asked, his confusion turning to excitement.

"Let's see, in her car, in her elevator, on her kitchen table, in her shower, and – oh yeah – I think, she made contact on her bed."

To his horror, Jensen began to laugh. "Are you saying you had sex with her?"

"She's not human, you know…" Matt trailed off, wondering how detailed he was required to get given the circumstances. He stood slowly, then flushed the toilet and exited the stall to find Jensen standing there with a raised eyebrow.

"Did she ask you any penetrating questions?"

"Nope, she left all the penetrating to me!"

Another man walked into the restroom, his eyes flicking curiously from Jensen to Matt, who was leaning weakly against the stall door.

"Would you pardon us?" Jensen said with a cursory glance in his direction. "We're having a meeting."

The man looked from Jensen to Matt. "You're having a meeting in the john?"

"Yes," Jensen snapped, "and a classified one. Leave, now." When he had gone, Jensen turned back to Matt, his expression softening. "You don't have anything to be concerned about."

"I fucked a spy," Matt shot back angrily. "Isn't that treason?"

Jensen bit his lip in an unsuccessful attempt to control his laughter. "Well, technically…" he began, then held up his hand when he saw the look on Matt's face. "Okay, seriously, you're in the clear. We have independent confirmation that she was planning to approach you, so it sounds like she is totally setting you up."

Matt took a deep, ragged breath as the full import of Jensen's words hit him. "Setting me up…"

"For sure, and you had no way of knowing." Jensen paused. "But Matt, didn't you think twice about getting involved once you found out she's Russian?"

"I thought she was German!" Matt moaned; then, responding to Jensen's raised eyebrow, added, "She sounds more like Kissinger than Dobrynin!"

"Okay, Matt, okay." Jensen put an arm around Matt's shoulder, a surprising attempt to offer comfort. "Actually, this is excellent."

"If this is so excellent," Matt said, fighting the urge to squirm away, "why do I feel like I was the shield in a shit fight?"

Jensen nodded understandingly, but Matt could tell he had already moved on, probably to figure out how to use the situation to his advantage.

"We'll run an operation. Keep her busy. That way we can control this thing and keep her away from some other unsuspecting jamoke."

"Oh, thanks," Matt shot back, wiping his running nose.

"It was just a figure of speech," Jensen said, sounding slightly embarrassed as he realized his faux pas. He then guided Matt to the sink and grabbed a handful of paper towels. "Go ahead, splash some cold water on your face."

Matt did as he was told, feeling somewhat like a child being comforted after a run-in with the school bully. Even as the cold water refreshed him, he knew he was still in shock and, like in those seconds of holding one's breath after banging an elbow, the real pain would come later.

"This is really an exciting opportunity," Jensen repeated as he held the paper towels out to him. "We'll run a counterintelligence operation, suck the bastards in. You will be our 'asset'…" He hooked his fingers into air quotes, "…a hero."

"I can't be an asset!" Matt exclaimed, then attempted to clarify when he saw the surprise on Jensen's face. "This woman…she pretended… we…she has ruined my life!"

"Wait, you know what an asset is?" Jensen asked.

Matt nodded, adding sheepishly, "I read a lot of le Carré novels."

Jensen raised an eyebrow at him, then sighed as if remembering how very young Matt was. "Take a minute, try to get yourself together, then come back to my office and we'll sort through this, okay?" He then slipped out the door.

Matt returned to the conference room to find the photo of Anna still on the screen and the three men again seated around the table, leaning in toward each other as they spoke quietly. This time, however, when they stood up at attention, their expressions were more relaxed, friendlier, and something else that Matt couldn't quite place.

Walking around the table with his hand outstretched, Agent Nelson said, "I want to congratulate you."

Matt shook the man's hand, but asked, "Why does everyone want to congratulate me for being victimized by this woman?"

The three men exchanged confused glances. "Why don't you tell us about your experience with her, and we'll explain how we're approaching this."

Matt nodded, then they all settled around the table. For the next twenty minutes he told them all he could remember of his encounter with Anna, from their meeting at the diner and the night he bumped into her at the bar to their tour of the monuments and the days they had met up since. This was followed by two painstaking hours of questioning from the men, mostly Nelson, about every detail. How often did they speak? Had he spoken to her while at the White House? And what had they spoken about? Had Anna given him any details about her life in Russia? Her family? Had he met any of her friends or colleagues? Had she taken any phone calls while he was at the apartment? And the big one: had she asked Matt anything related to his job? The questions went on and on, and for the most part yielded no additional information. Then, to Matt's horror and despite his best attempts to avoid the topic, they delved into their sexual escapades, wanting to know how, where, and the number of times.

Finally, he put his foot down. "No! It's none of your business! What could you possibly gain from this?"

Agent Nelson cleared his throat. "We understand this is uncomfortable for you, Matt, but believe it or not information about… um… *preferences* is very important for us in creating a profile of new foreign operatives, or identifying ones we are already familiar with."

Matt snorted indignantly, but he realized he didn't know enough about such things to argue the point. He also understood that they weren't giving him a choice. With the heat rushing to his face and his eyes moving about the room – anywhere but the faces of his interrogators – he described each time he had slept with Anna. Then, without thinking about it, his gaze landed on the photo of her on the screen.

"Holy shit!" he shouted, interrupting his own recounting of the shower they'd taken together the previous morning. He turned and stared at the men across the table, who had startled at his outburst. "I knew I'd seen her somewhere before!"

"What do you mean?" Nelson asked slowly.

He pointed to the photo. "I saw her on the street… she was crossing the street… my God, the limo almost hit her!"

"What are you talking about, Matt?" Jensen said. "What limo? When was this?"

"When I first started at the White House. I was in a limo on the way to deliver a package and she stepped off the curb. The driver had to stop short. She was wearing a dress just like that…" He paused miserably. "She was beautiful."

Nelson leaned forward in his seat. "Matt, did she see you?"

"Yes! We looked right at each other! She saw me, I'm sure of it!" Matt brought his fist down on the table hard enough to hurt. "I knew it! I couldn't remember where, but I knew it when I met her at the diner."

"…when she started talking to you at the diner…" Jackson added.

"Yes. She sat next to me."

Nelson nodded thoughtfully. "Okay, this lends credence to the idea that she targeted you specifically. Maybe that's the first time she saw you as well."

"Yeah," Matt muttered, "she saw me in the limo and thought I was important."

"You *are* important, Matt," Jensen snapped, "You regularly leave the White House with top secret documents in your possession."

Nelson shot Jensen a warning look. "Also," he added with a gentler tone, "they would have considered your, um, lack of status to their advantage because they could groom you for a long-term relationship, gain your loyalty –"

"That would never happen!" Matt exclaimed, even as he shivered at the thought.

"I'm sure it wouldn't," Jackson replied, "but it's not always as simple as being a patriot. These people are very manipulative. They work their way into people's minds, they find things to blackmail them with… and oftentimes they use good-looking women to do it."

Matt opened his mouth to protest again, then closed it as memories of his time with Anna flashed through his mind. Anna, looking at him with that small, teasing smile tugging at her lips, or with an unexplainable sadness in her eyes. Anna, completely unselfconscious as she dried herself off after a shower, padded naked across the living room, or pulled him back to bed. His breath caught in his throat then, for though he hadn't been aware of the stakes there had definitely been moments when he'd thought he would do anything for her.

The sound of Nelson clearing his throat again brought him back to the present. The agent's eyes were slightly narrowed, making Matt wonder if he could read his thoughts.

"Bottom line, this is really good news for us," Nelson said, echoing what Jensen had said to him in the bathroom. "We would like you to continue meeting with Anna again, find out what she wants from you. That will give us an idea of what her country is focused on in terms of spying on us."

"I'm really not sure I can do this…" Matt interrupted. "I don't want to do this! Why can't I just end it and go on with my life?"

"You can, Matt," Nelson said smoothly, surprising him. "And then Anna and her 'comrades' will target some other unsuspecting person, someone else just like you who thinks this woman cares about them. And maybe we won't catch it in time. God help us all then."

Matt's stomach clenched, as much from the thought of Anna "bumping into" another guy at a bar or diner – and taking him home with her – as any thoughts of espionage. Could it really have all been an act?

"This is the deal," Jensen said sharply, his patience with tiptoeing around Matt's feelings clearly at an end. "We are *at war*. It is a cold war, but a war, nonetheless. Our adversaries fight in many ways, one of which is to reach out to unsuspecting and innocent Americans who can serve their purpose, and use them for that purpose. Make no mistake, her motives are one hundred percent adversarial to our country. You have the opportunity to help our country by cooperating with us. Find out what they are after, and we will figure out how to go from there. And with regard to your concerns as to whether you can or want to do this, let me remind you that the cemetery right across the river is full of men and women who answered the call of their nation. This is your call, and you *will* answer it."

Hearing this, Matt was overcome with shame. He recalled his first day, when Keith warned him about Jensen blowing red, white, and blue smoke up his rear end. But this was not just smoke, and if they were right, if Anna was indeed a spy, he had no choice but to do what they asked.

Agent Nelson stood up, signifying an end to the meeting. "I think we've heaped enough on Matt's shoulders for today." He looked down at Matt. "Go back to work, clear your mind. We'll be in touch in a day or two." He pulled a card from his jacket pocket and placed it on the table. "Here are my office and page numbers. If she calls you to arrange a meeting before then, call me right away."

He then shot a look to Jackson, who ushered a reluctant Jensen out of the room.

"Don't pay attention to that asshole," he said, referring to Jensen when he was gone. "Anyone would be scared in your situation – I know I would be. But don't worry. This is what Jackson and I do for a living, and we're damn good at it – the whole team is. We'll train you, work with you, and I think we can have a little fun by screwing the fuckers who are out to screw our country." He gave Matt a wink that was supposed to instill confidence but fell short of the mark. "Just one more thing – and I cannot stress this enough. You cannot tell anyone, and I mean anyone, about this."

Matt walked back to the Secretariat, a tennis match of dizzying thoughts rallying in his mind. Could Anna really be a spy? It seemed much more likely that it was a case of mistaken identity, or maybe she was an innocent immigrant being manipulated by her fellow countrymen? On the other hand, he couldn't deny the way this had unfolded – seeing each other in the street and their "accidental" meetings at the diner and the bar. Either way, he had no choice but to find out – not just out of duty but for his own peace of mind. He took a deep breath, trying to allow his natural optimism to resurface. Certainly, it would be exciting working with the FBI, and for now, that would have to be enough.

CHAPTER EIGHTEEN

Matt reached the door of the Secretariat at the same moment as a young man carrying a box that seemed far too large for his slight frame. A vague feeling of dread filled Matt as he held open the door, his eyes flicking between the box and the guy's grateful expression.

"Are you Mr. Sanford?" the young man asked Glen, who was standing in the middle of the room.

"I am, and this is my young man who is going to help you," Glen said, pointing to Matt. The man put the box down on Keith's desk. He never offered his name, just that he was from the White House lawyer's office. Turning to Matt, he explained that the Watergate Special Prosecutor investigating President Nixon was demanding to see a collection of White House documents so voluminous the lawyers were unable to perform a thorough review of each one. This brought him to the reason for his presence there – and Matt's foreboding: they needed copies of each document so at least they had records of what was going out of the White House. They were aware of the Secretariat's "gopher" and had reached out for permission to conscript him.

Given the sensitivity of the material, it was agreed that no one but Matt would have access to the information. The young man waited just long enough for Glen to craft a sign reading "Special Project – Do Not Enter" and post it on the door of the copy room, then departed without saying what to do when Matt finished – a clue, for sure, that he did not expect Matt to finish any time soon. As Matt opened the box, he mentally repeated the instructions he did have: no one was to enter the room but him; he should copy the documents in the order he found them in the box and replace them in the same order; and the copies should be put in a second box in the same order.

When Matt picked up the first document, he immediately saw why all the secrecy was necessary. The legal-sized paper, which bore the name of a bank in Key Biscayne, Florida in large fancy script across the top, was the mortgage on the home belonging to Richard and Patricia Nixon. Matt leafed down through the box to discover it was full of personal documents belonging to the President. There were calendars, notes in Nixon's own writing, and White House message logs documenting discussions between the President and several of his top, and by now infamous, aides.

"Wow!" he exclaimed aloud, though he was the only one in the room, "This is real shit!"

Most of the documents pertained directly to the investigations into the President's finances and what he might have known about the Watergate break-in. To say it was interesting was an understatement, and Matt was sorely tempted to lean back and read through them. Maybe he would find the nugget of truth the whole world seemed to be looking for, the "smoking gun" linking the President to the break-in. He might have, too, if not for fear that the lawyer would return to check on his progress. With a sigh, he took a stack out of the box and got to work, placing the copies in one box and the originals in another, careful to preserve the order of both.

It was an excruciatingly tedious task, one Matt waded through with one eye on the clock, trying to get a feel for how long it would take. It was hard to gauge. Some documents were regular paper; for those he had only to take out the staples, put a page in at a time, and hit the copy button. But others were bound calendars, which required more care so as not to destroy the binding. Still others were legal size and required changing the paper in the machine. The good news was it took his mind off Anna, the FBI, and the tightrope he would be walking between them. By 11:15 a.m., he'd been at it a couple of hours and had gone through roughly three-quarters of the box. At this rate, he would be finished by noon, and all he wanted was to get a sandwich, go sit in Lafayette Park across from the White House and try to make sense of the situation he found himself in. That all went down the drain when the young lawyer reappeared, another box under his arm.

"How's it coming?"

"I thought it was going okay," Matt said, stifling a groan, "until I saw that box."

"I'm afraid there's plenty more where these came from." There was a note of apology and resignation in the man's voice that told Matt he wasn't the only one suffering.

"What's that mean for me?" he asked, unsure that he wanted the answer.

"There are maybe ten or eleven more."

Matt slumped over the copy machine in a pretend faint. "And it all has to be copied?"

"I'm afraid so," the man repeated.

"Sounds to me like this could take days…"

"I am afraid we don't have days. We're working against a legal order that gives us until tomorrow morning."

"Tomorrow morning! I'll be here all night!"

The man nodded matter-of-factly. "I haven't gotten a good night's sleep in weeks."

Had this been a month ago – heck, had it been a day ago – Matt would have sucked it up without complaint. Now, all he felt was the mounting pressure and his complete lack of control over his circumstances. As soon as the man left, he shot out the door like a bullet, marching past Keith into Glen's office. Keith, noticing Matt's intensity followed him.

"Glen," he said loudly, "They tell me there are eleven boxes and they have to be done by tomorrow morning!"

Glen looked up at him over half-rimmed reading glasses. "I figured it might be a big job." He sighed, "But I don't know what else we can do. The front office said we'd help out. I think we're stuck."

"What you mean is that *I'm* stuck," Matt shot back.

A look of genuine surprise flashed across Glen's face. "Son –"

Matt cut him off. "Every time you start out with 'Son,' I get screwed." He heard Keith's chortle behind him and silenced him with a glare. "I guess I better get back to the dungeon!"

He turned to head back to the copy room, leaving Glen and Keith open-mouthed at his outburst. Halfway through the Secretariat, however, Matt realized he wasn't really upset. Sure, copying the mounds of documents was a total pain in his ass, not to mention his back, but it also presented him with access to the biggest thing happening in the country – information beyond what was printed in the papers or put out by the White House. He was, literally, holding the documents that might tell the true story. Still, he thought, a devilish smile splitting his face, he was glad he had made the point with Glen. After a lifetime of doing what he was told, speaking his piece brought a sweet feeling of liberation.

As soon as he stepped back into the cramped room, however, his exuberance was replaced by an almost overwhelming weight. For just a moment, he just stood there before the copy machine and tried to process everything – the revelation that Anna was likely a spy and the expectation that he would help the FBI stop her, and now his lowly but vitally important role in the President's defense (or, as the case may be, his downfall). He halfheartedly raised an arm to pinch himself, then dropped it to his side. Everything he had seen and heard that morning was real enough, and there was no use trying to make sense of it.

Over the past few months, he'd become adept at copying and perusing the documents as he went. And, like most, the majority of these were pretty boring. Knowing that checking the time would only make it pass more slowly, he kept his eyes from the clock. To deal with the monotony, he adopted a Horatio Alger state of mind, imagining he was a great detective on the verge of finding the smoking gun. It worked. Matt became so engrossed in his task that the knock at the door caused him to jump as if jolted with electricity. He turned to see Keith's amused smile and knew he probably looked like a mad professor. A glance at the clock brought another shock: six hours had flown by.

"You need a break, Bud. C'mon out here."

Matt paused for a moment as if debating whether to stop the flow, then he smiled wearily and followed Keith out. The smell of the Chinese food hit his nostrils before he reached the main room of the Secretariat and he realized how famished he was. There on the desk was a small feast, probably from Glen's favorite place on the corner of 18th and G Street, of wonton soup, kung pao chicken, and three fat eggrolls. Without a word Matt picked up one of them and took a large bite, thinking it was the best thing he had tasted since those dinners he inhaled after an afternoon of drills at military school.

Glen and Keith looked on sympathetically, even laughing when, halfway through his reward, he finally offered them some. Glen shook his head in the negative, while Keith stepped forward and snatched one of the remaining eggrolls off the plate. Between bites, he informed Matt that he'd become somewhat of a celebrity. Apparently, several staffers had stopped by wanting to know why they couldn't use the copying machine, and when they found out Matt was holed up in there on a secret mission for the President's lawyers, the news spread like a firestorm.

The break was cut short by the return of the young lawyer, another heavy box of documents in his arms. If possible, he looked even more exhausted than before, though he did come to life when he saw the boxes of completed copies – the results of nine hours Matt would never get back.

"No rest for the wicked," Matt sighed as he returned to the copy room with a second can of Coke provided by Keith. At least his stomach no longer felt like it was touching his backbone. A few minutes later, Glen called through the door that he and Keith were leaving for the night.

Matt grunted in response to his "Hang in there, son," then heard the footsteps fading down the hall. He glanced at the clock that had now become his enemy – dragging interminably and yet racing toward the deadline. It was after eight and he was in for a long night ahead.

Over the past several months Matt had learned that some of the most mind-numbing tasks required the most fortitude. If one knew how to focus, however, they could also be incredibly liberating. Preparing himself for the mental marathon, he renewed his resolve to avoid looking at the clock and instead tear into each box as if it was an exciting new challenge. He was like a machine, pausing in his work only when the heat in the room, produced by the overheated copier, got to be too much – discarding his tie, then unbuttoning his shirt, and, finally, sliding off his shoes, which he tossed carelessly across the floor.

About ten o'clock, he nearly jumped out of his skin when a uniformed Secret Service agent popped into the room. Amused that he had startled Matt, the guard flashed a smile then rounded the machine to see what he was working on. Normally deferential to the agents, Matt instead reacted from his stress and exhaustion – not to mention the need to protect the files from prying eyes – and sent him packing.

By two a.m. he couldn't take it anymore. His back was spasming and his eyes were so dry his vision was clouded. If he didn't take a break, he wouldn't make it. A jog around the floor was helpful, but eerie. The long corridors were dark and had no sign of life, not even the office cleaners who did their work after hours. It reminded Matt of when he was a little boy, scared in the house at night, only worse. Back then, his fear was tempered by the knowledge that his parents were asleep a few doors down; tonight, he was in one of the most protected and safest places in the world, yet it felt like a creepy old mansion.

After a few laps he slowed down to a fast walk. It was then, as he caught his breath and wiped the sweat from his brow, that he saw through to the truth of that tedious night. Of all the White House staffers, his was the work that couldn't wait until the morning. It was too important. *He was important.* Then came the other thoughts, the ones he had been tamping down all night. The thoughts of Anna, the possibility that she was indeed a spy, that she had been using him – and worst of all, in light of the former, that he still cared about the latter. The realization shook him to his core, and yet he knew in that moment that his work with the FBI would be, at least in part, motivated by his need to uncover the truth of her feelings for him.

Still taking deep breaths, he passed the closed door leading to the Vice President's suite and headed down a staircase past the President's first-floor office. Like the Vice President's, it was closed, with no sign of the Secret Service agents who normally stood outside. He cut down the hallway in front of the President's office and headed toward the 17th Street corridor and down another staircase.

"Little early in the morning to be wandering the halls, isn't it?"

"Oh!" Matt exclaimed with a start as he saw a man dressed in a crisp suit and tie, making him uncomfortably aware of his disheveled appearance. "I didn't think anyone else was here."

"Just me and the mice," replied the man amiably. That's when Matt noticed the small table and telephone in front of a door on the underside of the staircase.

"You're protecting the stairs?"

"In a way," replied the man with a sigh. He pointed to the door, which had numerous little tape seals across the opening as though it had been sealed closed, opened, and re-sealed several times. "The tapes."

Matt realized the man was referring to The Oval Office tape recordings, made by President Nixon, that were center stage in the Watergate investigations. Because of their importance, they were under twenty-four-hour guard and, like Matt, the man was spending the wee hours doing mind-numbing but critical work.

"Watergate," Matt said, nodding wearily, "That's what I'm doing here. Copying Watergate documents…all night."

"Sounds painful," the man said, "but good for overtime pay!"

They laughed, and after a few more minutes of commiserating, Matt bid him goodnight and said he was going to get some fresh air. He exited the building through the ramp entrance by the West Wing and walked down West Executive Avenue toward Pennsylvania Avenue.

To his right was the front lawn of the White House, bathed in the light of the moon. It was a tranquil scene that completely belied its role in the current turmoil.

As he approached the Pennsylvania Avenue gate, a guard in his early forties stepped out of his booth. They talked for a few minutes about having to work so late, the guard chuckling when Matt admitted that he had never been up at such an hour and also been sober. Matt then left the grounds and headed across Pennsylvania Avenue to Lafayette Park. The night air was unusually cool and crisp for this time of year; there was light dew on the pavement that reflected the moonlight. Traffic lights blinked on and off and shined on the glistening street like tiny lights on a Christmas tree. The city was still and serene, and combined with his exhaustion, created an almost dreamy feeling within him.

Matt broke into a light jog for a few minutes, then sat on a bench for a few more to take in the beauty of the night. As he looked across the street at the quiet and stately White House, his mind drifted back to what lay ahead for him. He had the strange sense that this never-ending day marked a turning point in his life. Not twenty-four hours earlier, he had been enjoying an exciting new relationship – his first; now, like the country itself, a piece of his innocence had been ripped away. What it had been replaced with was as yet unknown.

With a sigh, he realized he would get no answers tonight. All he could do was focus on the considerable amount of work he still needed to do before the rest of the world woke up again. In a final push to break himself free from his malaise, he dropped to his feet and did ten push-ups, then jogged across Pennsylvania Avenue toward the gate at West Executive Avenue, leaving his serious reflection for another time.

When he reached the White House gate, the very one he had exited less than twenty minutes earlier, he flung it open and confidently walked through. There was no sign of the amicable guard he'd just joked with; there was, however, movement inside the booth. Instinctively, he froze in his tracks, and as the door to the booth opened, he realized he wasn't wearing his White House pass.

"I work here," he said with a quiver in his voice.

"Where's your pass?" a voice from the booth demanded.

"It's in my wallet."

"Let's see it!" the invisible voice barked. "Slowly!"

Matt slowly retrieved his wallet from his back pocket, then pulled out his pass. As he held it up, the door opened all the way to reveal an older, sterner-faced guard coming toward him. As Matt saw him return his gun to its holster, a chill ran up his spine. He remained frozen like a deer in the headlights of a semi-truck, afraid to move.

"You shouldn't come blowing through the gate like that," the man growled. "I was damn near ready to shoot you!"

"I just walked out this gate twenty minutes ago and talked with the guy on duty," Matt explained, "I assumed you were him."

The guard grunted, but his face softened slightly. "We just rotated shifts." As he got closer, Matt could see his hand trembling. "Man, am I glad you stopped!"

"I'm glad you didn't shoot!" Matt exclaimed.

"We both have a story to tell our kids," the guard said with a sigh.

Matt returned to the Secretariat, energized by the surge of adrenalin but shaken to the core about his close encounter with death. The thought that this day was a pivotal one in his life had just taken on a whole new meaning.

Glen and Keith arrived for work a little before seven a.m., just as Matt was finishing up what he hoped was the last box.

"Son," said Glen, "you should get a medal for this! What is that, sixteen hours of overtime in one day? I don't know how the hell you show that on a timecard. Do you, Keith?"

While the two men engaged in a discussion of federal overtime policy, Matt slumped in a chair and started to fade to black.

"Son, you're taking a car home," Glen said, then directed Keith to order a White House limousine.

Fifteen minutes later Matt walked into the apartment just as Walter and Grossman were about to leave for work.

"How you doing, lover boy?" Grossman teased, assuming that Matt's late night was due to another rendezvous with Anna. "Was she as frisky this time?"

"Nothing that exciting," Matt quipped as he walked past them to his room, "I was at work." He hoped that would be the end of it and was deeply annoyed that Grossman followed him.

"Helping Tricky Dick weasel out of the shitstorm? Good luck with that!"

Matt shot him an ugly look as he fell back on the bed, shoes and all. In truth, he was dying to tell them what he had been up to, that he was copying Watergate documents all night and, most of all, about Anna and his conscription by the FBI. But since that was not possible, he just wanted to be left alone.

As usual, Walter was the voice of reason. "Give it a rest, Grossman," he shouted from the door. "We're gonna be late!"

"Yeah, you're gonna be late," Matt growled, "Now get out."

"Alright, alright," Grossman muttered, "But this is to be continued…"

Matt's eyes followed him out, then he glanced around the room, almost unable to believe the interminable night was over and he was really back home and in his bed.

Just then, Walter popped his head into the room. "Oh, yeah, that girl called for you."

Matt groaned, eliciting a laugh from Grossman, whose head appeared behind Walter's shoulder. "I knew you were with her again!"

"No, man," Walter clarified, "That other girl, the one from school, the one who left you the record."

"Catherine?"

"Yeah, that's it. She left you the number where she is in New York; it's on the kitchen table."

Walter paused for a beat as if he wanted to say something else, then he turned and walked out.

Matt glanced over at the Roy Orbison record gathering dust on his turntable, then everything went dark.

CHAPTER NINETEEN

Awaking was an arduous process, like he was pulling himself from a long tunnel with weights on his ankles. Matt lingered for several minutes in that space between consciousness and unconsciousness, not quite sure where he was, though he had the vague sense from the light streaming in through his slitted eyes that it was at least late morning. Holy shit! His eyes flying open, he rolled over and grabbed his watch off the night table to find that it was indeed noon. Shit, shit, shit! He bounded out of bed, surprised by how much energy he had, and padded to the kitchen for something to eat.

"Grossman," he muttered as he rifled through a fridge full of condiments and takeout containers; it was not the first time his roommate had conveniently forgotten it was his turn to do the grocery shopping. When he pulled out half a loaf of moldy bread, he resigned himself to grabbing an egg sandwich on the way to work and picked up the phone to call Keith.

"No way, Bud," his friend replied when Matt said he'd be in shortly. "The boss says you got the rest of the day off."

"But –" Matt began.

"No ifs, ands, or buts, Bud. Glen was serious." Keith's voice held a hint of amusement as he delivered the news. "Just take it easy and we'll see you tomorrow."

Matt grunted into the phone, then hung up, furious. Any day, perhaps any minute, the House would vote on whether to hand down articles of impeachment, and the thought of having to watch it on the news with the rest of the world was unfathomable.

His hunger forgotten, he turned toward the table and the note, hastily scribbled by Walter, with Catherine's name and a number in Manhattan. He picked it up, his frustration about work momentarily replaced by curiosity.

Maybe she finally dumped that putz Michael, he thought, then decided she was probably just calling to see if he'd gotten the record. Either way, the polite thing to do was return the call and thank her for the gift.

He was staring at the phone, debating whether to call, when it began to ring. Matt grabbed it quickly, sure it was Keith telling him to come in after all.

"I can be there in twenty minutes."

"Really?" Anna purred. "I was hoping we could meet tonight but this is even better…"

"Oh, shit!" he said, shoving the piece of paper in his pocket. "I mean, Anna, good to hear from you…"

"Is it?" Anna replied, sounding miffed. "I thought the words 'oh, shit' meant something undesirable."

"Yes…I mean…no!" Matt said, starting to sweat. "I thought it was someone else is all. I'm sorry."

Even as the words came out of his mouth, Matt's every instinct was telling him he should not be talking to Anna. Though he had never revealed anything he shouldn't have about his work, he now felt like he was walking through a landmine. If he had learned anything from his time at the White House, it was that even the smallest tidbit of information could affect the country, and therefore the world. What if he said the wrong thing, gave her that piece of information her handlers were looking for?

"Apology accepted," Anna said smoothly. "I was calling to ask you to dinner tonight.

Matt swallowed hard. "Tonight?"

"Yes, I want to see you again." She paused. "And I need some advice…"

Advice? Matt's mind raced. He had to speak to Nelson, immediately.

"Matt? Are you there?"

Hoping he was making the right decision, he blurted out, "Yes, that would be great!"

They arranged to meet at seven at Clyde's, a popular restaurant in Georgetown, then Anna abruptly hung up.

"What the fuck?" he said aloud, already running back to his room, *"What the fuck!"*

He found Agent Nelson's pager number tucked away in his wallet on the nightstand. Now, he committed it to memory, then ripped up the paper and threw it in the trash before returning to the phone.

The FBI man called back so fast it was as if he'd been staring at his pager, waiting for Matt to reach out. Not surprisingly, he was also very excited by the development – especially Anna's mention of "advice" – and insisted he and Matt meet beforehand. Saying it was best they stay away from the White House, he suggested Whitey's Eat Bar, just across the river in Arlington.

"We need to make sure you and I are never seen together," he added.

Matt bit back a retort about his stating the obvious, then told Nelson what time he and Anna were meeting and where.

"Okay, see you at five," Nelson replied, then hung up, leaving Matt staring blankly at the phone for the third time in the space of an hour. He placed it in the receiver, then sat at the kitchen table, his head in his hands. What the hell had he gotten himself into?

The question triggered a wave of anger over the sudden lack of agency over his life. First, he had been told he couldn't come to work; now he had been forced into meetings with Anna and Nelson, and he didn't know which he dreaded more.

His growling stomach interrupted his thoughts, reminding him that he hadn't eaten since the Chinese food the evening before. Pushing the disturbing thoughts of the future from his mind, he went to his room, quickly dressed, and headed for the deli down the street. Ruminating about everything he couldn't control wasn't going to solve anything, might as well focus on what he could control: food. Twenty minutes later he was back home and parked in front of the TV, munching on a roast beef sandwich and watching for news of Nixon's fate. It never came, and Matt was again filled with frustration that he wasn't at work to catch the whispering of staffers or simply feel the energy at the White House. He also wasn't used to doing nothing, and boredom, coupled with lingering exhaustion from the night before, conspired to make his lids heavy. After fighting it for a few moments, he closed his eyes "just for a minute," only to jump up two hours later with just twenty minutes to take a long-overdue shower and dress for his meeting with Agent Nelson.

At precisely ten minutes to five Matt's taxi turned onto Washington Boulevard in Arlington. When the driver pulled up in front of Whitey's, a local favorite Matt had heard about, he was surprised to see it was pretty much a dump. He paid the man and slid out, his eyes scanning the sidewalk for signs of Nelson, then headed for the door. The place was even more run-down inside, and had that familiar sour smell of a bar badly in need of cleaning. It was sparsely populated, with the after-work crowd yet to arrive. Matt was about to order a beer when he saw the FBI man waiting for him at a table just off the bar with two beers in front of him.

"Good choice," he said as he took a seat, "It looks like a place people would meet to plot something."

Nelson laughed as he slid one of the beers over to Matt. "Next time we'll meet at happy hour, because the beers are cheap!" He paused. "So, this is happening…"

"Apparently, I don't have a choice," Matt replied sourly.

Nelson gave him what was supposed to be a sympathetic nod, but the lingering grin on his face betrayed his excitement.

"Look, I get it. You're nervous. But it's going to be okay. You're already seeing her, right?"

"Interesting term," Matt observed, eliciting another laugh from Nelson, "And, yes, I have been 'seeing her.' But this is very different!"

"It's not as different as you might think." He took a sip of his beer, then neatly folded his hands on the table. "Now, let's set some ground rules, okay?"

Matt nodded, all ears.

"Number one: first names only. Mine's Roger. Number two: I am here to protect my country. That is my only goal, *our* only goal, and, make no mistake, that *is* what we're talking about here. Number three: I am your partner in this, and I understand you will need some assurances. I'll work on that, but know the FBI will backstop you. That, you can take to the bank! Number four –"

Roger cut himself off mid-sentence when a young waiter appeared at the table. He was probably about Matt's age, but that's where the commonality ended as much of his face was obscured by a scruffy beard and slightly greasy hair that hung down to his shoulders. Roger offered the waiter a polite smile, then, with a gesture to their full beers, sent him on his way.

"As I was saying," he continued when the waiter slunk off, "this is an FBI operation. Jensen will interject himself, but you report only to me, and you will have to get comfortable reminding him of that. The White House does not run counterintelligence operations. I will keep him informed, but we have to keep his egotistical ass out of this."

"Sounds good to me," Matt said, relieved that he would not be under Jensen's thumb. Roger inspired a sense of confidence; he was in charge and seemed to know what he was doing. Mostly, Matt appreciated the fact that the agent was a straight shooter, a quality he had been raised to trust and seek out in others.

"Now that we got that covered," Roger continued, "We need to talk about tonight's date with your femme fatale." He looked at his watch and sighed. "I wish I had more time to get you comfortable, but I'm already running late for some other stuff at headquarters."

"Don't worry," Matt shot back, "she has a way of making me comfortable." He realized his error when Roger burst out laughing. The man thought this was a joke!

"Roger," he said slowly as if that would make his feelings clearer. "I'll go through with this. I know it's important. But seriously, I don't want to have sex with her again."

"Don't worry! If she tries to make the evening into something more, just tell her you can't because you have to be at work very early."

Matt nodded blankly, but he was already thinking how this could go sideways. What about tomorrow night, and the night after that? Given the passionate route their relationship had taken early and often, how would he continue to put her off? He said nothing to Roger, though, because right now he was focused on getting through the next few hours.

Roger leaned in toward the table. "I'm not sure what is going on here," he admitted. "The fact that she wants to see you shows that you're valuable to them in some way, but Anna is new to us and we know next to nothing about her. Normally, their modus operandi is to have a 'catcher' make contact with a 'mark.'"

Matt took a sip of his beer to cover up his nervousness. "In other words, me. I'm the mark."

"Yes, and once you're dragged in, they turn you over to a more seasoned counterintelligence officer to work you – probably use the sex as a threat. The good news is that you're not married – that is a whole other level of coercion – but they can still threaten to expose you as a traitor to the U.S."

"I would never!" Matt blurted out, his stomach jolting at the thought.

Roger held up a hand. "I know, I know. I'm just telling you how these people work. I'm actually thinking, though, that since it got so personal so fast, they might just let her continue the relationship rather than risk a transition to someone else. We'll just have to play it by ear."

Roger checked his watch again. "I'm late. Let me just give you some quick thoughts. Just meet her like always, like she is a friend…or whatever. There is no reason to think that she knows anything has changed, that you know who she really is."

It was a comforting thought, but just as Matt started to relax, Roger added, "On the other hand, she probably suspects that you know. They *always* suspect. It is vital to their survival. Be ready for her to say, 'What have you told the FBI about me?' If that happens, I've found the best thing to do is to just lie. Lying is easy if you laugh it off. Just snicker and ask, 'Why would I tell them about my friends?' Challenge her a bit; ask why she would be concerned."

Noting Matt's wide eyes, he said, "Look, a lot of this comes down to going with your gut in the moment. Right now, I'm very curious to hear what kind of 'advice' she is looking for. How much has she said about her work at the embassy?"

"Nothing," Matt replied, thinking that they hadn't done all that much talking. "Just that she started working there a few months ago when she got to the U.S."

"Okay. Be sure to ask her questions, but don't be too invasive. Ask what she does there, how long she expects to be in D.C., what she does for fun. And what about America? What does she like about it, what does she not like about it?"

"She likes films," Matt replied glumly as he remembered how much fun they'd had discussing movies in the car the night of their first real date. He also remembered how the night had ended and felt the heat rising to his face.

Roger signaled the waiter for the check, then reached for his wallet, pulled out a five, and placed it on the table.

"This oughta cover it." He stood to go, then smiled down at Matt. "Good luck with Wonder Woman tonight and give me a call in the morning. We'll set up a time for a debrief."

Then he was off, leaving Matt in disbelief that the short pep talk had been the extent of his preparation for meeting with a Soviet spy. He looked at this watch and realized nearly an hour had passed. It was the height of rush hour, and he would have just enough time to get back over the bridge in time to meet Anna. He hailed a cab, and as the driver fought traffic he sunk into deep thought, replaying Roger's questions and guidance. He prayed they were enough.

CHAPTER TWENTY

Matt arrived at Clyde's fifteen minutes early – a good thing, because he needed some time to calm his nerves before Anna got there. He grabbed a booth across from a long oak bar, which gave him a view of the entrance, and took a deep breath, allowing himself to take in the atmosphere. Clyde's location, including its proximity to Georgetown, George Washington, and American Universities, drew an eclectic crowd, to say the least – a regular mix of students, the wealthy and those eking out a living. It also attracted government and business professionals – which made Matt wonder if that's why Anna had chosen it. Was it a place she frequented in search of … what was the word Roger had used…? *Marks,* he thought glumly, *easy marks, like me.* Taking another deep breath, he shoved the thought from his mind and forced himself to focus on the task at hand.

Mission, he corrected himself. *Focus on the mission.*

By the time Anna arrived at ten past seven, Matt had begun to wonder if she was going to show at all. Those ten minutes were long enough to send him on an emotional roller coaster, alternating between relief and anxiety. All of that changed when she walked through the door. She scanned the room, her eyes landing on his, her full lips parting in a smile of genuine warmth. As she closed the distance between them, he held her gaze while also being very aware of the heads turning to stare at the stunning woman who moved with almost catlike grace. She was wearing a pair of tight blue jeans that accented her long, slender legs – a change from the dresses she usually favored but just as sexy. Her white button-up shirt was open just enough to expose the top of her cleavage, and her dark hair fell in gentle waves to her shoulders. The diamond studs in her ears were sparkly but irrelevant; she would have been just as radiant without them. Matt felt his stomach drop, and in that moment, he wanted more than anything to believe that Roger Nelson was wrong about her.

Anna slid into the booth across from him and gently placed a small purse next to her on the seat.

"It is so good to see you," she said in a tone that suggested they had been separated for a long time, though it had only been a couple of days.

Hearing the warmth in her voice, Matt's breath caught in his throat. It sounded so genuine, it seemed impossible that she was the person Roger and Jensen said she was.

"Anna," he blurted out before he could stop himself, "Why are you interested in me? You could have any guy in this place!" He paused. "And I am clearly younger than you."

"That's it," she said, not missing a beat. "I love that you're honest. Most men, especially older ones, just want one thing. They are all pigs. I am attracted to sincerity."

Matt exhaled, a reaction that conveniently could have passed for relief that the object of his affection desired him as well. He almost laughed then, for he remembered the observation Grossman once made about Matt's "bullshit Midwestern sincerity." Bullshit or not, it appeared to give him credibility in this caper between the two superpowers.

"I knew when we spoke at the diner that you were sweet," she continued, seemingly oblivious to the effect she was having on him. "But when I saw you with your friends the other night, throwing back those shots, I thought, that sweet guy also loves life! I am new here. I don't like the party scene, and I so wanted to find a friend to help me learn my way in this country. You have been that person for me, Matt, and that is why I am interested in you!"

"Wow," he said, again struck by the fact that beneath the subterfuge his emotions were all too real. "I mean, um, I figured you kinda liked me, you know, um…"

"I am so embarrassed!" she interjected, and he was surprised to see that she actually blushed. "I've just been so lonely since I came to this country." She lowered her eyes for a beat, then raised them to meet his. "I might not have been very ladylike."

"Oh, you were very ladylike," he joked, and couldn't help feeling smug when her blush deepened from pink to bright red. "All kidding aside, though, I've told you so much about me and I know next to nothing about you." He leaned forward, "Let's start over, pretend we just met. I want to hear all about your life."

She snorted. "That would take much more than an evening…"

"Okay, so let's start with why you came to America…?"

"I came here to study. I am very fortunate that my country allowed me the opportunity to study in the U.S. It is a great honor. I want to be successful and make the most of it. And I have to be brilliant because my government is paying for my education. I have a lot of pressure to succeed. My study is world affairs; don't you think I am lucky to study in Washington, D.C., the capital of the great superpower?"

"I completely understand," Matt replied truthfully, adding, "I feel the same way working at the White House."

"Yes! This is why I asked you for help tonight. I need to know as much about your country and your government as possible. It will be so helpful with my studies. For example, what do you think is going to happen to Mr. Nixon?"

Before he could answer, a waitress appeared. He looked at Anna and said, "No shots tonight. I have to work tomorrow."

Anna ordered two shots of vodka anyway, "just in case." She then tossed her head back and laughed mischievously, a delightful sound that Matt barely noticed because he was so fixated on the sight of her quivering breasts. Suddenly, the vow he'd made to not be intimate with her again seemed like empty words. He told the waitress he would take a pint of whatever they had on tap.

The waitress said she'd give them some time to decide on food, then left to get their drinks. As Anna perused the menu, Matt glanced around the room, anything to stop himself from staring at her. Suddenly, he stirred in his chair when he saw Jensen walk through the door and up to the bar. What the hell was he doing here? Of course – Nelson had told him about the meeting and he was checking up on Matt. Matt felt a hot flush of anger creep across his face. He had enough problems without Jensen nosing about. He glanced at Anna to see if she had noticed his reaction, but thankfully she was still pouring over the specials.

Matt forced himself to make conversation while trying to keep an eye on Jensen. What did he hope to accomplish, if not to make some kind of trouble for him? Fortunately, he finished his beer quickly and left, but Matt had no doubt he would have something to say in the morning.

Dinner went as their other dates had – fun and casual, with plenty of flirty banter thrown in. Matt was surprised at the lack of pressure he felt to make it so, once he surrendered to his circumstances. When he did attempt to go deeper with some questions about her background, Anna continued to remain evasive and steered the conversation back to her studies and how important her success was. She also reiterated her belief that Matt was indeed the ideal "friend" who could help her learn more about the U.S. government. To Matt, the implication was clear: she was referring to his job at the White House. He played dumb, saying that he would be happy to "tutor her on American history," and she let the matter drop with a *tank you,* the accent more pronounced in his ear now that he knew its origins. He smiled back at her, more confused than ever. If she was a spy, wouldn't she be pressing him harder?

Around nine o'clock he told her he needed to call it a night. As he paid the bill, Anna pulled out a tiny book from her purse.

"Can I get your work phone number?"

Matt froze, then cursed himself for allowing his discomfort to show on his face.

"Um…sure," he replied, for in truth he couldn't think of a good reason not to. He gave her the number, then repeated it, noting that she wrote it right below his name and the address and phone number of his apartment. In the brief glimpse he got before she closed it, he saw other pages filled with notes but couldn't make them out.

They left the restaurant and walked a short way down M Street. It was a beautiful evening with a clear sky. Anna stopped by a little Ford Pinto and proudly pointed to it.

"Do you like my American car? I've never had my own car before."

Matt made a show of walking around the Pinto to admire it, all the while thinking that owning a vehicle in her country was more about status than one's ability to afford it. Had targeting him earned her this perk?

"Wow, that's really something, Anna. Congratulations."

"Would you like to ride in it? I could give you a ride home."

Matt stared at her for a moment, the inner tug-of-war beginning again as he weighed the offer. In her eyes, he saw a mixture of innocent exuberance over the car and something else he couldn't put his finger on. It seemed like she knew she had him, though whether it was the confidence of a beautiful woman speaking to a man smitten with her, or the arrogance of a spy who had her prey in her sights, he didn't know. And, in that moment, he told himself it didn't matter.

"Sure, that would be great," he said, trying like hell to keep his voice casual. What harm would it be to prolong the evening just a little longer?

*   *   *

The next morning, Matt returned to work, fueled, as usual, by a mixture of caffeine and adrenalin. He had avoided spending the night with Anna, albeit narrowly, after she pulled out all the stops in the Pinto parked in front of his building. In truth, it was only his refusal to bring her under the watchful eyes of Grossman and Walter that stopped him. He didn't know if Anna was dangerous or not, but he was already juggling too many worlds to risk them colliding now – not only for his roommates' sakes, but his own. Still, it took every ounce of willpower to extricate himself from her embrace, and the sense of victory he felt as he slipped into bed alone quickly turned to ruminating over the hold she had on him. He had spent the rest of the night staring at the ceiling and the following morning thanking God it was Friday.

Thankfully, once he walked through the Secretariat doors there was plenty of chaos to distract him. Attention on the White House was at a fever pitch, as if Watergate was the only thing happening in the entire world. Rumors were flying about, the most prominent being that if articles of impeachment were indeed handed down, Nixon would resign rather than face a trial in the Senate.

Even at the early hour Matt arrived there were protestors marching in front of the White House. Many held placards, imploring passing motorists to "Honk for Impeachment." Others simply read, "Impeach the Cox-Sacker," referring to the former Watergate Special Prosecutor, Archibald Cox, whom Nixon had fired. At the gate on West Executive Avenue, where Matt was nearly shot two nights earlier, photographers were gathered three deep, hoping to get a photograph of the President crossing the street to his OEOB office. Their cameras, with long telescopic lenses, were perched atop spiny-legged tripods looking like something from a sci-fi movie. It was all so surreal, and for Matt, the other staffers, and countless other Americans, heartbreaking.

His first order of business was to call Roger, who suggested meeting for happy hour that afternoon in Arlington. He had just ended the call when Keith informed him that there was a woman on hold for him on another line.

"She sounds like a babe," he said with a wink.

Matt groaned inwardly. Just days ago he would have loved that Anna was calling; now, he was dreading having to be "on guard" so early in the morning and with no warning. He thought for a moment about telling Keith to say he was busy, then decided there was no point. In fact, it might even give him something interesting to report to Roger.

He picked up the phone and answered, hoping he sounded more relaxed than he felt.

"You're a hard man to track down, Matt Thomas," said a cheerful, vaguely familiar voice that was most certainly not Anna's.

"Excuse me?"

"It's Catherine…you know, Catherine Martin, from class…?"

"Oh, hey, Catherine," Matt sputtered, "I meant to return your call, I've just been so –"

"Busy, I know," she interrupted. "Your roommate – Walter, I think – said you're hardly ever home. I think his words were something, like … 'between his work and his extracurricular activities…'" Catherine trailed off in a giggle. "Did you take up a sport or something?"

Geez, Walter.

"Yeah, something like that. How has your summer been going?"

"Oh, you know, New York is great…"

"Actually, I don't know. I've never been," he replied.

"What?! Never been to New York? It's amazing!" She paused. "We'll have to get you up here one day. I would love to show you around."

Oh yeah, you, me, and your boyfriend, Michael, he thought.

"Yeah, sure, that would be fun…I guess."

Catherine was telling him about an exhibit at the Guggenheim when Jensen stormed into the room, walked over to Matt, and with his right index finger pressed down the receiver, ending the conversation.

"You realize that was the President?" Matt quipped sarcastically.

"Screw the President! What the hell was going on in Georgetown last night? And why the hell did I not know about it?"

Matt had always prided himself on being able to stay cool, a skill cultivated while dealing with the handful of knuckleheads at military school. But the stress of the last few days, coupled with Jensen's constant riding him, pushed him past his limit. He stood up, inched toward Jensen, invading his personal space, then glanced around to make sure no one was in earshot.

"You know, Mr. Jensen," he said in a quiet, steely tone, "I didn't ask to be in this position. You forced me into it. And since you need me, I think you should be more supportive." He smiled smugly as he saw Jensen's face go slack with surprise at being challenged. "Another thing – I am just going to put this out there – I honestly don't have a fucking clue how to handle this. I'm way over my head here. And since I'm on the subject, I think you need to get your shit in one bag and work out your relationship with the FBI. Agent Nelson told me that I report to him. What did he call it? Oh yeah, an 'FBI thing.'"

Jensen took a deep breath. "I see."

At that moment Glen's voice rang out. "Son, I need my morning Pepsi."

Matt fell back into his chair, slumped his shoulders, and let out an exasperated gasp.

Jensen looked down at him with something akin to sympathy. "Okay, Matt. You did the right thing going to Nelson. I'll work out the turf issue. You keep your end. I apologize."

With no response on the Pepsi front, Glen stuck his head into the room.

"I'm on it, Glen," Matt said as Jensen turned, nodded to Glen, and left.

"Son, what was that about?"

"He's pissed that I have not taken the security briefer on document control," Matt said, unable to believe how easily the lie rolled off his tongue.

*   *   *

Late that afternoon, Matt walked into Whitey's to find it much more crowded than the previous day. It was even more surprising, then, to see Roger sitting in the rear without his suit coat and his shoulder holster exposed for all to see. Matt sat down across from him and gestured to the pistol.

"You really good at shooting that thing?"

"Have to be!" Roger replied cheerily as he took a slug of his beer.

"How good are you?"

Pointing to a patron in a window seat at the front of the restaurant, Roger said, "I could take that woman out with a single shot to the head."

"Really?" Matt asked, impressed and slightly unnerved by the gruesome example.

Roger just smiled, then suggested they get down to business. Matt pulled out a little piece of paper with numbered points he'd prepared to be sure he told Roger everything. As he ticked off the list, he could tell from the FBI agent's expression that he was pleased with his meticulousness. And while he agreed with Matt that the information gleaned from Anna was lackluster at best, he was encouraged that she wanted to continue their tryst. Matt also noted that Roger didn't ask if he had slept with Anna, which he assumed meant the Bureau didn't want to be seen as encouraging this. The elephant in the room was that continuing the sexual relationship was undoubtedly necessary lest Anna start to think something was wrong.

Then Matt told him about Jensen's appearance at Clyde's.

"Son of a bitch," Roger said in amazement. "He called me to say he talked to you, but he didn't mention that. Sorry you had to take some shit. That won't happen again. I'll be better about keeping him informed."

"Not a problem," Matt replied smoothly, "It gave me a chance to put him in his place, which felt pretty good."

Roger smiled. "He is a pompous ass."

"One thing that bothered me," Matt admitted. "My boss Glen caught our confrontation and knows something is up. I am sure he has no idea it is anything like this, but he knows Jensen and I had words."

Roger shook his head. "Security people love to think they're spies. I'll let him know he screwed the pooch, and you let me know if your boss brings it up again. I'll read him in if I have to, but I really prefer to keep the circle tight."

Matt nodded, relieved that Roger had his back and was willing to be open with Glen. He had come to think of the older man not only as a boss, but a friend and mentor, and he'd hated to lie to him.

They were about to leave when Matt said, almost as an afterthought, "Oh, Anna asked for my phone number at work. I hated giving it to her, but I couldn't think of a reason not to."

Roger shrugged. "I can't see any harm."

"Great! I was worried." Matt wiped his brow, pretending to throw away the concern. "It is a little weird, though, knowing that a real-life spy has my name and phone numbers in her little book!"

"Whoa, whoa. What now?" Roger leaned forward; his eyes narrowed. "She has a book?"

"Yeah, she put my work number right next to my apartment phone number. I could read it."

"Did you see any other names?"

"No – I mean, I saw other writing in the book but I couldn't make it out."

"How big is the book?" Roger demanded.

"I'd guess four or five inches by about three. It's a little black book."

"How thick is it?"

"I guess an inch or so."

"An inch or so… that's a lot of names and numbers…"

"I suppose so." Matt was not entirely sure what to make of the interest.

Roger thought for a minute. Then, with a seriousness Matt had not seen before, he said, "I need that book." He saw Matt's puzzled look. "Yeah, I need it. That book could tell me if she is playing this game with anyone else from our side, not to mention names and numbers of her associates. That would be a major, major get!"

Roger sat back in his chair and stroked his chin thoughtfully, reminding Matt of a mad scientist. "We need to figure out how to get it from her, so I can take pictures of every page without her knowing."

"She keeps it in her purse, maybe you can steal her purse!" Matt offered, trying to be helpful.

"That won't work." Silence ensued as the pair contemplated this new opportunity.

"You might have to fuck her in your apartment so I can swoop in and get the book…"

Matt's eyes widened, surprised as much by the crass language as the suggestion itself.

"Speaking of things that won't work. What are you going to do, hide under my bed? And I have roommates. Besides, I don't want to…er…fuck her again."

"Really not about what you want," Roger reminded him. "This is our highest priority. We need to come up with a plan."

"Seriously, Roger, it's not a good idea for me to keep fooling around with her. It'd be…" He searched for the words.

"Playing with fire?" Roger smiled, but his tone had a hint of warning in it. "You better learn to keep your wits around you, Matt. Keep your mind on the mission, not what's between Wonder Woman's –"

"I get your point," Matt said, holding up a hand.

Roger flashed him a lascivious grin that brought to mind a bragging session in a boys' locker room. "Oh, I know you do."

As they left Whitey's, Matt's stomach was in knots. He knew Roger was serious about sleeping with Anna to get the book – and about Matt seeing it purely as a tactical maneuver. Matt had no doubt he could do the former; it was the latter, he thought as Anna's smiling face flashed through his mind, that was the problem.

CHAPTER TWENTY-ONE

"What a difference a day makes," Matt muttered as he entered the Secretariat that Monday, "Or in this case, two days."

Matt's jaw tightened as he recalled the night before, when he and his roommates returned to the apartment and found *The Washington Post* flung carelessly in front of the door – its headline about the House Judiciary Committee's recommendation that President Nixon be impeached and removed from office glaring up at them. Instantly, any sense of well-being he'd enjoyed over the weekend was replaced with shock and profound disappointment.

The three had gone to northern New Jersey, where they joined Tex and some of the other brothers for an impromptu camping trip. It was the most relaxed Matt had been in months, from the moment the three of them piled into Walter's jeep at six a.m. on Saturday and, after a brief stop for supplies, fled the stifling heat of the city.

In the afternoon, after meeting up with the others, they rented canoes and embarked on a voyage down the Delaware River. It was wide and surrounded by deep, thick woods. The forest along the banks showed no signs of habitation, and Matt mused that the journey could easily have taken place a hundred years earlier. It also brought back memories of boyhood outings with his father and grandfather on Lake St. Clair in Michigan. Of course, those trips had not included filthy frat songs belted out as the five-canoe armada of sweaty young men lazily maneuvered downriver. Even as he sang along with the others, Matt's face reddened at the thought of what his elders would say if they heard him. It was then, with a warm smile, that he recalled his father too had been in a fraternity and likely sang similar ditties.

A few hours later, their enthusiasm for the outdoors was rapidly waning, at least so far as it required such intense physical exertion. A rebellious contingent led, not surprisingly, by Grossman was lobbying to stop for the day, while the others wanted to continue in search of the perfect place to make camp. The canoes grouped in the center of the river, held together by the brothers like a big barge, as a passionate debate ensued. A few, including Matt, hung back and quietly observed the spectacle, waiting for the inevitable breakdown in negotiations they often witnessed at fraternity meetings during the school year. Even the usually outspoken Tex, exhausted from the canoeing and too much sun, abdicated his role as president and debate facilitator. It was Walter who finally put an end to the thing.

"Okay, assholes," he bellowed between puffs on his cigar, "here's what we're gonna do."

Whether it was the authority in his tone or the general weariness of the group, Matt didn't know. He just smiled and trailed behind the others as, like a bunch of kindergarten children, they followed Walter's canoe to the side of the river.

Walter issued simple and direct orders, where to pitch their tents and where to build a fire. He even directed the cordoning off of an area for a makeshift latrine. Once they made camp, Walter shifted to the role of chef, preparing a delicious meal that had Grossman and Matt complaining why he never cooked at home. After dinner, they gathered around the fire, where talk soon turned to their various summer romances. Matt laughed along with the others at some of the raunchier tales, his mirth coming to an abrupt end when Grossman announced, to his horror, that Matt had "defected" to the dark side.

"Tell them about Anna," he said.

Damnit, Grossman, Matt thought, as immediately a chant of "Anna, Anna, Anna" rose up from the crowd.

His mind racing, he turned the tables on his roommate by bringing up the girl he had seen slinking out of Grossman's room earlier that week. Like a pack of wolves, the brothers quickly turned their attention to his roommate, and Matt breathed a sigh of relief. The last thing he needed was for the fraternity brothers to be delving into his fledgling espionage operation.

Though it had blown over within seconds, the incident stayed with him the rest of the evening. Even the next day, when Tex, his hands wrapped around two sweaty beer bottles, took him aside and asked him to be rush chairman, Matt's knee-jerk reaction was to refuse. An honor by all accounts, Tex's offer instead felt like one more burden on his shoulders – and a reminder of the double life he was living.

And then they returned home to see the news about Nixon.

Holy shit, Matt thought as he went to grab the paper, but Grossman beat him to it.

"Told you, boychik," he said gleefully as he clutched the paper in his meaty fingers and waved it at Matt. "Tricky Dick is going *down.*"

"Shut up, Grossman," Matt snapped, his tone drawing a genuine look of surprise from his roommate.

"It's true, Matt," Walter drawled as he appeared behind Grossman, "The man is, in fact, a dick."

Ignoring them, Matt grabbed the paper and began skimming the article. In truth, it wasn't his roommates who ticked him off, but that he had worried needlessly about missing something on his day off, only to have it all blow up over the weekend. Then, of course, there was the sadness and disappointment that a President he had admired was, as Grossman so coarsely stated, was "going down."

All twenty-one of the Democrats on the Committee voted to send three articles of impeachment to the full House, with six of the seventeen Republicans joining in. As expected, the charges against Nixon included the cover-up of the Watergate break-in and related illegal activities. And it likely wasn't over, with the article predicting that the Committee would also hand down another article related to his alleged abuse of power on Monday. Not that it necessarily mattered; if a majority of the House approved just one of those articles, it would be sufficient to impeach the President and send it over to the Senate for trial. Removal from office was a separate matter and would occur if two-thirds of the Senators voted for it.

Though nothing he read came as a surprise, the words were like a punch to the gut. In that moment, Matt realized how fervently he had been hoping the President's name would be cleared. Ignoring Grossman's snicker, he tossed the paper to the ground and headed for his bedroom before he said something he regretted. He peeled off his clothes and slipped into bed, emotionally and physically drained yet knowing there was no way he was getting any sleep that night.

*   *   *

Just a couple of miles but a world away, Anna sat on her couch, pretending to inspect her new manicure – anything to avoid Vadim's stare.

"You're losing him, Annuska," Vadim said, clucking his tongue in that way that sounded mocking but, Anna knew, signified something much more threatening. "It is time to take things to the next level."

Anna looked up at him with feigned horror. "What exactly are you suggesting, Vadim?"

"Only that you demonstrate your commitment to our mission here." He leaned forward, his eyes narrowed. "The boy has not called you *all weekend.*"

"He has been busy," she said with a shrug. "Isn't that why we wanted him… because he has an important job…?"

"He and his job are of no use to us if we do not have access. If *you* do not have access."

"It was just two days…"

"It was not just two days!" Vadim snarled. "It has been *weeks*, and you have gotten *nothing!*" He paused, his face returning to its usual flaccid mask. "It is time to, as the Americans say, 'pull out all the stops.'"

Anna sank back into the cushion, inwardly sighing with relief that she had followed her instincts and kept her mouth shut. If Vadim knew she was already sleeping with Matt and not getting results, she would be on the next plane to Lubyanka. Vadim's ignorance had brought her a reprieve that was now coming to an end, and she still had no idea how to approach the situation.

She never doubted her decision to go to bed with Matt that first night. Some men needed the chase to stay invested; others, due to a lack of confidence, experience, or both, had to be pursued. It was the age-old dynamic of predator and prey; one simply had to decide which role they played and step into it. There was no question of roles here – Matt definitely fell into the "prey" category – but this went beyond her mission. Brutal honesty with herself was also paramount and she wanted him, pure and simple. The problem was, though she knew Matt liked her, was perhaps even falling in love, that was a far cry from getting him to betray his country.

She nodded reluctantly, and when she looked at Vadim again she did not have to fake the fear on her face. "I will do what needs to be done."

He stared at her for a long moment; then, he loudly clapped his hands and turned to the kitchen. "Okay, then. What do you have to eat?"

*   *   *

Around five-thirty p.m., Matt was walking through the West Wing on his way back from a minor task. The day had passed in a surreal blur in which he and the other staffers went mechanically about their business, all the while feeling as if the skies were about to fall down around them. The public had the luxury of distracting themselves with the banalities of life, but for those within the eighteen acres there was no escape.

He stopped in the Press Office to get a soda and saw through the windows a group of reporters gathered on the driveway out front. Popping the can open, he wandered outside toward the group, doing a double take when he saw three men walk out of the West Wing. They were three senior Republican members of Congress, and they were about to hold a news conference.

Matt smiled as he surveyed the approaching statesmen. He had always liked Senator Barry Goldwater, who, after a particularly divisive campaign, had lost his bid for the presidency to Lyndon Johnson in 1964. Though Matt was just a kid at the time, like millions of Americans, he respected Goldwater's straight talk. Now, as then, the Senator was a real character, his tall, slender frame dressed in a sharp grey, pin-striped suit, contrasted by pointed cowboy boots – a nod to his Arizona roots.

Senator Hugh Scott of Virginia could not have been more different; dressed in a rumpled suit and Hushpuppy shoes, he looked more like a college professor than a Washington powerbroker. The third man was Congressman John Rhodes, also from Arizona. He'd served as Minority Leader of the House of Representatives since Gerald Ford became Vice President the year before. As the three approached microphones, honking horns from protestors outside the gates could be heard in the background.

Goldwater spoke first. "Congressman Rhodes and Senator Scott and I have just concluded a visit with the President. He invited us down this afternoon to disclose to him what we feel the actual conditions in the House and the Senate are relative to his situation. We had a good, thorough discussion, and I think I speak for my two colleagues when I say that we were extremely impressed with the uppermost thought in his mind, which is that whatever decision he makes, it will be in the best interest of our country. There has been no decision made. We made no suggestions. We were merely there to offer what we see as the condition on both floors."

Matt knew, as everyone did, of course, the decision Senator Goldwater referred to was whether Nixon would resign.

As soon as he was done, reporters began pelting them with questions like little kids in a snowball fight.

"How do you evaluate that situation?" one called out.

"How do we evaluate the situation?" Senator Scott repeated. "Well, we informed him that the mood on Capitol Hill is gloomy and reflects the very distressing situation this country is currently in. We offered other opinions as well, but I think we will keep that amongst ourselves."

Another reporter shouted, "Gentlemen, when you say that the situation was gloomy, what, specifically, did you mean?"

It was the confident and affable Congressman Rhodes who put everything into context.

"I think everybody knows what I meant. It is well known that the situation on the floor of the House has deteriorated to the extent that impeachment is a foregone conclusion."

Talk about a tense conversation, Matt thought as he envisioned the three Republican leaders breaking the news to Nixon that he would be impeached.

Hungry for more details, the reporters continued firing away.

"The gentleman in the center," one reporter called out, clearly unable to recall Senator Scott's name.

"Oh, you mean the leader of the Senate?" Goldwater replied, obviously enjoying the reporter's embarrassment.

A laugh broke out among the crowd, bringing much-needed relief to the otherwise subdued proceeding. Matt glanced around awkwardly; was he the only one here uncomfortable by the levity under such sad circumstances? Then he noticed a familiar face approach. It was one of President Nixon's senior advisers. The man stood on the periphery of the group, right next to Matt. He listened for a few minutes; then, catching the attention of a White House press assistant, he raised his hand slightly into the air and twirled his index finger – an unmistakable order to end the session.

Immediately, the press assistant said loudly, "Thank you, gentlemen."

It was not unusual at such events for one of the White House staff to thank a speaker, thereby signaling to reporters that the last question had been asked. Yet, even as the reporters politely disbanded, Matt could sense their frustration at having to leave without the answer to the question on the minds of millions around the world: would Nixon resign, now that he had been told by three trusted Republican allies that he would unquestionably be impeached in the House, or would he fight it out in a trial in the U.S. Senate?

An hour later, Matt walked into the apartment to find Grossman and Walter parked in front of the TV. Their heads swiveled in unison to look at him like he was a soldier returning from war. Despite his exhaustion, Matt managed a smile, in part as an olive branch for biting their heads off earlier.

"Your girlfriend called about five times. I think she misses you," Grossman announced.

"You know what they say," Matt quipped, even as he groaned inside, "when you got it, you got it."

At that very moment the phone rang and Matt moved to answer it, praying it was anyone but Anna.

"I need to see you tonight," she said without preamble.

"Anna, it's been a very long day –" he began, but she cut him off.

"Please, Matt, my professor wants us to do a presentation tomorrow on what is going on at the White House. I have read your papers and watched the TV, but there is so much I do not understand."

Before being recruited by the FBI, Matt would never have let a lack of sleep stop him from running out the door to go see her. Now, all he could think about was that she was trying to bring down a country already in danger of imploding.

"Please, Matt, I really need your help."

The tone in her voice gave him pause. *She really is nervous*, he thought, though he was under no illusion that it was because of schoolwork. It was also very clear what he should do: call Roger, apprise him of this development, and get advice on how to deal with her. Yet, the idea of even sitting across a table from her was unbearable, let alone doing any-thing else. He was embroiled in an inner conflict between the responsible young man the world saw, and a new, unfamiliar person who was tired of always being "on," always being perfect. A flash of anger rose within him, that this burden had been placed on his shoulders. All he had done was respond to the advances of a stunning woman, for crying out loud, like any other red-blooded American male!

"Matt?" Anna said, pulling him from his thoughts. "Are you there?"

"Look, Anna," he replied tersely, unable to believe the words that were coming out of his mouth. "I would love to get together tonight, but it's late and I have to be at work very early."

"Please, Matt…"

"I'm sorry," he said, and for a moment he actually meant it. "It will have to be tomorrow after work."

"Oh, thank you!" she gasped, her relief palpable.

"Of course." He paused, then added, "You know I would do anything to help you, right Anna?"

"Yes. I do know this. You are a very good man, Matt."

What you mean is that I'm a patsy who's thinking with his you-know-what! he thought, the anger bubbling again – perhaps because there was a kernel of truth there. He managed to keep his voice neutral as they made plans for the following evening.

"I cannot wait to see you again," she said quietly, and he almost believed her. Then he heard the dial tone buzzing in his ear. She had hung up.

He was about to do the same when another thought hit him. Ignoring Grossman's call of, "Trouble in paradise?" he strode into his room and toward the khakis that, for the first time in his life, he had left crumpled on the floor. Fishing through his pockets, he pulled out the piece of paper with Catherine's number in New York, then picked up the phone on his nightstand. He paused then and looked at the clock, wondering if it was too late, and realized he didn't care. She answered on the second ring.

"Hey, Catherine, it's Matt."

"Matt…hi…" she said, sounding almost cautious. "I –"

"I'm sorry about the other day. I didn't hang up on you."

"Um, sure seemed like you did…"

"I mean the phone *was* hung up, but it was a colleague. He's a bit of a jerk."

"Well, clearly he's a jerk if he hung up on me," Catherine said, laughing. The sound was sweet and unaffected – innocent, almost – bringing to Matt's mind their early interactions freshman year.

"Anyway, I didn't get a chance to thank you for the record – I play it all the time."

In truth, Roy Orbison had been collecting dust all summer – between work, his friends and Anna, Matt had not even given music a thought. Though the lie was a small one, it seemed to be a growing trend, and it disturbed him.

"Oh, I'm so glad you like it." She paused. "I just felt like things were a bit awkward the last time we saw each other…you know, with –"

Matt cut her off. "With Michael."

"Yeah, he can be…"

"Possessive," Matt added, again finishing her sentence.

"Possessive…? Do you mean romantically?" She laughed again, but this time there was a slight edge to it Matt didn't understand.

"Michael is a family friend," she said firmly, "And he has more interest in my father's business than in me."

"Really?"

"Yes. His father has worked there since Dad started the company, and Michael has interned there every summer since we were in high school. I think he sees himself running the whole thing one day."

"Well, he certainly sticks to you like glue…"

"I know, and it can be too much sometimes. I know he'd do anything for me, but it's really not for me, you know?"

"Not really…"

"It's the business he really loves, and that doesn't leave room for anything else… just like my father."

She sounded a little sad, almost bitter, and for the first time it occurred to Matt that he had misread the situation – and Catherine – completely. Maybe it was just a distraction from his own problems, but he found himself wanting to know more. Before he could ask, she changed the subject.

"But tell me how you're doing. I can't imagine what it must be like working at the White House right now!"

Her question opened the floodgates – the love Matt had for his job and the people he worked with, as well as the sense of purpose it had given him, even the most mundane tasks. He had always loved the country, but that had been something ingrained in him since childhood by his parents and later in military school. It was the experience of working at the White House, however, that had shown him how truly incredible America was, not only in terms of its citizens but as a force for good in the world. He also told her about the deep sense of disappointment he felt about what was happening with the President – who he still admired in so many ways.

"I know it sounds corny," he said, embarrassed at how he had rambled on.

"Not at all," she said. "This is affecting everyone, but I can't imagine what it must be like to be in the middle of it all!" She paused. "Haven't you had any fun at all this summer?"

Well, there's a loaded question, Matt thought, thankful Catherine wasn't there to see his face reddening. He had been having entirely too much fun, and it had gotten him in a heap of trouble.

CHAPTER TWENTY-TWO

The next morning, Matt was a mass of contradictions as he walked into the Secretariat. He was physically exhausted, thanks to a marathon call with Catherine that ended after one a.m., followed by an hour of lying in bed, eyes staring at the ceiling as he replayed everything they said. Yet he also felt an odd sense of lightness, even exuberance, at being able to voice his feelings after what seemed an eternity of keeping a tight lid on everything. This, he realized, had much to do with Catherine herself.

He'd been surprised when she told him that she was of no particular political persuasion, nor was she very interested in the White House happenings. Yet she had listened with genuine interest to every word he said, which confirmed his initial impressions, nearly a year ago, that she was intelligent, kind, and engaging. Now, without that interloper Michael around, she made him feel heard in a way few people had. Of course, he hadn't shared his biggest burden – the situation with Anna – which, though necessary, made him feel like a total heel.

Today, his first order of business was to apprise Roger of his upcoming meeting with Anna at Ireland's Four Provinces on Connecticut Avenue, halfway between their apartments. He dialed the FBI man's pager, then sat at his desk, debating how much to tell him about the night before. Surely, Roger would not be pleased that Matt had refused a meeting with Anna, but he didn't care. Matt knew he was no espionage expert – hell, he wasn't even sure he believed she was a spy – but he intuitively felt that he needed to maintain the upper hand with her, or at least the illusion of it.

Usually, Roger returned pages immediately, so Matt was surprised when nearly a half-hour went by without a response. He sat at the desk, growing increasingly anxious with each minute that passed. The not-so-subtle clearing of Glen's throat reminded him that it was time for a soda run, so he reluctantly left his post and headed for the basement. From there, the day spun into its usual whirlwind of copy-making and package deliveries both within the White House and to the CIA, which provided temporary respites from thinking about the meeting that was to take place in just a few hours. Every time he returned, he checked with Keith and Glen to see if he had any messages, until finally each man separately took him aside to ask if everything was okay. When the day wound down without a word from Roger, the answer to that question was a resounding no.

With time to kill before he met Anna, Matt decided to walk home, hoping the physical exertion would help him release anxiety. Instead, he found himself trying to strategize. So far, she had not pressed him for sensitive information, but if the urgency in her voice was any indication that was about to change. He didn't know what he could safely tell her, if anything, to keep her interested. If he shared the wrong thing it could hurt the country; if he shared too little she might decide to try to get information elsewhere – maybe from some married guy she could seduce and then blackmail, someone the FBI couldn't track. He briefly toyed with the idea of canceling on her but figured that would only cause other problems.

He entered the apartment sweaty from exertion and found his roommates perched, as per usual, in front of the TV with the news on.

"Boychik," Grossman said, spreading his arms like a waiting grandmother, "Come. Join us."

Matt shook his head as he headed toward his room. "No can do. Having a drink with Anna."

Grossman turned to Walter in mock horror. "Our boychik is forgoing current events for a piece of –"

"Whoa," Matt said, cutting him off. "I'm not foregoing anything. I live this all day, remember? I don't have the luxury of turning off the TV."

"Still," Walter replied, "you are going to miss all the excitement tonight."

"I'm not missing anything. Nixon will resign tomorrow. If you want to know how I know this, watch the press conference with Barry Goldwater. I was standing next to him on the front lawn."

Walter raised an eyebrow at him, possibly indicating that he was impressed. "Oh, by the way, Catherine left you a message. Said she had a great time talking to you last night."

Grossman sat up straighter and, in an excellent imitation of Walter's sage tone, said, "Confucius say, man who juggle two women, loses balls."

Matt tried to shoot him a warning look but burst out laughing instead. Sometimes, Grossman's bullshit was just what he needed to take the edge off.

An hour later, after a long, hot shower and a quick meal of Grossman's leftover Chinese, Matt arrived at Ireland's Four Provinces to find Anna waiting at a table in the corner. Their eyes met, and for a moment everything Roger had said to him fell away, leaving only his feelings for her. Was it love, or just lust? Matt didn't know, but it was all-consuming. Her face, devoid of makeup except for deep pink lipstick, was even more stunning than usual; her hair was pulled back into a demure ponytail that gave her an almost innocent look. Matt approached the table and, with great effort, reminded himself that he knew better.

"Matt. I've missed you," she said, reaching out for his hand.

He intertwined his fingers with hers. "I've missed you too. Things have just been so hectic…"

"I know!" she exclaimed as if she had been waiting for an opening. "I cannot believe everything that is going on with your President Nixon. Incredible!"

"Incredible is certainly one way to describe it," he said soberly, for even after all he had seen he could still barely believe it.

"What is going to happen to him? What will happen to the country if he is no longer President?"

Matt inwardly sighed with relief as he motioned for a waiter. Her questions were more an invitation to join the public discourse than an inducement to give up classified information. He asked the waiter what they had on tap, then ordered a pint of Harp Irish Lager. Anna ordered a Stoli martini, straight up.

Of course, Matt thought, stifling the impulse to burst out in nervous laughter, *What else would a Russian spy order?*

"There was a press conference today on the front lawn," he said, lowering his voice slightly as if to suggest the conference was a guarded secret, "with the Republican leaders of the Congress. They told Nixon he was going to be impeached and if he is, he will be convicted in the Senate. My guess is he will resign tomorrow rather than fight a losing battle."

Anna leaned back a bit in her chair. "I do not understand you Americans. You elect a man to be your President, and then you say he is a pig. What does that say about you?"

Matt drew back in surprise, for he had never heard her be critical of the United States before. Then again, criticizing the country seemed to be the national pastime these days, even among Americans.

He waited for a moment as the waiter set down their drinks, then lifted the pint to his mouth.

"Not bad," he remarked, still pondering her comment. "What it says about us, Anna, is that we choose our President, and if he does something wrong, we can throw him out. He is accountable to us. That is what it means to live in a democracy."

"You were there today?" she said, sidestepping his comment. "You heard these leaders say this?"

"Yes, I heard it right from the horse's mouth," he said. And it was the truth, wasn't it? Even if one of her comrades had caught the press conference – and Matt standing next to Goldwater – they would have no way of knowing he just happened to wander onto the lawn. Indeed, he looked at Anna over the rim of his pint and saw her staring at him with new appreciation.

"I wonder if America will remain in the war without him…?" she mused casually.

Matt offered only a shrug and a small smile, hopefully implying that he had more information he just wasn't willing to impart.

"Well, I'm exhausted," he said, stretching his arms above his head. "I have to go to bed."

To his surprise and relief, she didn't argue with him. "Yes, go get some sleep." Then, looking into his eyes again, she added suggestively, "I want you to be rested the next time we see each other."

He laughed. "Yes, the next time we see each other. I promise."

Roger will be so proud of me, he thought, *if he ever answers his damn page.*

*   *   *

The following morning, Matt arrived at the White House feeling more rested than he had in weeks. Though he still didn't know what he was doing with Anna, he felt he had said just enough to keep her interested until he received more guidance. The stress of the hours leading up to that meeting had drained him, leaving him incapable of ruminating or replaying what he and Anna said. He'd fallen into a deep sleep and woke with the vague sensation of a pleasant dream, though he couldn't recall anything about it.

This time, when he paged Roger, the FBI man called right back, profusely apologizing for dropping the ball and promising not to do it again.

Matt wasn't going to let him off the hook that easily. "If you do, I just won't meet her," he said simply. "I mean it, Roger. If you think I'm doing this alone –"

"I told you, Matt. We have your back. I have your back."

Matt was silent for a beat. "Okay."

After making plans to meet at Whitey's for a happy hour debrief, they ended the call.

Matt sat there for a moment with the phone in his hand, thinking about what Roger had said. Bottom line: he had no choice but to believe he could trust him.

He didn't know if it was the notion of "trust" that triggered the memory of the dream, but his mind was suddenly flooded with images of

Catherine's smiling face. Before he even realized what he was doing, Matt was dialing her number, surprised by how much he was looking forward to hearing her voice again. But it was not to be, because Keith bounced into the room, pressed the button on the phone to end the call, and dropped a file in front of Matt.

"Sorry, Bud," he drawled, "this has to get to Presidential Correspondence, ASAP."

Matt was headed toward the ground floor, where the Presidential Correspondence office was located, when something told him to pass by Nixon's hideaway office on the first floor. The hallway was deserted, but for a lone uniformed Secret Service officer sitting behind a desk by the door of the office. Matt returned his smile and shrugged, thinking his curiosity had been misplaced, and hurriedly continued down the stairs.

The second Matt entered the Presidential Correspondence office, he knew something was afoot. He had been there many times before and the staff was always busy but friendly. This day, however, there was a subtle but noticeable shift in the energy. As they went about their work people were looking about, exchanging glances, like innocent grass-eaters on the Serengeti, sensing the presence of a predator.

Matt made his way to the head clerk and handed her the package.

"Something up?" he asked with a casualness he didn't feel.

She furtively looked around the room at her co-workers, then leaned forward.

"We were just directed by the Chief of Staff's office not to put the President's signature on any more documents," she said, barely moving her lips as though that would prevent others from hearing. She then withdrew and studied him, waiting for a reaction, and was rewarded by Matt's sharp intake of breath.

He looked around and realized that everyone in the room was staring at him. They all knew how to interpret the order. For efficiency's sake, the office regularly used a mechanical autopen that literally replicated the President's signature; thus, if the President's Chief of Staff's office directed his signature be withheld, surely it was because the President was about to *not* be president.

Matt's first reaction was to bolt for the door and call his roommates. But as he left the office, he quickly dismissed the notion – in part because he didn't want to hear their gloating. He would have to deal with that as soon as the news broke, and then likely for the foreseeable future. He decided instead to detour through the West Wing on a little reconnaissance mission to see if he could get any more information.

Matt entered the ground floor of the West Basement, and, finding it quiet, quickly ascended the stairs toward the Oval Office where Sergeant Van had been reassigned to watch the President's office.

"I noted you weren't at your usual haunt by the basement door," Matt said, looking into the empty Oval Office.

"Shit," said the sergeant, glancing into the office, "a light is out."

Matt stretched his head into the Oval, careful not to place his feet inside, knowing Sergeant Van's job was to guard against unauthorized access. Sure enough, there was a dark spot on the far wall above the doors leading to the Rose Garden, where a hidden indirect light had burned out.

"I'll never get GSA to fix it in time. The President is on his way over to meet with the Veep. Shit!"

Seeing he would learn nothing else at the moment – and knowing it was best not to loiter, given the impending arrival of the President and Vice President – Matt wished Sergeant Van luck and returned to the Secretariat. Still bursting to give someone the news, he was frustrated again to find Keith out on an errand and Glen on the phone, his door shut – for all Matt knew, discussing this very news.

A half hour later, with Mat's imagination running wild, he wandered back toward the West Wing. As the elevator opened on the ground floor of the OEOB, a Secret Service agent stood before him and stepped slightly aside for Matt to get out. Directly behind the agent, and no more than a few inches in front of him, was a somber-faced Vice President Gerald Ford, a retinue of agents at his back.

Matt had bumped into The Vice President at the elevator before and Mr. Ford was always quick to offer a friendly greeting. Not this time. Clearly deep in thought, the Vice President didn't acknowledge or even seem to notice him. The Secret Service agents, also stone-faced, followed Ford onto the elevator without offering the usual nod or wink.

As Matt watched the doors close behind them, he could easily surmise what weighed so heavily on the Vice President that morning. He had likely just been told by Nixon of the resignation, that he would be the next President of the United States. It was a job nearly every Veep wanted, but not under such unimaginable circumstances. At the end of the day, Matt was absolutely sure of just one thing: no one in that meeting noticed that one of the ceiling lights was out.

And I thought I had problems, he thought as he continued toward the West Wing. As he crossed West Executive Avenue, he saw the uniformed agent normally positioned in the booth near the entrance to the ramp of the OEOB standing instead in the middle of the street. This, Matt knew, meant the President was about to cross. He halted near the guard, and sure enough saw the West Basement door open, then President Nixon, trailed by five Secret Service agents, dash out and toward the OEOB. As they ascended the outside staircase leading to the President's OEOB office, Nixon appeared to be hunched over, smaller somehow. Near the top of the steps, he stopped, as did the Secret Service agents scattered on the steps behind him, and, for a brief moment, turned toward Pennsylvania Avenue, where news photographers and protestors were circling like wolves around the dying embers of a campfire.

Matt watched as Nixon took it in. He heard the horns honking for his impeachment. He saw the array of cameras waiting for just such a glimpse of him. He saw the protestors' posters and placards. And he heard the voices of angry Americans calling for him to resign. Matt tried to imagine what must be going through Nixon's mind and heart right now and knew he could never come close. All he felt was a knotting in his own stomach as Nixon turned and retreated into the OEOB, looking very much like an animal trapped, caged, and tormented.

Matt passed the guard and saw a tear flowing down the man's face.

"It's sad," Matt said in a moment of solidarity.

The guard opened his mouth a few times, struggling to get the words out. "No matter what you think about the man, it's not easy to watch someone go through this!"

They bobbed their heads in agreement, looking toward Pennsylvania Avenue where the hordes of media and protestors were chanting and honking.

Sad, Matt thought, didn't begin to cover it.

Matt entered the West Basement through the same door President Nixon had just exited. Down the short hall, Sergeant Van was back at his usual post in the lobby, standing, as he always did when the President came through. As Matt approached, he also noticed an elfish smile on the cherubic sergeant's face and could not help but return it. Van leaned toward him, and though no one else was in the lobby he grabbed his arm and whispered in his ear.

"Mrs. Ford is coming through with interior decorators." He then let go of Matt's arm and searched his face for a reaction.

Matt accepted the statement as the sergeant's gallows humor. "You're too much. Sarge!"

Van acknowledged the comment with a curt nod. "Hey, I hear there is going to be a press conference upstairs."

"Thanks."

Matt continued through the West Basement up the stairs toward the Press Office. The briefing room was packed like a sardine can. Not even standing room. Thinking he could gain access from the outside, he whisked through the West Wing lobby and out the front door, past the Marine on guard. When he got to the outer doors of the briefing room, he saw they were wide open with reporters overflowing, some even standing outside. Accepting defeat, he contented himself with joining them.

As they awaited the announcement, something in the corner of his left eye caught his attention. Turning his head toward the White House kitchen area under the North Portico of the Executive Mansion, he saw someone climbing out a window from the far end of the briefing room. Matt laughed when he realized it was White House correspondent Dan Rather. Evidently the room was so crowded it was the only way to get from the back of the room, where CBS had a small recording office, to the front. Rather walked up the driveway, then offered Matt a polite nod as he came to stand next to him.

"Aren't you going to try to get in there?" Matt asked.

Rather shrugged. "No need to. I already know what they're going to say."

"Really?" Matt asked, though it was less out of surprise than a desire to engage the newsman.

"Yeah. At exactly noon, Ron Ziegler will come out and say that the President will address the nation this evening at nine. Then he'll turn and walk away without taking any questions."

"What makes you so sure?"

Rather just smiled as if unwilling to reveal a trade secret; however, Matt was well aware that when the White House wanted to get airtime for the President to make an address, they called the networks to make the arrangements. People in the network then notified staff to keep them apprised. Of course, Rather could have just gotten the story from an inside source, and that may have explained the mysterious smile.

Sure enough, at noon on the dot, Ronald Ziegler, the maligned press secretary who served as a lightning rod for the President, appeared at the podium. His statement was exactly what Rather had predicted, as was his abrupt exit when he finished. The energy, both in the room and outside, was frenzied. Matt knew everyone believed Nixon would resign, yet this was overshadowed by uncertainty of what would happen to the country afterward.

As he left work to meet Roger, Matt pushed the country's crisis to the back of his mind and focused on his own. He knew he had gotten off easy with Anna last night, and that this would likely not happen again.

Roger was seated at his customary booth in the rear, a pitcher of beer and two glasses, one half-full, in front of him.

"Little thirsty, Roger?"

Roger grunted. "Happy hour started at four-thirty, so why not?" He poured a beer for Matt and pushed it to the other side of the table. "Tons of stuff happening at the big house."

"Crazy times," Matt said, shaking his head. "He'll resign tonight."

"You sure 'bout that?"

Matt told him what he had heard at the Presidential Correspondence Office.

"Shit! It is really happening then," Roger said, taking a sip of beer.

"I thought about calling you after that," Matt said, "I also thought about calling Anna… but I already gave her the 'big scoop' last night."

Roger raised an eyebrow at him. "Do tell."

Matt recounted his conversation with Anna about the three lawmakers – how he was with them on the front lawn, and heard their prognosis that Nixon had no options.

"I told her he would quit, and it looks like that is happening tonight!"

Roger leaned back in his chair and eyed Matt with new appreciation. "Brilliant. You gave her what seemed like inside information. And the fact that you were there is fantastic, shows you have access." He sighed contentedly.

"But she already thought I had access," Matt pointed out, "Otherwise she wouldn't have approached me."

"True, but you also 'predicted' the resignation. Definitely a step in the right direction."

Roger laughed when Matt told how Anna had called Americans pigs. "Fucking commies! They wouldn't even know what to do with democracy. But we'll do what we can to teach them, right?"

"Heck, yeah," Matt said with a confidence he didn't feel as he raised his glass to his lips.

"You said I took *a step* in the right direction."

"Yeah…"

"So, what's the next step?"

"You know what it is, Matt." Roger leaned forward. "We need Anna's book."

"And how am I supposed to get that?"

"We had this conversation," Roger said, his eyes suddenly steely. "You get it however you get it."

Matt met his stare. "Yes, and you are going to have to hold up your end too."

"What the hell does that mean?"

"It means I got lucky last night…"

Roger was all smiles again. "Now we're getting to the good stuff…"

"Screw you, Roger," Matt snapped, surprising himself as much as the agent. "I mean I got lucky with the press conference. She's going to ask for more information, and if you want to keep this thing going you need to give me something to pass on to her."

Just then, the waitress appeared at the table with the check. Matt sat there, his frustration mounting as he waited for her to leave so they could resume the conversation. Instead, as she turned to leave, Roger cried out, "Hey! These are regular prices. I should get the happy hour price."

"You ordered before happy hour," the waitress replied.

"No, no, no," Roger said, pointing at his watch for emphasis. "I got here at four-thirty."

She looked at him stony-faced. "You have to order *after* four-thirty to get the happy hour prices."

"You can't be serious! It was four-thirty. I get the happy hour price. If you can't make that happen then go get your manager."

She paused for a moment as if considering it, then decided it wasn't worth the trouble. "I'll adjust the bill, this time. Next time, you pay full price."

Roger glared at her as she walked away in a huff. "Geez, what a pill that woman is. I guess you have to order happy hour beer at four thirty-one. From now on, that's what I'm calling this place: four thirty-one."

He pulled out some money and placed it on the table.

"Now that that is settled," Matt said, his jaw clenched, "Can we get back to our conversation? What about the information for Anna?"

For the second time that night Roger looked at him with new respect. "You're right. I will get on that, and you, my friend, will get back on Wonder Woman if that's what it takes to get the book."

* * *

That night at nine p.m., the world watched as Richard Nixon, thirty-fifth President of the United States, announced his resignation. Matt, who sat glued to the television with his roommates, could almost feel the collective sigh of relief rippling throughout the nation. There were those who hated Nixon and were glad to see him go. There were those who hated the media, blamed it for the whole Watergate mess, and were angry about Nixon's departure. And there were those who were simply glad to see the Watergate nightmare that had polarized the country come to an end.

Matt belonged in the final camp. He didn't hate Nixon; in fact, he felt sympathy for the man. He also didn't hate the media, he believed they brought wrongdoing to the light of day. What saddened him most was the reason Nixon gave for resigning: he no longer enjoyed the support of Congress. It was the same sentiment expressed by Congressman Rhodes on the front lawn of the White House. Impeachment was a forgone conclusion, and Nixon's resignation simply a political decision between winning and losing. If there was any higher principle, it was that he was going to spare himself, and the country, the pain of impeachment. However, to Matt and many others, that left an open wound because there was no closure on the violations of law, integrity, and trust that comprised Watergate.

The following morning there was a farewell ceremony where, for one last time, Nixon spoke as president. Hundreds of staffers crowded the White House East Room, together with reporters covering it for print and on live television. There was no way Matt was missing this, and after convincing Glen to forgo his ten a.m. Pepsi, he rushed out of the Secretariat, groaning when he saw Jensen striding purposely toward him.

"I'm in a hurry," he said without slowing down. "Glen said I could go to the Farewell."

"Cool," Jensen replied, his tone uncharacteristically friendly. He turned and kept up with Matt as he moved down the hall. "I just wanted to tell you that I spoke to Roger this morning. He says you are doing a great job with our 'little operation.' Says you are a natural." He then stunned Matt by patting him on the shoulder. "Keep up the good work. You are making us all look good."

Matt paused for a moment. "Great," he said evenly. "I mean, that's the goal, right? To make all of us look good?"

He then rushed down the hall, leaving a slightly stupefied Jensen in his wake.

Minutes later, Matt ascended the marble staircase from the basement to the first floor of the Executive Mansion. When he reached the top, he found a strange confluence of emotion, sight, and sound. The Marine Corps brass band was playing music as though it was a celebration, but the faces of the assembling staffers bore a different testimony. Some were able to mask their feelings with carefully cultivated blank stares, while others were openly sullen.

Never forget this moment, Matt told himself, though he knew such reminders were unnecessary. Most of his White House experiences were indelibly imprinted on his brain, but none so much as this.

He continued to take mental snapshots as he entered the East Room, where presidents entertained royal families and Abraham Lincoln and John F. Kennedy had lain in state, and edged as close as possible to the podium. The first few front rows were reserved for the "A" list – soon-to-be President Ford and Mrs. Ford, Henry Kissinger, and the entire cabinet – and they all stared ahead, careful to show no sign of uncertainty or fear as the band played cheerfully, and painfully, on.

Finally, the music stopped – a sign that the President was arriving. But when Nixon entered the room, there was no traditional fanfare, no ruffles and flourishes, no Hail to the Chief, no baritone voice announcing, "Ladies and Gentlemen, The President of the United States of America." Instead, Richard Nixon silently entered the room with his family. When he reached the podium, some people clapped, while others, including Matt, sat or stood quietly, unsure of the proper etiquette for a presidential resignation.

Nixon began to speak, his voice cracking as he thanked the staff for all their assistance over the years. He then went on to talk about his last night in the White House. He had consoled himself with the writings of Theodore Roosevelt, or "TR," as he affectionately referred to him, specifically an exposition about whether one wins or fails is not important. "In the end," Nixon said, quoting the twenty-sixth president, "the victory goes to the one who is in the arena, trying." Nixon was obviously trying to convey that although he had lost his political fight and was being forced out of the White House, he had never, until now, stopped trying.

Then, without warning, the speech took a sad, if not tragic, turn as Nixon rambled aimlessly back to his childhood. He spoke about his mother, whom he praised as a saint, oblivious that the atmosphere in the room had shifted to the morose. Nixon was an accomplished speaker, known for his lawyer's precision, always moving toward a well-reasoned point. This morning, however, as tears filled his eyes and he wiped his runny nose, the analytical cogence had been replaced with frailty and remorse. It was like watching a ship slowly sink. Some people even began to sob.

Please leave, Matt thought, a sentiment no doubt shared by everyone in the room.

Finally, he left his past behind and moved to what Matt hoped was the closing.

"Always remember, others may hate you. But those who hate you don't win unless you hate them. And then you destroy yourself."

It was the closest thing to accountability he had expressed since the whole fiasco began. His White House was hated by people who opposed its policies. The White House also had a list of enemies. Now, he was acknowledging that the hatred he permitted to fester was what brought about his demise. He paused for a beat, then, blessedly, bid the country, "Au revoir."

The moment Nixon finished speaking, Matt rushed out of the room and down the grand stairs to the ground floor. Heading toward the Diplomatic Reception Room, he came face to face with a grim foursome of the President, First Lady, Vice President Ford, and Mrs. Ford. Matt scooted quickly in front of them, through the ornate and bright oval-shaped Diplomatic Reception Room and out the door onto the South Grounds where Marine One, the President's helicopter, awaited. Vice President and Mrs. Ford escorted the Nixons down a red carpet to the waiting helicopter. A few hours later, Gerald Ford took the oath of office in the White House, and Nixon's presidency officially ended on Air Force One somewhere over the Mid-west while en route to his home in California.

Matt's final "snapshot" of the morning was when they turned and waved goodbye, and slowly climbed onboard. He once again felt that rush of desire to spread the news, but this time it wasn't Roger's or his roommates' or even Anna's face that flashed through his mind. It was Catherine's.

CHAPTER TWENTY-THREE

For the first time in his life, Matt couldn't wait for summer to end. Student life, which a few months earlier felt like a distraction from the excitement of the White House, now beckoned for its normalcy. The slow burn of Watergate during his freshman year and its more recent explosion had left him chronically sleep-deprived and hypervigilant, always waiting for the other shoe to drop. He worked more twelve-hour days than he could count, then fell into bed exhausted but too wound up to close his eyes. Nixon's departure had brought no respite either. As the country turned its attention to who President Ford would choose as Veep, White House staff were working overtime on a transition that was not exactly unexpected but certainly unusual. When he wasn't overwhelmed with work, Matt's brain was on overdrive about the situation with Anna – specifically, how to get the book of names, and God knew what else, that she carried in her purse.

Matt had always been an action-oriented person, not really given to daydreaming. Now he found himself slipping into vivid scenes in which he was enjoying outings with friends or just relaxing with a book. Most often, though, he imagined spending time with Catherine, which simultaneously surprised, confused, and excited him. Since that first conversation lasting long into the night, they had spoken several times a week. He would call her on slow mornings at the White House, she would call him to say goodnight, and though these chats sometimes only lasted a few minutes he deeply enjoyed and looked forward to them.

As mid-August approached, he tried to look past this physical and emotional limbo and focus on what lay ahead. In addition to the start of classes, the fraternity was returning, and with big plans – the rush for new pledges, with its endless series of parties designed to entice new students and endear the fraternity to the potential candidates. Against his better judgment, and after several phone calls from Tex, Matt had eventually agreed to be rush chairman. Part of him felt like a wimp for not standing up to his frat brother, while another part wanted to embrace the role – and the life of a normal college student that he felt had been stolen from him. And what about Catherine, who was also soon to come back to D.C.? Where did she fit into that life? Did she see him as just a friend, or potentially something more? How did he see her? He filed these questions in the back of his mind, figuring he'd circle back to them when he didn't have other pressing matters, like international espionage, on his plate.

*   *   *

One Friday a couple of weeks after Nixon's resignation, Matt returned with Glen's afternoon Pepsi to find Keith sitting at his desk with the phone in his hand.

"One moment, please," he said, then placed the call on hold and looked up at Matt. "Bud, you got a phone call on line two."

"Thanks," Matt said, a sinking feeling in his gut. He had, as usual, been burning the candle at both ends and was looking forward to a rare night out with his roommates, but something was telling him that was about to change. He ducked into Glen's office to deliver the Pepsi, then picked up the phone.

"Hello, Matt here."

"Matt, I am so glad to catch you," Anna said in that abrupt, almost breathy tone she used when she was about to ask him for something.

Matt inwardly groaned. He'd managed to avoid seeing her since the resignation, telling her that with all the chaos at the White House it was not possible for him to get away. He had been giving Roger the same excuse, whenever the FBI man questioned him about what he was planning to do to get the book.

"Hey, Anna, I'm really busy right now," he began, drawing a raised eyebrow from Keith, as it had been an unusually slow afternoon.

"I am having some friends over to my apartment tonight and really want you to come."

Shit, shit, shit.

"That sounds like fun, but I have plans with Walter and Grossman tonight."

"Oh, please. It would be so fun to have you meet my friends." She paused, then added throatily. "I miss you, Matt. We have not been together in so long."

Matt gulped. He knew what she meant by "together," and, to his horror, he realized that beneath all the avoidance and strategizing, he missed her too. It was all the more reason to stay away. And what about these friends she spoke of? Were they Russian friends? Fellow spies? Would he be walking into a dangerous situation? What if this was his chance to get some valuable information for Roger? The man would blow his stack if Matt passed on such an opportunity.

"Okay, Anna," he said finally, "I will come for a while and then meet my roommates."

"We will see about that," she said, the confident laugh returning. Then the phone went dead.

Roger returned his page almost before Matt put the phone down.

"Anna wants me to come to a party tonight at her apartment. She says she wants me to meet her 'friends.' She's never mentioned friends before. What the hell, Roger?"

"Just calm down, Matt, and let's take a look at this. It might be what we've been waiting for."

"I thought you would say something like that…"

"It might be a chance to get the book…" Roger added thoughtfully.

"What?! How am I supposed to do that with a bunch of Ruskies hanging around?"

Roger laughed. "Don't get ahead of yourself, kid. She's in school, right? For all you know, they are people she knows from class."

Matt inhaled as Roger's logic hit home. "Yes, yes, that's true."

"And you haven't seen her in a while, right? She's probably just trying to re-establish contact."

"Oh, she's trying to 're-establish contact,' alright…"

Roger laughed again, this time with that slightly sleazy tone Matt hated, then abruptly switched gears as he formulated a plan.

"I have to go to my kid's soccer game, but that will be done by early evening. I'll run over and stake out Wonder Woman's apartment building. I'll park about one block going north on Connecticut Ave., toward Maryland. When you leave and I see you drive past me, I'll let you pass to make sure no one is following you. Then I'll follow you for a while to make absolutely sure you are not being followed. When I flash my lights, make the first right turn. Follow that street 'til I flash my lights again, so I can verify one last time you are not being followed. Then you make the next right turn and park. We'll talk in your car."

"That is a pretty impressive plan, Roger," Matt said sarcastically, "but what am I supposed to do when I'm in there?"

"You'll be fine. Just try to relax and remember the names of anyone you meet." He paused, and became more serious. "Do what you can to see where she keeps the book, but don't take any stupid risks, okay?"

"You don't have to tell me twice! Really!"

Roger continued his pep talk for a few more minutes, then reiterated the arrangements for their post-party meeting.

A second after Matt hung up, Keith yelled from the outer office.

"Hey, Bud. Sounded like that woman who called for you was Russian!" He chuckled. "Anything you want to tell us?"

Matt's head jerked up in surprise. For all the times Anna had called him at work, this was the first time Keith answered.

"She did, didn't she? She works in the AU housing office. They messed up my room assignment for this year."

His heart racing, he slowly got up and stepped out into the outer office. Fortunately, Keith had spilled what was probably his twenty-fifth coffee of the day and was preoccupied. Continuing past him, Matt walked down the hall intending only to get some air...until his gaze landed on Jensen's office door.

When he saw Matt's face, Jensen drew back in surprise. "You look like hell. What happened?"

Matt took a seat across from him, then told him about Keith's comment. He held himself back from revealing Anna's invitation or the plan with Roger, for though he desperately wanted support he doubted he would get that from Jensen.

"What if Keith suspects me of colluding with the enemy?" he rasped. "And he yelled it so loud, Glen definitely heard!"

Jensen laughed. "Colluding with the enemy? You've been watching too many spy movies. As far as I know, no laws have been enacted against speaking to a Russian. Let it go, and if Keith says anything else, let me know."

Thanking him, Matt left the office, relieved that, at least for the moment, he didn't have to worry about being accused of treason. He could only pray the "party" at Anna's went as smoothly.

*　　*　　*

Matt arrived at Anna's apartment shortly after eight, but he felt like it was closer to midnight. Exhausted from another long workday and the stress of the unknown, his body had the strange sensation of being both drained and animated by a nervous energy. He took a deep breath, trying to release the tension in his shoulders, then placed a smile on his face and knocked on the door. To his surprise, it was answered not by Anna, but a stocky, rather unattractive woman in a frumpy outfit. She looked him up and down as if assessing his worthiness to enter, and the jury definitely seemed to be out.

"Hi, um, I am looking for Anna...? I am Matt."

The woman's eyes flickered with recognition at the name. Dark and long-lashed, they were definitely her most attractive feature. Her full face was framed with sideburns, her lips were thin and drawn permanently into a tight line.

"Yes, Matt. I am Galina. I am Anna's roommate."

Her accent was much thicker than Anna's, and Matt had the distinct feeling that any further conversation would require the aid of an interpreter. Fortunately, Anna saw him and rushed to the door.

"Matt! I am so glad you're here," she said, planting a soft kiss on his cheek. She smelled of a new fragrance that somehow reminded him of woods near his home in Michigan – like earth and flowers and sunlight. "Come, meet my friends."

It was a small gathering. Everyone was Russian and, with the exception of Anna and Galina, all of them were men. They were also much older. Anna walked him 'round to introduce him, and he tried to look casually friendly as he shook hands with Gleb, Yefim, Sergei, Pavel, and Vadim. Each was wearing a suit and tie. One of them had a stench of cheap cologne, which tainted them all. Except for Vadim, their accents were heavy.

Gleb, Yefim, Sergei, Pavel, and Vadim, he repeated to himself. *Gleb, Yefim, Sergei, Pavel, and Vadim.*

He tried to keep the names straight as they asked him questions about school and life in America. They seemed nice enough, but Matt couldn't shake the thought that he had stepped into some sort of ambush. Sure, they could hear his pounding heart and see the sheen of sweat on his upper lip, he slipped off as soon as he could to the bathroom to regroup.

"Gleb, Yefim, Sergei, Pavel, and Vadim," he whispered as he splashed water on his face. He had an excellent memory, but given his nervousness he feared he couldn't rely on it. If only he had a pen and paper! Maybe, he thought, as he dried his face and hands on a small towel, he could improvise. Sure enough, in the medicine cabinet he found an eyeliner pencil.

He tried writing the names on a piece of toilet paper, but when that proved to be too thin, he pulled a five-dollar bill from his pocket. Quite pleased with his Boy Scout-like resourcefulness, he scribbled names on the edges of the bill then returned it to his wallet and went back to the living room.

Anna immediately approached him. "You were gone so long we were about to send search party for you."

"Oh, I," Matt began nervously, then saw she was smiling. "Ha, ha."

"Come." Threading her arm through his, she led Matt through a set of sliding glass doors onto a balcony, where a beer keg was sitting in a large ice bucket. There was a stack of red plastic glasses, the kind found at every college party, on a small table.

"I'm so happy you came. I hope more of my friends show up. I didn't mean for this to be just guys."

Matt smiled. "You and Galina make up for the others."

She squeezed his arm, then slipped free to pour two beers and handed one to him. Matt raised his cup and said, "To Anna and Galina."

Anna was leaning in to kiss him when the sliding door opened and Vadim stepped onto the balcony. He poured a beer for himself, lit up a cigarette, and exhaled contently.

"Ugh," Anna exclaimed, waving away the cloud of smoke. "Why do you guys have to smoke?" Then, telling Matt she would return, she went back into the apartment, leaving Matt with Vadim. Matt looked over to see the Russian studying him.

"So, Anna tells me you work in the White House…" His English was clipped and near perfect, revealing an excellent education. He was also more polished and social than the other men; he had an air of status.

"I am very interested in what is happening there. So unusual for a leader to give up his power. And now you have a new president. Do you know Mr. President Ford?"

"Not personally, but we are both from Michigan," Matt said, as if that factoid would somehow cement him as an insider. "I see him all the time."

"What an honor for such a young man to work right in the White House. You must be very smart! In our country, to be that close to the leader, one needs much experience and education!"

Matt thought for a moment. "This is America. You can do anything as long as you work hard." His tone held a slight challenge, and he was rewarded with the slightest flash across Vadim's face.

Just then, the sliding door was thrown open. Galina waved her arms. "Must keep door open. Too much smoke here." She retreated back inside.

Vadim shook his head. "Music too loud," he exclaimed, shutting the door and dismissing Galina's request.

"Tell me, Matt," he continued, "do you know Dr. Henry Kissinger?"

"I see him coming and going, but I do not know him personally."

"Anna told me you knew Mr. Nixon was going to resign before he did. How did you know this?" He exhaled without bothering to tilt or turn his head, sending a cloud of smoke toward Matt's face.

Matt shrugged. "I had a heads up."

"And how did you get this, as you say, 'heads up'?"

Matt decided again to taunt Vadim. "Oh, I couldn't say. You know, national security."

Vadim came closer.

"You must know a lot of things, then?"

Matt smiled. "I get around."

Again, the sliding door opened. Again, Galina waved her arms. And again, she said, "Must keep door open. Too much smoke." She said it as though she had not made the request before. Then she turned and disappeared.

Vadim pulled on his cigarette, turned, and while he was closing the door for the second time, exhaled into the room.

"Tell me, Matt, you are student, right? How can you work in the White House while you are in school?"

Matt thought a moment. "I work full time in the summer, up to eighteen hours a day. During Watergate, I had to help the President's lawyers and I worked twenty-four hours in one day. But during the school year, I will only work three mornings a week and Saturdays."

Vadim was processing this with a serious look. "And do they pay you?"

"Hell, yes!" Matt exclaimed. "I wouldn't do it for free. You know what they say, 'Money is good. More is better!'"

Vadim laughed, put his arm on Matt's shoulder, "A true capitalist!"

For the third time, Galina opened the sliding door and waved her hands. "Must keep door open," she said without exhibiting the least frustration. "Too much smoke."

For the third time, Vadim closed the door, then poured another beer.

Matt suppressed a laugh at the exchange between Vadim and Galina. *If these are the best of the best the other side has, I think we will win the Cold War.* He got the impression Galina was a prop, used to make Anna's life as a foreign student appear legitimate. He idly wondered what Galina had seen and heard in the apartment, and what would happen if she was ever no longer needed "on set."

Damn, I have read too many spy novels.

He leaned over the balcony, looking down onto Connecticut Avenue, wondering if Roger was in position yet.

Vadim appeared at his elbow, startling him. He had two fresh beers in his hands. Matt accepted one with thanks, then said, "Hey, can you chug?" hoping to hide his discomfort.

It worked.

"Chug, ya?" Vadim said, letting go a deep laugh.

They raised their red plastic glasses and went for it. It was no contest. Matt downed his fast enough to put his cup down on the balcony railing before Vadim finished his. The Russian looked at the competition's glass on the railing, raised his, and shouted, "To the chugger!"

Just then Anna stepped back onto the balcony, walked over to Matt and put her arm on his shoulder. "Vadim, Matt has to leave early. He has plans tonight."

Vadim drew back. "What plans could possibly take you away from our Annushka?"

Matt met Vadim's eyes. "Nothing that exciting. But I gave my word."

Vadim nodded and reached for Matt's hand. "I would like to meet with you, Matt. Maybe we can have lunch or dinner sometime."

"That would be fun! I'll give you a chance to win back your honor."

Vadim was pleased. Even though Anna was standing right there he said, "I will ask Anna to arrange."

"Before you go, Matt, I have something for you."

She escorted him down a hall to her room at the rear of the apartment, then told him to wait before disappearing into a little closet. Matt glanced around the room, and noting the window was open, stepped over to look down on Connecticut Avenue to see if he could spot Roger. Then, through the corner of his eye, he saw Anna's purse on her dresser and contemplated checking to see if the book was inside. It was a heart-thumping temptation. The door was ajar, and he could hear voices in the other room and see them moving about. What if one of them caught sight of him rifling through her purse? What if Anna did? Either way, he'd be majorly screwed. He stared at the purse, body frozen, mind racing.

Suddenly, he heard the bedroom door close. Matt turned to see Anna standing before him, completely naked and looking more glorious than ever. His eyes drank her in for a moment, even as his mind told him to flee, but there was no time. She pounced on him like a wild animal, wrapping her legs around his waist, arms surrounding his shoulders, pressing her breasts into his chest. Her hands grabbed his head and her mouth enveloped his. His heart pounded. Every instinct told him to escape. But her hold was tight. Escaping would have required physical force. He thought about the people in the other room. He thought about the purse. He thought about his own emotions, which in the moment were very much conflicted. And then he didn't think at all. Her thighs were clamped around his waist so tightly it produced heat. The taste of her moist mouth was intoxicating. He felt like a zebra being suffocated by a lion. One tranquilizing bite of the lion's jaw and the conquered animal becomes still. Anna was doing her part in the Cold War, and Matt did his. They fell to the bed. Anna reached down beside it to a prepositioned glass of ice, grabbed a cube and thrust it under his groin. It was shocking. The cold ice caused his body to immediately constrict, thoroughly enhancing the moment. It was like the Fourth of July, with rockets' red glare bursting in his brain. After several minutes he rolled on his back, dazed and breathless. Nothing he'd read in any le Carré novel prepared him for this.

"That was amazing. Where did you learn to do that ice trick, at some communist sex camp?"

Anna laughed as she got on top, pinned his arms with her hands and dangled her breasts in his face. "No. Communists are not that imaginative! I read it in the *Penthouse Forum*."

"Really? You read *Penthouse*, do you?"

She laughed. "I found it in the lobby."

Anna rolled on her side, casually laying her head on her arm, and watched Matt get dressed. For what seemed like a long time, they said nothing. In another time and place, he could easily have envisioned a lifetime of those moments with her.

"Anna, why are you interested in me?"

She didn't point out that he had asked the question before. She simply nodded her head toward the door. "They are what I have to work with here. I have more in common with you."

"Speaking of them, what should we say when I leave?"

"Just tell them we were looking at my pictures from home."

Matt left the room and received a very unapproving glare from Galina. He shook hands with the men and got out as quickly as he could. Though he had done nothing to arouse any suspicion, he couldn't help but feel like he escaped with his life.

As he headed for his car, Matt was careful not to look around for Roger in case he was being observed. Once inside, he put his hands on the steering wheel, gripping it until his knuckles went white.

"What the hell am I doing?" he asked himself, then pulled into traffic.

About five minutes later, the car behind him flashed its headlights. Following Roger's instructions, Matt made the next right turn. He drove another five minutes until the next signal was given. Again, he made an immediate right turn and pulled into the first parking spot he came across. The car behind him pulled up next to him. Roger, dressed in a ball cap, jeans, tennis shoes and a red jersey, got out of the passenger side and slid into the passenger side of Matt's car. The other car proceeded for a block, parked, and turned off its lights.

"Nice outfit," Matt said, then gestured toward the car. "Who is that?"

"My back-up," Roger said, adjusting the cap. "This shit takes teamwork."

"Should we wait for him?"

"Nope, he is on watch so we can relax." He turned and looked at Matt. "And how is Wonder Woman?"

"She lived up to your description of her. I'll tell you, Roger, if this is what war is like, no one will die."

Roger narrowed his eyes. "What? Weren't there other people there?"

Matt nodded. "There were. We went into her room." Then, as Roger burst out laughing, he added, "I had no choice. She is not human. She is fast and strong! And she does something with an ice cube –" Matt cut himself off when he saw Roger's eyes widen.

"Fuckin' A!" Roger exclaimed. "She is Wonder Woman! Fuckin' A."

The mood became more serious as Matt gave him a minute-by-minute recap of the evening, starting with his introduction to Galina.

"No idea who she is," Roger said, then started laughing again as Matt showed him the names he wrote around the edges of the bill with the eyeliner pencil. "Impressive! I'm going to have to remember that one for my memoirs."

Roger studied the bill. "I don't know about Galina, but the rest of these guys are part of the intel team headed by Vadim. We've been onto him for a while. It was him and Pavel who were tailing you at the beginning of this thing." Roger looked out the side window for a moment, then faced Matt. "It is not too subtle of them to have you over and meet the team. Usually, they do something like that in a friendlier, open setting, so as to not create suspicion. They are moving unusually fast here, a real odd departure from their normal protocol. I'm having a hard time figuring out what it means. Maybe it was some kind of test to see if she could get you to show."

Matt shrugged his shoulders.

"It might be good. She gave no warning of the invite. If you stalled, or said no, they might figure you need to get approval to attend. The fact that you showed up tonight might be construed as you truly acting on your own. Maybe they are moving fast to compromise you."

"Roger, it's your job to figure out what all this means. I am just good-time Matt, the sex toy." Then he told Roger about Vadim on the balcony and the sliding glass doors.

"Dumb shits!" Roger said, with an air of superiority. "Really sloppy tradecraft!"

Matt went on to relay Vadim's questions. Roger was impressed. "I love how you positioned yourself, not the most important guy in the White House, but you are there and have access to people and events. That is exactly what they want. They want a good plant, not too high up but someone who has access."

Finally, Matt told Roger about seeing Anna's purse and debating whether to open it to get a glimpse of the book.

"This is such a departure from what I have seen in the past," Roger said again, "She disappears with you and has sex with the rest of her colleagues outside. They certainly knew what was up. I gotta think about what this one means."

Matt grimaced. "I'll tell you what it means, Roger. It means I am in this thing deeper than I want." Then his voice got low. "You know, though, she seems vulnerable. I bet in a different place and time, she –"

Roger stuck his finger in Matt's chest and thumped it. "Don't even think this is anything but a ruse. She is doing her job and she will cut your throat if they tell her to." He thought for a second. "It is confusing. Maybe she messed up, went too fast the first night, and feels compelled to continue the ploy pretending she has an interest in you. But maybe she is also telling us something. Maybe she is looking for a way out. I like the fact that she said she has more in common with you. We'll have to think about that and see what happens." He paused again. "First, though, we have to figure out how to get our hands on that book."

CHAPTER TWENTY-FOUR

On Friday, precisely at noon, Matt was about to dig into his lunch when Jensen called and stiffly ordered him to appear. As he replaced the phone, Matt's hunger pangs were immediately replaced with a wave of nausea. A week had passed since the party at Anna's and the conversation with Roger. Assuming that's what Jensen wanted to talk about, he placed his burger back in its container and with great effort forced himself to head to Jensen's office, when all he wanted to do was run the other way.

His worst fears seemed confirmed when he walked in and saw Roger also there waiting for him. Jensen, who was on an unrelated phone call, waved him in then returned his attention to a stack of paperwork on his desk. Matt and Roger locked eyes, then Roger jerked his head toward Jensen and mouthed the word "asshole."

Matt covered up his laugh with a cough, earning an annoyed glance from Jensen that seemed to confirm that he was, indeed, an asshole.

His business concluded; Jensen hung up the phone then neatly folded his hands on his desk.

"Good afternoon, gentlemen," he said, "thank you for coming here so promptly."

"Interrupted my lunch," Roger grunted.

Matt nodded, thinking longingly of the burger going cold on his desk.

Ignoring their reaction, Jensen said, "It's been a while since we've spoken and I thought it was time to review the status of Matt's mission."

Here we go, Matt thought, his stomach tightening. *This is when they start talking about the book.*

Instead, Roger offered him a smug smile. "I've already 'reviewed the status,' as you say, with some senior counterintelligence people at the Bureau and the Agency, and they agree that it's going quite well. What, specifically, would you like to know?"

Matt watched as Jensen attempted to cover his annoyance behind a blank stare and realized the true purpose of the meeting: a good, old-fashioned pissing contest. He eyed the opponents, sizing them up. Jensen, as usual, was nattily dressed in an expensive tailored suit with matching tie and hanky neatly formed in his jacket pocket. His shoes looked like finely made Italian leather that were buffed to a spit shine. He had coiffed hair that touched his ears and a smattering of dark hair on his upper lip – an attempt to grow a moustache that, instead of the desired gravitas, gave him the appearance of an overgrown adolescent.

In sharp contrast, Roger's suit was wrinkled and his shoes, Florsheim wingtips, were in need of a polish. Yet he exuded a quiet confidence that came, not just with age, but experience. Matt didn't know the extent of what Roger had seen as an FBI agent, but he sensed that if he ever went to war Roger would be the one he'd rather be in the foxhole with.

"What I would like to know," Jensen said stiffly, "Is the plan moving forward."

"We – the Bureau, that is – believe this has a lot of potential and want to keep it going." He paused for a moment, then decided to throw Jensen a bone. "Look, I know right now the situation seems vague. We really do not know what these people are up to – in other words, whether this is a real attempt to recruit Matt or just a ruse to distract us from something more sinister somewhere else. In the meantime, we're going to keep them busy by feeding them disinformation and see where the shit comes out. I'll be working that part with the intel community. In the meantime, we're also trying to learn as much as we can about Anna. I'll keep you in the dark, Matt, to avoid any inadvertent slip of the tongue, but if there is anything that needs to be shared, I will do that."

Matt nodded, then glanced at Jensen, who seemed to accept that explanation for the time being, and waited for Roger to talk about the book. Instead, he turned and gave Matt a pointed look. "I know you have real concerns with the personal aspects of the relationship, but we need your continued support. It is important."

Matt squirmed in this chair. This thing had spiraled out of control and he couldn't fathom how it was going to end up. After all this time, the only "plan" was for him to use Anna and allow her to use him. That meant continuing the sexual relationship – a big problem for him, and clearly not for anyone else.

"One question, Roger. How long do you think this thing will last?"

He shrugged. "Don't know. Sometimes they fizzle. Sometimes they go on for years."

"Years!" Matt yelled, shifting forward in his chair as if to launch himself out of it. "There is no way I –"

Realizing his mistake, Roger cut him off. "Whoa, whoa, whoa. There is no reason to think that will be the case here, and we will do everything to ensure that it doesn't." He attempted a smile. "So calm down, okay?"

Matt nodded, but Roger's words had rocked him; his attempt to walk it back, woefully inadequate. Matt didn't believe the FBI was going to ensure anything except a successful mission, whether that took ten weeks, ten months, or ten years. The thing was, he would have wholeheartedly agreed with them, if not for the fact that it was his own future on the line.

Then, after reminding them for the umpteenth time that the mission was classified SECRET/NOFORN – strictly "Need to know" – Roger stood to signify this meeting was over.

"You need to eat something, kid," he joked as Matt followed him out of Jensen's office, "You're as pale as a ghost."

Matt hadn't been in a fistfight since he defended a friend against the playground bully in the sixth grade, but in that moment he felt an almost overwhelming urge to connect his fist with Roger's jaw. Instead, he took a deep breath and allowed common sense to prevail.

"Why didn't you tell Jensen about the book?" he said once they were out of earshot.

Roger chuckled. "I said this was need-to-know, right? Well, right now that doesn't apply to Jensen."

"Ahh, the pissing contest," Matt said, slightly alarmed by the bitterness in his voice.

"Maybe," Roger admitted, "But mostly I was trying to keep him off your back – at least until we have a solid plan."

Matt looked at him, thinking maybe he had judged Roger too harshly.

The FBI man's lips twitched slightly. "In the meantime, you just keep being the irresistible boy toy."

*   *   *

Instead of returning to the Secretariat, Matt headed to Lafayette Park, where he had found some measure of solace during the Watergate all-nighter. Now, as he sat down on a bench and closed his eyes, he hoped the beautiful early September afternoon would have the same effect. But try as he might to focus on the sunlight and soft breeze on his skin, his mind raced with questions for which he had no answers. How far would this mission go? Could they force him, possibly for years, to continue a physical relationship with Anna? What if he wanted to be with someone else? Have a different career? Would his life ever be his own? He felt helpless, as though he was on a train racing toward an unknown destination that promised nothing but pain and loneliness. And even if he could, would he, in good conscience, walk away from something so important to the country? Patriotism, at least in his book, meant doing not just what was convenient or brought him accolades, but doing whatever was required.

With a shake of his head, he dismissed his soul-searching as a waste of time and mental energy, both of which he had precious little. There were too many unknown variables for him to anticipate how he would react, and to pretend otherwise was to create the illusion of control – again, something he was lacking. For the better part of a year he'd been fumbling in the darkness and didn't see that changing anytime soon.

He opened his eyes and stared across the street at the White House. There were some days he still couldn't believe he worked there. He couldn't believe he had witnessed the unfolding of the historic events that summer. He couldn't believe he was, along with Roger and Jensen, part of a wall protecting that building and everything it represented. He realized there was only one way to approach things: wake up in the morning, get out of bed, and do what had to be done.

Like so many times before, the memory of the first solo flight came to the forefront of his mind. Taking a deep breath, he imagined himself back in that little plane, how he felt the fear creeping through his limbs, threatening to paralyze him completely, and how he conquered it. That had truly been the victory, much more so than his technical skills in the cockpit.

He then remembered what the White House guard said on the night of the Watergate all-nighter: "Someday we'll have a hell of a story to tell our kids!"

The way things are going, he thought perversely, *my kids will be quoting Lenin and demanding borscht for dinner.*

Chuckling despite his dark mood, Matt got up and walked toward the OEOB, determined to let go of his worries, if only for a few hours. Easier said than done, and as he was so busy trying *not* to think that he almost didn't hear someone calling his name. When he finally turned around he saw Murph, a mild-mannered, middle-aged guy who worked for the National Security Council.

They exchanged the usual pleasantries – which these days included commentary about the recent upheaval at the White House, then Murph asked some questions about his workload and the start of the school year. The chattiness struck Matt as odd. Murph was so painfully shy that Matt sometimes wondered if his horn-rimmed glasses were worn primarily as a personal protective barrier. Plus, they were just casual acquaintances, so why was he suddenly so interested in Matt's life?

As if on cue, Murph asked, "So, Matt, would you be interested in coming to work at the NSC?"

Matt stared in surprise as Murph briefly described the position – a rush of competing thoughts flooding his mind.

"Really! Wow, Murph," he said finally, "that's an amazing offer. Can I take some time to think about it?"

Murph smiled. "Of course. I'll circle back to you by middle of the week and we can get into the particulars."

Matt profusely thanked Murph for the offer, then the two parted ways. As he continued toward the office Matt slowed his usual gait, as if taking more time would help him process this new development. No doubt, Murph had just presented him with a cool opportunity. The NSC was at the top of the White House power structure; more importantly, it would involve different work that, while administrative, required thinking, as opposed to his current role as a messenger. The hours alone – weekdays from five to nine p.m. and Saturday mornings – were an inducement, allowing him to be on campus all day.

There were two downsides, however – one emotional, one practical, both significant. Accepting Murph's offer meant leaving Glen and Keith, with whom he had built a close relationship. Since day one Glen had had Matt's back, teaching him the ropes, and defending him to Jensen and others when he slipped up. Would Glen see his leaving as an act of disloyalty? The other issue was that the NSC was the focus for all national security and intelligence activities for the President, the White House, and the entire federal government. Clearly, Murph would have to be read in on the Anna situation. Would Roger authorize this, and if so, would Murph withdraw the offer?

Matt spent the rest of the day going about his usual tasks; he smiled at all the right times, joked with Keith, and good-naturedly rolled his eyes at Glen before agreeing to stay late for a rush copy job – all the while, tossing Murph's offer around in his mind. It was as if he had slipped on a mask of his former self: the aw-shucks, Midwestern kid who didn't even know duplicity existed, let alone engage in it. What alarmed him was how comfortable he had grown with that mask, and how each time he put it on, that kid inside seemed to fade a little bit more.

*   *   *

"Don't even think about it!" Matt said the next morning as Grossman sat down on the bed by the window.

With only two days until classes began, they were moving back onto campus. New room, same dorm, and same bullshit from his roommate.

"Already called it, boychik," Grossman said as he slid off his shoes. "Besides," he added, adopting an officious tone, "you need to be closer to the door. It saves time in the morning when you're dashing out to save the world."

Biting back an angry retort, Matt glanced at the other bed in the corner of the room, sandwiched tightly between the desk and the dresser. After a summer of having his own room he'd known it would be tough to share such close quarters with Grossman again; he also knew that if he argued every time Grossman did something that annoyed him it was going to be a very long year.

When he turned back to Grossman, he saw he had also removed his pants and, clad only in tightey-whiteys and a t-shirt, was laying prone with his head against the pillow.

"I hope you don't think you're done," Matt said, gesturing to several full boxes scattered about the room.

Grossman smirked. "But you're so much better at unpacking." Then, seeing Matt's face, he added. "Chill out, boychik, geez. I was just taking a break." Grossman groaned as he scooted off the bed. "Had a few too many brewskies last night."

"When *don't* you have too many brewskies?" Matt snapped rhetorically, knowing his annoyance was in part due to envy. The night before, while he stood hunched over the copy machine at the White House, his friends had gathered for pre-semester drinks at The Tavern.

To his surprise, Grossman didn't offer a comeback, but just grabbed the nearest box with his name on it and ripped it open. As a blessed, if somewhat awkward, silence settled over the room, Matt's thoughts drifted back to the previous day, and yet another complication added to a life that already had far too many.

He'd spent the last night in their apartment as he had so many others – twisting and turning as he agonized over his circumstances, with no one in whom he could completely confide. It was like freezing at the controls of that plane. He gave up the entire runway until it was a choice of pulling back on the yoke and lifting the nose off the ground or running right off the end of the runway into a field. As the first light appeared in the sky, he came to the inevitable conclusion: he either had to tell Murph he wasn't taking the job or have a man-to-man with Glen. Each was equally unappealing.

"You're even weirder today than usual," Grossman observed, breaking the silence. "What gives?"

Matt turned to him, as so often the case torn between the urge to smack him and burst out laughing. At least in this case, the decision was easy.

"*I'm* weirder than usual?" he said, unable to keep a straight face.

Before Grossman could reply, they heard a soft voice call out. "Yeah, Grossman, if that's not the pot calling the kettle black."

They jerked around to see Catherine standing in the doorway. And though she had spoken to Grossman, her eyes were locked on Matt.

CHAPTER TWENTY-FIVE

The next morning, Matt sat at his desk, a cup of steaming coffee in his hand, his right leg bouncing frantically up and down as if it had a mind of its own. A few feet away, Glen sat in his office, door half ajar, his ear glued to the phone. Matt told himself it would be rude to interrupt, when really it was his own dread of telling Glen of his decision to work for NSC. He knew it was a good move for him, was even excited about it, and yet he couldn't shake the guilt over abandoning people who had given him so much support.

"Yup, yup, got it," he heard Glen say, followed by the sound of the phone being replaced on the receiver. Matt stilled his leg and went to stand, then sat back down when it rang again.

"Dammit," he muttered, even as he felt a rush of relief.

He raised the coffee to his lips, grimacing at the bottom-of-the-pot taste, and tried to remember the last time he had any sense of peace. The feeling, one of constantly being split in two, was exhausting and confusing, making it difficult for him to recognize the good things coming into his life. Instead, everything was viewed through a lens of mistrust and fear that he was about to make some awful, irreparable mistake.

He'd had much the same feeling when he saw Catherine the previous afternoon. He was surprised when she showed up at his door – not by her appearance there, but the jolt of excitement that flooded his body. After allowing her and Grossman the briefest exchange of pleasantries, he ushered her out of the dorm before his roommate could say something stupid.

They went to a new coffee shop a few blocks from campus that she'd been wanting to try. For weeks, Matt had thought about Catherine's return to D.C. and whether the rapport they developed during their calls would hold up in person. Any worries were soon proved unfounded, for from the moment they sat across the table from each other it was as if everyone in the crowded coffee shop faded away. It was the strangest thing – Matt felt like he knew Catherine forever and yet was looking at her for the first time. He had always thought her pretty, but now he noticed her flawless and creamy skin, the light smattering of freckles on the tip of her nose and at the base of her long neck, and the warm, generous smile that revealed perfectly straight, white teeth. Most striking, though, were her eyes – dark pools that revealed kindness and yet held a sense of mystery. They also, when Matt looked into them, seemed to see right through him. And therein lay the problem.

They laughed as they swapped summer stories, then moved on to discuss the classes they were taking this year, but inside he felt himself pulling back as the faces of Roger…and Anna… flashed through his mind. He was really starting to like this girl and suspected she felt the same. How could he drag her into the mess that was his life?

"Son," Glen called out, interrupting Matt's thoughts. "Isn't it Pepsi time?'

Matt glanced at the clock, then jumped up. "Sure is – sorry, Glen. I'll be right back."

He was almost at the door when suddenly he couldn't wait another minute.

"Glen…"

"Yeah, son," Glen replied, peering over his half-rim glasses.

"Something has come up and, well, I have a decision to make. Murph at the NSC asked me if I would come to work up there and I don't want to leave but the work and hours are different and I don't know but I think that I –"

Matt cut himself off when he saw Glen, his hand to his mouth, was laughing.

"Son, I know all about it."

"You do?" Matt sputtered, slightly annoyed that Glen had let him ramble on.

Glen leaned back in his chair and clasped his hands behind his head. "Murph came to me before he offered you the job."

"Wait, what?"

"It's a courtesy, son. No agency wants to be seen as raiding another." He paused, then said seriously, "Anyway, I say go for it. Great opportunity."

Matt realized then that beneath Glen's laughter was support and admiration for his loyalty. He listened in surprise as Glen told him that the new president didn't appear to have much interest in their organization. It was even rumored that President Ford was going to nominate their boss to be an ambassador, and his departure could leave the organization's future in doubt.

"Now, son," Glen added, putting the matter to bed, "how about that Pepsi?"

Matt smiled with relief. "Yes, sir!"

After delivering Glen's soda, Matt headed to the NSC, located on the third floor, and told Murph he was accepting the job. He would start in two weeks, allowing for the appropriate transition for Glen and Keith. On his way back down the massive marble stairs, it suddenly occurred to Matt that Jensen should know about this latest development.

True to form, Jensen sat there with a constipated look as Matt told him about the job; then quipped sarcastically, "I'm sure they won't mind having a spy working up there."

Matt felt the angry flush rising to his face. "I am *not* a spy. I am trying to *stop* a spy. And, in case you've forgotten, I was pushed into it – by the Russians, by the FBI, and by *you*."

Ignoring the comment, Jensen rubbed his forefinger against his temple, and then ran it across his lips, appearing to be in deep thought.

"Maybe this is a good thing," he said, as if the NSC job had been his idea. "It certainly will make you look more important to the commie assholes – like you're on the up escalator." He smacked his palms lightly on the desk. "Okay, let me talk it over with some people."

"Talk it over with some people?" Matt sputtered. "I've already accepted!"

"Cool your jets, 007," Jensen said with a smirk that made Matt long to punch him. "It's mostly a formality. I'll get back to you quickly."

*   *   *

Just as Matt's time with Glen and Keith was coming to a close, his duties as rush chairman were ramping up. Despite his earlier reluctance to accept the position, Matt now found himself grateful for the distraction from his other, much more serious opportunities – not to mention the two assistants who came with the job. The three worked tirelessly, planning parties, setting up an elaborate process for identifying rush candidates – much like the one Tex had used when approaching Matt the previous year – and making sure each fraternity brother knew the candidates so they could conduct missionary work whenever they crossed paths with them on campus.

The rush process was a competitive one, not just for the pledges, but the different fraternities vying for fresh blood. Realizing that Walter's natural leadership and culinary skills would go a long way toward impressing potential recruits, the frat decided to go all-in with real food instead of the traditional pretzels, potato chips, and popcorn. Walter would decide on the menu and arrange for the procurement of supplies; then, on the eve of the big party, the brothers would gather at some predetermined spot off-campus to prepare the food. A recent graduate volunteered the backyard of his rental home, but gratitude turned to sur-prise when they got there and learned that a) Walter's plan called for the barbecuing of one hundred and fifty pounds of chicken legs, and b) there was only one barbecue grill available. Loyal to the core, the brothers took turns in pairs tending to the grill, and under Walter's watchful eye and while imbibing copious amounts of beer. Those not cooking gathered in small groups in the yard or around the keg in the kitchen.

Grossman, beer in hand, dutifully presided over each batch of chicken to ensure that it had the right amount of spicy sauce. One beer turned to many, and the more he drank the more sauce he added, earning the nickname "master baster," which he accepted with pride.

As the wee hours approached, the group dwindled to a few stalwarts, some of whom fell asleep on the living room floor. By three a.m., Grossman, Walter, and Matt alone tended to the mission. All fortified by beer and none of clear mind, they were oblivious to the unusual amount of smoke billowing out from the filthy grill.

Walter was the first to hear sirens in the distance.

"Man, only us and the fire department are stupid enough to be up this late!" he remarked, looking at his watch.

"Must be a big fire," Matt slurred, "Sounds like a lot of them!"

"Must be nearby," Walter added. "They're getting closer."

A few feet away, Grossman stood over a tray of chicken, swaying slightly. Matt and Walter heard him grunt in surprise as a freshly basted chicken leg slipped from his fingers and landed on the ground. Maybe it was the late hour or their dulled senses, but for a moment the three just stared at it in the dirt. Then Grossman reached down, retrieved it, and held it up in the moonlight to examine the light dusting of earth encrusting it.

"Whacha doin'!" he snapped as Walter unceremoniously tipped his beer over the leg, not only soaking it but Grossman's arm as well.

"Hate to waste good food…" Walter replied, still feebly trying to rinse the chicken.

Suddenly, from around the corner of the building, three eerie figures appeared. They reminded Matt of Beelzebub in *Lord of The Flies*. They were big, wearing heavy overcoats with iridescent marks that picked up the light of the fire and radiated it back at the boys. Their helmets emitted beams of light that penetrated the darkness and nearly blinded the barbecuers. The axes slung over their shoulders looked like the swords of medieval warriors. Their movement toward the boys was accompanied by strange sounds, like the clinking and clanking of metal and the kind of slushing sound that big rubber boots make. They were firemen!

The realization that the source of their early-morning fire alarm was a barbecue manned by three inebriated college kids failed to amuse them. After an awkward moment, Grossman broke the silence. He held out the dirt- and beer-encrusted drumstick and slurred, "You guys want some chicken?"

*   *   *

The following morning, Matt woke with a hangover the likes of which he hadn't experienced in nearly a year. He lay in bed for a minute, trying to remember the number of beers he'd had – anything to distract him from the brutal pounding of his head. Unsuccessful on both counts, he forced himself out of bed, pulled on sweats and a t-shirt, then dragged himself down the hall to the bathroom. Just the touch of the toothbrush over his fuzzy tongue made him want to throw up, but he knew he needed to put something in his stomach if he wanted to feel human again. With great effort, he resisted the urge to get back into bed and headed for the cafeteria.

He had nearly reached the entrance when, to his dismay, he saw Catherine coming out, a smile on her face and coffee in hand. Matt grunted in embarrassment, unable to believe that this was what several days of avoiding her had come to: she was as fresh-faced as a daisy, and he looked, and smelled, as if he'd spent a week in a brewery.

There had been an additional bonus to serving as Chairman: it gave Matt an excuse for not asking Catherine out. He knew she was waiting for an invitation; though neither said it during their calls over the summer there was an anticipatory energy that they would spend time together when she returned. And it wasn't that he didn't want to see her – quite the opposite – but every time he thought of it he would remember Anna… and Roger's expectation that he would get her notebook by any means necessary. Since starting a relationship with Catherine under these circumstances was unconscionable, he had kept his physical distance while continuing to speak with her on the phone. This was a timing issue, he told himself; he just needed to keep the lines of communication open until he could free himself.

Most girls would have been put out by his lack of availability, but not Catherine. In fact, she'd told him many times how much she respected his ability to juggle the moving parts of his life; her own, she said, was so narrowly focused. Now that she was back in D.C., she was a student one hundred percent of the time, the phone calls with Matt her only real distraction.

In turn, he admired the power of her concentration, and her enjoyment of the cycle of learning, that resulted in a mastery of studying. Matt, on the other hand, wasn't the studying type. He enjoyed learning new things well enough, but then he wanted to move on. He preferred social interaction, be it with his fraternity brothers or with other staffers at the White House. And he rarely had to go looking for a diversion, especially not with Grossman around, always looking for a way to avoid his own schoolwork.

Catherine was in awe of his constant mad dash between activities and his casual attitude toward school. She even told him that his ability to "keep all balls" in the air would take him far in life – which only made him feel like more of a heel. If she only knew those "balls" included a ring of Russian spies, one of whom he was sleeping with!

He was debating whether to approach when he saw Michael follow her out the door. Matt felt his lips twist into a scowl, an effort that brought about the sensation of a nail being driven into his temple.

Coffee be damned, he thought as he turned to go back to the dorm.

"Matt?"

The surprise in her voice was not so much about seeing him as it was about his disheveled appearance.

"Oh, hey, Catherine," he replied hoarsely.

"Um, how are you?"

As she leaned in and gave him a kiss on the cheek, Matt caught the scent of her perfume. Subtle and slightly sweet, he would, under normal circumstances, have found it divine. In his present state, it sent waves of nausea rising up from his stomach to his throat.

"I'm good…" he trailed off, using every ounce of his strength not to vomit all over her dainty white sandals.

Michael smirked as he gave him the once over. "Someone really tied one on last night…"

Matt shot him a sour look, then turned back to Catherine. "What are your plans for the weekend?"

She shrugged. "Just studying. You?"

"Rush party."

"Right." Her eyes met his. "I know you're busy, but maybe we can get together this week."

Matt was about to rattle off all the events and obligations he had to tend to, but the urge to wipe the smile off Michael's face was too great to resist.

"Sure!" He thought for a moment. "Why don't you come by the White House for lunch? Say, Wednesday?"

Catherine rewarded him with a smile so radiant it sent an electric shock through his body.

"That sounds great!"

"Okay." Matt glanced at Michael, noting his annoyed expression with satisfaction. "Well, I'm gonna go grab some coffee, but I'll call you tomorrow."

As they parted ways, Matt realized two things: his headache was gone, and for the first time in months he didn't care about Anna, Roger, or that little black book.

CHAPTER TWENTY-SIX

That Wednesday at noon, Catherine arrived at the White House for their official first date. At least Matt, in his more confident moments, thought it was a date. Other times, he wondered if Catherine considered him merely a friend, and a rather scattered one at that. As he went down to meet her, he decided it didn't matter – it was a beautiful late summer day, and for an hour or two he could pretend he was just a regular college guy having lunch with a gorgeous girl.

When he saw her, his jaw quite literally went slack. She had dressed for the occasion, eschewing the fashionably torn jeans and peasant blouses she usually wore on campus for a lovely, sky-blue dress that ended just above the knee. Sandals of the same shade and a low heel accentuated shapely ankles and calves. Her hair – had she gotten it done? – playfully touched her shoulders, and her cheeks were highlighted with a touch of color that contrasted her beautiful eyes and white teeth.

"You look great!" he sputtered, then immediately chastised himself for his lack of coolness.

"Don't sound so surprised," she said, but she was laughing and her cheeks flushed with pleasure at the compliment.

They bought sandwiches at a nearby shop and ate on Matt's favorite bench in Lafayette Park. Later, he would barely remember what they had talked about, only that when he looked at her everything else fell away. She was lighthearted, and yet he sensed a strength of character and the awareness of a much more mature person. And then there was that odd feeling that, while she might not know all the details of his life, she knew *him.*

"Thanks for lunch," she said, "but you probably have to get back."

Matt, always so conscious of the time, was surprised when he looked at his watch and saw that ninety minutes had passed.

"Oh, wow, I do," he said as they stood to leave. "Sorry I've been so busy – there's just so much going on here right now."

At least *that* was the truth.

"I get it. And actually…" She paused, as if weighing her words to gauge how they would be received. "I was thinking – hoping – that maybe we could get away from here for a bit, spend some time together."

"Get away?"

"Yes, like a weekend trip… my dad has a beach home in South Carolina and it's empty this time of year."

A thousand thoughts ran through Matt's mind, from the logistic complications to the implications of her invitation – but all that registered on his face was deep shock.

"Um, er, I didn't mean…" Catherine fumbled, her face turning beet red. It was the first time he had ever seen her nervous, and, if possible, it made her even more attractive.

At that moment, he saw three thick white blobs fall from the sky and land on the shoulder of her dress. In Matt's opinion, the pigeon's timing couldn't have been better – as if it was intentionally distracting the humans below from an awkward moment … only Catherine didn't notice. Matt's chuckle earned him a puzzled look, which only made him laugh harder, and her furrowed brow, harder still.

"Matt, what in the world is so funny?!"

It totally overtook him. He tried to eke out words but could only point at her shoulder. Finally, Catherine turned, saw the gooey mess, and burst out with a mixture of laughter and groans of disgust.

They returned to the OEOB, where Matt guided her to the nearest lady's room. As she cleaned herself off, he waited outside, still letting out an occasional chuckle as he recalled the pigeon's assault.

A few minutes later, she came out, looking disheveled and somehow even lovelier.

"Well," she said, flashing him a rueful grin and pointing to the huge wet spot on her shoulder, "This dress is for the birds."

Matt roared at the corny joke, and she joined him. Then, changing the subject, she said, "It must really be exciting working here," as if realizing it for the first time. "Have you seen the President?"

"Sure," Matt said in a casual tone that did no justice to the excitement he felt at each sighting.

"Wow, I've never seen a president! I mean, except on TV, of course."

Smiling, Matt glanced at his watch. It was one forty-five, and by his memory, President Ford had a photo opportunity at two sharp.

"C'mon," he said, grabbing her hand.

"What's the hurry all of a sudden?"

"You'll see. I promise there are no birds involved!"

"I smell like mint," she observed, the result from washing her dress with hand soap.

"Better than the alternative," Matt quipped and led her in the direction of the West Basement. As they neared the entrance to the West Wing, Jensen appeared. He was moving quickly, though he managed to smile.

"That issue we discussed the other day…" he said to Matt, "I got the go-ahead. We're all set."

Matt sighed with relief, knowing that his move to the NSC had not been jeopardized by his spy activity.

Immediately upon entering the small vestibule, Sergeant Van picked the two young people up on his visual radar screen, standing up as they approached. Matt smiled, for he knew the man normally only got out of his chair for the President and other dignitaries. The polite treatment now was most certainly for Catherine's benefit.

"Hello," the Sergeant said with his customary wide smile.

"Hi, Sarge. This is Catherine Martin. She's never seen a President before. We're gonna change that."

The older man chuckled as they briskly continued down the corridor past the President's barbershop and up the stairs.

On the first floor of the West Wing, the door to the Cabinet Room was open. Kent and another Secret Service agent were standing duty on either side. As Matt and Catherine approached, Kent smiled and playfully outstretched his hand, pretending to shoot an imaginary pistol at Matt. That was it. No challenge. Totally on the spur of the moment, Matt effortlessly guided Catherine through the protected corridors and into the Cabinet Room, where at the center of the elegant cabinet conference table sat Gerald R. Ford, President of the United States, surrounded by distinguished members of Congress.

Matt placed his hand on Catherine's shoulders and guided her to the center of the room. Then, at the center point of the table, directly opposite the President, he gently maneuvered her sideways between two photographers. With one hand on each shoulder, he twisted them so her entire body shifted, ever so slightly displacing the photographers off center by a few inches. There Catherine stood, directly opposite and no more than a few feet from President Ford, who seemed to catch the maneuver and subtly smiled in amusement. Not so the two photographers, who glanced down at Catherine in annoyance. Photographers were always furious when someone got between them and a perfect picture of the President. But they were helpless. There was simply no way to muscle out the diminutive young woman.

Matt could feel Catherine tremble as she faced the President, and he could relate after so many similar surreal moments he'd experienced at the White House. The President sat there, as regal and serene as a giant lion, while flashbulbs lit the room and cameras whirred as photographers took as many pictures as they could. Occasionally, he would turn to the person seated next to him and make a comment. This was theater at its best, though there was a deeper purpose behind the show. The White House created such opportunities for the world to see the President holding court – in this case, with the leaders of the Congress.

It was over in a minute, when a voice called out, "Thank you, gentlemen!" That was the signal for visitors to leave.

"Wow, that was incredible!" Catherine exclaimed, looking slightly dazed.

"C'mon," he said, smiling as he took her hand, "I'll grab you a cab."

"I'm fine. Going to walk for a while. I'll talk to you later, okay?"

Matt nodded; then, as she turned to walk away, he said quietly, "Catherine?"

"Yeah?"

"South Carolina – let's do it."

*　*　*

"Guys, give me a break," Matt said as he quickly folded a shirt and placed it in his suitcase. "The beer will still be there in ten minutes."

"You said that ten minutes ago," Grossman retorted. Beside him, Walter emitted a grunt of agreement.

"I'm going as fast as I can. Catherine and I are leaving very early tomorrow morning and I want to make sure I'm all packed."

"Blah, blah, bah…" Grossman picked up his binoculars and headed toward the window, hoping to see a couple having sex with the shades open – or even just a nude woman. "Seems our boychik has a new set of priorities to go with his fancy new job and fancy new car…."

Matt rolled his eyes. Grossman had been busting his chops for a week, ever since Matt bought the Oldsmobile Omega. He drained his savings to do it, but he needed a car, and the Omega was just too sexy to pass up.

Ignoring Grossman's comment, Walter walked over and spit a chunk of his unlit cigar out the window, his dramatic *p'tooey* coinciding with the ringing of the phone.

Grossman reached it first. "Thomas residence," he said officiously, earning an eye roll from Matt.

"Oh Ma-att," he singsonged. "It's one of your girlfriends." Then, at Matt's questioning glance, he added, "I'll give you a hint: she probably makes a mean borscht."

Shit, shit, shit.

From day one, Anna had the uncanny ability to call at the least opportune moment and she never called just to shoot the bull. Tonight was no different. Running out to meet her was the second-to-last thing he wanted to do – the first being telling Roger he didn't go. For a second he thought about simply not mentioning the call, but he dismissed this just as quickly. If he wanted to get through this and truly be free, he and Roger had to be able to trust each other.

"Okay, fine," Matt replied when she suggested the Irish bar where they'd met previously, then he hung up and reluctantly turned to his stony-faced roommates. From the heat of their stares, they'd clearly gotten the gist of the conversation and weren't about to let him off the hook so easily. Matt felt his own face go red. Cancelling their plans violated the code of brotherhood; plus, given the fact that he was about to spend the weekend with Catherine, it made him look like a complete cad.

Realizing the awkward silence had gone on too long, he improvised: "That dumb shit. She's drunk and needs me to pick her up and take her home."

Walter's eyes widened for a split second, betraying his surprise at the harsh words, while Grossman just shot back, "Didn't sound drunk to me. Probably just horny."

"Yeah, well, *that* isn't going to happen!" Matt replied, trying to convince himself as much as the guys. "It is possible, you know, to just be friends."

"Possible but not probable," Walter interjected, "Especially when you've already done the deed."

Matt couldn't argue with that logic. "I'll make this quick and meet you guys in The Tavern pretty soon."

"You know, you are living dangerously," Grossman pointed out. "If Catherine finds out, you will look like a schmuck."

"Unless one of you tell her, that will never happen. And, really, I *am* allowed to have friends!"

"Whatever you say, Matt," Walter said, then issued one last p'tooey out the window for emphasis before heading for the door.

"I think you ought to invite Anna to South Carolina," Grossman challenged as he followed him out. "That would take some balls!"

Once they were gone, he shoved the last few items in the suitcase, set it by the bed, and hurried out to the Omega. As he headed to the bar, he felt that familiar anxious feeling in the pit of his stomach. He was always nervous before seeing her, and even more so when he didn't have time to speak to Roger beforehand. He told himself that he had handled Anna on his own several times, but this was little comfort, especially now that the black book was in play. If he tried to grab it and got caught, he would lose her trust. If he didn't try, he might never get another chance. Either way, game over.

Anna was sitting at a table when he arrived. "Hello," she said, standing up to give Matt a warm hug.

"What's up?" he asked over her shoulder, and hearing the slight brusqueness in his voice gave her a squeeze of reassurance.

"I have a paper to do over the weekend," as she released him and sat down. "Can you help me with it?"

Matt groaned inwardly at the timing, but there was no debate: he was not going to cancel his plans with Catherine.

"Wish I could, but I am going away."

"Oh, okay." Anna dropped her shoulders in disappointment. "Actually, the paper was only part of it. I was missing you too. You haven't had as much time lately." Her eyes searched his. "Matt Thomas, are you – how do you say – getting tired of me?"

In a flash, he had a moment of clarity. Maybe she needed help with a paper, maybe she didn't. Either way, this meeting was really about gauging whether he was still on the hook. Had Anna felt him pulling back, or was Vadim suspicious and exerting pressure on her? Matt didn't know and he didn't care – for the first time since meeting her, he felt a sense of power.

"Tired of you?" He reached out and clasped her hands. "Of course not!" He sighed. "But I really can't cancel my plans. When is your paper due?"

"Monday," she replied almost absently. "What are these amazing plans?"

"I'm visiting friends in South Carolina. We've planned it for a while." He leaned forward. "Tell me about the paper. What's it about and what do you need help with?"

"Oh, let's just forget it and have a beer."

Matt watched her as she caught the waiter's attention with nothing but a smile – probably because the poor schlub had already been stealing glances at her. It was as if Matt was seeing her through a new lens, one unobscured by lust – or whatever – though that was certainly still present. Every word, every mannerism – from that smile to the casual wave of her hand, mixed with a subtle tone of disappointment, as she'd told him not to worry about the paper – was calculated to elicit a particular response. Later, Matt would remember that moment as the one when he truly started to believe what Roger said about her. The epiphany was disturbing, and one he was more than happy to drown in a pint.

As they drank, he told her about the new job in the NSC and was surprised to hear she had never heard of it. He launched into a primer on the organization of the White House, noticing the subtle shift of her body language as he moved into the NSC's place in it, coordinating foreign, defense, and intelligence policies. That shift became more pronounced when he described his new job, embellishing just enough to give the impression that his standing had grown.

"Vadim will be so pleased to hear of your promotion," Anna said with a smile. It was for Matt an opportunity to go on the offensive.

"Really. Why would you tell *Vadim* about my job?" he said, allowing suspicion to creep into his tone. "Who is he to you?"

It worked. Anna leaned back and tensed her lips, possibly wondering if he was exhibiting romantic jealousy.

"I am a student, remember? The government is paying for my education, and I help Vadim in exchange for a stipend that pays my rent. I would tell him because he was very impressed by you." She laughed, and Matt was surprised to hear it tinged with bitterness. "He will take the news as evidence of his own good taste."

"What does he do and how do you help him?"

"He is an attaché. I help him with understanding your government. That is why you are so helpful to me."

"An attaché?"

Anna's eyes narrowed almost imperceptibly. "Surely, working at the White House you know what an attaché is. Vadim is a *cultural* attaché – he helps our people understand your culture and to help your people understand ours."

Matt smiled. "Really? That sounds a little loosey-goosey. Are you sure he's not some kind of secret agent?"

He caught that flicker in her eyes again, and for a second Matt thought she was going to ask, as predicted by Roger, whether he had spoken to the FBI about her. Instead, she laughed and shook her head.

"You Americans watch too many James Bond movies, I think."

Matt laughed too. "You got me there! Real life just doesn't happen the way it does in the movies!"

"I wish my life was that exciting. Working and being a student is such a bore." She met his eyes. "That is why I am so glad I have you."

Matt's smile froze in place when she reached for her purse and pulled out the object that had caused so many sleepless nights and contentious conversations with Roger.

"Tell me your phone number at your new job," she said as she flipped through the book.

"I don't know it offhand yet." Matt pointedly eyed the book. "Can I see that? I want to see how many guys you are friends with."

She dramatically pulled it to her chest. "It's top secret. I can tell you that you're the only one I've slept with."

"We haven't done a lot of sleeping," he joked, then looked at his watch. "I really have to go Anna. Sorry."

She accepted his need for a quick departure without protest – possibly, Matt thought, to tell Vadim about the NSC. As she said goodbye, she enveloped him in a strong embrace and did not easily give it up.

"You know, Matt Thomas," she whispered in his ear, "I find you particularly pleasant to be with."

Matt said nothing, just planted a gentle kiss on her cheek. But as he walked away, and despite everything, he couldn't deny to himself that he felt the same.

He caught up with Grossman and Walter at The Tavern a good hour before closing time. Both three sheets to the wind, they gave Matt an overly exuberant greeting, then returned to a heated debate about who the hottest girl in their civics class was. Normally, Matt would have laughed at their verbal sparring, but tonight he just found it insipid. Any annoyance he felt toward his friends was quickly transferred to himself. Walter and Grossman were just being themselves, while his appearance was an insincere one, intended only to prove that he prioritized his brothers over a girl. He interjected a comment or two, then slipped back to the dorm and called Roger.

CHAPTER TWENTY-SEVEN

The drive to the eastern shore of South Carolina was a long and boring one, mostly on straight, interstate highway. It didn't help that Catherine dozed off within minutes of their hitting the road, leaving Matt alone and at the mercy of his own thoughts. He pressed the pedal of the Omega as if he could try to outrun them. Instead, each passing hour seemed to bring him down a rabbit hole in some area of his life, from the excitement of his new job at the NSC to the stress of the Anna situation… and finally, the status of his relationship with Catherine, which after an awkward start that morning was definitely in question.

He'd arrived at her dorm room at six and knocked softly so as to not awaken others. There was no answer. He reluctantly raised his hand to knock again when he saw Catherine at the end of the hall; dressed in a robe, her hair still wet from the shower.

"So sorry, Matt!" she mouthed as she scurried toward him, mumbling excuses for not being ready. Her words barely registered, though, because her robe had parted to reveal her nightshirt clinging to her damp body.

"Come on in," she said, her lips parting in a small smile as she noted his stare.

Matt had raised his eyes to hers; he wanted to follow her but felt as though his feet was stuck in cement.

"Um…" he began.

"I'll just be a minute," she muttered quickly and went inside, leaving the door ajar and Matt to stew in the knowledge that he'd just ruined an opportunity any guy would kill for.

Shit, shit, shit.

Now, as he snatched glances at her, so beautiful and innocent as she slept in the car, he wondered if he would ever get that chance again. But what other choice could he have made, when the night before he had been drinking with Anna, still lusting after Anna, and would likely have to sleep with her again in order to get the book? He may not be able to tell Catherine the truth of his life, but he could protect her from its messiness.

Who are you kidding, Matt? he thought, *You're going away with her for the weekend!*

He could almost hear Grossman and Walter's voices in his head, alternately congratulating him and calling him putz and schmuck and other Jewish words he didn't understand.

"You're no mensch," Grossman would say, "Two-timing the *shaina maidel* this way."

"No," Walter would add between bites on a cigar, "definitely not a mensch."

"What 'ya thinking?" Catherine asked, startling him.

Matt glanced at her, searching for words, then returned his gaze to the road – and the rearview mirror, where he saw a police car rapidly approaching his bumper.

"FUCK!"

"Excuse me?"

"I'm doing ninety!" he yelled, "And there's a cop on our tail!"

Catherine saw the flashing lights in the sideview mirror and calmly crossed her arms.

Infuriated with himself, Matt pulled off to the side of the road, put the car in park, and sat quietly as a burly cop swaggered up to the driver's window.

"See your license and registration," the man demanded in a deep southern accent. He bent down and peered into the window as Matt removed his wallet and began searching for the documents.

"I know the registration is here somewhere," he said as he handed his driver's license to the officer.

"What is this?" the officer asked, pointing to the White House parking pass tucked into the windshield.

"Oh, that's just my pass for work," he muttered, then leaned over to the glove box in search of the registration.

"You work in *the* White House?"

"Yep," Matt replied absently, annoyed that he was having no luck finding the registration.

"Can I see your ID?"

"Nope," Matt said, "I am not allowed to give it to anyone. Really!"

"You a little young to be working in the White House?"

"I'm just a part-time employee, sort of like an intern. I'm still in college."

"Shucks, son," the officer said, faintly reminding Matt of Glen. With a slightly awestruck expression on his face, as if Matt was an exciting movie star, or something, he said, "Let's just consider this a warning to slow down a notch. Courtesy of the state!"

Matt glanced at Catherine just long enough to see the same surprised look, tempered with amusement, on her face.

"Thank you, officer, that's very nice of you." Matt couldn't see the connection between his offense and his job – it was certainly no reason to get away with speeding – but he was not about to question his good luck.

"My pleasure, son."

"Courtesy of the state?" Catherine snickered as the officer slowly ambled back to his patrol car.

"Go figure." Matt offered a casual shrug, as if this was just the way he moved through the world. "Hey, you're not going to fall asleep again, are you?"

Catherine sat up straighter in her seat. "No way! You might get us into more trouble." She glanced around and noted a sign on the side of the road. "Actually, we'll be coming up on my dad's exit in about a half-hour or so."

"Great, any place good to eat near his house? I'm starving."

"Me too! And yes, there's a diner nearby…great burgers."

They spent the last leg of the journey exchanging light banter that consisted mostly of Catherine teasing him about his being a "big shot" and getting out of his "run-in with the law." Matt accepted the good-natured ribbing, relieved at the distraction the incident provided from the mental gymnastics that had plagued him earlier. Finally, they approached the exit, where Catherine directed him through woodsy backroads to the diner – a cozy joint with food every bit as delicious as she said. They were now within spitting distance of the house – and a market where they could stock up on supplies to fill the fridge, which would be empty in the off-season.

When Catherine had nonchalantly mentioned the "beach house," Matt had pictured a small, quaint cottage likely worn from years of exposure to salt water and sand. His first clue that this was a faulty assumption was the large wrought iron gates that sequestered the community from the rest of the world. His second was the guard sitting at the gate knew Catherine on sight, addressed her as "Miss," then quickly moved to unlock it for them. A smattering of homes decidedly larger than "cottages" was his third clue – but even they didn't prepare him for the Martins' summer getaway. Sitting right on the ocean, the u-shaped structure was easily large enough to fit three of his parents' house back in Michigan.

"Um… wow."

"What? Oh, yeah," Catherine said with a wave of her hand. "Daddy's pride and joy." Her tone held that hint of bitterness always present when she mentioned her father, but whatever the issue was there it didn't seem to effect Catherine's overall cheery attitude. To Matt, this was indicative of a strength even more attractive than the way she looked in her robe.

"Wow," he said again as she opened the front door and they entered a huge sunken living room flanked on each side by the bedrooms and bathrooms. She then guided him into a kitchen that would have made his mother weep with joy, and through glass doors to the outdoor patio with a huge barbecue and a brick fire pit surrounded by comfortable furniture.

Catherine set the bags containing beer, wine, and food for breakfast on the kitchen counter, while Matt got to work building a fire. It wasn't long before she joined him, an open bottle of wine and two glasses in her hands. Matt was halfway through his second when Catherine set her glass down on the table and stood.

"Let's take a walk on the beach."

A slight chill arose as the dusky sky turned dark. There were long stretches where nothing was said. Words would have been a distraction from the soothing sound of ocean waves breaking into foam that washed across the smooth sand, still warm from the sun.

"This is nice," Matt remarked, gently clasping her hand as they turned back toward the house. Catherine sighed contentedly and took a deep breath of the fresh ocean air. The rising moon cast light on the water.

"This morning," she said softly, "What was that?"

Matt's heart raced, knowing she referred to the moment outside her dorm room. "I know…I mean, I don't know."

He thought she would be annoyed by the vague answer or at least question him about it. Instead, she stopped dead in her tracks, then turned to face him, staring deep into his eyes.

"There are a couple of things," she said in an almost officious tone, "I want to bring to your attention."

Beneath hundreds of twinkling stars in the night sky, she pulled her top off, then with the sleight of a magician, slipped her hand into his pants.

"Let's plant the flag!"

Struck speechless for the second time in as many hours, with fumbling hands Matt pulled out his wallet.

"You don't have to pay me," she chuckled.

"I'm looking for my raincoat."

She drew her nose point to point with his so that her warm breath soothed his face. "Have you been a bad boy, Matt Thomas?"

Swallowing hard at the implications of that, he searched for the words to wiggle out of the situation and decided he didn't want to.

"I'm no boy," he said in a thick brogue. "The name is Bond, James Bond."

She tossed her head back and let out a very uncharacteristic howl. Laughing at her abandon, he pulled her into a tight embrace. But beneath the levity, he was angry, for in that moment, as he and Catherine sank slowly to the sand, he felt Anna, Roger, Jensen, the FBI, and the White House were all there too.

CHAPTER TWENTY-EIGHT

"You're taking Wonder Woman on a trip," Roger announced in between bites of a greasy burger. A glob of ketchup liberated itself, landing on his white shirt. "Shit."

"What?" Matt gritted out, keeping his voice low so no one from the lunch crowd at Whitey's overheard. Due to Matt's new work schedule, set to begin that evening, they would now be meeting at midday instead of the usual four-thirty.

"The wife's going to kill me," Roger muttered, dipping his napkin into his water glass and wiping the shirt, making the mess worse. "Yeah, we're thinking Ft. Lauderdale."

Thirty minutes earlier, Matt had walked into Whitey's feeling like he was on top of the world. After an amazing weekend with Catherine, he returned to D.C. looking forward to his new job and believing, for the first time in a long time, that life was going to fulfill its promise. He could barely wait until they ordered before launching into his last conversation with Anna four days earlier. He recounted how she had quickly dropped her request for help on the school paper once Matt indicated he was still interested in her, and, more importantly, her reaction to the news of his new, sexier job. Roger burst out laughing at Matt's impression of Anna's voice and accent – "Vadim will be so interested to hear of your new responsibility" – and praised him for questioning her on that statement.

"You're definitely keeping her on edge," he said when Matt described how uncomfortable Anna became. "That is great!"

Matt confidently continued his blow-by-blow account of their conversation – her description of her relationship with Vadim and his position as an attaché. He grinned smugly when Roger agreed with his assessments of their exchange: that the paper was a ruse to see if Matt was still on the hook, and that she had definitely been thrown by his "joke" that Vadim was a spy. He was particularly interested, though, when Matt told him that Anna spoke of how boring her life was and that Matt was a bright spot.

"Hmmm," Roger said, raising an eyebrow. "There may be something there. If she really is bored or lonely, that's something we can exploit. You're really doing a fantastic job, Matt."

Then, just as Matt was giving himself a well-deserved pat on the back, Roger had dropped a shitstorm at his door. Matt didn't know what angered him more – the agent's plan, the fact that he waited until Matt had gone through the whole debrief before springing it on him, or the fact that it was presented as a fait accompli.

"Ft. Lauderdale?" he snapped, leaning forward, his brow knitted. "No way! Why would I take Anna to Ft. Lauderdale?"

"Calm down, kid. This is not a punishment."

"It certainly feels like one!" Matt exclaimed, then glanced around and lowered his voice. "Why are you doing this to me? I have a life…I have a girlfriend!"

If Roger was surprised by that revelation, he gave no sign. He simply smiled and spread his hands magnanimously. "We think you could use some sun…?"

The attempt at humor only served to enrage Matt more. "Fuck you, Roger! I want the truth!"

"While you are there, you are going to get that book from her…"

"Of course, the book! What happened to the idea of giving me dummy information to supply to Anna? She has let it go so far, but she is going to want that information – Vadim is going to want it – especially now with my new job."

"I know," Roger said simply, "But our mission has shifted focus."

"*Our* mission?" Matt snorted. "I'm the one out there, risking my entire future for 'our mission,' with no idea if or when I am going to be free of this, and all you can say is that it has shifted focus? Now, what about the fucking book is so important? You better tell me, Roger, or so help me God…"

Roger leaned back in his chair and glanced down at the remnants of his burger, his lips pulling into a tight smile. Matt didn't know if the agent was debating whether to finish off the burger or tell one of his crass jokes but if it was the latter he was out of there. Matt felt his whole body tense in preparation to spring from the chair and leave. Then Roger's eyes met his, and for just a moment, he looked like a completely different man – world-weary and yet with a steely resolve worthy of any battle-hardened general.

He sighed. "We believe Anna's book might possibly contain the name of someone in our government who's working for the Russians. Matt, we have a mole."

*   *   *

Over the last year, Matt had leaned heavily on his ability to compartmentalize – something he learned in military school – to carry out tasks despite competing stressors pulling on his heart, mind, and body. That skill was put to the test like never before when he reported for orientation and tried to shift his attention from Roger's bombshell to his new home within the White House.

And what a home it was. The NSC was one of, if not the largest, concentrations of power on the globe, comprised of the President himself, as well as the VEEP, National Security Advisor, Chairman of the Joint Chiefs of Staff, Director of the Central Intelligence Agency, and the Secretaries of State, Defense, and Treasury. Also on tap were experts on every geographical region of the globe and vital subjects like arms control and terrorism. It was literally the epicenter within the epicenter of American strength, influencing its course and thus having an imprint on everything happening in the world.

Murph had already filled him in on some of the logistics. The NSC was located in the OEOB; however, the President's National Security Advisor, for whom the NSC staff worked, had his office on the first floor of the West Wing. The Situation Room, on the ground floor of the West Wing, was also staffed and operated by the NSC. The NSC's administrative Secretariat was the nexus for everything, and Matt would be one of a handful of students who meticulously recorded in a computer system every piece of paper, literally hundreds a day, coming into or going out of the White House. Each document or letter was tracked and monitored to make sure nothing critical to the security of the United States was lost in the vast bureaucracy. Even more than in Glen's office, Matt would have an inside view on everything that affected America's national security.

This new level of access necessitated an even greater level of security clearances – above and beyond the top-secret clearance he already had. Upon his arrival, Matt was taken to the NSC security office where, in a small room with a window overlooking a dingy courtyard, a distinguished-looking man in a nicely tailored pinstriped suit and polished shoes was waiting. He introduced himself as Mr. Sheridan from the Central Intelligence Agency.

As soon as Matt sat down, Sheridan walked over to the window and peered out, then lowered and closed the venetian blinds so tightly that not even the slightest glimmer of light could pass through.

"Can't be too careful!" he exclaimed as he turned to Matt.

Too careful of what?

Matt knew every nook and cranny of the OEOB; he knew the courtyard that the small window overlooked was on the interior, surrounded by secure OEOB offices. No outsider could peer through the window, let alone a spy. Besides, they were on the third floor!

"As I said," Sheridan repeated as if reading Matt's thoughts, "we can't be too careful when it comes to the security of the United States."

He then reached for a black valise resting against his chair and extracted a manila envelope, ripping it open with his index finger. Inside was a second sealed envelope marked in bold red letters "Top Secret Code

Word." Mr. Sheridan again used his index finger to rip open the second envelope and remove several documents.

This rather odd little ceremony kicked off a two-hour indoctrination into the world of national security. Speaking in a monotonous tone that bordered on maddening, Sheridan began by confirming something Matt already knew: that he would now have access to information so sensitive it could, in the hands of an enemy, result in grave danger to the United States. Merely labeling such information "Top Secret" was insufficient, so the government set up "fences" around specific programs and operations and limited access on a "need-to-know" basis – only employees whose duties required it had said access. Each program was given a code word and those with need-to-know status signed a secret document promising never to reveal or discuss the information.

The NSC was a focal point for these programs. Working there required access to many code word programs. To attest to the seriousness of these programs, Mr. Sheridan, launched into the story of Enigma, the super-secret machine used by the Nazis to code and decode Hitler's orders to his commanders. The British managed to purloin one of the machines and, with great effort, learned how to make it work so they could listen in. Those who had broken the code were true heroes, credited with changing the tide of the war. It was a truly fascinating piece of history that Matt had already read about in a high school history class, which made Mr. Sheridan's long, protracted monologue even harder to sit through. He did, of course, appreciate Sheridan's purpose in telling the story – to illustrate the gravity of Matt's new position. More than that, he was blown away by the similarity of his situation to the spy novels he loved so much.

Little did Sheridan know that his young trainee was knee-deep in a "need-to-know" operation, and that he, a loyal member of the nation's top spy agency, was opening the kimono to someone in close contact with the enemy. For months, Roger had been hammering home the importance of Matt's role, but in this moment the weight of his responsibility, and the possible danger to him, and to the nation, truly hit home.

The Anna thing was not a game; nor was it just about his feelings for her, Catherine, or anything else for that matter. It was, as Roger said, about one thing: the welfare of the United States and its people.

Next on Mr. Sheridan's agenda was a lengthy lesson on the several different types of intelligence – human, communications, electronic, signals, and photographic – followed by examples of each one. He described how American spies had bugged Soviet limousines, allowing U.S. intelligence to listen to senior Soviet leaders as they drove around the Kremlin. He also showed Matt photos, taken by SR71 spy planes and a new, super-secret spy-in-the-sky satellite, of various locations deep inside the Soviet Union. Each capability was protected by a code word and after finishing each part of the briefing, Matt had to sign a classified document promising never to reveal any of the information relating to the programs. Because the documents were actually classified, he wasn't even allowed to keep a copy of the agreements he signed!

Just when Matt thought the briefing would never end, Sheridan sat back in his chair and offered closing comments punctuated with several warnings.

"You have been put in a position of trust by your country. You now know about several of our most important national secrets…secrets that will come across your desk routinely. Hopefully, I have done my job to educate you about what these secrets are and how critical it is that you protect everything about them."

Matt nodded, thinking again how Sheridan had no idea his words hit so close to home.

As if on cue, Sheridan added, "Be wary. Protect yourself! Suspect everyone – especially those who express undue interest in your work – and never, ever let your guard down. Don't drink or take drugs! Impaired judgment is an invitation for trouble."

Matt shook Sheridan's hand with sincere gratitude – and a vague sense of pity for this man who had gone through his carefully constructed "curriculum" ignorant of who he was really speaking to. Over the past several months, this had been the case with most people in Matt's life – a fact that he both abhorred and, to his horror, found somewhat exciting. There was no conflict, however, when it came to the trust the government had placed in him. It was awe-inspiring and humbling.

The panic didn't set in until he was headed back to his new office. Sudden flashes of alcohol-infused memories with Anna ran through his mind like a film. How many nights had begun throwing back shots in bars and ended with them stumbling into her bed? It wasn't the first time he'd replayed their time together, but now, instead of a romance or a comedy of errors, these memories were the stuff of an espionage thriller that ended with the main spy left out in the cold – or worse. How stupid, to be so vulnerable with her!

His heart pounding and sweat breaking out all over his body, he ducked into a nearby – and, thankfully empty, men's room. As he splashed cold water on his face, Matt forced himself to flip the script. While his naivete was not in question, he was sure he never revealed anything to Anna that could harm the country. He had also managed, in more than a year at the White House, to avoid telling his friends about sensitive goings-on there. Yes, the information he would now be privy to was more critical, but that was only a matter of degree. His commitment to keeping it safe and the means to do so remained the same.

Gradually, his breathing slowed and his temperature cooled. With a shiver, he patted his face dry and continued to the NSC Secretariat and a waiting Murph. Matt stepped into his boss' tiny office, expecting a "welcome to the team" chat that would inevitably include the weather – Murph's fallback topic in moments of awkwardness. Instead, Murph, with uncharacteristic confidence, outlined the Secretariat's security policy.

Matt would be given a code word for logging onto the computer system. It would be changed frequently. Murph stressed the importance of entering the code correctly. An incorrect entry would alert the Secret Service, and lead to an embarrassing scenario he didn't want to deal with. Matt, recalling his own confrontation with the Secret Service, didn't need to be told twice.

Murph went on to explain that all classified paper trash must be torn up. He demonstrated with a sheet from a pad on his desk, tearing it into four sections. It must then be deposited without staples or paper clips into a "burn bag," designated by bright orange stripes. All burn bags and papers were to be locked in the safe before leaving at night. Regularly, the burn bags were taken to the CIA for destruction.

Finally, Murph stood up and led Matt out of his office to a small room roughly four times the size of a telephone booth. In the center sat a computer printer on a small stand.

"Printers," Murph informed him, "are dirty, dirty machines."

Exhausted and a bit punch drunk from information overload, Matt giggled, immediately earning a warning look from Murph.

"They produce all sorts of electronic signals that can be intercepted by hostile intelligence organizations, even through the walls of the building. That's why it's kept in this shielded room. The door to the printer must be closed at all times!"

Matt nodded. "Got it."

To demonstrate its effectiveness, Murph closed the door behind them and turned on a small portable transistor radio. Silence. Then he instructed Matt to open the door. The moment the door was cracked, music filled the small room.

"You see, with the door closed signals can't get in or out. If you leave the door open, anything coming over this printer can be intercepted. So always make sure the door is closed!"

*   *   *

"What took you so long?" Grossman whined when Matt walked in the door. "You have to get over to The Tavern and chug with the new Pledges."

"Yes, dear," Matt replied, as if talking to a nagging spouse. "And I'll take the trash out." He caught Grossman's raised eyebrow. "Sorry – I had a long day at work."

"Well, hurry up. You are setting a bad precedent."

"Since when do you care about being on time?" Matt asked as he discarded his suit and tie.

"I don't. But Tex said if I don't get you over there, he will make the pledges strip me and tie me to a lamppost in the quad."

Matt grinned. "So, what's it worth to you for me to show up?"

Grossman didn't miss a beat. "I won't tell your girlfriend that you have another girlfriend."

Matt almost asked which girl Grossman considered to be his main squeeze, then decided it didn't matter. If either Anna or Catherine learned of the other it would spell disaster, just for different reasons.

"Anna is not my girlfriend. She's a friend. We got off on the wrong foot."

"Don't you mean the wrong side of the bed?" Grossman quipped, thoroughly enjoying this.

The door had just closed behind them when Grossman announced. "Oh, by the way, Anna called and wants you to call her."

"Nice of you to tell me halfway down the hall."

"I can't afford to be any later," Grossman replied, clearly envisioning himself naked for all of campus to see.

They got to the elevator bank just in time to see Catherine step out of an arriving car.

"Hey!" she said, planting a kiss on Matt's lips. "I just came to see how your first day went."

"It was very… educational," Matt replied, ignoring Grossman's smirk at having seen the affection between them.

Matt longed to wipe that smirk off his face, though of course it wasn't Grossman he was angry about, but the situation. The mention of Anna a few seconds before Catherine was in earshot was too close for comfort and a reminder of how easily things could blow up in his face.

CHAPTER TWENTY-NINE

For the next couple of weeks, Matt settled into a routine that mimicked a normal life. Every weeknight he arrived for work a little before five o'clock. And every night, Murph was standing by the door with his unfaltering welcome: "Say, how's the weather out there?" Matt would then take his place among the other students and for the next four hours enter information from piles of documents into the computer, initialing each document to show that it had been processed. Matt quickly became quite good at judging the workflow. If things were slow and the pile was small, he would take his time and read the document he was processing. As a rule, they closed up shop at nine and he was back on campus by nine-thirty.

His days were much more challenging as he attempted to juggle the other aspects of his existence. The fraternity, his friends, and to a large extent, his schoolwork, quickly faded into the background to make room for Catherine's growing importance in his life. At least twice a week they had lunch or strolled slowly around campus, hands intertwined; when Grossman or Catherine's roommates were out, they stole moments alone in the dorm. No matter what, though, they spoke on the phone every day, sometimes more than once. The closer they got, the more Matt realized how much he cared for her – and that he had mistaken the lust he felt for Anna for something more. Unfortunately, alongside this epiphany came the fear that Catherine would find out about Anna and leave him – rightfully so.

Then there were the meetings with Anna, each preceded and followed by a meeting, usually over burgers at Whitey's, with Roger. Matt didn't know which frayed his nerves more. With Anna, he walked a constant tightrope between keeping her interested and keeping her at arm's length. He would talk about his access to data critical to U.S. security and how stringently that information was protected; however, unlike his time in Glen's office, he could not even give her the slightest breadcrumb without crossing into treasonous territory. Instead, he would carefully note the subtle shift in her gaze and body language and wait on tenterhooks for the day she asked for something substantive, perhaps attaching some sort of threat to that request. More difficult was acting disappointed that he was too busy to go back to her apartment, or, worse yet, pretending, when he did go, that he wanted to be there. On those nights, he slunk to his room not sure who he hated more, himself or Roger. The FBI man had made it clear: Matt had to keep the relationship going until they could grab the book; he always fell short, though, of discussing what happened after that.

Whenever he sat across a table from Roger he was also waiting for the other shoe to drop – that shoe being that the Bureau had finalized the plan for him to take Anna to Ft. Lauderdale. Matt spent much of the time between those meetings trying to come up with a story about the trip that would be plausible to Murph, his friends, and Catherine. But the weeks came and went without a word, and as he prepared for a short Thanksgiving trip to visit his parents in Michigan, he fooled himself into believing the powers that be had ixnayed the idea. Indeed, of all the things he had to be grateful for that year, not having to run off with a spy topped the list.

Another was his job at the NSC. It had quickly become his refuge; the singular focus it demanded providing a respite for his overtaxed brain. There was no telling what might come through the Secretariat. Sometimes there were CIA analyses and intelligence estimates. They might be on the military strength of a certain country, or background papers and talking points from the Department of Defense, CIA, and Department of State to prepare the President for meetings with foreign leaders.

Talking points were a favorite of the students. After the President had used them, they were sent back to the Secretariat for processing and filing. Each paper that went to the President went into a manila folder with the name of the foreign visitor typed across the front. After taking the notes off the President's desk, his secretary would stamp the folder with red letters, "The President Has Seen," then initial the stamp to certify it. Oftentimes the President himself would initial the folder, and occasionally the paper inside, to indicate he had, in fact, read the contents.

The papers were filed in the President's files, but the folders couldn't fit in the files and no longer served a purpose. To the students, they were valued souvenirs of their days in the White House. They vied for each one and traded them like baseball cards. When the President made a trip to another country, briefing books were prepared that covered the gamut of issues between the United States and the other country. These, too, came to the Secretariat and provided interesting reading.

Frequently, Matt handled issue papers on specific topics, such as Vietnam or U.S. strategies for nuclear, chemical, and conventional arms talks. Some of the most fascinating documents were old ones. The CIA, Defense and State Departments often sought to declassify documents so they could be turned over to the public or academics studying U.S. policy. Many of these related to the early years of the Cold War, the Cuban Missile Crisis, the ill-fated invasion of Cuba at the Bay of Pigs – skeletons from the country's deepest, darkest closet. The NSC had to approve their declassification, so they all came through the Secretariat.

Around six each evening the group would elect an emissary to run out and pick up sandwiches from a deli on G Street or a McDonald's on New York Avenue. They didn't stop their work to eat, though, but kept a steady pace so they could close up and head back to school at nine.

Sometimes, unusual tasks were put upon them. Both the House of Representatives and Senate were investigating the CIA for abuse of power and other improprieties. In the House, Congressman Otis Pike held hearings while, in the Senate, Senator Frank Church did likewise. Both investigations peppered the Administration, and the CIA in particular, with requests for information on secret CIA activities, such as its numerous attempts to assassinate Fidel Castro. As the NSC had to review any documents and approve their release to Congress, the CIA would collect the documents and pass them along to the Secretariat, placing any information inappropriate or too sensitive to reveal in brackets. There, Matt and the rest of the crew would help "sanitize" them, blacking out the bracketed portions with heavy magic markers, then copy the entire document so the copy could be turned over to the investigators on Capitol Hill. It had been discovered that even after redacting words with magic marker the originals could be read from the back of the page – not so with copies. But Matt and the other students could read the sensitive parts that were "sanitized," giving them a real history lesson.

This was pretty heady stuff – and, for Matt, scary as well. At times he would read the documents, which contained the most secret information about the government's covert actions, and try to forget what he read for fear he might let a nugget slip. He limited his drinking to one or two beers at most, always refusing shots no matter who tried to egg him on or, in Anna's case, seduce him.

His job also created a new barrier between himself and his friends that was both exciting and frustrating. Whereas the coverage of Watergate was accurate and often reported developments in real-time, the information he was privy to now either never reached the light of day or was misconstrued. Once, while watching Walter Cronkite, Grossman began ranting and raving about a particular policy announced by the White House. Matt, whose knowledge on the matter exceeded that of America's most trusted newsman, left the room rather than submit to the temptation to defend the White House. In moments like that he'd never felt so honored to be in the know – or so alone.

*   *   *

"Got the green light this morning," Roger said as he wiped his greasy fingers on the napkin tucked into his collar. It was the week after Thanksgiving and the two were at Whitey's for what Matt thought was a brief catch-up.

"Green light on what?" Matt's head whipped up from his shepherd's pie.

"Ft. Lauderdale." Roger's lips stretched into a small smile but his eyes were serious. "You know… you, Wonder Woman, the op we've been planning…"

"Yes, Roger, I remember," Matt said, hearing the irritation in his voice. "I guess I thought it wasn't happening…"

"Oh, it's happening… these things take time to plan." This time Roger's smile was one of genuine mirth. "We gotta protect our star asset, right?"

Hearing the word asset, one used so often in the books he loved, Matt emitted a chuckle tinged with bitterness. "And when is this taking place?"

"Soon – a couple of weeks." Roger reached his pointer finger into his mouth to extricate a piece of stuck meat. "Just hang tight."

*   *   *

A few days later, on December 1, Trans World Airlines flight 514 crashed into a peak in the Blue Ridge Mountains, about fifty miles west of D.C. A terrible tragedy that took ninety-two lives, it also affected national security because it occurred near the top-secret underground installation that would serve as headquarters for government officials in the event of nuclear war. For obvious reasons, the government had not previously acknowledged the existence of this facility; now, given the media attention to the crash and response activities, it had no choice. The facility, it was revealed, was operated by the Office of Preparedness, the entity responsible for continuity of government in a time of national disaster.

Matt wasn't surprised to hear from Anna when the news of the facility broke; what surprised him was the level of urgency she had never displayed before. There was no flirtation, no promise of a night of drinking and wild abandon, just a demand to see him right away and that it was "extremely important." She wasn't exactly thrilled when Matt said he could meet at lunchtime the next day, though he did detect a note of relief in her voice. The whole conversation was a red flag – something he pointed out to Roger the minute he and Anna hung up.

At promptly noon the next day, Matt parked on Connecticut Avenue, about a half-block from the Irish bar where they usually got together. He was about twenty feet from the door when he saw Anna striding briskly toward him.

"What's up?" he asked.

"I'll explain in a minute," she said as she grabbed his arm. "But I would rather meet privately."

"I thought we were going to have lunch," Matt said as they walked past the restaurant. "I'm hungry."

Anna didn't reply, just led him to her parked car. He opened the door for her, then rounded the car and got in the passenger side.

"I need you to help me," she said as she turned to face him. "You won't like this, but I need you to help me."

"What is it, Anna? I've never seen you so upset."

As the words came out of his mouth Matt realized his concern was twofold – for her and for the country – and that it was mixed with excitement. Was this the moment Anna admitted she was working to undermine the United States?

"The plane accident the other day. You know about it, yes?"

"Of course. It's all over the news."

"I need to know about the underground facility where it crashed."

Truly surprised, Matt turned to look out the passenger's side window. She had fished for information plenty of times, but never had she stated a request so forcefully.

"If you're asking about it, you know it's a secret facility. I've never been there."

"But you work in the White House. You can get me information."

And there it is, he thought. She had indeed told Vadim all about the access his new job afforded him. The crash and revelation about the facility had provided the perfect test of his malleability.

"Anna, even if I could find it, any information would be classified." Matt paused, knowing that the quiver in his voice was quite real. "Giving it to you would be treason!"

She reached over and put her hand on his shoulder. "I told you I need help. Vadim knows where you work. He expects me to get information. We are friends, and friends help each other, no? Please, Matt, find out for me, how big is this facility? Who works there? How many people? How far underground is it?"

Matt shook his head and ran his hand through his hair. "Anna, you are scaring me. You know I could get into big trouble. I don't think I can do this."

"I cannot disappoint Vadim! He will have me sent back home in disgrace." She paused. "Or worse."

"Or worse? What the hell does that mean?" Matt didn't wait for a response. "Anna, is this why you've been interested in me?"

Anna drew back, stung. "How can you say this to me? Friends help friends, they don't let them get hurt. We're friends, aren't we, Matt?"

"But *I* could get hurt if I do this!"

"No one will know," she said, her voice lower now, as if someone could overhear them in the car. "Vadim has no interest in letting your people know he has the information. If he did, it would be useless."

Matt took a deep breath, then nodded quickly to indicate that he understood her logic, but he said nothing.

"You must try for me, Matt. You must try!"

He forced himself to look into her eyes. "I'll call you in a couple of days."

She leaned over and kissed his cheek. "I knew I could count on you!"

"This is *not* a deal, Anna. I need to think about it and see if I can even get the stuff you're asking for."

"I believe in you. You will not let me down." Then, as if flipping a switch, she smiled and said casually, "Want to go inside and get something to eat?"

"Ummm…I sort of lost my appetite," he said, suddenly feeling the need to get as far from her as possible.

Twenty minutes later, Matt arrived back on campus replaying the conversation over and over again. Had he played his role convincingly? It seemed so; then again, Anna might just be the better actor. Matt couldn't worry about that right now; far more important was how Roger was going to help him – whether that meant getting doctored information for Anna or coming up with a plausible excuse to give her as to why this was impossible.

He entered the dorm room, mentally thanked the gods that Grossman was out, and made a beeline for the phone. Though he didn't say anything specific over the line, Roger knew that an immediate meeting was in order.

"Come to Jensen's office at four," he said, then ended the call.

*   *   *

"Well, this just got interesting," Jensen remarked as Matt crossed the threshold into his office.

Matt paused for a second, thinking how he had longed to punch Jensen.

"For some of us," he said evenly, "it has been 'interesting' for quite some time."

Roger, who had looked equally ecstatic about this development, saw the set of Matt's jaw and sought to diffuse the situation.

"What Jensen means is that Anna has suddenly upped the ante, and in a big way, right Jensen?"

"Well –"

Roger cut him off. "Matt, I know you start work soon – why don't you tell us about your conversation with Anna."

Matt nodded, then took a seat and repeated the exchange in Anna's car word for word. Roger and Jensen listened attentively; then, when Matt was finished, Roger said, "Excellent work, Matt."

"Yeah," Jensen added, "Especially how you played scared."

"I was *not* playing!" Matt snapped, then turned his stare to Roger. "I bought a little time, but I am going to need something to give her soon."

"I'll get with our intelligence people to concoct what they want to position," Jensen said. "This is a fantastic opportunity to see how the Russians are operating, and how they report purloined classified material. Outstanding! We might also place some disinformation, make them think we have five-foot dicks! That would really fuck with them."

"Agreed," Roger said, "How much time do you need, Jensen?"

"A few days should do it…" Jensen went on to explain that experts would have to fabricate information and coordinate among several government agencies to ensure nothing important was revealed.

"Okay," Roger said. "Matt, wait to follow up with Anna until then."

Matt left the meeting and headed to the NSC's office, taking some consolation that at least, according to Roger and Jensen, he had adeptly handled the situation.

He found Murph waiting by the door. "Hi there, Matt. Say, how's the weather out there?"

"Great. Really great!" Matt exclaimed, well aware that his overexuberant response had to do more with his own nerves than the conditions outside.

"Really? I heard it was going to rain." Murph gave him a perplexed look. "Say, can I have a word with you?"

"Sure, Murph," he said, following him into the cubbyhole he called an office. When Murph sat down, his desk chair, which was so old it should have been retired long ago to some dusty government warehouse, emitted an obnoxious groan.

"Say, that wasn't me!" Murph exclaimed.

Matt laughed at the man's discomfort. More different from Glen, he couldn't have been.

"Matt, do you know Ed over in the Sit Room?"

"I don't think so…"

"Takes care of administrative matters over there. I'm sure you've seen him around."

Matt nodded.

"Ed wants to take a couple weeks off at Christmas and I'm hoping you might like to fill in for him. Can't afford to lose you here, so it'd mean working days plus your usual evening shift. Of course, you'd get overtime."

Murph was trying to sweeten the pot, but there was no need to. Matt had wanted to see inside the Situation Room ever since reading an article in *The New York Times* describing it as the most secret room in America.

"You got it, Murph!"

It wasn't until he took his place among the other students for his shift that the full import hit him: he was gaining even greater access to the country's secrets just hours after a Russian spy hit him up for information.

CHAPTER THIRTY

"It's number one..." Grossman muttered almost unintelligibly as he reached toward Matt's bunk and handed him the phone, "... or number two... I forget which number she is..."

Matt opened his eyes, glanced at the clock, and groaned. It was seven a.m., and the ringing phone had just awakened him from his best sleep in weeks. He sat up, hung his legs over the bed and slipped off the top bunk, landing unceremoniously on the floor.

"Hello..." he said, praying it was Catherine; fearing that wasn't the case.

"Do you have something for me?"

"Huh?" Still half-asleep, Matt had the vague sense that having this conversation in the presence of Grossman was not a good idea. "Don't worry about it, Anna. And, not that I care, but my roommate is really pissed you woke him up!"

She got the message. "I am sorry. Let me know as soon as you get something."

"You'll be the first to know!" Matt said testily, then hung up the phone.

"Waiting for the results of your pregnancy test?" Grossman drawled.

"Screw you, man." Matt got up from the floor and started getting dressed. Since he was never going to fall back to sleep, a run to get some caffeine was his only hope of feeling human again.

When Matt arrived at the NSC that evening, Murph met him at the door with a note in hand. It told him to stop by Jensen's office as soon as he got in.

"Be right back," he told Murph, then ran downstairs, his mind racing.

Sure enough, Roger and Jensen were waiting for him, a manila envelope between them on Jensen's table.

"That's your package," Jensen said, jerking his head toward the envelope.

"Hold on a second," Roger said as Matt grabbed it. He took the envelope from him, opened it, held it over the table, and wiggled it so another envelope slipped out and plopped on the table. "Fingerprints," he said. "The outer package has Jensen and my fingerprints on it. This one is clean. Your prints will be the only ones on this shit, in case our asshole friends get smart and analyze it."

"It also means I'm the only one implicated," Matt snapped.

"Relax!" Jensen said with a smile. "You have done worse; you diddled a spy."

Roger cut him off with a look of annoyance.

"Matt, you are backstopped. You are doing a fantastic job. Just keep up the good work. There is no way this thing will come back to haunt you. In all seriousness, we are here to protect you."

Jensen looked down at his shoes in embarrassment, then looked back up and nodded his head. "Seriously, Matt. We are watching out for you. You are totally in the clear."

"So, what do I do with this now? I probably shouldn't take it upstairs with me. Someone might see it and ask about it."

Jensen thought for a second, then pointed to his desk. "Put it in the top drawer. I'll leave the office door unlocked. Just come by when you are leaving tonight, get it, put it under your shirt and walk out like you own the place."

"Excellent, I'm not only turning over government docs to a spy, I am stealing them from your office."

Roger laughed but Jensen let out an exasperated sigh.

"Okay," Matt replied. "So, should I read this stuff, in case she asks me about it?"

"I wouldn't worry about it too much," Roger responded. "She'll be so excited to get it, she'll take it and run."

"Is it classified?"

Jensen nodded. "There's enough in there to make it real. It's also sprinkled with bullshit so we can trace their reporting network. An inter-agency group developed it, so for sure there will be no harm to the country from you handing it over the fence."

Matt looked at his watch. "I should get upstairs. Murph's probably already wondering why you called me in."

Roger and Jensen stood, each shaking Matt's hand.

"Give me a call as soon as you make the handoff," Roger said.

For the first time since joining the NSC, Matt struggled to focus on his work amidst the barrage of fearful thoughts and stolen glances at the clock. He didn't know what he dreaded most – taking the envelope out of the White House or giving it to Anna. What if she wasn't home when he called? He didn't want to keep it in the dorm overnight where it might be subject to discovery by Grossman. By the time the end of the shift rolled around, he was so wound up he nearly wept with relief.

Matt joined the others in closing up the office; then, as the rest of them walked to the nearest exit, he wished them goodnight and ducked into the nearest men's room. A few minutes and several deep breaths later, he went to Jensen's office and found the envelope in the top desk drawer, exactly where he had put it earlier.

Everything is going as planned, he told himself. So why was his heart racing and his gut convulsing? He tucked the package under his shirt and tightened his belt so it would not dislodge; his winter coat would help conceal it as well. Then, as he had done a thousand times before, he walked casually out of the building, past the Secret Service post, and down West Executive Avenue through the southwest gate of the White House. There, after clearing another Secret Service post, he headed toward his car, which was parked on the Ellipse behind the White House.

He had just pulled open the driver's side door when he heard a friendly voice say, "Hello there. Working late?"

Matt turned to see a Park Police officer; his partner, an enormous German shepherd, stood beside him, eyes fixed on Matt.

"Yep," he replied, hoping his cheerfulness didn't sound too forced.

The officer nodded. "Well, have a nice evening."

"You too," Matt said, struggling to get in the car because the documents in his belt did not bend at his waist when he sat down. As soon as the door was safely shut, he allowed himself a moment of humor.

"Just stealing national secrets to give to a spy. How's your evening going, Officer?"

The lightheartedness quickly faded as he drove back to AU. Sure, Roger and Jensen said he was protected, but what if something happened that they couldn't anticipate? What if they both got hit by a car tomorrow? Who would be around to exonerate him if, say, a Park Police officer noticed his awkwardness while getting into the car? Matt was all too aware that he was technically committing treason and they were the only two people – at least the only two he knew – who could exonerate him.

He told himself he was being overly dramatic. He was one of the good guys, working with the real good guys. And, while Jensen and Roger were his points of contact, there was a bureaucracy, albeit a top-secret one, that knew about the operation and his central role in it.

As clarity and calm returned, he decided he didn't want the envelope in the dorm at all. He pulled over on New Mexico Avenue, just outside the campus gate, and contemplated his next move. He could go to Anna's, but her roommate would likely be there, or even Vadim. That was definitely a conversation he did not want to have. After a couple of minutes, he decided to go to the Irish place and have Anna meet him there.

The place was pretty busy, and it was loud. He went straight to the pay phone in the back by the restrooms. It was nine forty-five.

"Can you meet me right away?" he asked without explanation.

"Where are you?"

"The Irish place."

"I'll be right there."

"Anna," he barked before she had a chance to hang up, "I will be in my car in the parking lot."

The next fifteen minutes were interminable and yet they went by too fast. More than once he thought about leaving before Anna got there, of telling Roger and Jensen to get someone else to string Anna along and find the mole. But he was just toying with the idea, just pretending that he had the guts or the cowardice, depending on one's perspective, to walk away. Then, before he knew it, Anna walked up to the passenger side and climbed in.

"Where is it?" she demanded, having assumed his purpose.

"This is serious shit, Anna," Matt said, genuinely surprised by her cold demeanor. "I could get in a lot of trouble. I hope you appreciate that."

He pulled the package out from under his shirt. Anna stared at it, almost hesitating, then she grabbed it.

"I know this is hard for you," she replied, but her voice still lacked its usual warmth. "I am grateful." She leaned over and gave him a quick kiss on the cheek, then slid the package under her coat and hopped out of the car so fast that it slid out and plunked to the ground.

Matt closed his eyes, biting his lip and dropping his head so his chin landed on his chest. Anna never looked back – she just picked up the envelope, put it under her coat, and disappeared into the night with her hands shoved into her pockets to hold it in place.

"This can't be the way it works in the real world!" Matt said aloud.

Returning to the dorm, he called Roger to say it was done.

"Dumbass," Roger said, laughing when Matt told him she dropped the package. "Now we wait to see what happens next. Oh, and I'm sure this is the last thing you want to hear tonight, but it's time to invite Wonder Woman to Florida."

Matt groaned. "When exactly is this to take place?"

"Within the next two or three weeks," he said, "before you go home for holidays."

"Not going home," Matt replied, then explained how he'd agreed to fill in for Ed in the Sit Room.

"You know, kid," Roger joked, "You're a bona fide workaholic. Ever consider joining the Bureau?"

At that moment, Matt had had more than his fill of Roger and his jokes. He was about to say as much when Grossman entered the room.

"You look uptight," Grossman observed.

Matt looked from his roommate to the phone, then said, "Talk to you later, Dad," and hung up on Roger mid-sentence.

"Grossman," he said, noting that his appearance was even more disheveled than usual. "Next to you the Dalai Lama would look uptight."

"Next to you the Dalai Lama would look uptight," Grossman repeated in a surprisingly accurate imitation of Matt. He slid into his bunk and rolled over to face the wall.

"Rough night?"

Grossman grunted in response as the phone rang. Thinking Roger had forgotten to tell him something, Matt grabbed it.

"Haven't you said enough tonight?"

"Excuse me?" Anna said tentatively.

"Oh, sorry, Anna," Matt said, eliciting a chuckle from his roommate. "I thought you were a friend."

"I am a friend of yours…"

"I know, um, I mean –"

"That is why I am calling. I wanted to tell you how appreciative I am for what you did for me – and apologize for being so rude earlier."

"It's fine, really. I understand."

"It's fine, really, I understand," Grossman mimicked, then crawled from bed and left the room, presumably to head for the bathroom.

Matt took a deep breath. "Everything is fine. As a matter of fact, I was wondering…"

"Yes, Matt…?"

Matt noted the hopeful, almost innocent tone in her voice and hated himself for wishing it was genuine. He took another deep breath.

"You wanna go to Ft. Lauderdale next weekend?"

"Really?" Anna gushed, "Oh Matt, that sounds amazing! They have beaches there, yes? I've never been to the beach before –"

She went on about buying clothes for the trip, but Matt was no longer paying attention. He was already worrying what was going to happen when they landed in sunny Florida.

CHAPTER THIRTY-ONE

Two days later, Matt's body and mind were at odds as he got ready for his first day at the Situation Room. Over the past few months he had gotten used to an evening schedule, so rising at six a.m. was painful. At least he didn't have to deal with Grossman, who along with most AU students had headed home for the holiday season the day before. Matt felt guilty admitting it even to himself, but any sadness over not seeing his family for Christmas was tempered by the excitement of gaining access to the inner workings of the Sit Room.

He got to the White House early and, as previously directed by Murph, went to the lobby of the West Basement. Next to Sergeant Van, on the wall adjacent to the Sit Room door, was a phone. Only members of the Sit Room staff were entrusted with the secret combination for the cypher lock on the door. Matt had to use the phone to be let in. That was the last time he would have to do so.

The Sit Room was actually a series of rooms – a conference room, staff offices and an operations area with duty officers standing watch round-the-clock – located on the ground floor, literally seconds from the Oval Office. The operations area was the Sit Room's heart, where duty officers presided over consoles of sophisticated communications equipment capable of putting them in touch with anyone, anywhere on the face of the earth, at any second. Security was embedded in the Sit Room's design, protecting that equipment from emanating signals that could be intercepted by the eavesdropping antennae atop the Russian embassy. Protruding from the ceiling were three digital clocks, one with the letter

"L," indicating local D.C. time; another with the letter "Z" representing Zulu, or Greenwich Mean Time, used as a reference for international time conversions; and a third clock with no letter, just a small presidential seal to indicate the time wherever the President happened to be.

In the course of his work as a messenger Matt had met many of the Sit Room staff; others he knew by sight. They recognized him as well and accepted him as a teammate right from the beginning. The Director, a short, stocky man, approached and enthusiastically pumped Matt's hand.

"Appreciate you filling in for Ed. Today's his last day, so he'll be able to show you around. If you can hang tight for a while, I'll sit down and talk, but I'm under the gun to get the morning Intel brief for the Prez done by nine."

Matt nodded, then took what appeared to be a newspaper from the Director's outstretched hand. As he sat down at a large desk in the operations area to read, his eyes widened when he saw, emblazoned across the top and bottom of the paper, were the words TOP-SECRET – SENSITIVE. It was the President's Daily Brief, or "PDB," a summary written by the CIA each morning from reports of its worldwide network of spies and analysts. The PDB was so highly classified that only the President and a handful of his most senior aides received it. The copy Matt was reading was actually the President's personal copy, which he had read only an hour or so before. Matt was so engrossed that he didn't notice when the Director returned.

"Come on in for a minute," he said, gesturing to his small, cramped office. Matt followed him and sat down in a chair next to the desk.

"Thanks again for sacrificing your Christmas vacation to work with us. I know you're giving up a much-needed break from schoolwork."

Matt smiled as a memory of those easy summer breaks before college flashed through his mind. Surely, he thought, those days were gone forever.

"One thing I can't emphasize enough," the Director continued, "and it will become obvious once you learn your way around here. This place is very special. We're so close to the 'The Man,' everything is of the highest sensitivity. That means anything you learn here must never leave here – and that includes your co-workers across the street in the NSC Secretariat. What you hear, read, or see must be handled with the utmost secrecy, okay?"

"Got it," Matt returned enthusiastically.

At that moment, Ed walked in. Matt had seen the slender and distinguished man before but never put the face to the name. Ed had an endearing smile and warmth that made new acquaintances feel comfortable right away – and that was the case with Matt as he led him to the back of the operations area to show him around.

Ed was an administrative staffer with many responsibilities – things Matt would need to know about while Ed was out of town. First was the President's overnight folder, which was sent to him every evening by the National Security Advisor and contained a brief memo on everything of importance that had happened in the past twenty-four hours. Very often, the folder would include extremely highly classified personal notes from the CIA director or the Secretaries of State or Defense. Matt's job was to "break it down," meaning if the President made notes or comments he would have to make a copy, file the original in the President's files, and send the copy by classified courier back to the originator.

"Always remember," Ed cautioned, "to poke your eyes out." Catching Matt's questioning stare he added, "That's right. I said poke your eyes out. Aside from the President's closest advisors and their private secretaries, you'll be the only one to see these things. Once you've read them, forget everything, as if you never saw them."

Next, Ed showed Matt "the files," which were located in a large electronic cabinet that reached to the ceiling and stretched horizontally about twelve feet. The mechanical monster had several long drawers, which rotated for easier access to any particular file belonging to the President. One drawer contained his personal correspondence, including letters and cables, with heads of state. The first one Matt saw was titled "Brezhnev." Another drawer was filled with the President's "Memcons," or formal records of his conversations with world leaders. Another drawer was marked "Telecons" and was filled with transcripts of the President's telephone calls. Then there were miscellaneous files. Ed called one the "Yellow Pearl." It was a book that contained the location of all U.S. military forces, even ships at sea.

Ed advised Matt to spend some time getting familiar with the files.

"Sometimes," he said, "they call from upstairs and want the record of a particular phone call or conversation, and you better get it upstairs asap! It could be that the President is having a call with a world leader and needs to remember what they spoke about last."

Satisfied that Matt had a grasp of the files, Ed took him on a tour of a few places he might have to know about. The first was a small room located in the basement of the OEOB next to the often-visited soda machine. The door was non-descript; the kind of place you could pass and never notice. In fact, Matt had unwittingly passed it many times while getting a Pepsi for Glen. On the door was a combination lock.

"You've gotta keep this under your hat," Ed said while he opened the combination. "Don't discuss this with anyone, okay?"

"Right!" Matt nodded firmly.

Ed entered the dark room and waited for Matt to follow, then closed the door before turning on the light, a precaution so no one in the hall could see inside. Matt squinted, momentarily blinded by the glare of the light; then looked around, wide-eyed, as his vision cleared. Was he imagining things? The room resembled a booty-filled treasure chamber in an old pirate movie.

Seeing his reaction, Ed smiled. "This is where we temporarily store gifts until they are picked up by the State Department and inventoried," he said, moving about the small room.

It was an amazing site to behold. There was an expensive oriental rug rolled up against the wall. On the floor was a magnificent wooden box containing two bottles of wine, a gift from the Shah of Iran. Next to it was an unopened box containing a new Sony television, with a note to Henry Kissinger from Barbara Walters, the famous newswoman. The most unusual object was the head of a boar mounted with the animal's feet, gifted to Kissinger by Leonid Brezhnev. It was, Ed told him, a souvenir from a hunting trip the two had made.

After exploring the treasure room, Ed guided Matt to the second floor of the OEOB, right across the hall from the Secretariat where Matt used to work. They entered a room that had a steel vault door inside leading to another room. Ed picked up a phone mounted on the wall next to the door. The phone had no keypad or way to dial. It was a direct line.

"This is Ed. I'm entering," he informed the party at the other end, then unlocked a combination lock mounted on the door. "We have to notify the Secret Service before unlocking, so they can turn off the alarm. If you don't, they'll be up here faster than you can think your name."

They entered the small room and Ed closed the door behind them. It was filled with racks containing dozens of brown cardboard boxes.

"Know what these are?" Ed asked; then, without waiting for an answer, he said, "They're message traffic from Vietnam. The history of the war is in this room. The messages are from the highest generals to the President, keeping him informed of the progress of the war."

There wasn't time for Ed to familiarize Matt with the details. He simply told him how the boxes were organized.

"If they ask for a file, just come over here and look for it by date, or subject, which are marked on the front of each box. I've put you on the access list, so you can get in."

"There are about a million people who would like to spend some time in this place," Matt observed.

Ed nodded. "Also, sometimes the air conditioner goes on and trips the motion detector. The Secret Service will call the Sit Room duty officer. They will ask you to come over and escort the Secret Service so they can reset the alarm. While I am gone, you will have to do that, okay?

Matt nodded, smiling at the thought that he would be "escorting" the Secret Service.

That was the end of the tour – and Matt's crash course on the Sit Room.

*　*　*

Matt arrived the next morning bright and early hoping and praying he would be able hold things together while Ed was away. He had only been in about ten minutes when the Director gave him an assignment.

"Could you read through these PDBs and summarize the important stuff? We have to put together a monthly briefing for the former President. It should be pretty straightforward, just summarize the big things. Here's a copy of the last brief we did as a reference."

Matt was stunned when the Director then handed him a top-secret memorandum addressed to none other than Richard Nixon. The Director explained that as former presidents were often sought after for advice and interviewed by the press, the White House provided them courtesy briefings to ensure they were aware of important national security issues and less likely to make damaging statements. What shocked Matt was that he was being asked to write a memo to the former president on his first real day on the job!

Matt eagerly attacked the task and quickly became so engrossed in it that he didn't notice the phone ringing.

"Grab that, would ya, Matt?"

He looked up to see the duty officer already holding two phones to his ears, then jumped to grab the other one.

"White House Situation Room," he proudly said.

"This is Signal," said an official male voice on the other end. "Wheels up, SAM 27000, Zero Eight Ten. May I have your initials?"

"Ah, ah, M.T.," Matt answered, mystified.

"Thank you. Signal out."

What the —?

The duty officer was still attending his phone calls, so Matt quickly jotted down the message and, as soon as the man was free, stepped over to him.

"I got the weirdest phone call!"

"What's the deal?" the duty officer asked.

Matt read the message from his notes, then looked up to see the older man smiling.

"Signal is the White House Communications Agency. They're just notifying us that at eight-ten, Special Air Mission, that's Air Force One, tail number twenty-seven thousand, took off with the President aboard. They will call back when it touches down too."

Matt nodded casually, but he stood a little taller as he strode to his desk, enthralled with his small part in the President's schedule.

He had no sooner resumed work on the memo when a secretary walked in and plopped a folder down in the box on Ed's desk. Matt reached over and retrieved it, noting that it was the President's overnight folder from the previous night. As Ed predicted, there were one-page memos to the President from Secretary of State Kissinger, Secretary of Defense Rumsfeld, and Director of the CIA, William Colby. Each one-pager was marked at the top and bottom with a classification. The classification ran two lines, the top one reading in bold capital letters "TOP SECRET." Evidently, this wasn't secret enough, because after that it read "SENSITIVE." And even *that* wasn't secret enough, because next to it, in bold capital letters, were the words "EYES ONLY," followed by – in case that was insufficient – "EXCLUSIVELY."

Talk about overkill, Matt thought, barely stifling a laugh.

On each paper, President Ford had clearly scribbled his initials "GRF" to indicate he read it; however, on the page from William Colby, Ford had also written a note. As instructed by Ed, Matt made copies, filed the original in the President's files, and then forwarded the copies by White House courier back to their authors – after reading each one, of course!

Another paper in the folder right off the President's desk was his schedule for the upcoming day. Like everything else in this new world, Matt absorbed it in amazement. The schedule covered every second of the day. There was even a five-minute block, from eleven-thirty-five to eleven-forty, marked "personal time," that Matt could only surmise was a toilet break. Another interesting thing about the schedule: at night, it noted the President was staying in the "Philadelphia White House," because, officially, anywhere the President stayed was considered the

White House. It was the same with any plane on which the President is a passenger: the aircraft would be considered "Air Force One."

After a long afternoon, Matt finished his work in the Sit Room and offered a silent thanks to Murph, who had given him the night off from the OEOB. The next couple of weeks were going to be tough, working in the Sit Room by day and the Secretariat from the usual five to nine p.m., the exception being when he was in Florida with Anna. That was not a comforting thought.

With nothing to do and no one to do it with, he decided to grab a quick dinner at Roy Rogers on the corner of Van Ness and Wisconsin, about a quarter- mile from AU's campus. Matt sat alone eating a roast beef sandwich, watching Wisconsin Avenue traffic and thinking about his busy day. It had flown by, largely because everything was so new and exciting. He savored each part of it, from walking through the front gate of the White House in the morning to leaving in the evening with a farewell by the Marine guard at the West Wing door, and every single thing that happened in between. He knew he was lucky to have such an amazing opportunity. What surprised him the most was that everyone from Ed to the duty officers and the Director welcomed him with the same openness and trust that Murph, Keith and Glen had. He was immediately accepted as part of the small, insulated team. It all seemed surreal – and scary, considering none of them knew he was being courted, albeit unsuccessfully, by the country's greatest enemy.

What if Anna, or someone like her, had gotten to someone a bit less loyal than him, or a bit more vulnerable? The mere thought cut through Matt's fear about continuing his work for Roger, his anger about being so conscripted, and even his bitterness at having been used by the first woman he ever cared about. The age-old question he'd so often asked – "Why me?" – was completely irrelevant. For whatever reason this situation had been handed to him, and he would see it through.

When he got back to his room, he was so exhausted he didn't even turn the light on. He simply plopped down on the bed, kicked off his shoes, picked up the phone, and dialed Catherine. Clearly, she had been waiting for his call, for she answered on the first ring.

"Busy day at the office?" she asked when she heard the weariness in his voice.

Matt laughed, loosened his tie, and told her all the things he had done, from writing a report for Nixon to going through the President's overnight folder and sending secrets back to the CIA director by special courier. He may have been tired, but he was excited too.

"You know what I am doing right now?" he asked. "I'm sitting in the total darkness and thinking about your smile."

He heard that smile through the phone now when she said, "Are you working on the weekend too? Maybe I could come down."

Her words hit him like a punch to the gut because they meant he would have to lie to her again.

"Oh, that would be awesome, but while I am filling in for this Ed I really don't have any control over my time. I would hate for you to come down and not be able to spend time with you."

"I figured," she replied, disappointed, "But it was worth a try. Anyway, we'll see each other soon."

"Not soon enough!" he said, feeling sick to his stomach.

When they hung up, he sat there in the dark for a few minutes, wondering if he'd ever forgive himself for what he was doing to Catherine – or for the fact that, despite everything, part of him was looking forward to the trip with Anna.

With a sigh he stood and stripped off is clothes and slipped between the sheets. He was just about to close his eyes when the phone rang. He grabbed it, hoping to hear Catherine's voice again to soothe his guilty conscience.

"Matt!" Anna gushed, "How are you?"

"Actually, Anna, I'm pretty beat… about to go to –"

Ignoring him, Anna went on about what it was like trying to find a swimsuit in Washington in the winter.

"I ran all over the city, and you know I could only find a couple of bikinis. There are plenty of coats and scarves, but no bikinis!"

Her enthusiasm was both comical and infectious, and Matt again found himself looking forward to the trip, even if a team of FBI agents would be tracking his every move.

"And all the while, I am thinking, if Vadim or anyone from the embassy finds out what I am up to, I am going to be in big trouble!"

"Really? You mean you haven't told your boss about the trip?" Matt asked, incredulous and wondering about the implications of that.

"No. Of course not! He would only tell me an assignment to get something from you. This is fun only! Right?"

Matt forced a laugh, his heart racing at what she had just revealed about Vadim. "Yes, Anna, this is fun only."

They ended the call with Anna promising to keep him updated on the "bathing suit situation." Matt sat there thoughtfully for a moment, his finger on the button, a smile lingering on his lips. The conversation had the surprising effect of lifting his mood, and he decided that, just for the moment, he would enjoy it without beating himself up. He released the button and dialed Roger's number.

"Very interesting," Roger said when Matt told him about Vadim's ignorance of the trip. "Of course, she might be lying about that, or it could mean she is not as committed to Mother Russia as we think."

With his official duties, overt and covert, completed, Matt curled into a fetal position and closed his eyes. But sleep eluded him. He couldn't stop thinking about his lies to Catherine, or wondering if Anna's excitement was that of an immigrant seeing the beach for the first time, or part of her work as a seasoned she-spy. Either way, she seemed to be less Mata Hari and more of a real down-to-earth girl – and more appealing.

*   *   *

Matt's first assignment the next morning was to "go upstairs and clean out a safe," in the office next to that of the National Security Advisor. When he arrived, a secretary directed him to a small safe; Matt was to remove all the documents and file them in the Sit Room. He spent the next few minutes emptying the safe, taking care not to disturb the files' order as he placed them in a cart borrowed from the mailroom. When he finished and closed the safe, he heard a curious sound, as though a paper was caught behind the drawer. He reached his hand inside and, sure enough, felt something behind the partially extended drawer. With some awkwardness, he twisted his shoulder to allow him to get his arm as far in as possible and extricate a brown envelope, crushed and worn with age.

Matt blinked twice when he saw the name scribbled by hand on the envelope – Frank Sinatra! He stared at it a moment, fighting the temptation to take a peek, then tossed it in with the rest of the files and returned to the Sit Room, where he immediately began to add the files to the huge cabinet of presidential files behind Ed's desk.

"Matt, get the door!" shouted the duty officer.

Matt knew the request meant someone who didn't have the Sit Room combination needed to get in. Quickly, he proceeded to the main door that opened directly behind Sergeant Van's desk. He heard a succession of three bells ring, the signal from the Secret Service Command Center to the Sergeant that the President was about to pass his station. In seconds, President Ford came down the small staircase by the elevator, just off the lobby. Ford seemed to know the purpose Matt was serving as he held the door open.

"Hello, young man. How are you doing?" he asked, smiling broadly.

"Fine, thank you, Mr. President!"

The President continued into the Sit Room, followed by a retinue of Secret Service Agents, each of whom either smiled or nodded to Matt with gratitude for holding the door open. He stood there, filled with pride and awe, and wondering how it could be that he, recently promoted messenger, insignificant college student and beer-chugging champion, was allowing the President of the United States of America into the most sensitive and secretive room in the White House!

When he closed the door and headed back to his desk, the agents had taken up positions in front of the conference room, waiting on their charge. The conference room door was closed, but the Director was standing in front of it, peering through a small peephole that allowed the Sit Room staff to keep abreast of the needs of the nation's leaders inside.

"May I take a look?" Matt asked.

"Sure." The Director agreed so casually one wouldn't suspect they were talking about peeking in on the President of The United States. Matt stepped up to the door, pressed his eye against the tiny brass eyepiece, and looked in. The small device gave a fisheye view of the room. Matt could clearly see President Ford at the head of the table. Henry Kissinger, who was seated to one side, was speaking. Across from Kissinger was General Scowcroft, National Security Advisor to the President, and next to him was CIA Director William Colby. Matt wished he could spy on them all day; it was such a neat thing to do with the complicity of the Director and the Secret Service agents. Since, on the other hand, he didn't want his interest to appear unusual, he returned to his desk in the back of the room and continued to file the contents of the safe.

His simple filing task soon became bogged down because he couldn't resist reading the documents. When a nearby voice asked, "May I use this phone?" Matt didn't even look up.

"Sure," he responded indifferently.

"Thanks," the voice said.

Matt remained so engrossed in his reading that he didn't take notice when the man sat down on the edge of the desk, or when he reached out and dragged the secure telephone toward him.

"Hello, Operator. This is Director Colby. I'd like to speak to Deputy Director Walters."

For Matt, hearing this was like being doused with ice water. He jumped up, sending his chair hurling back against the file cabinet, and saw that the man who had just seated himself on the desk beside him was indeed William E. Colby, Director of the Central Intelligence Agency. Colby noted Matt's deer-in-the-headlights look and offered a warm smile.

"Excuse me, sir! I didn't realize it was you. Please, take my seat." He guided the errant chair toward Mr. Colby, then turned to walk away. "I'll give you privacy."

"No! No! Don't let me interfere with your work," Mr. Colby commanded, waving his hand for Matt to sit back down.

Matt obligingly sat back down and pretended to read, but he couldn't concentrate. All he could think about was the head of America's spy organization, seated less than a foot away from him, having a top-secret conversation with his Deputy Director.

When he finished, Mr. Colby dropped the phone back into place. "Sorry to disturb your work."

"I apologize, sir," Matt began, but William Colby waved him away.

Then, looking him squarely in the eye, he said, "You know, we both have jobs to do. I am sorry for disturbing yours."

"No problem, sir!"

As Mr. Colby walked away, Matt looked around the Sit Room, relieved to see that the duty officers hadn't noticed the interaction.

Now continuing his task in earnest, Matt finally came to the mysterious envelope labeled "Frank Sinatra." His eyes grew big when he began to read it. It was a dossier that documented every aspect of the famous singer's life, organized by his acquaintances, finances, purported associations with the mafia, and even his sex life. Matt was so engrossed he hardly blinked as he ingested it all. When he finished, he stared into space, wondering what the file was doing there. It was like something one would read in a supermarket tabloid. He picked up the envelope and studied it, noting again the wrinkles and discoloration that occurs with age. The thing had apparently been stuck in the safe for years. In a flash, he recalled old stories about J. Edgar Hoover ingratiating himself with Presidents Kennedy and Johnson by providing information on people, from political foes to socialites. Surely, this was one of those files.

He looked the document over carefully, realizing it was written and packaged so as to not betray its origin. The paper was plain white paper, not government bond, which contained the watermark of the Seal of the United States. The envelope was plain, with no return address. Both could have come from any local office supply store. But one thing stood out: the document's straightforward and factual manner. It read like a government report. Details were presented like facts. An official investigator had authored it – and they clearly had vast resources at their disposal – sources capable of finding out minute details of a person's most private affairs, as well as the ability to bug phones and rooms.

Surely, Matt thought, *J. Edgar Hoover was behind this!*

He imagined Hoover in his trademark double-breasted suit, pulling the very document from a valise in the Oval Office and handing it to a President. Matt thought about the ongoing investigations on Capitol Hill for government dirty tricks, remembering that domestic spying was the catalyst for the fall of President Nixon. The document he held now was a clear invasion of privacy. Without further reflection, he stood up, walked over to a document shredder, and slowly fed the papers into the machine. He saw the minuscule pieces of diced paper drop into a clear plastic trash bag below the device. That paper was now only a part of the past, along with the people who created and read it.

The moment was broken by the senior duty officer. "Police up the conference room, would you please, Matt?"

Matt looked around the corner to see that the President and his national security team had left. As he was accustomed to doing in another conference room for Glen and Keith, he began to clean up, placing the chairs uniformly along the table. He sharpened pencils and placed them along the top of the White House notepads. As instructed, he tore off the top page of every notepad so the writer's imprint on subsequent pages was not left behind. He thought about what the President and the most senior government leaders were discussing in that very room just minutes before. Then he thought about William Colby's conversation with the Deputy Director.

When he came to the seat where Mr. Colby had been sitting, he noticed that the imprint made by the CIA Director's writing was particularly deep on the top page. Matt looked around to confirm he was alone; then, feeling very much like one of le Carré's characters, he took a freshly sharpened pencil and slowly rubbed the point sideways across the page. Like magic, the indentations created by Mr. Colby's hand contrasted against the black graphite. Matt read the paper – Colby's observations from the meeting – and decided that it too should be shredded. Leaving the room, he started to feel guilty. He promised himself that he would never again think about the Sinatra dossier or Colby's notes. Yet, even as he made this promise, he smiled at the thought that he spied on the nation's chief spy.

CHAPTER THIRTY-TWO

Matt told Anna he'd meet her at National Airport, which left him time for a last-minute prep meeting with Roger. Now, as he sat in the terminal waiting for her, he regretted that decision. Whenever he was alone with his thoughts the guilt over lying to Catherine ate away him like acid – not to mention what was surely to happen during that trip. It was one thing to avoid sleeping with Anna when he was rushing between classes and work, but he could hardly do that when they were staying in the same hotel room on a "just for fun" getaway.

Just a few days earlier, he'd dropped Catherine off at the same terminal for her flight to La Guardia.

"You sure you can't come?" she said, one of several invitations she had issued since she told him she would be spending Christmas in Connecticut, then heading to Manhattan for a New Year's Eve bash with high school friends.

Matt shook his head. "You know I would love to, but I'm committed to the Sit Room."

"Yes," Catherine said, "And you can't fool me, Matt Thomas. You love every minute of it."

Matt grinned. "I do. But I still wish I could be with you."

"Next year," she said, with a simple confidence that both gave him hope and broke his heart.

He squeezed her hand, feeling like shit. "Next year."

After her flight safely took off, he walked to his car and drove around the city, thinking it might cheer him up. Christmas in

Washington was remarkably beautiful, every sight like the scene from a postcard. The White House, which was decorated for the season, was like its crown jewel. Matt parked his car and went to stand by the North Gate at the Executive Mansion, festooned with garlands. While he stood there, a group of tourists wandered up and peered at it with wonder in their eyes.

What do they think when they look at this place? he'd asked himself. *Do they hope for an unlikely glimpse of the President? Do they imagine what it's like to live here?* Whatever, it seemed strange to him now that while he knew every nook and cranny of the place, he was still awestruck, like the people a few feet away.

He had then walked along Pennsylvania Avenue and down 17th Street to the Ellipse, known as the President's Park, where he came upon the national Christmas tree, lit just days earlier by the President. Surrounding the majestic tree were Christmas trees from every state and territory in the United States. Matt checked out each one, pausing longer at the ones from his home, Michigan, and Connecticut, where Catherine was spending the holiday. Behind the display of trees, Santa's reindeer were camped in a manger constructed by the U.S. Park Service. He watched the animals munch hay and wander about in their pen, looking back at the humans with curiosity. Among all this, in the shadow of the White House, a yule log burned. His sight, smell, and spirit were all touched, lifting his spirits as he turned back to his car.

Matt was brought back to the present by the slapping sound of shoes against skin. Anna. He knew it was her, even before he looked up and saw her crossing the terminal toward him, her lovely face split by a grin. She was dressed like she was already in Florida, with a flamingo pink dress, matching flip-flops, sunglasses, and a frivolous beach hat. The sight immediately lifted his spirits and for a moment he could pretend that Catherine, and even the plan to get the book, didn't exist.

"Aren't you freezing?" Matt asked as he half-stood and planted a kiss on her cheek, then settled back down in his chair.

"Where I am from, this is not cold," she laughed as she sat next to him and opened her bag to reveal a white bikini that left little to the imagination.

"You know, I have never been to the beach before."

"Yes, you told me. I'll have to teach you some things," he said, looking at her exposed toes with a grin.

"Like what?"

"Like you can get sunburned, for starters. Then, too, you can be eaten by a shark. It is a dangerous place."

For a second her eyes widened, then she realized he was making fun and swatted him playfully.

Suddenly, Matt was all too aware that they were in an airport during the busiest time of the year. Yes, he had been in public with Anna, but only in a couple of restaurants. He wasn't worried about someone from work seeing them – Roger could easily fix that – but his frat brothers or fellow AU students were a different story. To anyone, it would be obvious they were traveling together. He nervously scanned the terminal and was relieved to see no familiar faces.

"We'll be boarding soon," he said, "I'm going to hit the men's room."

It wasn't until he was standing in front of the sink that it hit him again: this was not a vacation with the sexy Russian girl, but an FBI-run "op" intended to bring down a Soviet mole in American intelligence. A sudden wave of nausea rose within him, and the chill that ran up his spine had nothing to do with the water he splashed on his face.

"You can do this," he whispered, then dried his face with a paper towel and headed for the door.

Anna stood as he approached the chairs. "Ready?" she said, threading her arm through his. "Let's go to the gate."

Later, Matt would recall what happened next as a scene worthy of the classic spy novels he loved so much but rarely had time for anymore. He had just handed his boarding pass to the ticket agent and was waiting for Anna to fish hers out of her purse. That's when he saw him – Michael, his nemesis and rival for Catherine – standing across the terminal. He was standing sideways as he too looked through his bag for something, yet Matt could make out the proud slope of his nose and his arrogant perma-smirk anywhere. With a lump in his throat, he spun around and walked toward the plane.

"Matt, Matt! Wait for me!" Anna called gaily as she rushed to catch up to him.

Matt stopped but could not risk turning around. If Michael saw him…

Just as he reached the plane door, he snuck a sideways glance and saw Michael, still staring off in another direction.

"Okay," he whispered on an exhale, "It's okay."

Anna fell asleep almost immediately after takeoff – likely exhausted by a week of non-stop shopping and anticipation – with her head gently resting on Matt's shoulder. Matt realized he was enjoying the subtle pressure, and the way her perfume mingled with the fresh scent of her hair, far too much.

What the hell am I doing?

He loathed cheating on Catherine, even if it was in the name of national security. It wouldn't begin to restore her trust if she somehow found out. He ordered a gin and tonic. It calmed him with purpose. Reflection brought clarity. He realized the only way to deal with the situation was to draw a divide between his responsibility and his personal life. He just had to get comfortable with the game.

A few hours later, they arrived at the hotel in Fort Lauderdale, where Roger had made arrangements for them. They approached the front desk together.

"Mr. and Mrs. Thomas," Matt announced to the clerk.

Anna joked, "Still feels like we are newlyweds when you say that, doesn't it, sweetheart?"

The clerk looked at Matt and the two shared an uncomfortable stare.

Maybe, Matt thought, *the guy is trying to figure us out. Anna, after all, is noticeably older. Then again, maybe this guy is an FBI Agent.*

Anna surveyed the lobby. "This is a nice hotel. I'd like to take a look around. May I have a key, sweetheart?"

Matt gave her a key, which she traded for a kiss on the cheek.

"See you soon," she said as she walked away, leaving her suitcase with him. For a split second he was excited at the thought of access to her luggage; then he noticed her clutching her purse, undoubtedly with the black book inside. He definitely had his work cut out for him.

When the check-in process was complete, Matt took Anna's suitcase, along with his, and headed to their room. Roger had outdone himself, booking them a beautiful king-size suite overlooking the ocean. Matt threw their bags on the bed, opened large glass doors leading to a balcony, and stepped out. He placed his hands on the rail and took in a deep breath of fresh, salty ocean air. It was quite a difference from the wintry Washington weather he left behind only hours before. The view was stunning. He could see the curvature of the earth and the transition from the blue green ocean into a light blue sky, a few billowy white clouds moving across it. In the distance, a few large ships sat on the horizon. The sun had long passed over the hotel, yet it was still a warm and soothing presence.

Matt sat in a patio chair, placed his feet on a small table, and comfortably dozed. After a few minutes he opened his eyes, looked around, and wondered where Anna was. A glance at his watch told him it had been about half an hour since she had disappeared. He fell back to sleep again.

When he awoke next he was aware of two things: the bridge of his nose burning, and Anna standing beside him.

"This is so beautiful," she said reverently as she looked out at the ocean, "I am so happy you asked me."

Matt smiled and found he was genuinely pleased to have given her this experience. "See anything interesting on your tour?"

"Shops and sand," she said laughing as she disappeared into the bathroom.

Matt started to nod off again, only to be brought round by a resounding knock on the door.

"Who could that be?" he said out loud. As he jumped up from the chair and crossed the room it occurred to him that this could be a reverse set-up. With a nervous twinge, he pulled open the door half expecting to see Vadim. Instead, he found a man from room service.

"Two bottles of Bollinger, slightly chilled, for Mr. and Mrs. Thomas." He rolled a small cart past the surprised Matt. "Shall I open one, Mr. Thomas?"

"Of course," Matt replied, realizing what Anna had been up to while she was out. He opened his wallet, looking for a small bill to tip the man, but was dismayed to find he only had a wad of fifty-dollar-bills Roger had pressed into his hand at their last meeting at Whitey's.

"Do you have change for a fifty?" he asked, watching the man place a towel around one of the bottles. With ease, he then uncorked the bottle, producing a customary pop that echoed across the room. Before the man could answer Matt's question, the bathroom door opened. Anna appeared, stretching her arm along the door like a siren from an old movie. She was wearing her bikini. It looked more like three Band-Aids held together with dental floss than a swimsuit.

Matt turned to see the man from room service staring at Anna with wide-eyed shock. Muttering his thanks for the Bollinger, he placed both hands on the man's shoulders and guided him unceremoniously to the hall.

"Keep the change," he said, shoving the fifty at him, then closed the door in his face.

He turned back around to see Anna sauntering toward him.

"You know what to do with that?" she asked, gazing at the opened bottle.

Matt lifted the bottle off the cart and began pouring into a glass. She reached over, grabbed the bottle, and taking a step backward, with a calm, contented smile, poured its contents over herself with one hand. With the other hand, she seductively rubbed the bubbly stuff across her chest then let the bottle fall to the floor.

"Oops!" she said with a mischievous grin as she fell backward onto the bed. "Be a darling, won't you, Matt? Lick this cold champagne off me."

*   *   *

Matt was awakened from a sound sleep by an odd pressure around his waist. He opened his eyes to find the room dark, save a stream of moonlight coming in through the sliding doors. Anna, dressed in a T-shirt tucked into jeans and a ball cap, sat on him.

"Let's go."

"Huh? What time is it?"

"Time to get going."

He pulled himself up on his elbows. "Where?"

"To the beach."

"It's dark," he observed.

"Exactly!" Anna answered excitedly, "I want to see the sun come up over the ocean."

It took Matt a quick minute to hop out of bed and get ready. Anna waited on the balcony.

"C'mon," he said as he opened the door, "The sun won't wait for us."

Anna rushed toward him. Her purse was slung over her shoulder. Matt was quick to realize that if she took it to the beach, it would eliminate a perfect opportunity for Roger's agents to accomplish his mission.

"What are you taking your purse for?" he inquired.

"A lady always has her necessaries nearby."

Think fast, Matt!

"Okay," he said good-naturedly, stepping aside so she could pass. "But don't blame me if you get your necessaries wet and full of sand."

She paused. "You think that will happen?"

"It's the beach, Anna. I'm not taking my wallet. He pulled a wad of cash out of his pocket. "This is all I'm taking so we can get something to eat. I don't want my wallet getting soggy!"

Anna looked conflicted.

"The water isn't just in the ocean, Anna. It's in the breeze. Sand, too."

She bit her lower lip, affirming serious introspection, then stepped back into the room, wound her arm up like a pitcher getting ready to throw a softball, and tossed the purse onto the bed. She turned and ran down the hall excitedly calling out, "I'll beat you to the beach!"

Matt followed her to the elevator and sent up a silent plea to the agents.

Please, please make the best of this.

It was still dark as they crossed the street outside the hotel and walked to the ocean. They watched the water come and go for a few minutes, then sat down on the edge of its closest invasion. Anna put her arm around him and her head on his shoulder, igniting mixed feelings. He was comfortable being with her. Her warmth was easy to accept. He was smart enough to understand her motives, like getting him to sell out his country. He had no confusion about that. Roger and Jensen had drilled it into him. But there he sat with the woman who was not just beautiful but affectionate and fun-loving. Anna had the innocent curiosity of a child, wearing flip-flops in the cold Washington airport and wanting to see the sunrise over the ocean.

Matt shook his head as if to clear it of these disturbing thoughts. The horizon started to show a touch of light, announcing the sun's arrival.

"Are you thinking about her?" Anna asked, breaking the stillness.

Matt turned to stare at her in shock. "Thinking about who?"

"That college girl."

"But how –?"

Anna waved the question away as if to indicate it insulted her intelligence. "Women know these things. You love her, don't you?" she asked, but it was more a statement than a question.

"Yes," he admitted, "but I think I am confused. I am happy being here with you."

She tightened her arm around him. "You can't let yourself be confused. Men have lovers. Women have lovers."

"Where do you get that, Anna? Have you ever been in love?"

"I don't think in terms of love. I live for today. We don't own tomorrow. It is not ours." Anna tilted her head slightly and tightened her smile. "Don't be naïve. You know what this is. I adore how you make it easy and enjoyable. But I have a job, and you must realize that part of it."

For the second time in as many minutes, Matt was stunned. Was she being a friend or simply reeling him in tighter, knowing that through basic honesty she might ingratiate herself even more? He had no idea, and in that moment desperately wished Roger could hear what she was saying.

"What's there for you, Anna? Will you go home a hero? Have a nice life, knowing you wreaked havoc here?"

"It's not like that. I told you, I am living in this moment. I don't know what comes next."

"Really? 'Cause I can't imagine a life in a world of people like Vadim!"

Anna squirmed against him. "Let's not talk about it, okay?"

He didn't say another word. It wasn't necessary. She seemed conflicted, or at least uncomfortable, with the possibilities in her future. In that, they were united.

Traffic was starting to pick up on the road behind them. The day had begun. They walked along the beach for a couple of hours. Flip-flops in hand, Anna playfully dodged the water, every now and then catching a soaking wave, turning to splash him. Matt laughed at her schoolgirl spirit. Walking back to the hotel, they held hands. It was such a nice, relaxed time that they stopped at the hotel pool to lounge some more. A waiter appeared, and despite the early hour Matt ordered a couple of mojitos. He was enjoying himself, but he also wanted to give Roger as much time as possible.

"It's a Cuban rum drink," he told Anna when she looked him with a raised eyebrow. "You'll love it."

And she did love it, enough to order two more. By early afternoon, they were ready for something to eat. Returning to the room, they found it had been cleaned. Anna immediately went for her purse, which had been relocated from the newly made bed to a table near the television. For an instant she lost herself looking through it while Matt pretended not to notice. He watched through the mirror as she combed the contents, clearly taking inventory. Apparently, her concern was calmed, because after going through it she put the purse over her shoulder and calmly said, "Let's get something to eat. I am starving!"

*   *   *

They were seated in a restaurant overlooking the beach, just down the street from their hotel. Their table was near the front, affording a delightful view of the ocean just beyond passing traffic on A1A. It was a slice of heaven – fresh warm air, a light breeze and the enticing smell of the food that had been delivered to the next table. Seated at that table was a family, a husband, wife and two small children. Matt noticed the man staring at Anna.

He is too obvious to be undercover FBI, Matt thought. *Maybe he is from Anna's world? Or maybe he is just a guy, tired of the kids, thinking about life before parenthood – and perhaps marriage too.*

Regardless, the situation was unsettling – a reminder that this was not a normal weekend getaway.

"Be right back," he said to Anna and pointed in the direction of the restrooms. As he walked through the crowded eatery, his eyes flicked back and forth, seeing no one unusual. He had no sooner entered the men's room when he was pushed from behind into a toilet stall.

Matt grunted, then turned around, sure he was going to find Vadim or some other Russian thug. Instead, he was facing a woman's back. She was locking the door. The space was so small that when she twisted around to face him her nose nearly touched the tip of his, and their chests were lightly pressed together.

"What the—?" he said, but stopped when the attractive, athletic woman held her finger to her lips.

"Matt, I am a colleague of Roger's," she whispered. "He is here but staying out of sight."

"Okay," Matt whispered back, his limbs weak with relief.

"Our job was accomplished this morning. Roger wants you to know that we got what we came for. He is extremely satisfied. We are closing down."

"Okay," Matt said again. "What's that mean?"

"It means you did your job. Nicely, I might add. We have what we need. We're heading home. You will be on your own from now on. Roger said to continue to enjoy your vacation. He will catch up with you at the other end."

"Okay," Matt said; he seemed unable to say anything else.

She allowed herself a small smile. "Yeah, we were particularly impressed with how you handled it when your friend wanted to take her 'necessaries' to the beach."

Despite the small space Matt managed to jerk back. "Wait! Say what? How would you know that?" Matt peered at her. "Were you listening to us? You were. Did you take pictures too?"

She searched for a response.

Matt didn't wait for it. "You fucker! You were listening, weren't you?"

Again, she attempted to say something, but he spoke over her.

"You recorded this and took pictures. Of course, you are all like Hoover. I've seen his files."

She raised a curious eyebrow. He was highly agitated.

"Now you fucks have a file on me! You set me up to do this shit, and you are going to have a file that will follow me forever. You fuckers!" His voice became louder.

"That's it. I quit. I am out of here!"

He tried to push her aside but in the cramped space he couldn't get by. He reached behind her and jiggled the lock. In doing so, their bodies were pressed together.

"You can't go. You need to follow this through."

"What I need is to get the hell out of here," He raised his gaze upward as if looking to escape over the top.

Suddenly, the agent pushed him backward over the toilet. He gripped the wall to steady himself.

"I need you to focus," she said. It was not a request.

Ignoring her, he reached upward, putting his hands on top of the walls, preparing to raise himself. Without another word, she inched backward and pulled her top off, exposing her breasts. Stunned, Matt dropped down onto the toilet seat.

"Was that necessary? Really?"

She thought for a second. "It was that or my gun. I was afraid you were going over the top."

"I guess I should be glad you didn't go with Plan B," Matt muttered, thinking one day he might think this was funny, but that day would not come for a very long time. He took a deep, calming breath and sighed with resignation. "This whole thing has me bewildered in every direction. I'm not even going to ask what your deal is."

"I need to know if you are with me or if we have a problem…"

Matt thought for a minute. He looked at her breasts. Sheepishly, he said, "I'll do it."

"Look me in the eyes. Let me hear it again."

"It's a little hard to look you in the eyes with the 'ladies' staring me in the face."

She quickly put her top in place. Matt stood up and unintentionally brushed against her chest.

Her lips twitched in amusement. "Couldn't resist, could you?"

"How could I? You inspired me. I mean, your commitment!"

She shook her head, confident the volatile situation had passed, and turned to open the door.

"Let's keep this between you and me. No reason to broadcast it."

"What?" Matt shot back sarcastically. "You mean that isn't in your manual?"

"The manual only covers Plan B," she laughed, then turned serious as she pulled the door open.

"Tell me again, are we good?"

"Yes," Matt answered, almost apologetically.

"Okay, then. Let's get out of here."

When he stepped out, he saw in the mirror above the sink, a broad smile on her face as she preceded him. Then he saw a man washing his hands. It was the same man who'd had been admiring Anna, and just now saw the female agent emerge from the stall.

"It's a burden," Matt said, shaking his head and thoroughly enjoying the shocked look on his face.

There was a short service hallway leading back to the dining area. Matt stopped, leaned against a wall, and took a deep breath to transition from the FBI back to Anna. He could see Anna looking out at the beach. Her chin rested on her fists. She appeared to be enjoying herself.

"She really is a beautiful woman," he said, under his breath. He flashed back to his military school days, when he never could have imagined speaking to a girl who looked like her, let alone the situation he now faced with Anna, Catherine, and whatever just happened in the restroom. He remembered the hot secretary pressing her breast against his hand on the copy machine that first day at the White House and Glen's reaction, saying he was oversexed and underfed.

"I wish Glen could see me now!" he mumbled.

*   *   *

After returning from Ft. Lauderdale, Matt walked into four thirty-one for his meeting with Roger. His eyes scanned the room, spotted the FBI man at a table with his usual pitcher, and strode toward him with angry purpose. Immediately sensing something was amiss, Roger reached for the pitcher and began pouring.

"I thought we would toast our success," he said.

Matt didn't waste time with niceties. He slid into the chair. "Did you record me?"

Roger pushed a beer over to him. "Don't worry about it. We are required to destroy it in twenty-five years."

"I can't believe what an asshole you are. Did you take pictures, too?"

Roger laughed. "I'm kidding. There is no recording and no pictures. We did have a bug in your room, so yes, we overheard. But nothing was recorded."

Relaxing slightly, Matt decided to believe him. "It's still disturbing to think you were listening."

"Believe me, it's not my favorite part of the job," Roger lamented. "I felt like a creep. When we got the book, we pulled chocks and left. You were on your own after that – believe me!" He took a drink. "You did really great. Wonder Woman's book is a treasure trove. I can't tell you what we got, but it's a big service to us. There are some names in there that were surprising. Let's just say this was nearly a total success."

Matt took a greedy gulp of his beer. "That's great to hear, Roger. So now that you got what you wanted, let's claim victory and I'll just jump off the merry-go-round."

"Yeah, like that is gonna happen," Roger said unsympathetically.

"You just said this was successful; you got what you want."

"I said it was nearly a total success. Yes, we got names, but we don't have anything to indicate which, if any of them, is the mole." Roger paused as their favorite waitress approached.

"You guys want something to eat?"

"We'll have some tater tots and wings. That work for you Matt?" Roger asked.

"Whatever," Matt shot back indifferently.

When she left, Roger leaned into the table. "This is getting very interesting. You are getting to her. I can tell."

"That's not what I want to hear, Roger. Plus, it's not true. You know better than me, this is a game and she is playing me."

"True, but she let you get close. That is unusual."

"Roger, this is getting on my nerves. I'm confused. Sometimes she seems so real, innocent, and funny. I like her."

Roger leaned back, drawing a deep breath. "Okay, that is *not good*. She is a fucking spy."

"No shit! You think I don't realize that? Why don't you get to know her? You lick champagne off her. She is awesome."

Roger thought for a moment as if considering the possibility. "She *is* bodacious. And she is enjoying herself, isn't she?"

"She might fake some stuff, but I don't think she is faking everything. And neither can I."

Roger's eyes got big. "You know, I think you are at a critical point."

"Really!" Matt answered sarcastically. "A critical point, so let's kill it."

Roger leaned forward again. "A critical point in that maybe she is signaling us. Maybe she is trying to tell you – "

Matt cut him off. "She opened up to me." Roger hunched more forward. "She admitted to me she is a spy. And that this is a game. She is lonely."

Roger put his hands on his head.

"This is beyond awesome. She is trying to say she wants a different life! One we can give her!"

"It's too much for me, Roger. This is not what I signed up for. I am half in love with this she-spy. I need to forget all this and just go back to being a college student. Go to work every day…go back to Catherine."

"Who…? Oh, that girl from campus?" Roger waved him away. "Don't be ridiculous. This is your future. Someday you will write your own ticket, you can write a book –"

Matt interrupted. "I have no future with Catherine if she finds out about this Anna thing,"

"Wonder Woman," Roger interjected.

"Whatever, whoever," Matt continued. "It is making me crazy."

Roger gulped his beer. "Let's look at this for a second. She admits all the things you just said. She probably jeopardized herself going to Florida. That violated a restriction; she is not allowed to travel outside D.C. It is doubtful she told her boss about the trip."

"She told me she didn't," Matt reminded him.

"There you are," Roger said, thrusting both hands forward to emphasize his point. "We are close, Matt. Close to having a coup here. If we can turn her, it would be a fantastic win for us."

"You mean for you."

"For our side," Roger emphasized. "Seriously, we have come so far. Let's give it some time."

"What the hell, Roger. I have given it time. Look where I am. I'm getting in deeper."

Roger began a lecture. "You're being emotional. If you look at this objectively, you'll see how good you are at this. We have to give it a little more time. That is all I ask. I'm thinking she will slow down a bit back here in D.C., where fat ass – what's his name, Vomit?"

"Vadim," Matt corrected.

"Under his nose she will be more restrained. Maybe we'll get back to just plain old espionage. But we have to give her the opportunity to help us."

The waitress appeared with their food, indifferently shoving it across the table. When she left, Roger changed the subject.

"How'd you like our female agent down there? Pretty amazing, heh?"

"I only saw her for a couple of seconds!"

"Oh, yeah," Roger said, realizing the encounter was brief.

Matt could not help himself. With an impish grin, he allowed, "I didn't get a good feel." Roger nodded understandingly. Matt's impish grin grew into an uncontrollable laugh.

"What's so funny?" Roger asked.

Matt barely eked out a weak, "Nothing. If I don't laugh, I'll cry."

Roger changed the topic then, signifying an end to any discussion of Matt's freedom. The FBI agent was so fixed on his mission, he didn't care how it affected him. Letting it drop for the moment, Matt popped a final tater tot in his mouth; there were a few remaining crumbs on the plate, not worth the effort to go for. He stared at them absently as he considered his situation. He was scared by how much he liked Anna – loved her, maybe. He knew this thing could ruin his relationship with Catherine. If things kept going as they were, he might end up cold and lonely, like the crumbs in front of him.

CHAPTER THIRTY-THREE

The next ten days brought a strange lull in his dealings with Anna. She didn't call as often, and when they did speak she sounded cheerful enough, though somewhat distracted. Maybe, he thought hopefully, she and Vadim were losing interest in him; maybe they had moved on to someone else. Later, Matt would realize that her cheerfulness had a fragility to it, as if it could crack at any minute. In the moment, however, he was just relieved to have a little less stress in his life. While most of the country had slowed down for the holidays, for those doing the people's business, it was as hectic as ever.

Matt enjoyed working in the Sit Room – it was one of those extremely rare life experiences that one recognizes for the opportunity it is in real-time. For Matt, the enjoyment turned to a hyper-awareness, knowing that once Ed returned it would be back to the Secretariat and Murph's banal commentary about the weather. While he was grateful for that job too, nothing could compare to the excitement and access of the Sit Room.

One evening he was approaching his dorm room, take-out bag from the diner in hand, looking forward to quality time with a burger, fries, and his bunk. Those plans were dashed when he heard the phone in his room ringing before he got his key in the door.

"I need to speak with you now," Anna said without preamble, "Can we meet at the Irish place right away?"

"I'm just fine, thanks for asking," he said, not missing a beat. "Let me check my calendar. Looks like I have an opening, should I pencil you in?"

Anna uttered a half-hearted apology for the abruptness, then hung up the phone. With a groan, Matt zipped his coat back up and grabbed the white bag from the diner. He might have to forgo some sleep, but he was not letting a perfectly good burger go to waste.

Fifteen minutes later, he walked into the Irish pub, full but slightly queasy from wolfing down the burger in the car. Anna was nowhere in sight, so he grabbed the only unoccupied table, which, unfortunately, was adjacent to a game of darts. For the next several minutes, he was distracted by the occasional dart whizzing by, then he saw Anna arrive. As she walked across the bar and surveyed the situation, her face, already tense, tightened into a grimace when she saw his perilous location.

"There aren't any other tables…" he said, rising to greet her.

"I see that," she hollered over the outburst of a player who had just made a bull's eye. "Let's take a walk, okay?" She gestured toward the door, and he took her delicate hand and led her out.

"There. This is much better," Anna said outside in the quiet of the evening.

"What is so important?" Matt asked, getting right to the point. The hairs on the back of his neck were standing up, and it had nothing to do with the cold.

"Let's walk a bit," she replied, drawing in a deep breath and veering off busy Connecticut Avenue up a less hectic side street. It was dark out, but the combination of a bright moon and residential streetlamps lit the sidewalk. A few minutes seemed like a long time. Anna finally broke the silence, her words coming out in a torrent.

"I need to ask you for help. Vadim is pushing me to get information from you. Please help me, Matt. I've put him off for a while now. He is getting frustrated with me."

"Really?" Matt deadpanned. "That is a problem for both of us, isn't it?"

She squeezed his hand. "You understand me, don't you? I know this is not good for you, Matt, and I did not want to ask. I have no choice."

Matt turned to look her in the eyes. He wasn't clear if she was feigning her reluctance, if she thought he was a hero or a dupe. He was furious with himself for not being able to tell – and for having convinced himself that she might simply fade from his life.

"I'm terrified to ask, but what is it you need?"

"He wants information about Vietnam…what your country is going to do. Matt, he is wild; I have never seen him like this before. I'm afraid he's going to…" she trailed off.

Matt refused to take the bait, though at her implication he felt an uncomfortable flutter in his stomach. How far would Vadim go to get what he needed?

"I haven't discussed it with the President."

"Don't tease me, please." She reached out and clutched his arm, her fingers digging in for emphasis.

"Give me some time; I'll see what I can find out."

Without a word, she grabbed him by the shoulders and gave him a long, hard kiss. His heart thumped so loud he feared residents could hear it behind their closed doors.

"Anna, maybe it would be better if you walk in front of me. I'll follow and make sure you get into your car."

She hugged him again; then, to his relief, she turned around and began striding, relaxed but purposeful, ahead of him.

As soon as he got back to the dorm he called Roger at home. A woman answered the phone, then called for him, her hand over the receiver to muffle the sound. A moment later, Roger answered with tiredness in his voice.

"Oh, did I wake you?" Matt snapped. "Listen, my friend called. I went ahead and met her 'cause she said it was urgent and I didn't have time to call you. She asked for more information. Roger, she wants information about our plans in Vietnam!"

"Okay, calm down," Roger said, but he sounded excited.

"Also, she seemed scared, really scared."

"Do you believe her?"

"Who knows? She might be acting. But she said she put it off for a while and Vadim was seriously on her case about it. Roger, she stopped just short of saying he might do something to her if I don't get it…"

He could almost hear Roger rolling his eyes.

"Okay. Come to Jensen's before you start work tomorrow. Good job, Matt."

They hung up, and Matt sat down hard on the bunk and put his head in his hands.

The next day, Roger and Jensen were waiting for him in Jensen's office. It was a quick meeting. They were both pleased.

"This may take a little time, since this is real shit. It will have to be developed and approved by a few levels." Jensen said, rubbing his chin.

"How long is a little time?" Roger asked impatiently.

"I don't know. I'll expedite it."

Roger looked at Matt. "If Wonder Woman gets impatient, play scared and say something like, 'I'm looking for it. Don't push me. I have to be careful.'"

"I can handle that." Matt looked at his watch and saw he was late for work. "Gotta go."

As he turned to leave, Roger said, "Oh, and Matt?"

"Yeah, Roger?"

"Try to keep those feelings of yours under wraps – got it?"

Matt saw the look of surprise on Jensen's face as he left the room to rush down the hall. As he took the imposing staircase two stairs at a time, he wondered how long it would take Jensen and Roger to get the information for him to give Anna. Hopefully soon; he wanted, needed, to get this over with. He had a nagging feeling that something was coming to a head. He was also sure Roger and Jensen had continued their discussion about him after he left, and, for all he knew, were making decisions that would cement his future.

*　*　*

"Change of plans," Catherine said, her tone unreadable, when Matt answered the phone the following night.

"Oh, really?" Matt said, intrigued and nervous at the same time. Once upon a time, he'd liked surprises and spontaneity; these days, such changes sent him down a rabbit hole spanning from D.C. to Moscow. "Is this change good or bad?"

"Both, actually. My dad is insisting I come to the company Christmas party, something he hasn't done in years…"

"Okay…?"

"Somehow he heard I was seeing someone – well, seeing *you* – and he wants me to bring you. Matt," she said, her tone almost pleading, "Is there any way you can come to New York on the twentieth?"

Matt paused, mentally checking his schedule to make sure it didn't conflict with anything Anna-related. "The twentieth? That's this Friday…"

"Yes, and it's at the Pierre, a hotel on Fifth Avenue – really fancy," she said, half-joking. "Seriously, Matt, please come. I will never hear the end of it if you don't."

"Really?

"You don't know my father," Catherine said bitterly. "He's not in my life except when he sees a chance to control it, and he has this thing about my dating the 'right guys.'"

Matt took a breath. Despite everything going on, he didn't see a reason why he couldn't go. "I guess I can get a flight to New York after work."

"Oh, thank you! We'll have fun, I promise."

Somehow, Matt really doubted it. He also knew there was one way Mr. Martin could have heard about him: Michael.

*   *   *

It was Wednesday before Roger set up another meeting in Jensen's office. When Matt arrived, the two men were chatting around the conference table. A manila envelope was lying in the center.

"This is the most serious information we have turned over," Jensen said as Matt took a seat. "It has been developed and vetted by the intelligence community for you to release to your friend. It will really set the hook, Matt. They will be impressed and no doubt come back fast for more. We'll need to be ready."

Matt readjusted himself in the chair, displaying an element of discomfort. Roger reassuringly reached over and slapped his leg.

"You've pulled the wool over their eyes. This new load could be too good. It might impress them, or it might have the opposite effect and make them realize you are a plant working for us." His message, Matt noted nervously, was somewhat in conflict with Jensen's.

"I think you need to look nervous over this exchange," Roger said as if reading his thoughts. "Let's show her you are scared. Tell her you are scared. Tell her you need to cool it. Let her see you realize the seriousness of this. But don't overplay it; be natural. But let her see you are sweating, okay?"

Matt drew a deep breath and let it out slowly. "The way I am feeling right now, that won't be hard to do."

After his shift that evening, Matt returned to Jensen's office. Just like before, the envelope was in the top drawer of the desk. He stuffed it under his shirt, making sure it held firmly in place against his body by tightening his belt. It was a beautiful, clear evening as he walked outside the White House to his car. Despite the fact that what he was doing was at the behest of the FBI, he was terrified. The idea of walking outside the building again with classified information to give to a spy was frightening. He unlocked his car, got in and sat briefly looking at the illuminated White House.

This should be exciting, he thought, thinking of all the spy novels he had read. Instead, he was so fearful he could feel a line of sweat run down his spine. In many ways his life had become a terrifying experience. He turned the key in the ignition and adjusted the radio to his favorite station, laughing when he heard Johnny Rivers' "Secret Agent Man."

Minutes later, he found a parking spot on the side street where he had told Anna to meet him. He sat in his car, his heart racing. Roger's words came to mind. How funny it was that Roger wanted him to "play" scared. Of all the times he had met Anna, he'd never felt like this.

"Damn him for planting that idea!" he muttered out loud. Then, closing his eyes, he forced himself to think of that solo flight a few years earlier – the terror he had felt before and during takeoff, the exhilaration while gliding through the air, and the feeling of accomplishment when he landed after overcoming the fear. Nothing, before or since, had compared to those extremes, though his present circumstances certainly came in second.

Just as his pulse began to slow, he was jolted by a knock on the window. He turned, half expecting to see a cop. Instead, Anna was standing there with a perky smile. She had beaten him to the punch, finding his car before he got out to seek her. She passed around the front and jumped in the passenger side, leaned over and gave him a long and seemingly sincere kiss on the cheek. Awkwardly, Matt lifted his shirt to remove the envelope.

"Something for me?" she teased.

Matt could not match her lightheartedness. "Anna, this has me terrified. If I ever got caught giving you something like this, I would go to prison."

She leaned over, took the envelope with her left hand, while with her right hand she caressed the side of his face. "I would never let that happen to you. Trust me!"

He gulped. "I want to, Anna, but we have to cool it. This is really scaring me."

She leaned back in the seat, looked out the window. "You are helping me, and I will protect you. You have to believe me."

"I think I trust you. I am not sure about the rest of your colleagues."

She smiled. "Vadim is the only one who knows. No one else knows your identity."

"I have been seen at your apartment and the embassy."

"You worry too much. Maybe we need another trip to Florida to relax."

Matt grinned. "Not tonight."

When he got back to his room, the phone rang before he could take off his tie. "Thank you, darling!" Anna said, "Remind me to prove my appreciation."

Matt was in no mood for frisky conversation. He decided not to overplay the concern expressed earlier.

"Grossman," he shouted to the empty room, "quit picking your nose." Then he muttered into the phone, "He came back from break early." It was the best he could think of at the moment. Fortunately, it worked.

"I'll let you go then. You are the best. I am so grateful. Good night!" She hung up.

Matt thought for a minute, then called Roger at home to say he had done his job.

CHAPTER THIRTY-FOUR

That Friday at eight, Matt walked into the Pierre, feeling very much like James Bond in his rented tux. The best part of the short flight from D.C. had been his fellow passengers staring at him, apparently trying to place him as someone famous.

"It's black tie," Catherine had reminded him at least five times, clearly nervous about him meeting her father. Now, as he walked into the packed ballroom, he felt his stomach clench at the thought of it. He was playing enough roles in his life and in no mood to take on another.

He threaded the crowd of similarly well-dressed partiers, searching for Catherine and, seeing no sign of her, settled for the bar.

"A gin and tonic please," he said to the bartender.

"Very well, sir," replied the man, who was at least ten years Matt's senior. His tone was respectful yet mocking, as though he resented serving rich young brats.

A moment later, the rocks glass of cool, clear liquid appeared before him. Matt picked it up, turning around as he brought it to his lips. And that's when he saw her – Catherine, looking amazing, her natural beauty heightened by an afternoon at a salon. Her light brown hair was finely twisted into braids that brushed over her ears. A trace of dark eyeliner underscored her brown eyes, which contrasted with a slight rosy glow on her cheeks. Her fingernails were polished to a high natural gloss. Her dress was a sophisticated ivory color that clung to her shapely body. She looked like a movie star.

Catherine walked toward him, the color of her cheeks deepening under his stare.

"You're looking at me the way you did the first time in the cafeteria," she said.

At the truth of her words, Matt drew back with a small start. In that instant, he traveled back to that long-ago day when he first laid eyes on her, how he had felt. So much had changed since then – hell, he was barely recognizable to himself – and yet one thing had remained: he had loved her in that moment, and he loved her still. The moment of clarity made him weak in the knees.

"Well," he said, smiling as he took her gloved arm and allowed her to guide them to their table. "I guess I am."

After that, the evening would take a definite downward turn – indeed, a spiral. Matt and Catherine were the only young people at the table. She was seated next to her father, a distinguished man with silver hair and piercing blue eyes that seemed to be dissecting everything they looked upon. On the other side of the table were two older couples – long-time associates of Mr. Martin, Catherine explained under cover of the enormous centerpiece, and no doubt on the "A list" of New York society. They appeared to be stalled in an earlier part of the century, old and stodgy. Catherine's father made polite conversation with the other men, one of whom was evidently a congressman.

An orchestra was churning out classics from the big band era. When it played things appealing to the younger people, the adaptations were comically watered down. Largely left to their own devices, Catherine and Matt made their own fun, often by poking fun at some of the other guests as they danced. Every now and again, Matt would glance over to find her father watching him, his stare both cold and emitting an uncomfortable heat.

After a delicious and decadent meal consisting of duck and other things Matt couldn't identify, the orchestra began a more spirited number, which prompted Catherine to drag him into a throng of dancers.

As they moved around the dance floor, he softly sang in her ear "Pretty Woman," from the Roy Orbison album she had given him.

They were on their way back to the table when suddenly Matt felt Catherine slow her pace, then stop. When he turned and saw Michael, his hand on her elbow, Matt felt an unreasonable surge of annoyance that he sought to diffuse. *What the hell is he doing here? Calm down, Matt, he works with her dad. Of course he was invited.* He felt his jaw relax and even attempted a small smile that, to his surprise elicited only a steely glare.

"Catherine," Michael said solicitously, "Would you give me the honor of a dance?"

Catherine glanced at Matt, who magnanimously said, "Go ahead. I'll be waiting at the table."

As he walked away, the thought of being seated with Mr. Martin and company struck him as singularly unappealing. Making a detour to the men's room, he found inside a cabal of four other young men who, like himself, found loitering in a toilet preferable to the party outside.

"Welcome, brother," one said, holding out a pocket flask to share. "Not exactly a fraternity party, is it?"

Matt laughed as he took a complimentary swig, then listened as the others, clearly chums from one of Manhattan's elite private schools, briefly caught each other up on their college lives. Matt chuckled and nodded in all the right places and was again filled with gratitude for all he had experienced that went way beyond beer chugs and rush week.

He leaned up against the wall and helped himself to a second swig. The second was much larger than the first.

"Rocket fuel!" he said, wiping his mouth with his sleeve.

"How'd you get roped into this, friend?" one of the other fellows asked.

"My girlfriend's father managed to talk her into this."

"You're actually with your girlfriend?" another asked in surprise.

"Yeah. Aren't you?"

One by one, they admitted that they were there on blind dates with "appropriate girls" arranged by their families. Their real girlfriends were waiting back at their respective dorms, some hundreds or even thousands of miles away.

Well, looky here, Matt thought as the third swig hit him hard, *I'm not the only two-timer at this shindig.*

After a fourth and final drink taken at the urgings of the others, he bid them adieu and exited the men's room. As he made his way back to the table, he looked around for Catherine and Michael and saw them swaying slowly off to one side of the dance floor. This struck him as odd, as the song the band played – an unfortunate take on a Rolling Stones tune – was a fast one. He stopped, watching as Michael leaned in and whispered something in Catherine's ear, then Catherine's head jerk back and shake from side to side. *What the hell?* Matt thought, assuming Michael was issuing some unsavory proposition. Swaying slightly, he resumed his approach toward them, just as Catherine turned and faced him. Her jaw was clenched, her beautiful eyes steely beneath the tears. Beside her, Michael shot him a smug smile.

And in a flash, Matt knew.

Not knowing what else to do, he walked up to them and played dumb.

"Catherine…what's the matter?" he asked, bracing himself for the answer.

"The 'matter,' Matt," she said, her voice as hard as her stare, "Is that Michael just told me he saw you and some woman at the airport last week. I didn't believe him at first, but he was very specific, said you were boarding a flight to Ft. Lauderdale." She paused and looked at the ground, then raised her eyes to meet his. "Is this true?"

"Catherine, I um, wait…" he said, quite unable to form a coherent response.

"Is it true?"

He looked down and nodded.

"Michael, give us a minute. Please."

With another smug smile, Michael reluctantly headed for the table, where he would no doubt share the news of Matt's debauchery with Mr. Martin.

"Care to explain," she said, turning back to Matt, "what you were doing traveling with some woman when you were supposed to be working, when you couldn't spend the holidays with me?"

She was giving him every opportunity to clear himself, and, oh, how Matt wished he could take it.

"I'm sorry, Catherine," he said finally, with a drunken shrug that only served to trivialize his response.

Catherine took a deep breath then ran a gloved finger under her eyes. He thought in that moment that she never looked so beautiful, or so cold.

"Goodbye, Matt."

As he slunk out of the hotel, the winter air felt far less forgiving than when he came in. That's when he realized he'd left his overcoat in the coat check. Dammit, he thought, then forced himself toward the curb to hail a cab. No way he was going back in and risking running into Catherine, Michael, or worse, her father.

Mercifully, a taxi pulled up a moment later. "LaGuardia, please," he said as he slid into the backseat. Though he'd feared this for months, Matt couldn't believe it had actually happened – and in a way he never could have anticipated.

"Fucking Michael," he muttered.

"'Scuse me, sir?" the cabbie asked.

"Oh, sorry, nothing." Matt paused. "Hey, man, forget the airport. Take me to the nearest bar."

* * *

Matt jumped up and looked around, surprised to find himself back in his dorm. Grabbing his watch, he noted the time – two p.m. – and moaned as the night before returned in ugly flashes. The realization that he loved Catherine, followed by her realization that he was a piece of shit, followed by far too many gins and tonic – he lost count after five – in a dive bar in Midtown, where he also left the vomited remnants of the duck. It was close to three a.m. when he got to the airport, bought a ticket for the first flight out, and fell asleep in the boarding area. By six he was on the plane, and back in his room by eight-thirty, roughly twelve hours after he had left it. A quick trip that had completely upended his life.

Thank God I at least have the day off, was his last thought before drifting back off to sleep.

The room was dark when he opened his eyes again. He looked at his watch again, saw it was five-thirty, and with great effort peeled himself off the bed and headed for the shower. Fifteen minutes later he emerged feeling slightly more human and left the building to get something to eat. To his shock, he found Anna sitting on a bench out front. How long had she been waiting there? Did she know about his trip to New York?

She got up as soon as she saw him. He did not greet her, but kept walking without so much as a nod. In a few yards she caught up to him. He continued walking without looking at her.

"Anna, it is really bad for you to come here. You should go. I will meet you later." He walked faster to put distance between them.

"Vadim is here. He insists on talking to you." She motioned in the direction of a parking lot.

"What the fuck, Anna? What is wrong with you? You should not be coming to campus! This can hurt me! Really!"

"You must talk to him!"

"Okay," Matt said, figuring it was better to concede rather than risk a scene.

"Go back to the car. I will meet you there in a few minutes. But this is bullshit, Anna. No one from my life here can see you. Go!"

She slowed her gate to fall behind him and walked to the waiting car.

Matt walked across campus, then circled back toward the parking lot, being careful to follow a different route. He was infuriated – and scared to death – by the crossing of a boundary that had always remained intact.

He came up behind the parked car and got into the passenger side. The first thing Matt noticed was the overwhelming stench of Vadim's cheap cologne, hanging like a thick fog. Anna was in the back seat, Vadim at the wheel. Matt's anger was on the surface. He was about to launch a fusillade over their indiscretion, but Vadim beat him to the punch.

"You are good man, Matt. Your information is very helpful. You are good friend to Anna. But I must ask. The last information was very special. Where did you get it from?"

It wasn't so much the question that sent an icy chill through Matt's veins, but his polite tone. He looked at Vadim, then back at Anna, who wore an apologetic expression. He didn't know what their game was, but he quickly assessed the situation and decided to go on the offensive.

"First of all, Anna *is* a friend. But we have always kept our friendship away from my work and where I live. No one knows about our friendship and we must keep it that way. Coming here could be bad for me! Do you understand?" he demanded. "I will not be able to help her anymore if someone finds out."

"I understand," Vadim began, "and still, I must know where you got this information."

"Are you being intentionally stupid?" Matt asked, agitated. "You know where I work!"

Again, Vadim asked, "Where did you get it?"

Matt looked at Anna. She averted her eyes, as though to distance herself from the inquisition.

Matt leaned closer to Vadim. "Look! I don't know what game you are playing or what you expect me to say. You know where I work. This situation is making me very uncomfortable, coming here and asking me questions. Whatever you are up to, I don't like it. I can stop this, you know. So back off!" Matt turned to get out of the car.

Vadim grabbed his arm. "This is very special information. You could have trouble for giving it to Anna."

"Are you threatening me? Because if you are…"

"Believe me, friend," Vadim said, holding up his hands as if in surrender, "I apologize to make you nervous. Please be calm down."

"I will calm down when you leave."

"I am sorry to scare you. But I ask you to be friend to Anna."

Matt pretended to be surprised. "I thought I was. I don't know why you have to interject yourself. You coming here spooks me."

Vadim placed a hand, gentler this time, on Matt's shoulder. "Please, don't be bothered. I just want to say thank you!"

Matt got out of the car as nonchalantly as possible, but he was shaking from head to toe as he headed back to his room. Of two things, he had no doubt. The first was that Vadim's appearance on campus was indeed a threat, demonstrating that he could get to Matt anywhere and ensure the continued flow of information. The second was that in upping the ante, he and Anna were truly endangering Matt's real world, the one he hoped Catherine would one day to be a part of again, somehow. He immediately called Roger and demanded they meet.

An hour later, he was in Jensen's office across the table from Roger and Jensen, the latter of whom had slipped into a fresh suit even for the impromptu meeting on a Saturday.

Probably sleeps in it, Matt thought, and emitted a bitter laugh that elicited stares from the two men. He knew they suspected he was losing it; heck, he suspected it himself. He recounted the episode, leaving out the debacle in New York the night before. Their weak attempts at sympathy would only enrage him further.

As he spoke, Roger and Jensen leaned forward in their seats, as if that would help them listen more intently. He could see their minds working, calculating the significance of the campus interaction and how they could use it to advance a piece on the chessboard.

"Hmm," Roger said, stroking his chin, "lots to think about here. They love the last batch of shit we threw to them. They want more. The hook is definitely set! Question is, how much more do we give them?"

"Right," Jensen said. "We can keep this going indefinitely, giving them bad information, but will they eventually figure that out?"

Indefinitely! To Matt, that word rang out so clearly it was as if Jensen had shouted it.

"Listen, guys," he said. "I've been a team player, but now that smelly fuck Vadim is threatening me. They can destroy my life." He sighed and ran a hand through his hair. "Shit, they already ruined my relationship with my girlfriend. I know in the scheme of things that sounds like high school stuff to you guys, but…"

Jensen stood up and stretched his arms, as if to somehow release the intensity of the situation by physical activity.

"I wonder what the deal is with Wonder Woman," Roger said thoughtfully, ignoring Matt's concern. "Is she slacking off, so the slob has to get involved?"

"Can't be it," Jensen answered, stretching his legs. "She has produced information that has them pleased. I think this was simply them trying to jerk a knot, scare the hell out of young Matt so he comes up with more good stuff. I think this is a good development."

"Seriously, you guys gotta figure a way for me to get clean and get out. I can't do this anymore. Really!"

"We still don't know who the mole is," Roger said, meeting his eyes.

Matt held his stare. "I mean it. I want out. You two pros figure this out. I'm going home and crawling under my bed."

He stood then and left the room without waiting for a response. It was a bitterly cold night, but Matt barely felt it as he walked to his car. His footing was steadier than it had been in hours, his mind was clearer than it had been in months. Because in that meeting, he'd fully realized something for the first time: they needed him more than he needed them.

* * *

The following afternoon, Sunday, Roger summoned Matt and Jensen for an "emergency follow-up meeting" at a dump of a restaurant not far from the White House, where they were unlikely to be seen.

"We've been thinking this through," Roger said. "You have been great. You have done everything we asked. And we believe you have Wonder

Woman and Vomit buffaloed. They think you are the real deal – naïve and subject to their manipulation. So, this is a perfect setup for us. Now is the time for us to move."

"What does that mean?" Matt asked, ignoring the burger on his plate.

"I want to look her in the face," Roger continued in a conversational tone, "and tell her we have her on violations of the Espionage Act."

"What's that mean?"

"It means we can expose her and throw her out of the country. Declare her *persona non grata*," Jensen chipped in.

"She will realize that we played her. It will be a real embarrassment; she'll be seen by her people as a failure. But I'll offer her a deal. If she commits to coming over to us, and gives us information on what they are up to, what they know, what they want to know, and most importantly, who else they are following here, her life will be much easier. It will be up to her to decide. Return home in disgrace to an uncertain future."

Matt gulped. "Uncertain future?"

Jensen leaned into the table. "The Ruskies don't look upon failures kindly. She, possibly her family, will be disgraced. There will be consequences."

Matt felt the alarm rising. "Will they hurt her?"

"It's possible, we can't predict. But she will know the prospect is not good," Roger answered, noting how Matt squirmed in his chair.

"She has a way out," he continued. "That is to agree to work for us. It is a classic situation, but to make it work, I need to talk to her and put the pressure on her. We'll need you to lure her to meet with me."

Matt was still thinking about the "hurt" part. No matter who or what she was, the idea of betraying Anna made him sick. His stomach muscles began to tighten. He needed air. He excused himself and went to the restroom, where he bent over a toilet. His stomach was in turmoil, but nothing was coming out. After a couple of minutes, he went to the sink, splashed his face. Looking in the mirror, he saw his puffy eyes.

"What the hell have you gotten into?" he said aloud. He took his time returning to the table, for he instinctively knew they were discussing how Matt should offer up Anna's head on a platter. A few feet short, he stopped, turned, and walked out of the restaurant.

Dusk was overtaking the Capital. Streets were crowded with Sunday traffic. Matt ran down 17th Street, toward Constitution Avenue. He was not an avid runner, but it felt good to run and try to leave everything behind. He didn't notice cars slam on their brakes to avoid hitting him as he crossed Constitution Avenue. The more he ran, the faster he wanted to go. He began to feel pain. His stomach cramped. His head pounded. His feet began to hurt. He ran so hard and fast his lungs began to tighten, barely taking in enough oxygen to support him. Still, he ran, harder and harder. As he ran, he felt sicker and sicker.

Matt had walked along the Mall before, along the Reflecting Pool that stretched out before the Lincoln Memorial. In the past he'd enjoyed the beauty of Washington. This time, however, no emotional reaction to the surroundings could calm him. He was running away from everything. Up the stairs at the end of the Reflecting Pool and around the Lincoln, he bounded. Halfway across Memorial Bridge, he couldn't catch his breath. His legs and feet hurt too much to go on. He gave out, leaning against a guard rail on the bridge, vacuously gazing into the Potomac flowing below. His heart was ready to burst. His mouth was filled with harsh bile that crept up from his stomach.

"They say George Washington threw a dollar across the Potomac," a calm voice said from behind him. "I don't think it was here. River's too wide. Deep too, I'm sure."

Matt turned around in shock. How the hell did Jensen find him? He was about to ask, then decided he didn't care. He was too spent and too embarrassed.

"Don't take this so hard, Matt. We are in a good place."

"Then why do I feel so bad?" Matt asked caustically. "This has screwed up my life. I've lost the most perfect girl. If I live to be a hundred, I will never find another Catherine, and she's gone because I let this she-spy into my life, who, incidentally, I'm probably setting up to be murdered!"

Just then a police car pulled up and put on its flashers. A cop could be heard reporting into his radio, "We have a jumper on Memorial Bridge."

Jensen stepped over to the car, flashed his federal identification, and assured the officers he had everything under control. The police drove away as quickly as they had arrived.

Jensen returned to Matt, who was still leaning forward on the railing. "Just give this some time, Matt. You will look at it differently in a few days."

"Really?" Matt said, unconvinced.

"You need to take a deep breath, relax. Give it a couple of days and get some perspective. Trust me."

*   *   *

Matt got his orders from Roger. He was to call Anna and invite her to 431. When Matt pointed out that this would be an unusual, and possibly suspicious, departure from the Irish place, Roger shook his head dismissively. That bar was too crowded, he said, and not conducive to achieving their objective. On the other hand, he liked the set-up at 431. It was never loud, and it wasn't particularly busy, so a quiet conversation was possible. Also, there was a back entrance that was made for a discreet get away. Roger did concede 431's location was an issue; Anna might question why he was choosing a place across the river in Virginia. After much discussion, it was decided Matt would simply offer to pick Anna up in front of her apartment and then drive to 431. That way he wouldn't have to reveal the destination until she was a captive audience.

Matt sat in his room, contemplating the call. But before he could get his thoughts clear and summon the courage, Anna called him.

She got straight to the point. "I am sorry we made you so uncomfortable the other day. I did not intend to."

"Anna, that was a crappy idea. I have a life here. You and your attack dog would cause a lot of questions if any of my friends saw you."

"Yes, yes. I am so sorry; it is just that Vadim pushes sometimes."

"That is a big concern for me. I don't understand his intentions, Anna. I think we need to talk. Can you meet for dinner tomorrow night?"

"Um, yes Matt, but it is Christmas Eve. Don't you have plans with your American girl?"

Holy shit! He had completely forgotten about the holiday and had not even thought about calling his parents!

"Christmas Eve, right." He paused. "No, no American girl, but I am working until five. Let's grab dinner after that. I can pick you up in front of your apartment at five-thirty?"

Anna immediately agreed.

"One last thing, Anna. Don't bring Vadim, okay?"

"Of course not," she said lightly, as though he was joking.

Matt was a ball of tension that night. He hid in his room, not even leaving to eat. He called his parents back in Michigan seeking comfort, and found he only felt shittier for having to lie to them too. By eight-thirty he crawled into bed, where he lay wide awake the rest of the night.

The following afternoon, when he pulled up in front of Anna's apartment building promptly at five-thirty, she instantaneously appeared as if she had been waiting by the door. As she walked to the car, Matt thought how beautiful she was. She was unusually informal in a ponytail and jeans. Her gait was delicate, the essence of femininity. Watching her approach, Matt was amazed at the fact he really didn't know how old she was. He always guessed she was in her mid-thirties, but as she opened the passenger door, he figured she might be even younger, maybe just a few years older than him, though aged by a much harder life. Odd that he never thought much about that before.

Anna slid across the seat and gave him a kiss.

"Hey," she said casually.

His brain was in turmoil. *Please help me get through this!* he prayed silently.

"How you doing?" he asked; then, before she could answer he added, "I'm in the mood for a good hamburger. That sound good?"

"You Americans and your hamburgers," Anna said with a toss of her head and what seemed to be a genuine bit of excitement.

"There's this place just across the river in Arlington that's supposed to have the best burgers around."

"Sounds great."

That was all the convincing he had to do. The deception was in motion. Now he had to get through the next half hour or so until Roger would take over. The drive through Georgetown was slow and painful, partially due to heavy traffic. Matt tried to act normal, but his heart was sickened over what he was doing. He thought back to how he had successfully deceived Mr. Wallace just after starting at the White House, and he gained confidence he could carry out this ruse. After turning off Wisconsin Avenue onto M Street, he took a left toward Virginia across the Key Bridge. Beneath was the Potomac River, and just down river to the left was Memorial Bridge, where Jensen talked him out of a panic a few nights earlier. They kept the conversation light, though Matt did say that they needed to talk about this thing with Vadim. He told her it scared him; that she needed to keep him away and never let him openly approach him again.

"I don't control him," she said. Though her tone was matter-of-fact, Matt knew she was reissuing the threat from the other night. Given their destination, it was all academic at this point, but he still had to keep up a front.

"This makes me very nervous, Anna."

"Don't worry, I won't let anything bad happen to you."

Her words hit like a burning arrow through the chest.

When they pulled up in front of 431, Anna gave it a disparaging look.

"I know it's not much," he said, "but the burgers really are supposed to be the best." He paused, then added, "But, I mean, if you prefer somewhere more upscale…?" It was an attempt to keep her off-balance, albeit a risky one.

Roger will kill me if I foul up his plan…

Anna looked from the restaurant back to him. "Okay, let's get some good American burgers!"

431 was sparsely populated, its few patrons all clean-cut men. FBI, Matt surmised. Anna didn't seem to notice. As instructed by Roger, he proceeded to a table in the back of the restaurant and held out a chair for Anna, subtly guiding her to sit with her back to the entrance. This way, she would not see Roger arrive and approach their table. As he took his seat, he was reminded of a similar scene from *The Godfather*, when Michael Corleone took revenge against the family's nemesis, Sollozzo, and Captain McCluskey, the crooked cop who'd broken Michael's jaw. But this was no movie set and he was certainly no Al Pacino. It was real life, and he could only hope it turned out differently for Anna than it had for Sollozzo and McClusky.

She looked around. "As you said, this place doesn't look like much."

"If you don't like it, we can go somewhere else. Really!"

"Oh, no!" she said with a smile, "I hear their burgers are the best!"

Despite apprehension and guilt over the pending betrayal, Matt became calm, knowing it was going to be over soon.

Within seconds, the familiar waitress appeared. She was even more odd and distant than normal, probably having been instructed by Roger to pretend not to recognize Matt, lest she say something suspicious.

"Happy hour prices are still in effect. You like a pitcher?"

"Sure," Matt answered, looking at Anna for approval.

"Please," she said, "and two shots of Stoli as well." She looked at Matt. "Oh, come on – it's Christmas!"

"Christmas, right," he said, a hint of sadness entering his tone.

She gave him a look of sympathy he had never seen before. "Okay, Matt. I know heartbreak when I see it. Why are you not with your girl?"

"Actually, she is not my girl. Not anymore."

"I am sorry to hear that," she said.

"Are you, Anna?" he said angrily. He realized he was being distracted from the game plan, but he didn't care. "Because we broke up because of you. Because she found out we went to Ft. Lauderdale together."

"Oh, no. Did you explain we are friends?"

"Friends, Anna? No, I did not tell her we are friends. She would not understand our kind of friendship – the kind where we sleep together and I give you government secrets." He paused then, knowing this was a pointless conversation. Anna did not make him get involved with Catherine – he had done that all on his own. "I'm sorry, Anna. That is not your fault. Besides, I really messed it up the other night in New York."

"New York? What were you doing there?"

"She went for the break. She's still there. There was a party and – " Matt caught her odd expression. "What?"

"Nothing," she said, shaking her head. "I misunderstood something."

"What?" he said, leaning toward her, a nervous feeling creeping over him.

"Vadim told me earlier that she was in her dorm…this afternoon."

"Why," he gritted out, "would Vadim be watching her dorm? How does he even know about her? Wait – of course he knows, because *you* told him!"

"It is my job, Matt," she said sitting back in her chair. "There is no problem. He called her, how you say, insurance. But you are still helping us, so no problem."

Matt glanced around the restaurant, wondering vaguely how the FBI would react if he put his hands around her neck.

"I truly am sorry, Matt. I promise, I won't let anything happen to either of you."

He took a slow deep breath and realized he believed her, or at least that she meant it.

"Okay, Anna. Okay." He paused. "Anyway, Catherine must have come back to campus early, but I don't know because we're not speaking."

When the waitress arrived with a pitcher of beer, Matt poured one for Anna first, then one for himself.

"I'm not much in the mood for a toast," he said.

"So let me do it." Anna gave it thought. "We will drink to friendship."

Matt nodded, and as they clinked glasses, he saw Roger appear in the entrance, pausing for a moment, like a gunfighter surveying a saloon. Then he looked straight at Matt and nodded. It was the signal for Matt to make his move. Matt's heart stopped cold. Then, with a casualness that bore no concern, he said, "I better hit the restroom and make some room for this beer."

Anna smiled as he got up and stepped away. He paused to take one last look at her. The look on Anna's face was happy. She seemed inquisitive as she perused the unfamiliar menu. Matt was cold. It was difficult for him to believe that she was a treacherous spy, willing to destroy him. Yet, despite that ugly fact, he sheltered a fondness for her fun-loving nature. He shrugged his shoulders, thinking, *That's what makes her so good at what she does.* Then he turned and moved toward the back, knowing he would remember that look on her face for the rest of his life.

Just as he reached the men's room, someone pulled him into the adjacent kitchen.

"FBI," a man whispered. "Come with me."

There were two other agents with him. They grabbed hold of his arms, while the other led the group out a back door to a waiting car. One of the men politely ordered, "Get in, sir." The man placed his hand on Matt's head and guided him into the back seat where Jensen was waiting.

"Give me your car keys," Jensen demanded.

Matt pulled the keys from his pocket, every inch of him pumping with adrenalin. It made him nauseous. Jensen rolled down his window and issued an order to a waiting agent: "It's an Olds Omega. Park it at American University in the lot behind Anderson Hall. Leave the keys on the top of the front driver-side tire."

Matt heard him talking, but the words barely registered because he was thinking of something Anna had said.

He called her, how you say, insurance. But you are still helping us, so no problem.

"Come on, Matt," Jensen was saying, "Hand me the keys."

Matt was shaking. *I promise, I won't let anything happen to either of you.*

"No, no no…"

"No, no, no, what?" Jensen said. He was looking at Matt like he had gone mad.

"She won't be here to make sure nothing happens!"

Jensen's face darkened like a storm cloud. "Matt, what the fuck are you talking about!?"

Vadim said she's at her dorm…

Matt opened the door and rushed out of the vehicle, ignoring Jensen's shouts behind him. As he ran to his car, he expected the agents to grab him, but they didn't and he didn't stop to think about it. He jumped into the Omega, turned the key in the ignition, and sped off in such a fluster he made a wrong turn on Washington Boulevard, then another and soon found himself heading south, away from Washington, on Interstate 395. Panicked and unfamiliar with his surroundings, he was frustrated knowing he was wasting precious time. Within minutes he came upon the Capital Beltway. Knowing it was essentially a circle around the city, he decided to get on it and find another route back toward AU.

Please, he prayed as he pressed his foot to the gas, *just let me get to her in time.*

EPILOGUE

He came to slowly, as if trying to climb up from watery depths and feeling like something was around his legs, pulling him back down. It was reminiscent, though more severe, of some of his hangovers, and his first coherent thought was that he'd tied one on, and then some. Then the random flashes began, coming unbidden to his mind in no particular order – Anna, sauntering toward him in her white bikini; Roger, looking sheepish as ketchup squirted on his shirt; the face of the emergency medical worker leaning over him on the street. And finally, Catherine's eyes as she told him to get lost.

"Catherine…" he whispered hoarsely as he struggled to sit up.

"Oh, no you don't, young man," said a stern female voice. "You've been in quite an accident."

He opened his eyes just enough to see a white nurse's uniform. *Beltway. Crash. Vadim.*

He tried again to move, then heard the nurse say, "Miss, please come, he's calling for you," followed by the sound of heels. And suddenly, there she was, her lovely brow creased with worry.

"Matt, Matt, it's okay, I'm here."

"Catherine? You're okay. Thank God!"

"Actually, you can thank me," Roger joked as he stepped toward the bed.

"How?"

"They told me everything, Matt," Catherine said, gripping his hand.

"Normally we would only discuss such a sensitive matter with a spouse, not a girlfriend," Roger told him, then turned to Catherine. "However, we owe Matt a tremendous debt of gratitude. Our country owes him a debt of gratitude! We just thought we should tell you this was not his doing. He had the weight of the United States government pushing him. And he had a highly trained enemy agent manipulating him."

Catherine nodded. "I do understand. I don't like it, but I understand."

"What you did is nothing less than heroic," said another voice. Jensen. "You were there for our country. We are all here for you, Matt."

"You have a ways to go in your recovery," the nurse cautioned, "but you're young and strong and you'll be fine." She paused. "You are also very lucky."

"How long have I been out?"

"About twelve hours."

"Oh, God. What about my parents?"

"We didn't want to worry them," Roger said, "Figured we'd let you call when you could tell them yourself." He smiled. "When you call to wish them Merry Christmas."

"Right, Christmas," he mumbled, his eyelids growing heavy again.

"You rest now. I'll be here when you're awake." Catherine smiled again, then leaned in to plant a kiss on his lips. "Merry Christmas, Matt."

*   *   *

"Get in, quickly," Vadim growled as the man slid into the passenger seat, "Don't want anyone seeing us together."

The car was parked on a busy block of K Street, with a constant stream of pedestrians passing by.

"Calm down, my friend. I made sure I was not followed, and besides, it is better to hide in plain sight." He paused. "I am very good at my job."

Vadim paused. "Yes, I know this. You have proven it many, many times over the years."

"And my loyalty. Do not forget my loyalty."

Vadim narrowed his eyes at him. "What are you getting at?"

"Just that I take many risks to get you the information. What happened to the girl tonight demonstrated what could happen…to any of us. One false move," he paused to snap his fingers, "and it's all over."

"Anna was careless," Vadim said flippantly. "She insisted, against my advice, on pursuing the boy – and she allowed her…baser instincts… to make her decisions for her."

He glanced at the friend. "I will see what I can do about getting you higher compensation."

"It's never been about money for me," the mole replied. "Of course, it doesn't hurt. Has there been any sign of her at all?"

"I went to her apartment. Her roommate has not seen her. She is lost to us."

"I'll do what I can to find out what happened to her." The man paused. "And what of the college girl you had me follow?" He gave Vadim a pointed look, the implication clear.

"What, do you think I am animal? Besides, there is no point in doing anything to the American girl now. Matt Thomas has already, as they say, left the building."

"I think you have the saying confused with something else…" the man began, earning an annoyed glance.

"Who can keep up with your American sayings? They are as empty of meaning as the rest of your culture. The important thing is that your identity was not compromised." Vadim pulled out a pack of cigarettes and offered one to the mole, who declined. "In light of these events," he said, pausing to light one for himself, "I must await new instructions from Moscow."

"Do you think you'll be called back there?"

"Who knows?" Vadim looked at the cigarette, an American brand. "I would miss these, I admit."

"And I would miss our chats," the mole said. "But rest assured, our work will continue, regardless."

"Of this, I have no doubt. Goodbye for now, my friend."

The two men embraced, then the man slipped out into the cold D.C. night and blended seamlessly into the crowd.

ABOUT THE AUTHOR

Thomas Hutton retired in 2022 from a career in government services, specializing in Continuity of Government, Emergency Preparedness, Crisis Management, and Critical Infrastructure Protection. He is a graduate of American University where he earned both a BA and an MBA. He resides in Northern Virginia.

ACKNOWLEDGMENTS

Special thanks to Dana Micheli, whose kindred spirit and incredible collaboration made this effort possible. Special thanks also to Gail Woodard for her advice and support over the past ten years. Her kindness and encouragement kept me focused, even when my inner voice whispered, *"It's too hard."*

Thanks to so many people in my life—my fraternity brothers, co-workers, friends, and acquaintances—who provided inspiration simply by being part of my journey. There are pieces of so many of them in this story, some more obvious than others, yet without these personal relationships, this book would not have been written. I resist naming names for fear of overlooking anyone and diminishing my gratitude for all.

And finally, to those patient friends who, over the years, endured my storytelling—many of whom suggested, *"You should write a book"*—thank you. A special thanks to my wife, Patrice, who listened, never doubted me, and always believed. Thank you for being part of my life and my story.